Fallout

GJ Moffat

hachette
SCOTLAND

First published in 2010 by
HACHETTE SCOTLAND, an imprint of
Hachette UK

First published in paperback in 2011 by
HACHETTE SCOTLAND, an imprint of

1

Cataloguing in Publication Data is available from the British Library

ISBN 978 0 7553 1854 4

Typeset in Monotype Fournier by Ellipsis Books Limited, Glasgow
Printed and bound in Great Britain by Clays Ltd, St Ives plc

Hachette Scotland's policy is to use papers that are natural, renewable
and recyclable products and made from wood grown in sustainable forests.
The logging and manufacturing processes are expected to conform
to the environmental regulations of the country of origin.

HACHETTE SCOTLAND
An Hachette UK Company
338 Euston Road
London NW1 3BH

www.hachettescotland.co.uk
www.hachette.co.uk

GJ Moffat is a father, husband, writer and lawyer though sometimes he's not quite sure in what order. Although he became a lawyer, he always had the urge to write about good guys and bad guys and his thrillers bring them to life in glorious Technicolour. He is married with two little angel girls.

Praise for *Fallout*:

'This Glasgow based thrillfest may only be Moffat's second release but already he's claiming a place on the 'Unmissable' shelf next to Rankin, McDermid, McBride and Jardine'   *Daily Record*

'*Fallout* is a page-turner worthy of the term'   *Civvy Street*

'another storming success for G J Moffat... Its chases and tension are superbly written and it takes the reader a while - but not too long - to see through the twists and work out what is going on. Highly recommended'
                                                                eurocrime.co.uk

Praise for *Daisychain*:

'Positively crackles from first page to last... An astonishingly accomplished debut with Grisham-like élan... If you read just one thriller this year, make it this one'   *Daily Mail*

'Daisychain is a fast-paced, action-packed thriller . . . with buckets of blood . . . a gripping read'   *Scottish Legal News*

'If you want a confrontation with full-on firepower, this book is for you'
                                                                Scotsman

By GJ Moffat and available from Hachette Scotland

Daisychain
Fallout

For my parents – Christine and Jimmy

Acknowledgements

Thanks first and foremost to my family – Kay, Holly and Lucy – for putting up with me spending long days at work and then coming home to disappear into the study to write.

To the Hachette/Headline team for signing me up (twice now) and getting my books out there. Particular credit has to go to Bob, Wendy, Gillian, Joanna and Peter. And, latterly, Vicki and Alice.

In the creation of this book, a small band of people are due special mention for giving up their own precious time to share their experiences with me and I have no doubt that it is all the better for it. They are: Simon Leila, Diane Turner, Peter Brogan of HMP Barlinnie who looked after me so well on a miserable afternoon in February (though, in the end, the jail itself didn't make it to the final cut) and the woman at Fort William police station (I never took a note of her name) who answered my random questions on a sunny afternoon in September.

Finally, thanks to David Pike of DRP Webdesign for doing such a good job with my website.

prologue: contract

'How long is it now that you've been killing for me, Carl?'

Carl Hudson had never met the man sitting across from him but he knew the type: trying to be provocative just to get a reaction. Hudson ignored the question, lifted a white cup and sipped at his espresso.

'Don't be shy, now, Carl,' the man said. 'You're among friends here.'

He spread his arms out and smiled at his own joke because they were the only two people using the pavement tables of a nondescript coffee shop. The place had just opened for the morning trade and the baristas were still putting the last few tables in place outside.

It was a warm day in late August and the man sitting across from Hudson removed his suit jacket. The label inside flashed as he placed it over the back of his chair, disclosing that it was a very expensive piece of bespoke tailoring. He cinched up the cloth of one leg of his trousers and then crossed his legs, summer-weight wool brushing softly as he did so.

Hudson sipped again at his coffee and pushed his sunglasses up

3

his nose with the index finger of his free hand. He looked at the other man and, taking in the details as his companion leaned back in his chair, decided that he needed to give him a name.

Tag Heuer watch.

Armani glasses.

Silk tie by Paul Smith.

'I need to call you something,' Hudson said, still ignoring the man's question. 'How do you feel about Paul?'

'Fine. Whatever.'

'I'll admit that I'm curious,' Hudson said. 'Why is it that you want to meet me now? What's so special about this job?'

'I like to study history,' Paul said, lighting a cigarette and drawing in a deep lungful of smoke. He picked a piece of tobacco from his tongue and flicked it on to the ground; smoke from the cigarette drifted up into the glare of the sun.

'I mean, you can learn a lot from history,' he said finally. 'Let me give you some examples by way of illustration, OK?'

Hudson was beginning to feel the heat of the sun on his shaved head and wasn't really in the mood for small talk. But he had to give Paul his place; he was the one who wrote the cheques – figuratively speaking.

'This is one you might know about, given your . . .'

Paul's eyes darted around as he searched for the right word, 'background.' He smiled, satisfied with the word he had come up with, and carried on with his train of thought. 'Did you know, for example, that the first use of a car bomb in the West was . . .'

He paused and looked at Hudson. 'Sorry, that was a bit crass, wasn't it? What is it that you soldier types call it?'

Hudson knew that he was being toyed with but he had to play the game. 'Vehicle Borne Improvised Explosive Device,' he said matter-of-factly.

'God, it sounds so utterly banal when you say it like that, don't you think?' Paul asked.

Hudson took it for a rhetorical question and said nothing.

'Anyway,' Paul went on, running a hand through his thick grey hair. 'The first time one was used in the West was in 1920 in New York. Some Italian lunatic took a horse-drawn wagon loaded with explosives into the heart of the financial district in Manhattan and killed forty people. Terrible thing.'

Hudson wondered where this was going, but he could see that Paul was in full flow and that it would be a mistake to interrupt him at this point.

'But you've seen the results of one of those things up close, haven't you? Where was it – Iraq or Afghanistan or . . . ?'

Hudson nodded, but said nothing.

'But then al-Qaeda,' Paul said, shaking his head. 'I mean they really took it to new levels of ingenuity, you know. The American embassy in Beirut in eighty-three. And then look what they went and did on 9/11. The ultimate vehicle-borne device. They cost me a lot of money that year with the hit the stock market took.'

Hudson finished his coffee and wiped at the thin film of sweat beading on his forehead with a napkin. He got the feeling this part of the conversation was over.

'Like I said,' he started, 'what's so special about this job that you wanted to see me in person? Why not follow the usual lines of communication?'

What Hudson really meant to ask, but could not, was: what are you doing risking a meeting in public like this, you lunatic?

'It's . . .' again with the dramatic pause, 'delicate.'

'How so?'

'Well, maybe delicate isn't quite the right word.'

Get to the point.

5

'Have you ever killed a police officer?'

'You know,' Hudson said, 'you were absolutely right. Delicate is not the correct word.'

He stood, pulled a ten-pound note from his pocket and put it under his empty cup. 'The coffee's on me,' he told Paul. 'Let's not ever do this again, OK?'

'Five hundred thousand,' Paul said.

Hudson stared at him, wondering if he'd heard correctly.

'Five. Hundred. Thousand,' Paul repeated deliberately.

Ten times the biggest single fee Hudson had previously had from the man. He looked along the street and nodded at his back-up waiting in the car thirty yards away, indicating that he should sit tight for a bit longer. Then he sat back down.

'I thought that might get your attention,' Paul said.

part one: targets

1

Rebecca Irvine looked in the mirror and, for the first time in a while, was sort of pleased with what she saw. She'd been letting her hair grow for about a year now – since her husband, Tom, moved out of the house – and the previous blond dye job was gone, replaced with something closer to her natural shade of dark brown.

'Becky, come on. We don't want to be late,' her best friend, Hannah Fraser, shouted at her from the hall downstairs.

Irvine opened a drawer in her dressing-table and looked at the envelope from her lawyer that contained the final court order confirming her divorce from Tom. She felt as if she had lost a part of her life that she would never get back. Not that she regretted for a second the fact that the marriage had produced her son, Connor. But it was going to be tough holding down her job as a detective constable in Strathclyde Police's CID and trying to take care of her family.

Irvine picked up her mobile phone and scrolled through the contacts list until she found Logan Finch's number, her finger hesitating over the call button.

'You better not be calling *him*,' Hannah said, now leaning against the door of Irvine's bedroom. 'This is a girls-only night, you know.'

Irvine had not heard Hannah come up the stairs; she turned the phone over in her hand and looked sheepishly at her friend.

'Sorry,' she said. 'But it's still kind of new for us. I mean, we've only had five real dates. Plus, with all that Logan went through with Ellie, it's just, you know . . .'

She stopped herself from saying any more.

Hannah only knew the official story: that Logan's old girlfriend, Penny Grant, had been murdered and that her eleven-year-old daughter, Ellie, turned up in a state of shock three days later at Logan's flat. Logan was Ellie's father and so he'd taken her in and was doing the best he could to bring her up.

The real story was a little more complex and Irvine sometimes had to stop and remind herself that even those closest to her couldn't ever know the truth.

Hannah sighed. 'Look, just call him,' she said. 'I know you won't be happy until you do.'

'I was going to anyway,' Irvine said.

She dialled Logan's mobile number and put the phone to her ear. Ellie answered after a couple of rings.

'Hi, Ellie.' Irvine tried to sound cheerful. 'Is Logan there?'

'Hold on.'

Irvine was unsure how Ellie viewed this new stage in her relationship with Logan; couldn't work out if the girl's occasional bouts of sullen behaviour when she was round at his new flat in Shawlands was because of it or the fact that at thirteen Ellie was technically a teenager and supposed to act that way. Whatever the cause, Irvine was prepared to allow Ellie as much time as she needed to adjust after all that she had been through.

'Hey, Becky,' Logan said as he took the phone from Ellie. 'What's up?'

She heard the smile in his voice and couldn't help but smile too. 'Just checking in to see how you're doing.'

Hannah rolled her eyes at Irvine and turned to go back downstairs.

'I'm good,' Logan said. 'We're just about to go into town to grab a pizza.'

'OK, listen, I don't want to hold you up and we're heading out to the concert now anyway. I'll give you a call later when I get home. If it's not too late.'

'It's never too late,' Logan told her. 'Call me any time.'

They said goodbye and Irvine pressed the end button on her mobile, slipping the phone into her pocket and going down to join Hannah.

'Hey, look,' Hannah said, stopping Irvine before they left the house. 'I do like to kid around, you know, but I think Logan's good for you. You deserve better than Tom, that's for sure.'

Irvine smiled and hugged her friend. 'Thanks,' she said. 'And he is good, right?'

'Seriously. And he's kind of hot too, which always helps. Have you two, you know . . .'

Irvine didn't answer the question.

2

Ellie grabbed Logan's hand as they waited to cross the road to the restaurant. He was still getting used to being parent to a thirteen-year-old girl and wasn't sure yet what kind of relationship they had: somewhere between being friends and being father and daughter. Logan was happy allowing her to be the one who defined their relationship.

They ran together through a gap in the traffic and then walked to the Pizza Express on the corner of the opposite street. Logan felt his phone vibrate and frowned as he fumbled in his pocket for it.

'Who's that now, Logan?' Ellie asked.

She had gradually slipped into calling him by his first name after starting off calling him 'Dad'.

Logan pulled the phone out and put it to his ear.

'Can you come into the office tomorrow?' Alex Cahill asked without introduction.

'Hi to you too,' Logan said. He covered the mouthpiece and told Ellie who it was.

'Yeah, whatever,' Cahill said. 'Can you come in tomorrow?'

'Mr Grumpy. Remind me why I quit my job to come work for you?'

Cahill didn't reply. 'Are you going to tell me what it's about?' Logan asked. 'I mean, it's Saturday tomorrow.'

'Sorry, I'm a little pissed about this. We got a referral for some actress from London who's coming up here for a film premiere on Sunday and they want to get a contract signed up, like, right now. Which is messing with my weekend plans.'

'What's the story?'

'I only just spoke to her manager, but apparently she's been getting some weird shit in the mail; from some kind of stalker or something. And it escalated just in the past few days to some specific threat against her for this trip.'

'So she's looking for a close-protection detail?'

'Yeah.'

'It'll pay well, then?'

'Too right. Way that prick of a manager spoke to me, I'll add twenty-five per cent on top just for the aggravation factor.'

'Standard contract then?' Logan asked. 'I mean I can do that in an hour or so.'

'If only,' Cahill said. 'The manager is e-mailing me a contract from her lawyer. Some big-shot media guy from London. You got time tomorrow to deal with this? I mean, if it's going to mess up plans with Ellie . . .'

'It's OK, I can do it. Ellie's going into town with my parents so they can spoil her. Again.'

Ellie screwed her face up at him.

'What time you want me there?' Logan asked.

'Is ten good for you?'

'Yeah, that's fine. See you at the office then.'

Logan put his phone away and asked Ellie if she was OK with him having to work tomorrow.

'Sure,' she said. Which was her way of saying 'not really, but you're going anyway so what can I do about it'. She was economical with her words.

'I know I'll have to pay for it later,' he said, hoping to lighten the mood.

Ellie smiled slyly. 'Gran said maybe you should give me some money so I can get myself something tomorrow.'

'Always the cash with you.'

Logan couldn't help but smile back at her. As she grew (and she was growing fast), he was beginning to see more of her mother in her looks. She was going to be taller, though, because she was almost at Penny's height, five-two, already.

How different life would have been, he thought – for all of us – if Penny had told me she was pregnant and we'd worked it out. Maybe the strain of having a baby so young would have been too much for us and we would have split up anyway. And then I could have lost touch with Ellie.

But at least Penny would still be alive.

Such thoughts came to Logan frequently; usually at night when he lay awake listening to make sure Ellie was still in the room next to his.

Still breathing.

He tried to push it all from his head and to focus on the positives, on what they had now. But it wasn't always easy. And other images invaded his head in the night – colours of the dark rainbow: *Ellie's face, black and blue and purple; scarlet-slicked hands reaching for her; claret splatter of blood on snow.*

3

Irvine was determined to enjoy her post-divorce night out. Her mum and dad were looking after Connor, and Hannah was driving so she had the green light for wine over dinner before they headed out to the Exhibition Centre for the concert.

She had dated the band's singer, Roddy Hale, back when they were teenagers. His dream of making it big seemed like the usual fantasy, except that he'd gone on to global success. Trouble was, if the tabloids were to be believed, he'd also gone on to Class A drugs.

'God,' Hannah said, as they walked through the double glass doors of the centre, 'I need to go to the little girls' room. Maybe that second glass of wine with dinner was a mistake.'

'Yeah,' Irvine said. 'You're the designated driver tonight so take it easy, OK.'

'You've been on holiday for three weeks and you still sound like that policeman who came to our school to give us the "road safety lecture" when we were twelve.' Hannah did the quotation thing with her fingers and left Irvine to head for the ladies.

'I told you before,' Irvine shouted after her friend. 'It's not a holiday.'

Irvine had put in for a long holiday but her boss, DI Liam Moore, had ripped up the paperwork and told her she was to go away and clear her head and get back on the job when the divorce was done: compassionate leave. She had gratefully accepted.

'Whatever,' Hannah said, waving a hand at her as she ran.

Irvine walked to the side of the wide entrance corridor, next to a poster advertising future events at the centre. She watched people streaming in through the doors and noticed how young most of them were. She started to feel self-conscious and pulled at her T-shirt, smoothing it over her stomach, glad that she had managed to lose and keep off most of her baby belly since her son's birth. It hadn't been easy given the culture in the CID of long hours and fast food.

An older man with a closely shaved head and wearing faded jeans and an olive T-shirt came in behind a group of girls and glanced sideways at Irvine. He was good-looking in a very masculine way, with broad shoulders and muscled arms. He smiled at her and rolled his eyes a little and kept on walking. Irvine guessed he must be chaperon for the group of girls, and that one of them was probably his daughter.

'OK, babe,' Hannah said, coming back from the ladies, grabbing Irvine's arm and pulling her into the flow of human traffic. 'Let's rock.'

The interior of the main hall of the centre felt entirely alien to Irvine. She hadn't been to a major gig like this for years and had forgotten how cavernous the place was; and that the smell of mass-ranked youth was so distinctive. The queue for the overpriced bar snaked through a temporary roped-off area and the crowd at the merchandise stall was five deep, with young men – teenagers most of them – stripping off their existing T-shirts to expose pale, skinny bodies and putting their new ones on.

The PA system was blasting out while the crowd waited for the band to come on stage and Irvine felt the concussive bass thud of the music vibrating through her whole body. She was content to let Hannah lead the way and allowed herself to be gently pulled along through the ticket checkpoint, past the floor-to-ceiling soundproofing curtains and into the auditorium. She was unaware of the man in the faded jeans and olive green T-shirt, alone now, keeping pace with them about fifteen feet back.

'Come on,' Hannah yelled at her over the sound of the music. 'Let's get down near the front.'

'Do we have to?' Irvine shouted back. 'We can just stay back and still see everything, and maybe not get killed.'

'You want to have a good time, don't you? So let's go.'

Irvine followed Hannah into the crowd until they stood about ten rows back from the stage. She knew that the noise when the band came on would be thunderous this close to the PA system, but she tried to relax, wanting to let loose and have fun.

The man moved into the crowd directly behind her and stayed there, about seven rows back. He nodded in time to the recorded music but all the while kept his eyes trained on Irvine, feeling the ceramic knife strapped to his leg cool against his skin.

As the minutes passed, the hall really started filling up and Irvine felt the excitement of those around her grow as they anticipated the appearance of the main act. She wondered what it would feel like seeing Roddy again after all this time.

The spotlight operators started to ascend to their perches high above the stage. Irvine looked around and caught sight of the man in the green T-shirt some way behind her. He was looking at the stage and seemed to be on his own, not with the group of girls Irvine had seen him with earlier. Embarrassing-dad syndrome — he was allowed to drive them here and back but could not be seen to be with them inside.

Then the lights went out and a huge roar sounded as the crowd surged forward. Hannah looked at Irvine and laughed as bodies pressed against them on all sides.

A steady drumbeat started up and the crowd surged again. Irvine was shocked at the volume level. Did it use to be this loud, she wondered, or am I really getting older? She hadn't thought that being in her early thirties was all that old, until now.

Behind her, the man moved with the surging crowd, advancing towards Irvine.

The guitar intro to one of the band's best-known songs chimed out, undercut by a pounding bassline, and then the stage was bathed in blinding white light. Roddy Hale stood alone at the front with his head bowed.

The crowd around Irvine started to jump in time to the bass-line.

Hannah put her arm around Irvine's shoulder and they joined in.

Irvine felt alive.

The man in the green T-shirt moved forward until he was directly behind Irvine, then reached down into his sock and slid the knife out of its holder.

4

Carl Hudson kept all the gear he needed in the boot of his car or on his person.

He had two changes of clothes to enable him to blend into most situations: first, a fairly decent pair of linen trousers and a blue cotton shirt, and, second, a T-shirt and an old pair of jeans. He also had plenty of bottled water and protein-rich snacks; a ceramic knife that would pass through any metal-detector; two fully loaded Glock-19 handguns with spare magazines; a scoped sniper's rifle by Heckler & Koch and a ballistic vest.

Hudson was not ordinarily given to bouts of self-doubt. He killed people for a living – no point trying to put a gloss on it – and even though he considered himself one of the best, what the boss wanted on this job made him nervous. It was not a mindset he enjoyed and he wondered, not for the first time, if the money he was being paid had blinded him to just how difficult this might turn out to be.

He was working alone tonight because that's what the job demanded. Low-key was what was required for this particular event. You don't take out a cop and make a big show of it. You do it fast and ugly so that it looks like something random.

Hudson got the cop's home address from the boss a couple of weeks after that odd conversation with him at the coffee shop. He was not all that happy that the boss had seen his face. Usually if you saw Hudson's face it was because you were part of his crew, a genuine friend (of which, given his line of work, there were few), or about to die at his hands. To have someone else out there knowing what he looked like and knowing the name he was currently using, albeit not his real one, was something he could have done without. He might be the boss, but it was often the guys at the sharp end, guys like Hudson, that got sold out when the cops came calling.

He was also concerned about the boss's state of mind. He was paying well, *too* well, and it made Hudson think that he might want the job done for more than just sound business reasons. Being dispassionate and cold were solid traits in this line of work. Personal animosity was not. That, in Hudson's experience, didn't usually work out too well – for anyone. He'd seen too many guys come to sticky ends. 'Wetworks' called for discipline and control, not anger-fuelled, machine-gun kill sprees.

This one with the cop also had to be up close because that's the way the boss wanted it.

'Use a knife,' he'd told Hudson. 'I don't care if it's quick or slow, but you make sure you tell her who sent you before the light fades from her eyes.'

'It's pretty much always slow with a knife,' Hudson had replied. 'So she'll know.'

'Good. If you can make it painful as well, then, you know, all the better.'

It made for a difficult job, requiring more improvisation than

Hudson was usually comfortable with. He much preferred a distance shot with a rifle; a single tap to the skull and it was lights out.

When he had followed the two women into town and seen them go into the Indian restaurant he'd thought about calling it off tonight. The boss might set the mission, but Hudson was in control of how it all went down. Then he got lucky. The women were going to the concert, which would be perfect; big crowd, dark, lots of noise and there was *always* someone with a knife at these gigs.

Some quick thinking was necessary to get the thing in motion; in the centre's car park he had to change from his relatively respectable short-sleeved linen shirt into the T-shirt; strap the ceramic knife to his leg in case there were metal-detectors in the centre; grab some cash to buy a ticket from a tout and get going. He had to do all of this fast and keep an eye on the women as they walked towards the entrance. If he lost sight of them now it would be tough trying to find them in the crowd of ten thousand or more.

He got done just as the two women reached the door and ran quickly to catch up, paying the first price the tout asked so as to keep moving. The last thing he needed was to get into a negotiation.

He saw that the woman cop was waiting just inside the door. He latched on to the back of a group of teenage girls and got inside, even making eye contact with the cop in the process. That way she'd be more relaxed if she happened to see him later.

Inside the hall, he waited to the side of the doors and followed the cop when she came in with the friend. He figured the best time would be just at the start of the gig with the crowd surging and the sound of the band drowning out any noise. People fell over all the time at these things so it might take a moment for anyone to realise that she was really hurt. By that time Hudson would have faded back into the crowd to exit with everyone else as the panic started to spread when they found that the cop was dead. If he left straight away someone would remember him. The security staff were, by and large, amateurs, but they would at least recall an older guy leaving by himself.

All of which meant that he might not be able to deliver the message the boss wanted. So be it. When it got to this point, Hudson alone called the shots.

Once the band came on, he slowly pushed through the mass of tightly packed bodies, the cop's back firmly in sight. He was totally focused on the job in hand and ignored what was happening on stage.

He got into position behind the cop and bent slightly to pull the knife from the holder on his leg, his eyes never straying from the soft part of her lower back. That was where he would slide the blade into her flesh and then up into her vital organs in one swift thrust.

5

Irvine watched as Roddy Hale lifted his head, opened his mouth to sing and then fell forward over the edge of the stage head first into the security pit. The microphone was still in his hand as he fell, the cord yanking out of its socket, whiplashing through the air and bringing one of the amp stacks crashing over on to the stage. The crowd was so pumped up on the adrenalin rush of the moment that no one seemed to notice immediately.

Irvine felt another surge within the mass of bodies and was pushed heavily forward as a group of four drunken teenage boys barrelled past her, heading to the front of the crowd. She swung her head round as the boys passed by and saw the man in the green T-shirt being pushed away from her in their wake. She wondered for an instant why he was so close to her, but dismissed the thought.

The music faltered and descended into a buzz of loud feedback as the band members dropped their guitars and ran to the edge of the stage to see what had happened to Roddy. The stage started to fill up with other crew members who looked unsure of what to do until a thin young woman jumped down from the stage into the security pit.

The man in the green T-shirt lashed out at the last of the drunken boys, hitting him solidly on the back of his head and dropping him straight to the floor with the blow. The crowd started to part around him, no one wanting to get dragged into a fight.

The other three boys turned and squared up to him, the biggest of them lunging at him and getting in a glancing blow to his temple before the man pulled the boy's head down and drove his knee up into his face. Blood spattered the man's jeans and the boy went to the floor with a guttural shout.

The crowd started to move more forcefully away from the fight, and Irvine and Hannah were pushed towards the stage. Irvine started to fear that the combination of what had happened on stage and the fight now escalating behind her was going to end in a panicked crush.

People die in these situations.

Irvine saw that the crowd was starting to thin out at the front as the massed bodies pushed towards the side exits. She could hear people shouting and the high-pitched screams of scared young girls.

Reacting quickly, she saw that the shortest distance to safety was to the security pit down in front of the stage, which was now only about eight feet away. The security guys were allowing people to climb over the barriers and directing them to the emergency exits behind the stage area. She grabbed a handful of Hannah's top and elbowed her way forward.

The security guys didn't need any prompting and grabbed Hannah when Irvine pushed her friend towards them. Irvine herself vaulted over the barrier and leaned back against the stage, breathing heavily.

She looked for Hannah and saw her friend sitting on the floor with her head in her hands. Someone jumped down from the stage, one of the roadies, and ran past Irvine. She turned to watch him and saw that he had crouched down beside the still form of Roddy Hale some distance from her. The woman she had seen jump from the stage earlier was there, feeling for a pulse on Roddy's wrist as a slowly expanding pool of blood formed around his head and matted his hair.

Irvine went over to them and crouched beside the roadie, who was about to try to turn Roddy over on to his back. She grabbed his arm, and he looked at her sharply.

'You need to leave him,' Irvine said. 'He might have a neck trauma and if you move him it could kill him.'

'What?' he said, looking confused.

'I'm a police officer,' Irvine told him. 'I know about this kind of thing, OK. We need to get him some medical attention right now, so get one of these security guys to get the paramedics in here. They usually have an ambulance on standby outside.'

The house lights were up now and the remnants of the crowd were still pushing to get out of the limited exits. It had all happened so fast that the security teams had not had time to open more exits, so bottlenecks had formed at the doors making the crush much worse. A number of injured people were lying on the floor of the auditorium being tended to by distraught friends.

The roadie was now screaming at one of the security guys and pointing at Roddy's body. The woman who had been checking his pulse stood and stepped back, lifting her feet gingerly out of the blood on the floor. She looked to Irvine as if she was in shock. Irvine grabbed Roddy's wrist, pressing her fingers to his flesh and finding a weak pulse. The blood pool around his head continued to expand.

She pulled hair away from his face and put her hand under his nose to feel for the movement of air indicating that he was still breathing. Like his pulse, it was faint, but there.

'What's wrong?' the security guy asked, bending down to look at Roddy.

'He may have a serious head injury,' Irvine told him. 'Have you got an ambulance here?'

'Sure,' the guy said.

Irvine was getting pissed off now. 'Then call it for Christ's sake. He needs help now.'

6

Hudson was not happy. He'd taken an elbow to the side of his head from the biggest of the boys he'd been in the fight with and a knee to his thigh as he had tried to get out of the auditorium. Much as he'd wanted to, he resisted the urge to lash out with his knife and did his best to go with the crowd until he was able to squeeze through one of the exits.

After he got out, he headed straight to his car. He was annoyed with himself for losing his cool and getting into it with the boys; it was amateurish and potentially dangerous. Even for a professional the odds of four against one were not great. Fortunately, the speed and violence of his reaction had scared off the remaining two boys and he had been able to get out of the place pretty quickly.

The whole area was soon going to be crawling with emergency services vehicles and the press and he did not need that kind of publicity. Most of the crowd was spilling out into the car park wandering around in a state of confusion, so he was able to get through the exit barrier in quick time before driving sedately away and back towards his crew's flat in the east end of the city.

The flat was in a pretty run-down area but that was the whole point of it: to avoid attracting attention to their activities. The other members were out and, once inside, he grabbed some ice from the freezer, put it in a clear plastic food bag and pressed it against his throbbing face in an attempt to combat the swelling that he could feel tightening the skin where the elbow had caught him. He poured a glass of water from a bottle in the fridge and used it to wash down a couple of extra-strength painkillers.

He sat on the couch and switched on the TV, flicking through the news channels until he found a live feed from outside the Exhibition Centre. A woman reporter was doing her best to make it seem incredibly exciting, running through the crowd with her cameraman in hot pursuit; the images fractured and jerky.

Hudson leaned his head back against the couch and pressed the make-shift ice pack harder against his injured face. 'You can always trust civilians to fuck up a perfectly good plan,' he said aloud.

He switched the TV off and leaned over to pick up a mobile phone from the table in front of the couch. There were two – his personal one and another that was being used only for this job. He grabbed the temporary one and punched in the number for the phone he had given to the boss for such communications.

'Is it done?' was the first thing the boss asked.

'You're not watching the news then?' Hudson said.

'What? No.'

'The cop was at a concert and something happened just as I was about to get to her.'

'So?'

Hudson took a breath. 'I'm just telling you what happened,' he said. 'It didn't get done.'

'Are you still going to do it tonight?'

'I don't know. Maybe.'

'So call me again when you actually have something positive to report, OK.'

'Fine.' Hudson was about to end the call when the boss spoke again.

'How are the other preparations coming along?'

'We'll be ready when we need to be.'

'Good.'

'That one will definitely make the TV,' Hudson said. 'You still want it done like that? I mean, there are easier ways.'

'I'm looking forward to it.'

Hudson was not; but when someone waves a half million in front of you, you do what they say.

7

'Just drop me off at the hospital,' Irvine said to Hannah. 'I'll get a cab back home.'

Hannah was slowly picking her way through the traffic to get out of the Exhibition Centre. Irvine had explained to the paramedics who had loaded Roddy on to the stretcher that she was a police officer and they had been happy to tell her that they would be taking him to the Southern General Hospital on the south side of the city.

'What's going on, Becky?' Hannah asked. 'You did your thing and now he's going to get looked after by the doctors. Why do you need to be there?'

'I don't know,' Irvine said. 'I just kind of feel like I should see it through, you know.'

'Not really. I mean, did seeing the old boyfriend up there in rock-god mode do it for you?'

'No,' Irvine said shortly. She was normally attuned to Hannah's sharp sense of humour, but there was a snide edge to the last comment that annoyed her. 'It's nothing like that. It's just, I don't know, I want to see how he is.'

'You going to call Logan first?'

'I told you,' Irvine said, angry now, 'it's not like that. Just get me there, OK.'

'What? You think they'll just let you walk into his room?' Hannah said, sounding sullen.

Irvine took a breath. 'Look at me. I've got his blood all over my hands. And I'm a police officer who was at the scene, so I don't think I'll have any trouble on that front.'

Hannah went quiet and Irvine regretted having spoken so abruptly to her. They had both been through a lot tonight and there was no point in getting into an argument.

'Sorry,' she said. 'It's been a weird night. I mean, we're both pretty frazzled.'

Hannah puffed her cheeks and blew out a breath. 'I still think you should call Logan, you know?'

Irvine turned to look at her friend.

'He's a good guy,' Hannah said. 'I mean that. And I think you'd be crazy to screw things up with him after it's taken the both of you so long to hook up. Just call him.'

'I will,' Irvine said. 'When I get there.'

Hannah stopped the car outside the main entrance of the hospital and kept the motor running. There were already two news crews parked out front unloading their gear and trying to persuade a security guard that they should be allowed to film in the grounds.

'I hope you know what you're doing,' Hannah said, reaching over to give her a hug.

'I'm not sure I do. But I'm going to do it anyway.'

'OK, but I still think it's a bad idea. I mean, it makes no sense to me.'

Irvine unclipped her seatbelt and turned in her seat to look at Hannah. 'Did you see him up there? Roddy, I mean.'

'Yeah.'

'He didn't look too good even before he fell.'

'So?'

'I've seen so much of it since I've been on the force,' Irvine said. 'I've lost count of the number of junkies and alcoholics that I've arrested either because they've been involved in a fight or just because they're so far gone that they can't function. They go cold turkey overnight in the cells, and in the morning we're the ones who have to clean up the puke and . . .' She paused, recalling the stench and despair of those lost souls.

'Anyway,' she went on. 'They rarely get any better and we keep seeing the same faces every week until they move on or they die. And some of them trail around kids who'll grow up not knowing any better and the cycle repeats itself over and over. Teenage girls whoring themselves out to pay for their habit . . .'

Hannah looked through the windscreen and ran her hands over the steering wheel. Irvine felt bad for making her friend feel uncomfortable; most people would never have to deal with the stuff she'd seen while in uniform on the streets and maybe that was a good thing. Judging by the number of cops who were on sick leave due to stress or depression, there was a limit to the amount of misery most people could endure.

'I'm not some kind of crusader who thinks they can save everyone, because I know I can't. But I know Roddy, or at least I used to know him before he turned into . . . this.' She opened and closed her hands, frustrated at being unable to express herself more clearly.

'And you think that maybe you can help him,' Hannah finished for her. 'Save him from flushing his life away.'

'I don't know. I mean I can't really explain it in any rational way. When I saw his face tonight in all that chaos, I thought there was still some small part of the old Roddy visible there.'

'Like he wasn't all the way lost?'

'Right, yes.'

'I'm not saying it's a bad thing, you know?' Hannah said. 'To want to help someone. It's just that you've got a chance right now to be happy, and after all the crap you had to put up with from Tom . . .'

'I'll be fine,' Irvine told her. 'I'll call you tomorrow, OK?'

'Call me *tonight*,' Hannah said.

8

Irvine waved at Hannah as she pulled away from the kerb and turned to walk into the hospital car park. She didn't know the place very well, so went over to a large display board looking for directions to the A&E department. She saw it highlighted in red under the heading 'Zone 7' and traced her finger over the map until she found its location. She heard some excited voices behind her and the noise of running feet on the tarmac as a camera crew sprinted past.

Zone 7 was a U-shaped collection of buildings enclosing a large car park. The A&E department entrance was at the far corner of the car park and Irvine headed towards it at a brisk walk, seeing the camera crew set up outside with a woman reporter speaking direct to the camera.

It did not occur to Irvine that the reporter would have any interest in her and it took her by surprise when the camera swung round to focus on her. She put her hands up to shield her eyes from the lights. It looked on film as if she was trying to hide her face and the blood made it all the more dramatic.

'Who are you?' the reporter asked, thrusting the microphone at her.

She swatted the microphone away and went through the door. Once inside, she went to the admittance desk where a solidly built, middle-aged nurse sat behind a glass screen. The nurse looked up at Irvine and smiled as the reporter outside rapped her knuckles on the windows.

'Friend of yours?' the nurse asked.

'No,' Irvine replied without turning to look behind her.

The nurse took a form from a plastic filing tray and asked Irvine for her name, her pen poised over the first box on the form.

'Oh, no,' Irvine said. 'There's nothing wrong with me.'

The nurse looked down at Irvine's bloody hands resting on the counter and then back up at her face, raising her eyebrows.

Irvine pulled her hands down by her sides self-consciously. 'It's someone else's blood,' she said.

The eyebrows went up another notch.

'No,' Irvine said. 'It's not like that. I'm a police officer and I was at the concert tonight. The one in town where there was some trouble.'

'Yes,' the nurse said, drawing it out as if it was a word of three syllables.

'I helped one of the people that got hurt, Roddy Hale, and I need to know how he is.'

'Do you have any identification?'

'No, but I can give you my warrant card number if you want to check.'

The nurse remained sceptical. 'Why don't you do that, then,' she said.

Irvine gave her the information and a number to call at the police headquarters on Pitt Street. The nurse went to the back of the room behind the glass and picked up a phone.

Irvine turned and walked through the waiting area, which was empty except for a mother sitting with her arm round a young boy. He was holding a towel on a nasty gash on his forearm. She guessed that it wouldn't stay quiet for long, judging by the pictures showing on the TV mounted on the wall. There were several ambulances and police cars at the Exhibition Centre and the caption running along the bottom indicated that there were dozens of casualties. Some of the injured would no doubt be following Roddy here – and probably some fans as well once they found out where he was.

Irvine was about to turn and go back to the desk when a new scene flashed up on the screen. The sound on the TV was muted so she didn't know what was being said, but she saw herself on the screen approaching the hospital entrance and then throwing her blood-stained hands up in front of her face. The picture froze on that image with a caption about a 'mystery woman'.

'Christ,' Irvine said aloud, drawing a look from the woman with the boy.

The sturdy nurse was now outside the glass screen and motioned for Irvine to follow her. Irvine heard sirens outside; blue light flashed vividly as the sky darkened. She went after the nurse through a set of double automatic doors and into the interior of the hospital.

9

Hudson sat in the flat watching TV coverage from the hospital. Each of the major channels had crews out at both the Exhibition Centre and the hospital now. It was big news. As he watched, he saw the cop's image flash up on the TV screen.

There would be no chance of getting to her tonight. Hudson dialled the boss's number on the temporary mobile.

'It's not going to happen now,' he said when the boss answered.

'Why are you bothering me again with this? Do it tomorrow.'

'I can't. I need to get the other thing organised and I don't want to leave anything about that particular job to chance.'

'But the thing with her still needs to get done. I mean, you understand that, right?'

'I understand.'

'You don't get any more money unless it happens. So get it done. I don't care if it's you or someone else, just do it.' The boss ended the call.

Hudson set the mobile down on the couch. He would just have to get another crew member to deal with the cop. He didn't want to because it was a difficult job, but the other thing was far more complex and potentially dangerous so he needed to concentrate on that.

He was beginning to wonder if half a million was really worth it.

10

Logan was searching in the fridge in his narrow galley kitchen for the last bottle of beer from a six-pack he'd bought a couple of weeks ago, certain that he'd seen it in there last night. He found it at the back of the bottom shelf behind a half-used iceberg lettuce.

The flat was smaller than his previous penthouse in the city centre but it was also a good deal cheaper and had loads more character, with high ceilings and original case and sash windows. He didn't mind the narrow kitchen because it meant everything was within easy reach when he was cooking. Not that he was any kind of expert, but he liked to throw stuff together from scratch whenever he had the time. He popped the cap off the bottle of beer and poured a glass of Pepsi for Ellie.

It was almost half past eleven and he shouted for Ellie as he wandered into the hall, heading for the living room.

'Ellie, it's on in five minutes.'

They had a regular Friday night thing of sitting together on the couch and watching *Later With Jools Holland*. Logan almost always found something he liked on the show, but Ellie was still in a 'pop' phase and found a lot of the stuff more curious than enjoyable. Still, Logan was pleased that she humoured him, though he knew it was likely she did it just to stay up late as the weekend began.

He sat on the couch and took a drink of beer, relishing the cold liquid sliding down his throat. Setting the bottle down on the polished oak floorboards, he picked up his BlackBerry from the side table and scrolled through his e-mails before checking for any voicemail messages, hoping that Becky had called him. There was nothing and he assumed she was having too much fun to find the time to call. That was fine by him; he knew that the divorce had really taken its toll on her over the preceding year.

He was toying with the notion of calling her and leaving a message when Ellie came in, tying her long hair back, and threw herself on to the couch. He decided against calling Irvine and put the BlackBerry back on the table.

'Call her if you like,' Ellie said, smiling and taking a sip from her cola. 'Don't worry about me, Logan.'

'When did you get to be so sarky?' he asked. 'Maybe I should just tie you up and . . .' He stopped himself, suddenly realising the memories he would stir up for her. 'Sorry, Ellie. I didn't mean—'

'Don't be,' she said, cutting him off. 'I mean, it's fine. You don't have to treat me like I'll break or anything.'

Logan had been amazed at how well Ellie had adjusted to what had happened to her and to her new life over the last eighteen months; so much so that sometimes he wasn't as careful as he should be when talking to her. Her recovery and adjustment was, in part, testament to the excellent work of the counsellor that Irvine had put them in touch with, and her progress was such that he had stopped their regular fortnightly sessions the previous month. He didn't know yet if it was the right decision, but figured that they could always start up again if need be.

He'd only really known Ellie for a short time and he was the one who sometimes found it difficult to adjust to the fact that, for him, she was 'born' as a fully developed eleven-year-old girl. She'd seen a lot more in her life than most adults, more than anyone should ever have to, and he admired her resilience.

'Who's on tonight?' she asked, nodding at the television.

It was the big plasma screen that Logan had brought with him from the penthouse in the city and it looked monstrously out of place in this old flat. But there were some luxuries Logan wasn't willing to surrender, and this was one of them.

'Dunno,' he said. 'It'll be a surprise.'

'Surprise if it's any good,' she said.

Logan made a face at her and switched on the television just as the titles started to run.

When the programme was finished, Ellie gave Logan a hug and kissed his cheek before heading to bed.

'Brush your teeth,' he shouted after her.

'Done it, *Dad*.' Heavy sarcasm on the last word.

He knew she didn't intend it to sound mean, and kind of liked the fact that she could make a joke of their odd relationship. He considered for a moment picking up the guitar that was on a stand under the window, but he had not really practised in a while so settled instead for flicking through the sport channels before switching off and turning out the lights.

The front door of their flat was heavily secured and he checked and double-checked each of the three locking mechanisms before being satisfied all was in order. He wondered briefly if he was developing OCD in relation to his lock routine.

After that, he looked in on Ellie and found her asleep with a book lying open on her chest. He went in and gently lifted the book, setting it down on the floor next to the bed. His cat, Stella, slinked into the room as he was switching the lamp off, jumped on to the bed and assumed her standard position at Ellie's feet.

'You look after her, you hear,' he told the cat, pointing a finger at her.

She eyed him contemptuously and then licked her bottom.

'Classy,' Logan said. He leaned over Ellie, pushed her hair off her face and kissed her cheek. 'Night, honey.'

Logan was pulled from a light doze by the familiar ring of his BlackBerry from the living room. He got out of bed and ran through on his tiptoes trying to be quiet, and failing as the old floorboards creaked and groaned under him. The screen identified Irvine as the caller. He smiled broadly and pressed the call answer button.

'Hey, Becky,' he said, sleep slurring his speech a little.

She didn't respond, but he heard background noise including the distant sound of sirens.

'Becky?' A little worried now.

'What?' Irvine's voice sounded over the phone. 'Oh, sorry, Logan.'

'What's going on?' he asked. 'Where are you?'

'I'm at the Southern General.'

'The hospital?' he said, hearing his voice rise in pitch.

'Yeah. But, listen, I'm OK. I mean, I'm not here for me.'

She sounded distracted and he felt a little annoyed as he heard her speaking to someone else. He couldn't quite make out what she said, as if she had her hand over the mouthpiece.

'Becky?'

'Sorry, Logan. Christ, it's bedlam here like you wouldn't believe and this doctor's telling me to switch my phone off 'cause he says it'll interfere with their stuff but that's just crap.'

It sounded to Logan as if she was either high on adrenalin or maybe a little bit drunk. 'Look, what's going on?' he asked

She was silent for a beat. 'You haven't seen the news?' she asked.

'No. We watched *Jools* when we got back and then went to bed. You woke me up, in fact.'

'There was an accident at the concert. The crowd panicked and some people got hurt.'

'But you're OK?'

'Yeah, I'm fine.'

He felt the tension in him ease. 'What caused the panic?' he asked.

'It was Roddy,' she said. 'He fell.'

Logan was confused for a second before realising she meant Roddy Hale, the singer with the band – and her old boyfriend. He hated the small pang of jealousy he felt at her casual use of his name.

'But why are you there? Is Hannah hurt?'

'No, she's gone home.'

Irvine's mind clearly wasn't on the call and he still had no idea why she was there.

'Hey,' Irvine said. 'They're letting me into see him now and they'll take this phone off me if I don't switch it off. I'll call you in the morning, OK. You go to bed.'

'See who?'

'Roddy. Bye, Logan.'

Logan stood looking at his phone, not knowing how to take what had just happened. He realised one thing at least – that his feelings for Irvine were probably deeper than he had been willing to admit even to himself. Why else would he feel a knot of tension growing in his stomach?

Then he remembered something Irvine said about the news and switched the television on to the BBC News 24 channel. He caught the end of a report about the events at the concert and the picture of Irvine at the hospital flashed up.

He dropped the remote on the couch and sat heavily, staring at the screen.

11

The hall outside Roddy Hale's room was getting kind of tight for space what with the hospital staff, the other band members, who had brought with them assorted managers and personal assistants, and two uniformed police officers trying to keep some sort of order. Irvine had identified herself to the officers when they got there and asked them to keep everyone who was not a nurse or a doctor outside in the waiting area. But that had been three hours ago and there were a lot more people around now, including the woman who had jumped down from the stage to get to Roddy after he fell. She was standing in the hall taking little sips from a very strong-looking mug of hospital coffee.

'Are you ready now?' a nurse asked Irvine, holding the door to Roddy's room open for her.

It was one of the nurses who had been involved in treating his injuries. She was not much more than five feet tall and wore blue scrubs with a mask hanging loose at her throat. Blood spotted her tunic, the red turned to purple by the blue of her clothes and standing out in the stark lighting of the hall.

45

GJ Moffat

Irvine held the off button on her mobile until the screen went dark and then pushed the phone into the back pocket of her jeans, unaware of the concern in Logan's voice during their conversation.

'Sure, thanks,' she said to the nurse and went past her into the room, the woman with the coffee giving her a glare as she went.

The nurse followed her in, closed the door quietly and leaned back against it, crossing her arms over her chest.

Roddy was lying on a bed with the top part inclined so that he was half sitting. He was wearing one of those unflattering hospital smocks and his black leather trousers from the concert.

His head was heavily bandaged and he had a saline IV drip in his left arm. The hospital staff had wiped away a lot of the blood, but there was still some dried and crusted on his face and neck.

Very rock 'n' roll.

'Had a little trouble finding a vein for the drip,' the nurse said.

Irvine picked up the insinuation straight away – that they knew he was a regular drug user. 'Are you running any blood work?' she asked, without turning round.

'No, not yet.'

'Do you need to?'

The nurse said nothing for a moment. 'Not unless the police ask us to,' she said finally.

Irvine turned to look at her.

'Are you asking me to?'

'No,' Irvine told her. 'Is that a problem?'

'Not for me, if that's the way you want it.'

'I think he's probably been through enough tonight, don't you?'

The nurse shrugged and said nothing, meaning it wasn't any of her business and if that's what Irvine wanted it was fine with her.

46

Irvine stepped forward to the side of the bed and looked down at Roddy. His skin was pale and his ribs were prominent through the skin of his torso. She remembered that he had always been slim as a teenager, but he looked close to emaciated now and there were dark smudges under his eyes. She put her hand on his arm and it felt warm and damp.

'Do you need me here for anything?' the nurse asked.

'No. I thought maybe you needed to be here to monitor him or something, you know?'

The nurse walked forward and stood beside Irvine. 'Do you know him?' she asked.

Irvine though for a moment. 'Not really,' she said. 'I used to but that was a long time ago.'

'He's a junkie,' the nurse said. 'You know that, don't you? I mean you're a police officer so you've probably seen plenty like him.'

'He uses drugs, I know. But that doesn't make him a junkie. Maybe he's still the same guy underneath and he just needs . . . help.' Irvine realised that she was starting to sound defensive and looked away.

'Don't go getting your hopes up or anything,' the nurse said.

She turned away and Irvine heard her pull the door open, the noise of chaos outside briefly filling the room until the door slowly swung shut again. She realised then that she still had her hand on Roddy's arm and pulled it away, letting it hang by her side.

The doctor who led the treatment team had spoken to Irvine before she called Logan and explained that while Roddy had a large wound to his head and a concussion, he was otherwise in remarkably decent condition given that he had fallen head first off an eight-foot-high stage. The head wound had bled quite substantially, making it look worse than it was, but it had still

47

GJ Moffat

required twenty stitches starting at the top of his forehead and tracking back under his hairline.

Irvine suddenly felt very tired. She pulled a chair over to the bed from the corner of the room and sat, bowing her head and rubbing at eyes that felt heavy with fatigue. She looked at her watch and saw that it was almost one in the morning.

'What the hell am I doing here?' she said aloud.

And then it struck her: what did Logan think of the call she made to him? That had been such a bad idea. She looked up at Roddy's face and around the room, where the detritus of the treatment filled the bins and blood smeared the bedclothes. Coming here still seemed the right thing, though Irvine wasn't clear on the thought process that got her to this point. Nor was she sure what was going to happen from now on. Sometimes it was good to be spontaneous; sometimes not. She leaned forward and rested her head on the bed, and almost instantly fell asleep.

12

Irvine woke after an hour, her eyes heavy and her head foggy. She sat back in the chair and rubbed her hands over her face, certain that she must look a complete mess. She checked her watch again then looked at Roddy, and was startled to see him watching her.

'Hi,' he said. 'Um, who are you?'

His voice was surprisingly strong and steady, though his accent was one of those mid-Atlantic oddities that come from spending too much time in the States. He frowned and scratched at the bandage covering his head, wincing in pain when his nails passed over the stitches underneath.

'DC Irvine,' she said, the formality automatic in the circumstances.

Roddy pushed himself up on the bed.

'I'm clean,' he said. 'I haven't had anything for a couple of weeks, OK.'

It took a moment for Irvine to realise what he was talking about. 'No,' she said. 'It's not like that. I mean, I'm not here . . . officially or anything like that.'

He looked uncertain.

'I was at the show,' Irvine said.

'I don't understand,' he told her. 'Why are you here if it's not about, you know, the drugs?'

Good question.

'It's Becky,' she said. 'Becky Reid.'

He squinted at her and she saw recognition slowly dawn on him.

'Holy shit,' he said. 'Becky Reid.'

Irvine pushed her hair back off her forehead and then worried that it would look flirty and flicked it back down.

Yeah, like that helped.

'You're a cop, then?'

'I am.'

'But you said your name was Irvine before.'

'Oh, yeah, I'm married. Was married. I just kept the name because I've had it so long and my boy, my son, has his dad's name too. It would be too confusing to change it now.'

'You have a kid as well?'

'Yeah.'

He smiled at her and she saw a glimmer of the old Roddy, the boy she used to know.

'Are you really getting clean?' she asked. 'Or did you say that just because you thought I was a cop?'

'You *are* a cop.'

'You know what I mean. Don't avoid the question.'

'You going to arrest me if I tell you the wrong thing?'

'Roddy . . .'

'Yeah, I'm clean fifteen days now.'

'So, what happened tonight then?'

'It's tough, you know? Kicking a habit like that.'

Irvine nodded; she'd seen enough to know.

'I just feel like crap the whole time,' Roddy went on. 'And because me and the guys were rehearsing pretty much all day I guess I didn't eat enough and just passed out and crashed.' He made a diving motion with his hand to illustrate his fall off the stage.

'Maybe you should be taking a break. I mean a real break: from touring and everything. Give yourself a proper chance to get well.'

'Avoid the temptations of the road, you mean?'

'I didn't, actually, no. But that couldn't hurt either.'

'True.'

He looked away and Irvine wondered if he was telling the truth. She couldn't be sure from his physical appearance but his eyes looked clear enough. If he'd been high at the concert and that had caused the fall she reckoned he would still be showing some of the usual symptoms and she didn't see any.

'You didn't answer my question,' he said, turning back to face her.

'What question?'

'Why are you here?'

'Oh,' she said. 'That one.'

He watched her but said nothing.

'Honestly? I don't really know. I was at the show with my friend and after you fell the place went a bit mad and we pushed to the front to get out of the crush. I just ended up helping you out, and . . .'

'And what?'

'And then we drove over here and, well, here I am.'

She lifted her hands, turned her palms upward and rested them back on her knees. He looked at her, unsure what was really going on and trying to read her face.

'You looking to save me or something, Becky Reid?' he asked. 'Is that it?'

'Do you need saving?'

'What do you think?' he asked, smiling.

She didn't return his smile. 'I think maybe you do, Roddy.'

13

After a restless night Logan got up early and showered while Ellie was still asleep, setting the water as hot as he could bear it and feeling better for it. He rubbed his hair with a towel and decided to leave it to dry naturally. He'd grown it a bit longer after quitting Kennedy Boyd and kind of liked it deliberately unkempt.

'Fucking bed-head,' Cahill called it.

He was sitting in the living room drinking tea and eating a slice of semi-burned toast when he heard Ellie get up and pad barefoot into the bathroom. He'd given up coffee a while back: something else from the stresses of his old life that he'd left behind.

It was going to be a warm day again and light from the low sun streamed into the room through the open blinds.

Logan stared at the phone while listening to the sounds from the bathroom as Ellie got ready for the day. He wondered about calling Irvine, but didn't want to appear either jealous or desperate. After all, nothing about what Irvine had said, or the way she said it, could give him any real cause for concern. She was a police officer, albeit not actively on duty, and had gone to help someone she used to know. What was wrong with that?

Except it wasn't just someone she knew – it was someone she used to care about.

Ellie came into the living room in her robe, hair wrapped up in a towel.

'What do you want for breakfast?' Logan asked.

'Just some toast. And coffee.'

Logan looked at her and raised his eyebrows.

'All the girls at school drink coffee. What's wrong with it?'

In addition to selling his expensive flat and shopping at John Lewis now instead of Hugo Boss, Logan was paying private school fees for Ellie. He was determined to make up for being absent from her life for so long, and giving her the best education he could afford was something he wanted to do. If it meant that some of the luxuries he used to enjoy were gone, then that was a price worth paying.

'I doubt that they *all* drink coffee,' he said. 'And anyway, whatever anyone else does has no bearing on what goes on here.'

Jesus, I've turned into my mother.

'Tea then,' she said, pivoting and sweeping out of the room with a flourish. 'Please, Logan,' she shouted from the hall.

Logan smiled and finished his own tea. Looking at his watch, he saw that it was almost nine now and his parents had said they would be at the flat by half past to pick her up. He walked to the kitchen, put a slice of bread in the toaster and filled the kettle. He was getting comfortable with domesticity.

His parents arrived, as always, bang on time. His mum hugged him too long and too hard as usual: a habit she had only picked up after Ellie came into their life. She asked how he was doing with an exaggerated look of concern on her face while his dad stood behind her rolling his eyes. Logan smiled and said he was fine.

'Hi,' Ellie shouted, bounding into the hall and embracing his mum and dad in one move.

Nothing had surprised Logan more about the whole situation with Ellie than how quickly she had taken to her 'new' grandparents. She might call him by his first name, but for them it was always 'Gran' and 'Pops', and they were smitten with her right from the start. It didn't hurt that his dad spoiled her even more than he did his other grandchildren. When Logan tackled him about it, worried it might cause a rift with his brother, he was told that there was a lot of catching up to do with Ellie and there was no argument to be had about it.

Penny had been an only child and her father had died in a car crash before she was ten, leaving her on her own with her mother who died five years later after a long illness. He figured it maybe helped Ellie in bonding with his parents that she only had one set of grandparents.

She was wearing the Levi's and pink hooded Gap top that he had bought her a couple of months ago. They had been too big for her then by about an inch but they seemed to fit her now.

'Have fun,' Logan told them as they headed out on to the first-floor landing. 'And don't go crazy.'

'I'll go exactly as crazy as I want,' his dad said. 'Right, Ellie-bee?'

'Right, Pops,' she laughed, sticking her tongue out at Logan and then running down the stairs. His dad winked at him and followed her down. His mum paused on the steps, gave him the concerned look again and told him not to work too hard.

'I won't,' he said.

'It's Saturday after all and I thought you gave up the whole lawyer thing to avoid these long hours.'

'I'm still a lawyer, Mum.'

'You know what I mean. Just take it easy.'

14

Logan got to the office on St Vincent Street just before ten. He was dressed in his regulation black CPO polo shirt and combats, which was *de rigueur* even for the non-field operatives like him. Cahill met him in their reception area on the third floor of the building, also wearing his combats but with a plain white T-shirt on top.

'Cold enough?' Logan asked, rubbing his arms in the cool of the air-conditioned office.

'You starting already?'

'Just asking. Don't shoot me or anything.'

'I won't, but it's still early for a Saturday so don't wind me up. I've already had fifteen minutes with the manager guy this morning. He's taken up residence in the boardroom along with his own security guy.'

'Not on your Christmas card list, then?'

Cahill looked sideways and curled his lip in disgust, ushering Logan through into one of the smaller meeting rooms out of earshot of the actress's entourage. The core members of the CPO team were in the room already: Tom Hardy, Bailey Judd, Chris Washington and Carrie Richardson. They were waiting for a full briefing on the job once Cahill got the details from the initial meeting.

Logan couldn't tell if Cahill was genuinely annoyed or if he was just grumpy at having to put up with the demands of an actor. He'd made it abundantly clear on several occasions that celebrity 'babysitting' was not his core business and he only took on those kinds of job because they were very lucrative.

'So who's the actress?' Logan asked. 'Anyone I know?'

'Scottish girl,' Chris Washington said. 'She was in that big action movie last summer which has made her think she's the second coming of Angelina Jolie.'

Logan had formed more of a bond with Washington than with any of the others in Cahill's team, Washington having adopted Logan as his pet gym project to get him stronger and leaner. It was working, but Logan found it tough going. Washington set a gruelling programme and pushed Logan hard any time he looked like easing off. He had shaved off his goatee beard and let his hair grow a little, softening the blunt look he had had when Logan first met him.

The others looked the same as always: relaxed and professional.

'You mean Tara Byrne?' Logan asked.

'That's the one,' Washington said.

'I'm impressed, Alex.'

Cahill shrugged, trying to look nonchalant.

'Never mind him,' Carrie said, taking a sip from a cup of Earl Grey tea. 'He likes to pretend he's not bothered but he is really.'

Cahill ignored her.

'We going to meet her team now?' Logan asked.

'Sure,' Cahill replied. 'Let's go.'

'And are we hitting the gym later?' Washington asked as Logan opened the door to leave.

'Not today, OK.'

Washington shook his head and smiled, lifting the sleeve of his polo shirt and flexing an impressive bicep at Logan.

There were two people in the boardroom from Tara Byrne's entourage: a medium-height, youngish guy dressed in a black suit and black shirt trying his best to look tough, and a man in a pale suit with a pink shirt. He was clearly the manager who was causing Cahill so much grief, because he stood and walked round the boardroom table to shake Logan's hand firmly, taking control of the room immediately. Logan noted two things about him: that he was quite short, around five-six, and that his dark hair was excessively gelled. But he was well enough preserved for a guy who had to be in his late forties, though his nose was flatter than it should have been. Looked like he used to box.

'He doesn't look much like a lawyer,' the manager said to Cahill, turning his back on Logan.

And you don't look *much* like an asshole either, Cahill thought. Doesn't not make it true. 'We're all casual around here, unless a job calls for it to be otherwise,' was what he said instead.

The manager guy went back round the table to sit down, leaning back in his chair and putting his feet heavily on the table. Logan saw now that he was wearing tan cowboy boots, scuffed at the toe and worn a little at the heel.

Cowboy. Perfect.

'I'll do the intros then?' Cahill asked.

The cowboy nodded, either missing the sarcasm in Cahill's voice or choosing to ignore it.

'This is Devon Leonard.' Cahill nodded towards the cowboy.

59

'I'm Phil Hanson,' the other one said. 'Head of Miss Byrne's security and her driver. Anything about her safety and well-being goes through me.' Lean face framed by very neat, dark hair with a precision side parting.

The cowboy smirked at Hanson's comment. Logan was surprised Cahill hadn't killed the guy already.

Cahill nodded at Hanson, hoping that at least one member of the team knew what they were doing.

'So where are we with this?' Logan asked.

The cowboy, Leonard, put his hand on a document sitting on the table in front of him and pushed it across the table at Logan, who caught it just as it was about to slide off the edge.

'That's our standard contract. Baring Hawkes do them for us.'

This was clearly meant to be impressive. Baring Hawkes was one of the biggest law firms in London – part of the so-called 'Magic Circle' of firms with billings in excess of £1 billion each year and partners taking home more than a million. But Logan had seen enough when he was practising to know that there are good lawyers and bad lawyers in every firm, so he wasn't intimidated by Leonard's name-dropping.

'OK,' Logan said, flipping the contract open as he sat down. 'Give me some time to review this and then hopefully we can get it agreed and signed off.'

Leonard put his feet on the floor and leaned forward, placing his hands in front of him on the table. 'We don't really negotiate these things,' he said. 'I mean, we pay BH a lot and they're pretty damn good.'

Logan nodded, but said nothing, keeping his eyes on the contract and taking a pen from one of the holders on the table to make annotations. Cahill was in no mood to play nice with Leonard, so he ignored the comment and spoke instead about the security situation.

'Can you tell me exactly what's been happening?' he asked, looking at Phil Hanson. 'So as I can get an idea of just how bad it is.'

'Sure,' Hanson said. 'Though, like I told Mr Leonard, it's nothing that I can't manage.'

Leonard waved his hand at Hanson and leaned back in his chair. Clearly there was some tension about bringing additional security in on this and Cahill knew that he would have to be sensitive about Hanson's role. He got the impression that Hanson might be ex-military; something about the way he carried himself – very upright – and in the neat, well-groomed appearance. Old habits die hard for soldiers. Cahill was inclined to give him the benefit of the doubt and believe he wasn't an asshole like Leonard.

'OK,' he said, nodding. 'How did you come to get in touch with us?'

'You were recommended by a business associate,' Leonard said. He didn't offer to elaborate any further.

'And you need close protection for a film premiere, am I right?' Cahill asked.

'Correct,' Leonard said. 'Tomorrow night. Sunday.'

'Phil,' Cahill said, deliberately directing his question away from Leonard. 'Tell me what it is that's causing the concern.'

'Well, it just started this week. Miss Byrne receives a lot of fan mail, as you can probably guess, and her PA opens everything to give it a first look, you know? If there's anything dodgy then she brings it to me. We get lots of sex-type stuff, but most of it is pretty sad or just plain dirty. But we got this one thing on Monday that was out of the ordinary, so far as the sex stuff goes anyway.'

Logan was half-listening to the story while reviewing the contract, which was surprisingly balanced and fair. He had made a few notes and scored out a couple of the more biased clauses, but on the whole he was hopeful that this might not take so long after all.

'What was it?' Cahill asked.

Hanson shifted a little in his seat. 'It was a Barbie doll with the blonde hair coloured black using oil paint, which was still wet. The breasts had been roughly cut off the doll and then smeared with red paint to look like blood. And there was a note with it, typed on an old typewriter, that just said "Die bitch".'

'OK,' Cahill said. 'The threat is a little generic, but it does sound like something a disturbed mind possibly might come up with. What was next?'

'Tuesday there was another Barbie,' Hanson went on. 'This time the legs had been cut off and the, well, the lower extremities hacked at with a knife. There was a note that said, "How do you think Hollywood will like you after I've done this?"'

'More of a direct-type threat then.'

'More direct than "Die bitch"?' Leonard asked, raising his eyebrows.

'Yes. "Die bitch" is non-specific. The second one has a threat of actually doing something to her and it's linked to her success in the States. Were you able to trace where it came from?' Cahill again directed his question at Hanson.

'No,' Hanson said. 'It wasn't mailed through the post. It was hand delivered.'

'Don't you have security cameras at her house?'

'It was delivered to her fan club address, which is just a serviced office building in London. No security.'

'Did you speak to the staff there? Did anyone remember anything about the delivery?'

'Yes. And no. We got nothing.'

'Which means that whoever is responsible is going out of his way to stay anonymous.'

'And what does that mean?'

'Probably that the dolls themselves are not the end of the business. That most likely there will be an escalation.'

'And then yesterday we got this.' Hanson reached under the table and pulled out a plain brown box. He got up and walked round the table and placed the box in front of Cahill. Logan stopped his review of the contract to watch. 'We haven't shown her any of the stuff,' Hanson told Cahill. 'I mean, she knows that there's something going on but we've kept the details of it from her.'

Cahill opened the lid of the box and carefully lifted out another doll, this one with the eyes gouged out and most of the hair roughly cut off, with only a few wild clumps remaining.

'Was there a note?' he asked, closing the box and handing it back to Hanson.

'Yes. It said "See you Sunday".'

15

The room was quiet for a moment.

'What's so bad about *this* doll?' Leonard asked Cahill.

'Up to this point, he's been communicative but vague. Now we've got identification of a specific time for him to make contact.'

'The premiere,' Hanson said.

'Yeah. And judging by this you were right to come to me. I'd be inclined to take him seriously.'

'You keep saying that,' Leonard said. 'You keep saying "he". How do you know it's not a woman?'

'Again, just from what I've learned over the years I've been doing this, the anticipated level of violence and the fact that it is very specifically targeted at the symbols of her sex – the breasts and such – make me pretty certain that it must be a man. I mean, women, as a general rule, don't do that sort of thing.'

'I hate this part of it,' Leonard said. 'The sickos. Can I get some water?'

Cahill went to the sideboard and took a bottle of chilled water from a small fridge inside and a glass from the tray sitting on top. He poured half a glass of the water and then stretched across the table to place bottle and glass in front of Leonard.

Leonard took a sip of water, and Logan couldn't help wondering if his management fee got increased for dealing with this kind of stuff.

'You haven't gone to the police,' Cahill said. 'Why not?'

Hanson looked at Leonard, who took his time putting his glass down on the table before speaking.

'Bad timing,' Leonard said.

He lifted the glass and took another sip of water. Logan could tell that Cahill was getting annoyed by Leonard's propensity for short, cryptic answers from the way that the muscles in his boss's jaw tensed.

'How so?' Logan asked, thinking it might help to make a new voice heard.

Leonard looked at him and for a moment Logan wondered if he was going to respond at all.

'Well,' he sighed at last. 'Tara had a big hit last year and she's just signed up for two more parts in the States, parts that will make her a megastar, so she doesn't need the publicity right now. Big movie studios are notoriously fickle and nervous and we don't want them upset.'

'What's the premiere tomorrow?' Cahill asked.

'It's for a small, independent movie,' Hanson said. 'She did it for next to nothing for the director who's a friend of hers, and if she supports it now it's got a chance to make some money for him. She thinks he's a talented guy and he deserves it.'

Logan thought that Hanson seemed to know more detail about Tara's relationships than a security grunt ordinarily would. Leonard looked away from Hanson as he spoke. There was obviously some dynamic to the relationship that Logan was missing.

'And it helps her profile to be associated with UK independent film-making,' Leonard added.

'OK,' Cahill said, opening his pad and clicking his pen. 'I'll need to know the arrangements for the premiere.'

Logan saw that Leonard was fiddling with his watch. He unhooked the strap and without warning slid the watch across the table to Cahill, tracing faint scratches on the table top. Cahill caught it in his left hand and looked up at Leonard.

Leonard laughed. 'Do we synchronise watches now?'

Hanson looked embarrassed and angry and was about to say something when Cahill smiled and raised his hand to cut him off. He turned the watch face-over in his hand, seeing that it was a Rolex.

'That's good,' he said. 'Never heard that one before.'

Leonard frowned.

Logan wondered just what the hell was going on with Leonard. Was this his way of showing that he was in control – annoyed by Hanson's intervention?

'You can send me the bill for the repair to the table,' Leonard said.

'I will,' Cahill replied deadpan, throwing the watch back at Leonard in a hard, flat trajectory.

Leonard moved his head quickly to avoid getting caught in the face as the watch passed by him and landed on the floor. He pushed his chair back on its wheels, leaned down and lifted the watch by the strap, turning it over to check the face and the back plate. He glared at Cahill and then put it in his jacket pocket.

'Sorry,' Cahill said. 'Don't know my own strength. I guess we're even now.'

Fallout

'It's a Rolex,' Leonard said. 'It's still working just fine, thanks.'

'The premiere?' Cahill asked, looking at Hanson.

'It's at the GFT. We've to be there for seven p.m. and the film rolls at half past.'

'Where are you staying?'

'The Hilton. Plan is to drive from there to the GFT and then straight back. No parties or clubbing or any other detour.'

'Then we have an early morning flight on Monday to Heathrow and from there on to LA,' Leonard said.

'OK, that's good. The simpler things are the better it will be.'

'How do we handle it?' Hanson asked.

'I'll go out today with my team and check the possible routes to and from the venue. We want to avoid travelling the same way there and back. In fact, it might be best to go a long way round on the journey back so that the only thing that's the same is the entrance to the hotel. We'll also want to check everything else – your rooms, the hotel itself, the film theatre if you can get me access . . .'

'Shouldn't be a problem,' Hanson said. 'I can tell you that we have three rooms together at the end of a hallway in the hotel and motion sensors set up in the hall.'

'That's good,' Cahill said again. 'You should also get a list of guests going to the screening, and staff working at the theatre.'

'Already done,' Hanson said. 'I have the information back at the hotel.'

'Excellent. You and I can get together later to review everything and agree the schedule for tomorrow after I've done what I need to do. That'll give me a chance to check out the hotel at the same time. And I'll need to speak to Miss Byrne. She has to be a part of this too.'

'Seems like an awful lot of fuss,' Leonard said. 'I mean, it's not like there are terrorists after her.'

'It's the way I work,' Cahill said, the tone of finality clear in his voice, brooking no discussion.

'You'll want to check our car as well?' Hanson asked.

'No. We'll use my cars. I want one in front with two of my operatives, I'll be in the middle car with you and Tara, and two more of my people in the third car to monitor everything.'

'Won't that be a little bit conspicuous?' Leonard asked. 'I mean, for God's sake, we don't want Tara to come across as some kind of diva who needs a presidential-style security detail. Can't you just be in the car with her?'

'If you want me to do this, then it gets done my way. End of discussion. And she is the US President for as long as I'm responsible for her safety.'

Leonard tried to hold Cahill's gaze but looked away after a few moments and said nothing more.

'Looks like we're all set then,' Cahill said. 'Logan, how you getting on with that contract?'

Logan flipped through the last few pages and made a couple more minor changes before confirming that he was done. He passed the finished document to Cahill, who grabbed it and stood. 'I'll get this typed up now and we can sign it and get about our business,' he said, turning to leave the room. 'If you want any coffee, let Logan here know.'

Leonard stood as Cahill opened the door of the boardroom. 'I'll need to run that past BH,' he said, pointing at the contract in Cahill's hand. 'They've got a lawyer on standby waiting to hear from me.'

'No need, Devon,' Cahill said. 'You can tell your boy at BS to go home and enjoy his weekend.'

Logan hid a smile behind his hand.

'It's BH,' Leonard said loudly as Cahill left the room and closed the door quietly.

'I think he knows exactly what it's called, Devon,' Hanson said.

16

OK, Becky, just how far are you going to take this thing?

Irvine had found that the best way she knew to deal with difficult situations was to go at them full-tilt and keep going until she had no option but to stop; current case in point – Roddy Hale and his apparent desire to kick a serious hard-drug habit.

She was now back home, stepping into the shower to wash off the sweat, blood and grime of the previous night. That was her physical situation. Mentally, her state was a little harder to pinpoint. She tried to replay the end of her conversation with Roddy, not sure she was remembering it all quite right.

'You looking to save me or something, Becky Reid?' Roddy asked. 'Is that it?'

'Do you need saving?'

'What do you think?'

'I think maybe you do, Roddy.'

'So save me.'

'What?'

'It's pretty simple. I can't do this any more, at least not for a while and not in my current state. And I can't do it while I'm still living the same life. There's too much temptation. I need to get away from it.' He paused.

'What can I do?' Irvine asked. 'I mean, I'm a recently divorced single mother on the sick. What can I give you that you can't just go out and buy?'

'Sanctuary.'

She rolled her eyes.

'I mean it,' he said. 'Somewhere away from all of the bullshit that comes with what I do: the press, the fans, the agents and managers and record label execs. I can't take it right now. I really can't.'

'You want to live at my place? Are you crazy?'

'It doesn't need to be at your place. We could go somewhere. I just need a few days away from it all and I'll pay for everything.'

Irvine stared at him, certain that her jaw had done the cartoon thing: unhinged itself and dropped to the floor. Roddy saw the look on her face.

'It's not like that. I don't mean that we'll be together or anything, but I just need someone to be there, you know? To help me through the tough parts. Keep me from falling off the wagon. I know myself well enough to realise that I'm not strong enough right now to do it alone. I will be, just not yet.'

Isn't this why you're here, Irvine asked herself. It's what you told Hannah. But this is a step too far: reconnecting with someone you were in a bad relationship with out of some desire to Do Some Good.

If your kid's a problem for you, bring him along,' Roddy said. 'Maybe it'll be good for me; help keep me grounded, you know?'

'I can't bring my son into this.'

'OK, sure. Just you. Whatever works.'

'I didn't say I'd do it at all. You're only hearing what you want to hear. Still the same old Roddy, after all.'

He looked chastened; his cheeks turned red, making her feel bad. This was how it used to be with him, she remembered. Her trying to be a grown-up and him acting like a child, pouting and stamping his feet to get his own way. This could never work.

'I'm sorry,' he said.

She looked at him. 'I don't think you've ever said that to me, Roddy. Not back when we were together, that's for sure. And not after either.'

'This kind of thing,' he said, opening his hands, 'it makes you think about your life. And I know this probably sounds to you like some LA psycho-babble bullshit . . .'

'Yeah, it does.'

'. . . but it's true. And I have been in therapy. It works. Or at least it works for me, so you've no need to be snooty about it.'

Irvine felt guilty again. Maybe he had turned his life around. He certainly sounded like a different man.

'It's not any twelve-step, making-amends-to-everyone-in-your-life crap,' he went on. 'It's just about where I am right now. About needing some help with this. It's not easy, for me especially, to admit that I'm a mess and to ask someone else to help me get through it. I'm used to skating through life not caring about anyone but me.'

'I know you are. I was there once, remember.'

He sighed, rubbing his hands over his face. 'I said I'm sorry. And I meant it. Sorry about everything, OK?'

She watched him closely, trying to judge if he was for real or just telling her what he needed to so that he would get his own way. Despite her reservations about him – who he used to be – her defences were not holding up.

But what was she supposed to do? Take time out from her life just as maybe it was getting back on track? Just as she and Logan were starting something?

If you do it, Becky, she told herself, it's not about you. It's about Roddy and helping him. What's so bad about wanting to save someone for a change, instead of scraping them up off a pavement or throwing them into a cell?

When she thought about it like that, she found it difficult to argue with herself.

'Becky, look . . .'

'Roddy. Shut up and listen to me, OK? I've seen it all before. The most likely outcome of this whole thing is that if I do it – and that right now is a very big "if " – I'll leave you for an hour and you'll find a way to score something: glue or painkillers or whatever.' He started to protest but she shook her head. 'It's the way it is, Roddy. It just is. I'll come back and you'll be high.'

He stayed quiet, sensing that she might be on the verge of a decision.

'If that happens then we're done. No questions, no explanations and no apologies. We're just done.'

'What are you saying?' he asked.

This time she was the one to sigh, looking away from him and out of the window.

'I'll give you one chance,' she said, turning to face him again. 'Because I used to care for you and because you seem to be trying to turn it around. But it'll be no more than that, OK? If you try anything or if I . . .'

'What?'

'Never mind. Do you understand?'

'Of course. Yes.'

*   *   *

Irvine had a cabin bag packed with four days' worth of clothes and was still trying to work out what she was going to say to her mother to persuade her to look after Connor.

And what to tell Logan.

The first one was by far the easier. But telling Logan . . .

It had taken the best part of the last year and a half for them to get properly together. Neither of them had wanted to talk about themselves or their feelings for each other, with Irvine going through the break-up of her marriage and Logan committing all his energy to making a home for his daughter. And he'd done the very best that he could have. That anyone could have.

And, in the end, that's what had made her fall so hard for him. Past all the emotion of the death of Ellie's mother, of Ellie's ordeal and rescue, she had well and truly fallen. Watching him taking care of this girl whom he had never met, never known, and sacrificing everything that he had worked for in his life up to that point – the penthouse and the career and all of the aspirations he had – for her sake. Anything that stood in the way of giving Ellie what she needed was jettisoned. Maybe some of it was guilt on his part, but Irvine was close enough to see that mostly it was just how he was.

How could she not have fallen?

Plus, like Hannah said, he *was* also just a little bit hot.

It finally happened on a Friday night. They were back at Logan's flat and had just slumped on to the couch together after a day out with the kids. Ellie had gone to bed and fallen asleep almost immediately and Connor had done likewise on Logan's bed.

Logan had tilted his head back on to the couch and turned to look at her. She'd made the move. Leaning in to him, she opened her mouth on his, tingling at the warmth of it. And they had kissed for what seemed like an age, just holding hands until he slipped his arms round her waist and pulled her to him.

And that was their first date: the beginning and end of it.

Logan had waited until after their first *real* date to tell Ellie. Since then, things had cooled a little between Irvine and Ellie, which was understandable and why they were taking it so slowly. No sleepovers. But it had been close that last time. Irvine had felt it when they pressed together at the end of the night, standing in the gloom of her living room. She felt him kiss her just a little more urgently and pull her in more tightly. And she had felt the longing too. It had been a while for both of them.

But it ended as it always did – with him leaving to go back to the other girl in his life: to Ellie. So Irvine had been left to take care of her longing on her own that night.

Same old story.

17

Irvine got dressed and carried the cabin bag down to the living room. She called her mother, feeling like a nervous teenager calling home after the first time she had stayed out all night.

'Where the hell have you been?' her mum said.

Not the best start. But at least she didn't mention the concert; since her parents had retired they didn't watch much news or even read a newspaper regularly. Who needs all that bad news? was her dad's explanation.

'I need you to keep Connor for a bit longer please, Mum. Can you do that?'

Silence. Then: 'Why? What's wrong?'

'Nothing's wrong. I just need a bit of time for myself.'

'Is it Logan?'

'Yes.'

The lie seemed easier.

'For how long? I mean a day, a week or what? I've got a life too, you know. Just because your dad and me are retired doesn't mean we don't have things to do.'

'I know, Mum. And I appreciate everything you've done for me since Tom and me . . .'

'How long?'

'Just for the weekend; until Tuesday.'

Pause. 'Fine. What about clothes and stuff for Connor?'

'You've still got a key, haven't you? Just drop by and pick up what you need.'

'You're leaving *now*? You don't even have time to come and see him first and say bye?'

'It's easier if I don't. I've never been away from him for more than a night and I think it's better if I just do it. Otherwise we'll both be upset. He won't miss me anyway while you and Dad are spoiling him.'

'Where are you going? At least I should know that.'

Frosty now, but job done.

'I don't know yet. It's all a bit last-minute so I'll call you when I get there.'

'OK. Be careful.'

Irvine pressed the remote lock button on her car key and the indicator lights flashed as the central-locking mechanism opened the doors. The sun was warm on her back as she loaded her bag into the boot and slammed it shut a little too hard.

She sat in the driver's seat and put the key in the ignition. Then she paused and laid her hands in her lap, looking along the quiet street. Was this some sort of reaction against being on compassionate leave and feeling useless? Was she trying to reclaim a little part of her old self?

Whatever it was, it was done now and too late to change it. Or at least that's what she told herself. *Can't back down now.*

She lifted her mobile from the passenger seat and scrolled through her contacts list until she found Logan's number. She hesitated and then put the phone back down on the seat, deciding that she would go to the flat to see him. If he was there, she'd explain it all in person. If not, then she'd call him.

She pulled away from the kerb thinking again of that night with Logan in her living room; failing to notice the car that pulled out and followed fifty yards behind her.

18

Carl Hudson was sitting on a brown leather couch in an All Bar One in the city centre enjoying a mid-morning coffee when his phone for this job vibrated in the back pocket of his jeans. He grabbed the phone and looked at the screen, which identified the caller only as 'Three'.

'What's up?' he said after pressing the button to answer the call.

'She was at her house this morning.'

Hudson turned in his seat and looked out of the first-floor window on to the street below, squinting against the glare of the sun. 'And . . .'

'We followed her from there. She went to see somebody but evidently they weren't home and for the last half-hour she's been sitting in the car looking up at the building she just came out of. Looks like there's somebody she's pretty keen to see.'

Hudson watched a mother across the street with her two children, a boy and a girl. The kids must have been early teens or maybe a bit younger and were conversing in sign language. Hudson watched, fascinated, as the mother joined in. It looked to Hudson like the boy was the one with the hearing problem, from the way he carried himself and his strained facial expressions while signing. But they all behaved like any ordinary family in conversation: laughing, frowning and looking away even as someone was 'talking'. And it all looked seamless and so, well, normal. He made a mental note to call his wife after he was done with this conversation.

'What you want us to do?' Three asked.

'You have your assignment,' Hudson told him. 'So stick to it.'

There was silence for a beat or two.

'You want us to do it now?'

Hudson sighed; the cops and the spooks had pretty good surveillance these days and you had to be careful on mobiles. While Three hadn't really said anything incriminating of itself, he still wasn't sure that Three and Five were the best people for this gig with the cop. Trouble was, he really couldn't spare anyone else with the other job set to go down tomorrow and a lot of the preparation still to be done.

Three was his most recent recruit and he didn't know him that well. Sure, he had all the physical skills necessary, but at twenty-six he was very young and Hudson worried that he was too inexperienced. Case in point – do it now in broad daylight on a Saturday in Glasgow's residential south side?

Yeah, just you go ahead.

'No, I don't want you to do it now,' Hudson said, keeping his voice even. 'Just keep tabs on her and look for the right time, OK? Like I said – it has to be quick and random and you have to make sure of it.'

'Like at night?'

'Yes.'

'So it looks just like a street thing?'

'Yes.'

'OK. You want that we should check in with you later or only after . . .'

'After.'

Hudson pressed the button to end the call. He wanted to call his wife, but he had a meeting with someone the boss had put him in touch with this afternoon to get the last piece of the Thing. This was how Hudson thought about jobs, using bland words in his head so that he would never be caught out and say something incriminating aloud. It was always the Guy at the Place at the Time with the Thing.

He sat for a moment and decided the job had to come first. He had drained the last of his coffee from the mug when his temporary phone rang again. It was a number he did not recognise.

'Uh-huh,' was all he said to answer the call.

'Is this . . . this is you?'

Had to be the Guy; the one with the last piece of the Thing.

'It's me.'

'Um, well I have it. I mean the thing you need.'

'OK. Meet me where I said before. One hour.'

He hung up without waiting for a reply.

19

It was too hot to stand outside in the sun and too stuffy to sit in the car with no air con, so Irvine adopted the unhappy medium of letting the engine idle with the climate control at its coldest for ten minutes till it was nice and cool and then turned it off again to conserve fuel. But now the routine was getting kind of annoying and she didn't know how long Logan was going to be out.

'Five more minutes,' she told herself.

After another half-hour, Logan showed up. She was so preoccupied fiddling with the ignition that she didn't see him until he had jogged up to the door, where he put his key in quickly and then was gone.

Irvine pulled at the door handle and then stopped herself. She flipped down the sun visor for a quick check in the mirror. Not too bad. She fussed with her hair for a minute, thought about putting on some lippy and decided not to. She turned her face to view the different angles then stretched up to check the little bit of cleavage that was showing at the rim of her black vest.

'Killer,' she said, and then got out into the sun.

Heat shimmered up off the tarmac, twisting and warping the surface of the road. It was warm for September: close to seventy-five. Should have worn the shorts instead of the jeans, Irvine thought.

Walking up the path to the tenement door, she realised that she had not planned particularly well for this. She wasn't great at delivering news that, though not really bad in itself, needed a bit of work to make it sound better than it was. Still, too late now. Just blurt it out and it'll be fine. Really. Honest.

I'm going out of town for a break with Roddy. You know Roddy? My millionaire rock star ex-boyfriend.

'Maybe not,' she said aloud, and pressed the buzzer for Logan's flat.

'Yo,' he answered.

'Somebody's happy,' she said, smiling.

'Oh, hey. Come on up.'

The buzzer sounded, indicating that the door was open. She pushed against it and stepped into the hall: stark plaster walls painted red on top and yellow below.

The sound of the door to Logan's flat being opened echoed down the staircase. The inside of the building was much cooler than outside and gooseflesh popped up on the bare skin of her arms. She started slowly up the stairs, trying to breathe steadily but hampered by the big red muscle hammering in her chest and by the warm tingle growing in her thighs.

He was leaning against the doorframe with his arms crossed in his tight CPO polo shirt, showing off some of the muscle he'd been building in the gym with Chris Washington. Not that she was complaining: shoulders and chest were wide and firm. The biceps she could take or leave.

She stretched up and kissed him lightly on the mouth, that tingle shivering deliciously hot inside her, and then moved into the flat as he closed the door behind her. He caught up with her in the living room, the TV on mute with some Saturday lunchtime football show; talking heads going blah blah blah.

'I saw you on the TV last night,' he said. 'Fame at last.'

She knew that he was trying his best to make it sound casual and easy, but she heard the fear. She was a cop, it was what she did.

'Look, I'm really sorry about that,' she said. 'And the way I was on the phone.'

Logan stuck his hands in the pockets of his combats and shrugged, looking like a five-year-old boy being scolded.

'It was just, well, it was a weird night.'

'You're OK though?' he asked, looking down at his bare feet. 'I mean, it looked pretty scary from what I could see.'

'It was. But I'm fine. Big butch cop, me.'

She winced, feeling the strain in her voice as she tried to make light of it when she didn't feel that way. God, this was so awkward. Why couldn't it be easier between them? Maybe there was just too much history.

'Not so butch,' he said, looking up at her.

Kiss me, she almost said. Grab me and kiss me and pull these clothes off and fuck me.

But she didn't. Nice girls don't say 'fuck'.

Irvine sat on the couch and stared out of the window. Logan stayed where he was. Is this really how it's going to end, she wondered; before it's even gotten started?

'I was with Roddy at the hospital.'

'So I saw.'

Was that petulance in his voice now, an argument brewing?

'He's been in bad shape. Drugs and stuff.'

Irvine looked up at him, caught his eyes on her for a fraction before they flicked away to the silent TV. What had she seen in those eyes – anger? Maybe desire. Or was that wishful thinking?

Someone inside her head screamed.

She was hoping that Logan would make this easier, make it a real two-way conversation. But he was as mute as the talking heads.

She stood and spoke in a rush, words blended in staccato sentences. 'He asked me to help him, to take him away for some time to get away from it all. From the temptations. And I said yes.'

Logan remained still, looking at the TV. Irvine realised that she hadn't really seen him truly angry before and that maybe he was a silent one. A brooder.

'I'm going today. Now. I wanted to tell you, to let you know . . .'

He looked at her, eyes dark under the storm cloud gathering in his head. 'Is that it?' he asked.

Was that a tremor in his voice? Raw emotion?

Kiss me, the voice in her head shouted.

'No,' she said stepping towards him. 'Logan . . .'

What? I love you. I want you. What? Say something, Becky.

Then his mouth is on hers and his hands are at her back, grabbing and pulling at the vest. She feels the skin on her lower back exposed as the material rides up and an electric jolt when his fingers brush against her.

Is Ellie here, is all she can think before the hot tide rushes up and over her and their tongues are meshed in one mouth.

She doesn't wait for him; too many barren months are pushing her on. She pulls the polo shirt up over his head and puts her hands on his chest, her fingers pressing into the soft skin and hard muscle.

Then he's moving her out of the room and towards the bedroom, their mouths never parting.

They stumble through the doorway and he cracks his elbow on the frame. But nothing breaks their union.

They're in the room now; he leans back and lifts the vest up and over her head. The air touches her skin. Then he's behind her, his hands unclasping her bra and moving around until they are on her breasts. He slides them up, brushing her nipples.

After that it's difficult for her to remember details.

He pushes her on the bed, traces kisses over her stomach and then . . .

And then.

His kiss there; soft, warm and perfect.

She feels the tension in his muscles as he moves up on to her and then slides himself in. She opens her eyes and looks at his face above her; his eyes are locked on hers.

He moves inside her, convulsions brimming.

Sliding her hands on to his back, she curls her legs around: her feet press on him, pushing him on; pulling him in.

His breath quickens; the pace slows.

She feels him pulse inside.

They don't say anything for a while, lying side by side on the bed. Then she turns to him, grabbing his hand. 'I *so* needed that,' she says.

He laughs and nods.

Roddy can wait.

20

Irvine drove to the hospital, still feeling tremors in her arms as she turned the wheel, changed gears. Maybe this thing with Logan was for real; the sex certainly was.

Had it ever been as good as that with Tom, she wondered.

With anyone?

She didn't think so. Or maybe it had just been too long.

Pulling into the main grounds of the hospital she saw that the media presence had diminished, with only one crew outside the A&E door and even they didn't look that interested any more. The cameraman was sitting in the open door of the van drinking a can of Coke and looking bored. The vultures were leaving, now that it appeared no one was going to die, for which Irvine was thankful. Having been caught in the centre of the maelstrom she was surprised that it hadn't resulted in any fatalities.

Roddy was an injured celebrity, and so automatically fascinating to the media, but the fact that no one had died meant that the red tops and the TV news editors had nothing juicy to blame him for.

A broken leg and several concussions were the worst injuries she heard on the radio news.

Irvine hoped that she would be able to get past the news crew without a repeat of her reality TV star moment from last night. She went into the car park and then drove around for a while, hoping that someone would leave to allow her to park close to the exit, ready for a quick departure. She got semi-lucky when a tired-looking nurse in scrubs fell into a Ford Fiesta two rows from the exit and pulled out.

Once she had parked, Irvine tied her hair up with a black scrunchy, put her sunglasses on and pulled one of Logan's baseball caps over her head, pushing it down until the brim almost touched the top edge of her shades.

She walked away from the car, watching the news van and moving horizontally until she was behind it. Then she walked briskly straight towards the entrance and slipped around the back of the van, escaping the notice of both the cameraman and the reporter who was touching up her make-up in the front seat.

Inside, the A&E reception was fairly quiet with most of the casualties who had been brought here already treated and either sent home or on a ward somewhere in the hospital. She saw that the nurse who let her in last night was back on duty and, when she caught her attention, got waved through the automatic doors into the green womb of the hospital interior.

Irvine had read somewhere that green was supposed to be a relaxing colour, which was probably why most hospitals seemed to choose some shade of green – sort of turquoise here – to keep the inmates relaxed. Under the strong overhead strip-lights, combined with the clinical smell of detergent, bleach, blood and bodily fluids, it just made her feel nauseous.

She hated hospitals; had been in too many as a cop.

Seen too much blood.

Seen four deaths as a cop; four too many.

In her second month out of Tulliallan she'd been called to a complaint about a too-loud party on a council estate in the east of the city. When she got there with her older partner they rounded up several under-age kids in the street, drunk and letting everyone in the street know it. Three in the morning.

The party broke up fast when they got inside. Drugs flushed. Dealers bolted. Job done.

One last sweep of the house before they headed back to the station to write it up. Irvine had been the one to find the kid. He wasn't even three, curled up under his bed in the smallest room in the house. Little blond moppet. She thought he was sleeping and when she couldn't rouse him had to get on the floor and squeeze under the bed to try to get to him and shake him awake. That's when she found the methadone bottle in his hand; the empty bottle.

Faint pulse; blue lights; green-suited paramedics.

A long night in the hospital.

The longest night for the wee boy. Never-ending. Eternal.

That was the last time she had cried over something at work. Cried for six months while they went through the prosecution of the mother and father and she had to give evidence in the witness box against both of them. They couldn't plead out to the charges: no street honour in that. Remanded to Barlinnie – the Bar-L – and state aid to get the best QC around. Your tax dollar at work: defending the killers of the wee angel they were supposed to look out for, to raise until he was a man on his own.

Guilty verdicts notwithstanding, it made her sick.

Justice can't just be done; it has to be seen to be done. Innocent until proven guilty. Everyone is entitled to a proper defence, a fair trial. Human rights, you know.

GJ Moffat

Nemo me impune lacessit.

The motto on the coat of arms in every court in Scotland.

No one shall touch me with impunity.

How about jail sentences of five years each? Out after half of it served. He's in the ground; they're in the pub.

21

Roddy was sitting in a chair by the bed dressed in cargo pants and a faded black Sex Pistols T-shirt. He was sipping at a cup of tea in a cracked hospital mug and reading a three-month-old copy of *Hello!* magazine.

His band manager, a skinny woman with elfin features and short dark hair that only accentuated her otherworldliness, was the only other person in the room. She was striding from one end of the room to the other – which really wasn't very far at all – and talking on her mobile. Irvine recognised her from the concert as the woman who had jumped down from the stage after Roddy fell.

The manager frowned when she saw Irvine and ended her phone call abruptly with a curt 'Call you back.' Roddy looked up and smiled.

'Just what do you think you're doing?' the manager said to Roddy. 'Going on a holiday in the middle of a tour. We'll get our asses sued off.'

She was English: pure public school. But she talked like she'd much rather be an American. She probably called nappies 'diapers' and lifts 'elevators'.

'It's my ass,' Roddy said. 'Not yours.'

'You know what I mean.'

'And it's hardly a holiday. I mean, were you not there last night? Did you not see me take a header off the stage?'

'The doctor says you'll be fine in a week or so,' she said, surly now. 'And we've still got four more weeks of shows. Did you forget that because of your . . . condition, we could only get limited insurance cover?'

'I need to get away, OK? The decision is made and it's something I should have done a while ago. It's either this or I'll end up dead.'

'Maybe no bad thing,' Irvine said. 'Look what it does for sales.'

Roddy laughed. The manager scowled. 'I guess there's nothing I can do to change your mind?' she said.

'Nope,' Roddy said.

She sighed and toyed with her mobile. 'You realise the amount of crap I'm going to have to deal with? From the label and the promoter and . . .'

'It's why you get the big bucks. Don't sweat it.'

Irvine looked the manager up and down. She looked expensive, that was for sure. Manicured hands and pedicured feet, French polish on her nails, designer labels all round.

The manager looked like she wanted to continue the fight, but Roddy stood and, grabbing a 'distressed' green duffel bag that nevertheless managed to look brand new, said, 'Let's get going.' He walked gingerly around the bed and handed the bag to Irvine. 'You don't mind, do you?' he asked. 'I'm still a bit wobbly.'

'Should you be leaving so soon?' Irvine asked.

'No,' the manager said.

'I can't be in here for another minute,' Roddy declared.

Irvine took the bag and slung it over her shoulder, with Roddy holding on to her elbow. Irvine looked at him closely and decided that he was fit enough to travel.

'Well, if I can't stop you,' the manager said, 'at least let me help get you out of here without having to run the press gauntlet.'

'There're not that many left,' Irvine told her.

'They're probably just on a lunch-break, 'cause the doctor told them he was supposed to be in here for at least another day.'

'Oh,' was all Irvine could say, glad she'd been lucky with her timing.

'Sit tight here for now and I'll get someone to arrange for you to leave from a different door.'

'My car's out by the exit, at the far end of the car park.'

'Best go get it then, dear.'

Irvine breathed slowly and counted to ten in her head.

22

Three was pretty pissed off at the way Hudson had spoken to him earlier. He wasn't an idiot and didn't appreciate being treated like one; he'd had enough of that while he was an army grunt. Now that he was a private contractor he expected a bit more respect. Still, he knew that even out of uniform a chain of command was entirely necessary, so he sucked up any residual anger and got on with the job in hand.

Five had driven when they followed the cop to the hospital. He was two inches shorter than Three at five-eight and worked hard in the gym to maintain his tightly packed, muscular body.

They had decided to stay outside the main grounds of the hospital rather than try to follow the cop into the car park. It would have looked suspicious following her around in there and this way they could see more clearly when she was leaving.

Now here she was coming out of the A&E entrance and walking down to her car. It was almost two in the afternoon and the sun was hot in the clear sky. She had the baseball cap on again and walked quickly through the car park.

They were taking turns to catch up on some sleep when they could and Five was dozing in the driving-seat. Three nudged him and pointed at the cop with his chin. Five rubbed at his eyes and scanned the car park until he located her, just as she got to her car.

'Check the tracker,' he said, keeping his eyes on the cop.

Three opened the glove-box and switched on the handheld device that enabled them to monitor the GPS tracker they had fitted to the underside of her car while she'd been in the flat she visited earlier. The signal was strong this close to the vehicle and Three gave a nod.

They sat in silence and watched as she got in the car.

'She's on the move,' Three said, as the car backed out of its parking space and then drove out of sight behind one of the hospital buildings.

They waited to see it coming out of the hospital grounds but it didn't reappear. Three looked at Five and then checked the GPS.

'She's not moving,' he said.

Five rubbed at the short stubble on his chin. He was six years older than Three and had been with Hudson's crew for the last eighteen months; technically he had rank here.

'Go see what she's up to,' he told Three.

Three dropped the tracker in Five's lap and got out, jogging across the road and then slowly walking through the entrance and round to the area where he had seen the cop's car go.

The car was outside the general outpatients building, parallel to A&E. The cop was in her car and the singer was being helped into the passenger seat by some skinny woman who was dressed like a rock chick. When the singer was in the car, the cop pulled away and drove past Three's position. She glanced at him as they went by.

Three hurried back to the car and got in as the cop's car turned left ahead of them. 'Shit,' he said. 'She saw me.'

Five looked at him quickly and then back at the road.

'Sorry.'

'It's done now. Where's she going?'

Three looked at the handheld in his lap, watching for a minute or more to make sure that the cop had settled into her chosen direction of travel.

'OK,' he said. 'She's going north.'

'Sure of that?'

'I'm sure. And she's got that singer guy with her.'

Five looked at him and frowned. 'Call the boss and let him know. He's not gonna like it.'

23

Hudson was driving to the place where the rest of his crew were getting everything ready for the job tomorrow when Three called. He had just finished his meeting with the Guy, and the Thing was sitting in a brown paper bag on the passenger seat.

'Go ahead,' Hudson said when he answered the call.

'We've got her on the GPS, heading north.'

'Good. Get it done tonight if you can. I don't want this thing dragging on over tomorrow. I've got enough on my plate already.'

She's got someone with her.'

Hudson had his phone on hands-free and he had an excellent kit set up in his car, with a microphone set above his head and a speaker by the transmission tunnel. Still, he pulled over to the side of the road for this conversation.

'What do you mean she's got someone with her? Who?'

'Looks like the guy from the TV.'

Hudson had no idea who Three was talking about and told him so.

'The singer guy,' Three said. 'From the concert.'

Just what Hudson needed – a genuine celebrity in the way. If he got taken out at the same time it would be a media circus, even more so than just for a cop. He massaged his temples with his fingers, aware that the action was a cliché, but it felt right.

'What you want us to do?' Three asked.

'Just follow them for now, OK.'

'So we don't do it tonight.'

Hudson closed his eyes and took a breath. 'Not if she's still with him, no.'

'OK, but what if they stick together for a while? I mean how long you want us to wait?'

Hudson thought for a moment. His plan had been to have the entire job done by tomorrow night and he knew from experience that if things dragged out too far then the probability of screw-ups, and getting caught, increased exponentially. He thought that maybe the boss would like the simplicity of both hits going down simultaneously.

'It's got to get done by tomorrow night,' Hudson said. I want us all out of here after the thing in town; no hanging around.'

'So we wait till tomorrow and if they're still together . . . ?'

'Then you'll just have to improvise.'

'And the guy?'

'If you have to.'

Hudson finished the call, thinking: this is not going to end well.

part two: execution

1

Cahill drove along Waterloo Street towards the Hilton hotel and veered right at the end of the road. Tom Hardy was beside him in the front passenger seat with Chris Washington, Bailey Judd and Carrie Richardson following in a separate car.

The street ahead sloped down to the service yard at the rear of the hotel, curled to the right under an old telecoms building and then switched back to the left to get to the hotel entrance. Cahill slowed and parked at the side of the road, rather than going on and turning into the hotel driveway.

There was a taxi parked in front of Cahill's car with the now standard garish colours of an advertisement painted over the black of the cab; so much for tradition. He got out and waited for the others. The five of them walked along the path past the taxi and turned left on to the hotel's driveway. Cahill was aware that together they looked quite intimidating and in one way it was a deliberate choice for all of them to come here together: anyone who intended to do Tara harm might see them and perhaps think twice about it.

If they were here and watching. Any advantage, however small, was worth the effort.

'Cab rank goes all the way up,' Hardy said, pointing with his chin at the line of taxis taking up the whole of the left-hand side of the driveway.

Four or five of the taxi drivers had convened at the front of the queue of cars and watched the CPO team as they walked up the gentle incline of the driveway towards the revolving doors at the entrance. The hotel loomed high above them, its glass and brown-stone exterior reflecting the early afternoon sunlight.

Washington walked over to one of the taxis and pointed at a metal plate on the back beside the licence plate.

'They've all got these,' he said. 'Says that they are officially licensed as taxis by the City of Glasgow Council.'

'We should check when we get here tomorrow that all the cars have the plates,' Cahill said. 'Make sure that any that are here then are meant to be here.'

Washington nodded and re-joined the group as they continued up the driveway past the taxi drivers who, probably without even realising they were doing it, shifted towards their cars while keeping a close watch on them.

Stopping at the top of the slope, Cahill looked back down past the row of taxis, not liking what he saw. With the taxis taking up all that space, there was only a narrow entrance left for anyone else. Too easy to get stuck there while someone with a gun put several bullets into the car.

'Not great,' Hardy said. 'Just gives us a single-track entry and exit point.'

'Easily blocked and used as a trap,' Bailey Judd said.

Though Judd was the youngest of the team and still learning the job as a close-protection operative, he was getting more comfortable about expressing his views to the others. Cahill had him marked out as a potential team leader in future.

'Maybe if this was a war zone,' Washington said, shaking his head. 'I don't think we need to worry too much about getting boxed in and caught in a firefight on this job.'

Washington was the perfect operative in Cahill's view: strong, tough and always the first one into a fight. Even now, with a young son and another on the way, he never backed down. Maybe not leadership potential, but a leader always needed an able lieutenant: the way Cahill had Tom Hardy.

They continued to follow the road round past the entrance, Carrie nodding at the young, uniformed doorman and giving him her best smile, which was pretty good. She was not averse to using her femininity if it helped out on a job.

The road curved back down to the main street in a crescent shape, again fairly narrow. An electronically controlled barrier marked the entrance to the hotel's underground parking garage.

'I'll make sure that gets checked when we're leaving here tomorrow for the premiere,' Judd said, pointing at the garage entrance.

Cahill nodded in agreement, and then all of them turned round to look back up at the hotel entrance.

'If this was anything other than a babysitting job,' Washington said, taking off his sunglasses, 'I'd be worried. I mean this has just about everything that's bad about a location.'

Cahill knew that Washington was probably right, but he didn't want them to get complacent because of the perceived nature of the assignment. That went against his instincts, his innate professionalism.

'But we treat it the same as always, right?' Carrie asked.

'We have to,' Cahill said. 'Everybody needs to keep it tight.'

Carrie was standing beside Washington and nudged his ribs with her elbow.

'See, tough guy,' she said to him. 'Who's your daddy now?'

Washington looked down at her implacably and put his glasses back on. 'I'm a married man,' he said. 'Try to keep it in your pants, will you.'

She screwed her face up at him.

The taxi drivers watched them in silence as they walked to the entrance doors, Cahill nodding at them because he felt it was only polite. They went through the revolving doors into the plush lobby, with its marble floors and walnut-clad columns flanking a central seating space. Spreading out, they walked round the whole area, checking everything and making mental notes about the layout of the place. Carrie and Washington took out small notepads to write down what they saw. The rest of them kept it in their heads.

After a full circuit of the lobby area, they convened again round one of the tables in the seating space and ordered coffee.

'It's all way too open for my liking,' Hardy said to Cahill. 'Inside and out. Too many exit and entry points to cover comfortably; doors all over the place.'

'That one over there,' Judd said, pointing to a door to the right of the entrance, 'has access to a stairwell that goes all the way up to the top and also down to the parking garage.'

'I'll speak to Tara's security team and see if we can do anything about switching our departure away from here,' Cahill said. 'But we should prepare for the fact that they *will* want to leave from here.'

'What's the plan with her guys?' Washington asked. 'I mean, do we get to sit down with them and go over it?'

'Not all of us, no,' Cahill said. 'I'm planning on meeting later with Phil Hanson, her head guy, and then we can go over it tomorrow before we come out here.'

'You want some company when you go to see Hanson?' Hardy asked.

Cahill thought for a second. 'Might be a good idea, yeah,' he said. 'I'll meet Tara as well so it might be helpful if she sees a show of strength from us. Reassure her some.'

'Take the biggest, ugliest, hardest-looking bastard,' Hardy said, nodding.

They all looked at Washington.

'What?' Washington said, trying to look indignant but smiling all the same.

2

Roddy was lolling on the passenger seat with the window open and his head tilted so that the fast-moving air was rushing straight into his face. Irvine glanced at him as she drove, checking to see how he looked and paranoid that he might still be concussed. She was pleased that although he looked pale, bruised and far from his best (maybe ten years far from his best), at least he was alert and communicative.

'So where are we going?' Roddy asked for what seemed like the hundredth time in the last hour. 'I mean, is it a secret or something?'

'Yeah, it's a secret. So stop asking me.'

He turned his head further to the window and pretended to sulk, but she could see the smile lifting the edge of his mouth as he did it. She figured he was just happy to get away from it all and was kind of enjoying what passed for freedom in his cloistered world of recording studios, rehearsal rooms, TV shows and concert venues.

She'd had what seemed like a great idea as she drove from Logan's flat to the hospital but was starting to think that the buzz of the sex and the hot blast of Logan's shower – with him in there with her all wet and slick and . . .

Steady there, girl. Deep breath.

Anyway, this grand idea of hers to drive north towards Glencoe and Fort William and lots of other places so very *Scottish* was intended to reconnect Roddy with his past and with . . .

'What?' she asked herself.

'Eh?' he asked, turning to face her.

'Nothing. Sorry.'

'Are you mental?'

'Quite possibly,' she said, laughing. 'You've only got to look at what I've done in the last twenty-four hours.'

'You have a point.'

She noticed again the forced American twang of his accent – LA by way of Govan.

The countryside flashed by. God, she couldn't remember the last time she'd actually taken the time to see where she was going. Really see it for what it was. Twisting and winding along the side of Loch Lomond, shards of light from the surface of the water flashing in her eyes through gaps in the trees on the bank. The smell of . . . nothing really. Not the urban reek of Glasgow. Of humanity or what passed for it: cigarette smoke, exhaust fumes, booze.

A thought jagged in her mind from out of nowhere.

They must have gone this way when they went to get Ellie. Logan and Cahill and the others.

And with that realisation everything changed. The pure, clean smells were replaced by sharp, bitter tangs tugging at her gag reflex.

The smell of death, and of desperation.

Ellie's poor mum – Penny – lying on the floor of the house, her face a bloodied pulp. The taste of her own vomit, erupting after she went back and stole the clothes and the journal for Ellie.

Blood and piss and sweat in that bar where the man who was following Logan got shot.

Brain matter smeared red and white against the toilet-stall door.

It was more than mere memory; it was reality. A time machine transporting her back, making her feel the same raw, bleak emotion. And then the whole of the time since then with Tom and Logan and . . .

Irvine wrenched the steering wheel and the car skidded across to the other side of the road, the wheels skimming grass and dry earth, throwing dust into the air. Roddy grabbed the door handle and braced his other hand against the dashboard.

She braked hard, then soft, and the car rolled to a stop. The car behind screeched past them, the driver glaring at her and holding his hand firm against the horn in protest.

Irvine threw her door open without looking at Roddy and almost fell out of the car; gulping in the air and trying to clear her nose and mouth of the smells and tastes. But they were more than physical sensations.

Forever part of her.

She heard Roddy scrambling across the driver's seat to get to her as she sat heavily on the grass. Closing her eyes she saw the news reports from the cabin – the Scenes of Crime team all over it with their white coveralls and masks and the tents where they tagged and processed and preserved all the evidence.

TV crews and long-lens photographers out on the loch – the other loch – watching as the dead were carried out one after the other in bags.

I helped to do that, she remembered thinking: to kill them.

Cahill's refrain: 'Who gives a fuck?'

Maybe he was right. The investigation went nowhere and the media interest dried up after a week or two of lurid headlines about gang wars on Scotland's bonnie banks.

And everyone bought their story for Ellie. It helped that DNA from Penny's body was matched to the Russian killed in the bar when the police ran it through the database. The police always liked it when a case closed, so they didn't think too hard about how it all fitted together. They had a violent criminal tied incontrovertibly to the scene and the fact that he was dead saved on the cost of a trial and a prison term. All wrapped up in a neat bow.

They got lucky, that was for sure.

But Ellie had been traumatised, of that there was no doubt. Not that you could tell now with her so strong and vibrant.

Does she wake, like me, in the night? Does Logan? Do we all see the same ghosts?

Irvine's dream is always the same. She's back in Ellie's room, reaching for the journal on the shelf in the wardrobe when something moves at the back. She can't resist. Nightmares are like that.

Inexorable.

Unbearable.

She walks into the wardrobe, but it's nothing like Narnia. It's black. And then she sees it – the body bag. The zip starts to move down, to open from the inside. A hand reaches out . . .

Irvine opened her eyes and squinted in the sun. Roddy was kneeling in front of her, a light breeze tugging strands of hair across his face, that ridiculous bandage on his head. Were they trying to make him look like an idiot?

Sterling effort.

'What?' he asked, seeing a smile dance on her lips.

She reached up and pulled the hair from his face, tucking it behind his ear. 'It's all right,' she said, talking more to herself than to him. She closed her eyes again and breathed deeply of tree sap and clear water as a jet ski droned far away on the other side of the loch.

Roddy moved, dirt scraping under his shoes and knee joints popping as he stood and walked down the short slope to the water. She looked at him as he bent down, water splashing over his hands. She frowned, wondering what he was doing as he turned, diamond tears dripping from his cupped hands, rainbows refracted in the glistening drops.

He walked carefully back to her, spilling water as he neared, then opened his hands as she looked up. The water was cold when it hit her skin. Irvine allowed it to flow over her and then wiped it back off her face and into her hair, feeling the sun on her forehead. Roddy stood above her in silhouette with the sun behind his head.

She got up and thanked him – turned to go back to the car.

He said nothing for a half-hour as they cleared the loch and headed northwest towards Rannoch Moor and the valley at Glencoe.

'Seems like we *both* need a bit of a break,' he said finally.

'Thanks, Roddy. I mean for what you did and for not asking.'

'That's OK. But tell me. This guy – the one you went to see and left me dangling in the hospital for – is the good worth the bad? Worth what happened to you back there?'

She looked at him and he stared back.

'What else would have taken you so long after you left me at the hospital?' he asked in answer to her silent question. 'Saying your goodbyes?'

'Why do you assume that there's anything bad about my relationship with him?'

110

'That wasn't about him, back there?'

'Kind of, but not really. We share . . .'

How to put it?

'. . . history.'

He said nothing more and went back to his open window and the rush of air on his face.

3

Ellie came back to the flat with Logan's parents after dinner. Dusk was glowing pink in the night sky and the smell of the Indian summer filled the place through open windows.

It had been a strange afternoon after Irvine had left to go on her odyssey (if that was the right word) with Roddy. The electric jolt of their time together had faded, leaving Logan to wonder just what he was supposed to make of her decision to go with Roddy, but to come here first and do what she did.

He had picked up the phone to call her at least three times after she left, but didn't want to spoil what had happened by seeming needy and jealous – albeit he kind of was.

After listening half-heartedly to a few Springsteen tracks ('Who's the old guy?' Ellie had asked when she saw the photo on the cover of his last album) he went to his DVD collection and ran his finger down the shelves, stopping when he got to Hitchcock's *Rebecca*. And, like Irvine, he was assaulted by the past: his first time with Penny after the concert at the Barrowlands.

But this time, when he tried to remember her face in the rain – her lips on his – all he could see was Irvine. Maybe that was a good thing; maybe not. He couldn't decide.

He wondered if he loved her. Irvine.

'I love you, Becky,' he said quietly to the strangers passing below his window, testing how it sounded, how it felt.

It didn't feel awkward or embarrassing, but beyond that he couldn't really say.

He was dozing on the couch with some awful Saturday night programme on the TV when he heard Ellie's voice as she bounded up the stairs and pushed her key into the lock, laughing as his dad tried to keep up with her and failed. He stood as the door creaked open.

'Hey, Logan,' she said when she came into the living room, casually standing on tiptoe and kissing his cheek.

Suddenly the world was righted again.

He noticed the bags of clothes and shoes that his dad brought in behind her.

'You spoil her, Dad.'

'You're a lawyer. Sue me.'

Logan laughed.

Ellie grabbed the bag from Logan's dad and disappeared towards her room, shouting that she was going to try the stuff on for Logan to see. Then he heard his mum huffing up the stairs to the front door. His dad leaned in and whispered to him, 'She asked to go to Penny's grave, to put flowers down for her.'

'And did you?'

'Course not. I told her that she should ask you, that it was her father's job to do that with her.'

'I'll talk to her, then. Take her tomorrow morning.'

His dad nodded. 'Right, love,' he said as his wife's red face appeared in the doorway. 'Let's get home for *The X Factor*.'

'I just got here,' she complained. 'Am I no' even getting a cup of tea?'

'Get yourself turned round and leave the boy to the Ellie-bee fashion show.'

He ushered Logan's mum out into the hall and towards the front door, winking back at Logan as he went, and shouting goodbye to Ellie. Ellie ran into the hall and put an arm round each of them and then darted back to her room.

'Take care, son,' his dad said as he got to the front door.

He paused and turned to walk back to Logan, putting his arms round his son and kissing him brusquely on the cheek. It was the first time in many years that Logan could remember such an overt display of affection from the man.

'And you take care of her too, or it's me you'll be answering to. Understand?'

Logan nodded and his dad turned and closed the door. Logan stood staring at the door, feeling the dry kiss on his cheek, the day-long stubble brushing against his skin.

4

After Ellie had shown Logan her new clothes, they watched a movie together before Logan went to the kitchen to make hot chocolate for them both. He was leaning against the counter waiting for the milk to boil and wondering how he would broach the subject of going to Penny's grave when Ellie came in and did it for him.

'Pops said you would take me to see my mum.'

She always talked about Penny like that, like she was somehow still here.

'If you want to. Tomorrow, if you like?'

'Yes.' She twisted the hem of her jersey top in her hands.

'What is it?' Logan asked.

'Can we get her a card and some flowers?'

Logan told her that of course they would.

'I mean a funny card,' Ellie said. 'She told me that's what you always got her.'

Logan blinked hard as he turned back to the kettle and said OK. It was a day for memories, good and bad.

They sat in the living room sipping at their hot drinks and

enjoying the last of the day's warmth as the cool of the night started to seep in through the window. Logan got up and pulled it shut.

'Can I ask you about something?' Ellie said to his back.

'Sure.' He closed the blinds on the window and sat back down beside her on the couch.

'It's about when you and Alex found me.'

Logan said nothing, waiting for her to find the strength to ask whatever it was that she wanted to know. It was not something that they had ever really talked about much.

'What was it like? When you shot that man?'

It was not the question Logan had expected. 'What do you mean?' he asked.

'I mean, how did it make you feel?'

'I didn't feel bad about it because he wanted to hurt you; to hurt both of us. Do you understand that?'

'Uh-huh. But wasn't it wrong to, you know, kill him like that?'

'No. Not when you're doing it to save someone from getting . . . hurt.' Couldn't bring himself to say 'killed'.

'Do you, you know, think about it now? Or dream about it?'

'Like your bad dreams?'

'Yes.'

He put his arm round her and pulled her closer until she rested her head on his shoulder, her hands twisting and pulling at themselves on her lap. 'Sometimes I dream about it, yes. But then I wake up and I think about . . .' *what he did to your mother and how he deserved all he got* '. . . you, and what we have now, and the bad stuff goes away.'

She was quiet for a moment, still worrying with her hands. 'Why didn't the police ever ask me about it? I mean those men and the cabin and all of that.'

'You know that Becky's a police officer, don't you?'

Her muscles stiffened when he said Irvine's name, but she didn't respond.

'Well, she helped us to tell the police the story about how you got to my flat and they believed her.'

'Why couldn't you just tell them everything that happened instead of *her* lying about it?'

'We all lied about it, honey. To protect you and everyone who was there with me and Alex. The police might not have understood that we did what we had to do to save you.'

'But if it wasn't wrong, why did you have to lie about it?'

She'd make a good trial lawyer – probing all the time for the weak points. Logan almost smiled at the thought.

'Because it can get you in trouble. Sometimes the police don't believe it when you say that you did the right thing.'

'That doesn't sound fair.'

'It's not. But it happens.'

'But they can't come back and take you away for that now, can they?' Her hands slid round his waist and she pulled him to her tightly.

'No, they can't.'

Little white lies.

Ellie went to bed and Logan stayed on the couch, enjoying the silence and trying hard not to think about anything except new clothes and the strong embrace of his father.

He went in to see Ellie before going to his own bed, and as he leaned in to kiss her goodnight she opened her eyes and looked at him. She said nothing and he thought that maybe she was still asleep. She did that sometimes, appearing wide awake but dreaming instead; giggling and talking nonsense. It had totally freaked him out the first time it happened.

'Why do you like her?' she asked.

Logan sat on the bed, pushing dark strands of hair back from her face. 'You mean Becky?'

Ellie nodded.

'I don't know.'

'Because she's pretty?'

'Sure, but not just that. I like talking to her and just being with her.'

'More than my mum?'

'Your mum was special, Ellie. Becky can't replace her. But I like her a lot.' He put a hand on her cheek, felt it damp.

'Tell me about my mum, Logan, when she was young and you were with her and how she was and what she liked. Everything. Tell me about her.'

And he did.

They fell asleep together, curled as one: father and daughter and the fresh, raw memory of Penny. Not the lifeless body at the end, crushed and beaten and alone, but the real Penny: the Penny that they both loved and kept vibrant and alive inside their hearts.

5

Irvine pulled in to a café in Glencoe village and they stayed there for a couple of hours – much longer than Irvine had intended – eating, and drinking coffee, and catching up.

Roddy was more open that she remembered him, even making embarrassing admissions about dalliances with groupies on tour buses and in plush hotel suites.

'Booze and cooze,' he said, laughing. 'That's what Dougie called it.'

'I never did like him,' Irvine told him, smiling despite herself. 'Greasy wee shit.'

Roddy laughed briefly, then winced at the pain slicing into his head. 'Great drummer, though. You've really got to give credit where it's due, Becky Reid.'

He'd been doing that all afternoon, calling her by her full maiden name. It was good, she thought, because charming as he could be, he'd always be a bit of a dickhead. She wanted to be reminded that this trip was not a holiday or, God forbid, a romance. It was to get him out of harm's way.

GJ Moffat

He was less exuberant when it came to talking about the drugs.

'How did it start?' she asked him. 'I mean, someone must have helped you get into it the first few times. Was it that manager, the skinny bitch from the hospital? She looks the type.'

'No. She might come across as a bit of a bitch but she's the one that tries to keep us straight. In fact, she set me up with a couple of people when we were in the States. Addiction specialists.'

'So what went wrong?'

'I did. Never kept the appointments.'

'Too busy getting wasted?'

Roddy nodded. 'Or getting laid.'

'Don't spare my blushes, Roddy.'

'Oh, come on. You weren't so sensitive earlier.'

Irvine swirled the dregs of her coffee and swallowed it down, feeling the bitter grit and wincing as it grated down her throat.

'You didn't answer my question, Roddy. How did you get started on the drugs?'

He leaned back in his chair and looked around the empty café. The waitress who had served them was behind a low counter watching a small colour TV replaying the news from last night. Irvine saw her own face again and frowned.

'The booze just wasn't doing it any more, you know,' he said. 'I finally woke up one morning with the mother of all hangovers, puking and . . . well, just puking. A lot. I felt like shit all day and couldn't focus on the rehearsal at the venue.'

'Where?'

'What? It doesn't matter, does it?'

'Just asking.'

'I don't know. Charlotte, I think. Or maybe Portland.'

Irvine's US geography was not strong so she had no idea where those places were. She thought maybe he was going to say LA; she knew where LA was.

'Anyway,' Roddy went on. 'So this roadie, big fat guy, he took me outside and told me he could get me something to pick me up. Help me get through. That's how it started.'

'Then it's always chasing the same high, isn't it?'

He nodded, but said nothing.

'I know,' she said. 'I've heard the story a hundred times. Probably more.'

He shrugged.

'But at least you're trying now,' Irvine said, feeling that she'd maybe been a bit too mother-knows-best with him.

'And what's your story?' he asked. 'I mean, why no longer married?'

'Nothing dramatic. We just, I don't know. We got tired of each other. I got tired of him.'

'Couldn't match up to me, eh?'

'Oh, yeah. Such a hard act to follow.'

'I need to go to the rest room,' he said, standing abruptly and scraping his chair back on the tiled floor.

'Do I need to come and watch you?'

He stopped and raised an eyebrow. 'Not unless you want to.'

6

Irvine sat looking out through the big window on to the street as the day began to wither and the sun bled into the horizon. She saw a car parked across the road with two men in it. One of them, the passenger, had reclined his seat and was sleeping and the driver was reading a newspaper.

Something about the car, or maybe it was the men, nagged at her memory, like a dripping tap. The thought did not solidify and anyway she couldn't really see the men in the fading light, so she caught the attention of the waitress and asked for the bill.

The driver of the car across the street folded the paper and then drove off. Irvine figured it was just a couple of tourists taking a break; a bit like her and Roddy.

The waitress was removing a little plastic tray with the bill and Irvine's cash on it when Roddy came out of the toilet.

'You should have let me get that,' he said. 'This is my trip and I can pay for it. I want to pay for it. You shouldn't be out of pocket to help me.'

'You can get the next one. And the two rooms at the hotel. And everything else.'

'*Two* rooms?'

'Don't make me regret this, Roddy,' she said, elbowing her way past him to get to the door.

Back in the car, Irvine thought that Roddy looked a bit brighter now. Maybe the fresh air and the food at the café had revived him, and certainly there was a bit of a healthier tone to his skin than there had been when she picked him up from the hospital.

'Where are we stopping tonight?' he asked.

'Don't know; somewhere soon because I'm knackered.'

They drove on until they reached the bridge at Ballachulish and Irvine pulled off on to the Oban road when she saw a sign indicating that there was a hotel. The road curled under the bridge and the hotel came into sight by the side of the loch. It looked OK to Irvine, with a large modern extension attached to the side of an old house.

'We stopping here?' Roddy asked.

'Yep, looks good to me.'

The tyres crunched and skidded a little on the loose gravel of the car park and Irvine found a free space not far from the reception – on the ground floor of the main house.

'You wait here,' she told Roddy. 'I'll check if they have any rooms.'

He watched her walk into the building and then looked across the road at the dying orange-red glow of the sun reflected on the calm surface of the water. In the far distance, Ben Nevis loomed above the loch and he wondered, not for the first time, why he had ever left here to live in the States.

A car came down from the bridge and slowed as it approached the hotel entrance. Roddy paid no attention to it.

Five parked in a spot as far from the hotel entrance as possible, but not so far from the other cars as to be noticeable. He wanted to be discreet but not obvious.

'Guy's still in the car,' he said to Three, who turned his head to look out of his window. 'At this time of night they're probably just going to get a room and go to bed.'

'Yeah. Not much chance of getting at them here, then.'

'I'll go find out what room they'll be in.'

'How you going to do that?'

'Leave it to me, son.'

7

Irvine waited at the empty reception desk and cleared her throat a couple of times to attract someone's attention. She always felt that it was too brazen to ring the ubiquitous service bell.

After a minute or so, a young woman in a bright uniform of navy skirt, white blouse and silk tartan scarf came out of the door behind the desk and asked how she could help. Irvine asked for two adjacent rooms and was told that she could have a suite in the old part of the hotel but that was the best that could be done tonight. She said OK and the woman handed her a registration card to complete.

Irvine heard the reception door open and looked round, expecting to see Roddy. Instead, a sturdy guy about her age and height smiled and came to stand behind her.

Irvine was finishing the registration card when she felt the man behind her brush against her as he leaned forward and took a hotel brochure from a stand on the desk. She didn't see him glance quickly at her registration card to note the room number.

'Sorry,' he said.

Irvine said it was fine and finished what she was doing. She stood there while the receptionist went back through the door behind the desk to get the keys. She felt the man's silent presence at her back and felt uncomfortable, without really being sure why.

Then she heard him turn and leave, and assumed that having checked the place out and looked at the brochure he had decided it was not for him.

After getting the keys, Irvine walked along the hall and found a quiet spot to call her mum, knowing that her son would already be in bed and feeling a little too fragile to hear his voice. This was only the third time since he'd been born that she had spent the night away from him, other than when she was called out to a crime scene by her job.

'How's Connor?' she asked after a frosty exchange of hellos.

'He misses you. Said he wanted a cuddle from his mummy when I put him down for the night.'

Again with the guilt trip: ever since she split from Tom.

'I miss him too, Mum, so don't start, OK? I don't need a fight with you right now.'

She immediately regretted being so sharp. Her mum was an odd mix of steel and sentiment and could be cut quite easily.

'Sorry, Mum,' she sighed. 'It's been an emotional time for us both, what with the divorce being final and all.'

'I'm sorry too. You need support from me and I'm not very good at giving it to you sometimes. I know I can be too critical.'

'Can we start this conversation again?'

'Yes, let's.' Irvine thought that she almost heard a smile in her mum's voice.

'So how is he?' she asked.

'He's great. We took him to the park and then to dinner. He was tired out so he went to bed quite happily after his bath.'

'Thanks. I'll only be a few days and I'll call tomorrow to speak to him. Tell him that, OK?'

'I will.'

They said goodbye and Irvine stood for a moment, trying to maintain her composure and just about succeeding.

'Room twenty-three,' Five said as he got in the car. 'It's on the second floor.'

'You're good,' Three told him.

'I know.'

'So we take her in the room?'

'Maybe. I mean, it's an option. Let's wait and check it out once they're both settled down inside.'

They sat quietly and watched as Irvine came out of the hotel and she and Roddy got their bags from the car and walked back into the hotel.

'Should we check in with the boss?' Three asked.

Five nodded as the last glow of the sun disappeared, leaving the surface of the loch cold and black.

8

Cahill and Washington got back to the Hilton close to eight o'clock that night. Tara Byrne's security chief, Phil Hanson, rose from one of the couches in the reception lobby and waved at them as they came into the building. They walked over to meet him and shook hands. Hanson asked what they thought of the place.

'Well,' Cahill said, 'we checked it out earlier and I'd definitely stay here if I was in town, but for security purposes it sucks.'

'Bad entrance layout,' Washington said, nodding. 'Way too narrow and easy to get boxed in.'

'Can we maybe think about taking her out from the back, or is there another exit?' Cahill asked.

Hanson shook his head. 'No way,' he said. 'Devon's got the press primed for her leaving and he wants to make a big show of it. This is a career thing for Tara and she knows that she has to be visible.'

'I guess we'll just have to make do,' Cahill said.

'Want to see the rooms?' Hanson asked.

Cahill nodded and told him to lead on.

*　　*　　*

Hudson was sitting opposite his number two in the Hilton bar, facing out into the lobby and sipping at a bottled beer, when he saw Phil Hanson stand and greet the two men who came into reception.

'Somebody's here to see her security chief,' Hudson said, nodding at Cahill and Washington.

Two was Hudson's most experienced guy and knew better than to turn and look behind him immediately. 'What's he look like?' he asked.

'Two of them,' Hudson said. 'Definitely ex-military.' He leaned forward, resting his hands on his knees and straining to hear what the three men were talking about.

'Maybe American,' Hudson said. 'Can't be sure from this far away.'

Two nodded, stood and walked to the bar, looking out at the lobby and seeing the other men talking briefly before moving towards the lifts. He lifted a bowl of peanuts from the bar counter and took them back to their table, crunching on a couple of the nuts as he went.

'I think they must be the outside contractors,' Hudson said finally, after watching the men get in a lift and head up to the tenth floor.

'Yeah,' Two agreed. 'The black guy looks like a real hard case.'

'I could take him,' Hudson said.

Two knew that when it came to close-quarters fighting there were few people who could match Hudson. It was more than just his physical abilities; he was fearless in a fight. Almost as though he didn't care if he won or lost.

'Probably here to check the place out for tomorrow,' Two continued. 'They won't like it.'

'If they're good they won't like any of it,' Hudson said. 'From here to the cinema and back.'

Two smiled and pushed his dark fringe back off his tanned face.

Hudson's mobile vibrated in the back pocket of his jeans. He arched his back and lifted off his chair to get the phone.

'It's them,' he said to Two after checking the screen. He put the phone to his ear and listened, saying nothing for a while, and Two began to wonder if he was listening to a voicemail message rather than a live call.

'So it's not done is what you're telling me?' Hudson said finally.

He listened to the response and frowned at Two, who popped another handful of the peanuts into his mouth and crunched on them.

'It's your call. I can't tell you how to do it if I'm not there with you.' Another pause for a response. 'Call me later,' he said, ending the call and slipping the phone back into his pocket.

'Five will make sure it gets done right,' Two told him. 'It'll be fine.'

'I'm glad you think so.'

'I do. So just chill for now and enjoy your beer, OK?'

They finished their drinks in silence and Hudson stood to leave. Two got up and followed him across the lobby and out into the night air. They paused outside the entrance doors while Two lit a cigarette and then turned his head to blow the smoke away from his colleague, aware that he detested the stink of it. He'd once seen him knock a man out with a single punch after he blew smoke in his face.

Hudson shoved his hands in the pockets of his jeans and tried to remember the last time he felt any kind of emotion at the prospect of killing someone. He realised that perhaps the answer was never, and that this did not cause him any concern.

9

When they had checked the entire floor of the hotel where the rooms were situated, including the stairwell and the lifts, Cahill and Washington followed Hanson into Tara Byrne's suite.

Tara was something to behold in real life – as opposed to fifty feet high on a cinema screen. She was movie-star slim but retained enough curves to still resemble a real woman. Her dark hair was perfectly styled to appear elegantly tousled as it fell around her face and on to her shoulders. Her eyes were a striking shade of blue. She was sitting on a huge couch beside a tall, heavy woman of about twenty-five.

'Tara,' Hanson said, 'this is Alex Cahill and Chris Washington of CPO. They'll be helping look after you at the premiere tomorrow night.'

She nodded at both men and introduced the woman beside her as her PA. 'How does it look?' she asked Hanson.

'We'll manage just fine,' Cahill answered.

Hanson moved to the window and looked down on to the motorway as it snaked south of the city, depressing in its concrete monotony. Tara watched him, and Cahill wondered if they were more than just professionally involved; something about the way her eyes lingered on him as he stood at the window.

'That doesn't sound entirely convincing,' she said, turning to face Cahill. 'I mean, if you're trying to make me feel better you're not doing a very good job.'

She smiled, but it looked forced to Cahill. 'What can I say?' he told her. 'I can't promise that it's going to be easy.'

'No, I suppose not.'

The PA stood and went through a door to another part of the suite. Tara tucked her legs up underneath her on the couch.

'They won't tell me what this is all about,' she said to Cahill, her eyes darting off in Hanson's direction. 'Why I need extra security.'

Cahill went to the couch and sat beside her, leaning forward to face her. Hanson turned from the window and watched them. Washington stayed where he was, seeming to take up more space than anyone else in the room.

'Look,' Cahill said, 'I'll tell you what this is all about if you want me to. I don't like my clients not knowing what's going on around them. But maybe you don't want to know. It's up to you.' He leaned back on the couch.

She looked at Hanson again. 'Someone doesn't like me,' she said to Cahill. 'Actually, I know that it must go quite some way beyond that.'

Cahill nodded.

'That's as much as I need to know,' she said.

'I'll tell you some of what I told Phil when we met this morning,' Cahill said.

'OK.'

'The bad guy has the easiest job. That's the not-so-good news.

But they're usually also not as good as we are. Not as prepared and not as tough.'

She smiled weakly but said nothing.

'The best way for us to deal with these situations,' Cahill said, 'is to assume the worst. That way we minimise the risk of anything getting missed. Something like this, the weak points are the start and the finish – the hotel and the premiere – because they are fixed and certain. There's nothing we can do to change them so we have to be vigilant about it and check them thoroughly.'

'We look for anything out of the ordinary,' Washington added. 'A full three-sixty scan of the area, and we are the best in the business at that. And we know that with people, the first thing you look at is the hands.'

'Why?' she asked, appearing genuinely interested. This was a good sign for Cahill; if she was interested then it probably meant that she was beginning to trust them and would be willing to follow instructions.

'Because that's the most dangerous part of a person,' Washington said. 'The part that pulls the trigger or presses the button . . .'

Tara shifted in her seat, looking nervous.

'Listen,' Cahill said. 'I'm not going to pretend that this kind of thing is easy. The bad guy gets to set the plan: the timing, the where, the how and everything in between. What we do is the harder part because we're mainly reactive.'

'Is it true,' she said, 'that if someone is truly determined, then they can't be stopped? Like 9/11?'

Cahill sighed. 'With suicide bombers – which is really what the 9/11 crew were – then the answer is probably yes. But we're not looking at that kind of thing here.' He looked at her for a moment. 'And I haven't lost a client yet,' he said.

Washington nodded at Tara. 'It's true.'

Cahill could still see the tension in her. 'Listen,' he said. 'I know it all seems weird and kind of scary right now, but once we get started tomorrow it'll be fine. We'll all be dressed to blend in with the crowd so that the first any bad guy knows about us is the elbow in his ear and the foot on his neck after he hits the ground.'

'But there's no harm in you being a little bit scared,' Washington said. 'Because that means that you'll be alert to what's going on around you. And there may be things that will look out of the ordinary to you but not to us, and we want you to be a part of the team, not just a passive participant.'

'Have you done this kind of thing before?' she asked Cahill.

'You mean for a celebrity?'

'Yes.'

'Sure. I've done it for everybody from politicians to movie stars and from four-star generals to private businessmen. I know crowds and I know what to look for, but you can help us too.'

'He's right, Tara,' Hanson said.

She smiled again, this time looking more reassured. 'So how does it work?' she asked. 'I mean, from here down to the car and everything else?'

'Well, like I told Phil at the office this morning, there'll be three cars with you in the middle and that's kinda how we'll work it when we're on foot too.'

'What do you mean?'

'We'll work in three teams. Two of my people will be the team on point, including Chris here, meaning that they will go ahead and check everything in advance and only when we get the all-clear will we follow. And the other team of two will cover the rear.'

'And I'll be in the middle?'

'Correct. And you'll have me with you at all times.'

'But how does that work when we leave here? I mean, you don't need anyone covering the room after I'm gone, do you?'

'No. What happens is that the point team will start off downstairs in the lobby to check out that there's no one waiting down there for us. The rear team clears the corridor outside the room, the elevator and the stairs, and they keep that area covered until we're in the lift and headed down. Then they follow us.'

'Always someone with you, in front of you and behind you,' Hanson said, walking from the window and standing beside Washington. 'It'll be fine.'

'And you'll be in the car with me?' she asked Hanson.

Hanson looked at Cahill, who nodded. 'Just like always,' he said.

Cahill couldn't help but notice the edge in Hanson's voice.

10

Cahill and Washington went with Hanson to his room for a review of the guest list and to finalise arrangements for getting one of the CPO team into the cinema the next morning.

Cahill wanted to ask Hanson about what he thought he had seen and heard back in Tara's room – the connection he sensed between her and Hanson. Not because he was interested in gossip, but because it might have an effect on the operation. If Hanson was going to be with her in the car, then Cahill wanted to be certain that his mind would be focused on the job. He decided to wait for now, to see if Hanson would volunteer anything. If he was as professional as Cahill thought he was, he would bring it up at some point tonight.

Hanson's room was much smaller than Tara's suite – a standard twin room with two beds, a little table by the window and a flat-screen TV mounted above a sideboard on the wall opposite the beds. Brown and beige: the new glamour.

Hanson went to the sideboard and took out the guest list for the premiere – two sheets of photocopied A4 paper. He handed it to Cahill and sat on the sofa.

'Any chance this stuff she's been getting is from an old boyfriend?' Washington asked while Cahill scanned the list. 'Or maybe a low-level actor who's become obsessed after having a bit part opposite her?'

'No boyfriends on the list,' Hanson said, bristling slightly at the question. 'And everyone on the list Tara signed off on, so I think we're safe.'

Cahill stood in front of the TV, folding the list and putting it in his back pocket. 'Did *you* sign off on them?'

Hanson took a Coke from the fridge, sipped at it and stared at Cahill.

'It's your job,' Cahill said. 'Not hers.'

'I know,' Hanson said. '*We* checked them out before it went to Tara. Sorry, I should have been clearer.'

'No problem. Look, I know this is probably difficult for the people close to Tara and it's been a long day, but let's not fall out over it, OK? I mean, we have to work as one team.'

'Sure,' Hanson said. 'My fault. I'm just stressed by the whole thing and Devon is being a pain in the arse about it.'

'How so?'

'He's a pain at the best of times, you know. But he's been a total nightmare this week.'

'His golden calf's at risk,' Washington said.

'Yeah, maybe that's it.'

'I'll have one of my team call you in the morning,' Cahill said, 'to get access to the cinema. Then we'll all meet here later to get ready for the trip, OK?'

Hanson nodded. 'What route we taking?' he asked.

'You don't need to know. In fact, the fewer people who know in advance the better.'

'But I'll be driving,' Hanson said. 'I need to know the route before then.'

'No. I'm driving. That's the only way it works for me.'

'She's my full-time responsibility,' Hanson said. 'No disrespect, Alex, but you're only in it for this one gig. Don't you think you're taking it a bit too far?'

Cahill sighed. 'Phil, you seem like a decent guy and I get the impression you know what you're about. Which is good. But this is my job and my responsibility. I'm going to use the people I know and trust and that way it gets done right. We both know that these things can be inside jobs and so I need to have complete control.'

Hanson fingered the edge of the table and breathed heavily through his nose.

'I can see that she means a lot to you,' Cahill said, looking for the response now. 'Which is why I'm letting you stay in the car. But that's the only concession I'm going to make.'

He waited for Hanson to speak, but he said nothing.

'I need to know if you have any more vested in this than just a professional interest,' Cahill said finally.

'What do you mean?' Hanson asked, meeting Cahill's eyes now.

'I mean, are you and Tara involved?'

'No.'

Cahill thought the answer came too quickly. 'Phil . . .'

'OK, yes, we've had something. It hasn't really gone anywhere and, anyway, it would be difficult for her. Right now she doesn't really need any distractions, you know. Not with Hollywood knocking at her door.'

'I'm not worried about *her* being distracted.'

'I'm fine,' Hanson said, looking at Cahill again. 'You don't have to worry about me.'

'I hope you're right.'

11

Roddy was quick to fall asleep when he got into bed and Irvine left him alone in the bedroom, closed the door and sat down in the living area. She had taken bedlinen from the bedroom and intended to spend the night on the sofa, giving Roddy the time he needed to catch up on his rest.

The suite was not big, but had been put together well. Irvine thought that it must have been renovated quite recently because that new carpet smell was still fresh in the air. It was at the end of the second-floor hall and the living area had an original cast-iron fireplace dominating the main wall opposite the door. A brown leather couch sat in front of the fire, flanked by two tan leather armchairs.

Irvine laid the bedlinen out on the sofa and pulled a nightdress from her bag; really no more than an oversized pink and blue T-shirt with GRUMPY BUT CUTE on it. Tom had bought it for her for a birthday one year and she still kind of liked it, even though the colours were faded and the seams beginning to fray.

Before getting undressed she wanted to call Logan and say hi. She looked around for her phone before realising that she must have left it out in the car when they were getting the bags. She opened the door to the bedroom, saw that Roddy was deep in sleep and slipped out into the hall, heading downstairs to the exit.

The heat of the day had faded and been replaced by a mild chill. Irvine felt the cold on the bare skin of her arms and she hurried to her car under the weak overhead lights illuminating the car park, reaching into her pocket for the keys. She was heading for the driver's door when she saw a familiar car parked on its own a short distance away. It was empty, but she was certain that she had seen it before. She stopped and stared at it, trying to place it in her memory.

She heard laughter and turned to see two men coming out of the hotel entrance. Instinctively, she ducked down behind her car and then felt foolish for having done it. But she was now certain that she had seen the car, and one of the men, already today: outside the hospital and again outside the café in Glencoe.

Paparazzi, was her first thought. Or maybe just tabloid journalists. They must have recognised her from the footage on the TV and were now stalking her and Roddy to get the scoop that would make them rich.

Then she remembered that one of them had been at reception when she checked in. Probably got to see what room they were staying in too.

'Damn,' she said quietly to herself.

The gravel of the car park crunched under the men's feet as they approached her car. Only having had bad experiences with the press so far, she figured that her best option was to avoid them so she slid round the car as quietly as she could, keeping her head below their field of sight. As they passed her Irvine moved round again, lifting her head and peering through the glass to watch them as they went to their own car.

She dropped her head down again and heard the doors of the

car slam shut. She waited, hoping that they would drive away and allow her to get her phone and get back inside unnoticed. But the car engine did not start and instead she heard the muffled sounds of the men talking inside.

She risked being seen and looked quickly inside her car, spotting the phone sitting in the cup holder between the front seats. She knew that if she opened the door, the interior light would come on and the men would see her.

She turned her back against the passenger door and slid down until her bottom rested on the gravel. Why did everything have to be so bloody hard all the time, she thought, rubbing her hands through her hair.

Her stubborn inner self decided that to hell with it, she was not going to pay over the odds to make a phone call from the hotel – even if Roddy was picking up the bill. Even on someone else's tab she couldn't quite bring herself to be so wasteful, so she stood quickly and opened the car door.

Five had his back turned to Irvine's car when she opened the door. Three saw her immediately, and he opened his own door and was out before Five knew what was happening.

'Hey,' he shouted to Irvine as he walked towards her. 'Do you need any help there?'

Irvine was leaning into the car and he wondered if she had heard him. He heard Five get out of the car behind him and hurry to catch up. He quickened his pace.

'Hey,' he shouted again.

She stood up out of the car and closed the door, looking directly at Three. He had the impression that she was committing his face to memory.

12

Five lengthened his stride to catch up with Three. They were about twenty feet from Irvine's car when she closed the door and started to walk fast towards the hotel's main entrance. Five knew immediately that they were unlikely to catch her before she got inside. And then what would they do – engage in open warfare in the reception or on the stairs?

'Leave it,' he said to Three.

Irvine heard him, stopped and looked back.

They stood fifteen feet apart staring at each other as a low mist hung over the surface of the loch.

Irvine noticed that neither man was carrying a camera or anything else that made them look like journalists out for a story. Maybe she'd caught them by surprise, but she couldn't help but notice that they were also both in pretty damn good shape with narrow waists and wide shoulders. She expected journalists to have the paunch that came with long hours and bad food choices. The man closer to her was the younger, and from the way he stopped at the older man's voice she assumed that he was also junior in rank — if 'rank' was the right word.

The older of the two men walked forward until he was level with the younger one and Irvine walked backwards slowly, watching them. She was unnerved now by their silence.

'Just leave him alone, OK,' she shouted at them, wanting to say something.

She continued to back up until she felt she was close enough to the reception entrance, and then turned. She fought the strong impulse to run, not wanting to appear scared. She looked back as she reached the door and saw that they had turned and were heading back to their car.

Back in the suite, Irvine took a bottle of single malt from the mini bar, relishing the heat that burned as the liquid ran over her throat and down inside. Her hands were shaking a little as she picked up the phone and searched for Logan's number in her contacts list. She was about to call when she saw that it was after eleven. She hesitated and then pressed the button anyway, selfishly wanting to hear his voice.

The phone rang and clicked on to the answering machine. She was about to end the call when she heard Logan pick up the phone and answer groggily.

'Mmmyello,' he said.

'Hey, sleepy-head.'

'Becky,' suddenly alert now. 'What's up?'

'Nothing. I just wanted to say hi and see how things are with you?'

'Well, this afternoon was, um interesting.'

'Is that what you're calling it? Maybe I shouldn't have bothered you.'

GJ Moffat

'If every time is going to be like that, you can bother me all you want.'

She smiled.

'How's things with your man?' Logan asked.

'Fine. He's sleeping just now. I think he might be OK. I mean, it seems like he really wants to get better, which is the first step.'

'I guess so.'

'Listen, you get back to bed,' Irvine said. 'Sorry I woke you.'

Irvine wanted to say something else to end the call, but was unsure of what.

I love you?

It felt too soon. But it didn't feel wrong.

'Take care,' Logan said.

'You too.'

Irvine put the phone down and leaned back into the sofa. Best not to rush it, she thought. There's plenty of time yet.

Lots of living still to be done.

13

Irvine woke around eight, with a blade of sun warming her cheek through a gap between the curtains. She rolled on to her back and stretched, her hands pushing against the leather of the sofa. She was glad that, despite the lack of a proper bed, she had slept pretty soundly and felt better for it.

Her first thought was of yesterday with Logan. But the scene with the two men in the car park last night intruded and she shook it from her head. She went to the window and pulled the curtains back, revealing a glorious view of the loch and the hills behind it, the water sparkling in the early sun.

As she gathered the bedlinen from the couch, she became aware of the sound of the shower running and heard Roddy's voice singing something. She listened, straining to hear what it was before recognising 'The Dock of the Bay'. She made herself a cup of tea and was standing sipping it by the window when Roddy came out of the bedroom dressed in faded blue jeans and a grey polo shirt with ROAD CREW stamped on the back. He had a baseball cap on to cover the bandage on his head and she had to admit that he looked good. He paused when he saw her and looked her up and down, nodding and smiling.

'You're such a sleaze,' she said, putting her cup down and going past him to get to the bathroom.

They went down to the dining room for breakfast, loading up on sausage, bacon and eggs for the day ahead. She went with poached, he with fried. She wondered what Logan liked for breakfast and found herself looking forward to finding out.

'What's the plan today, boss?' Roddy asked.

'I thought we might move on,' she said. 'Check out of here and then drive over to Fort William for lunch. Maybe just wander around the town for a bit and do the tourist thing.'

Irvine actually quite liked the hotel and would ordinarily have thought about staying another night, but the encounter in the car park had soured it for her and she was keen to move on.

'This place is pretty nice,' Roddy said, looking around the bustling dining room. 'Why don't we stay here?'

'Let's keep moving. It'll be good to see different places. Maybe we'll even head over to Skye. Take the ferry for the scenic route rather than the bridge.'

'Whatever. You're in charge.'

They put their bags in the car after breakfast, Irvine looking at all the others to see if there was anyone inside and anxiously glancing at the road when anything came into view. This was supposed to be a relaxing break. At least Roddy seemed to have brightened up today.

Irvine stayed in the car while Roddy went inside to settle up the bill, his baseball cap low on his head to at least try to disguise who he was. The hotel guests were mainly older types and families though, and probably not that into his band. Predominantly, the audiences at his gigs were teenage boys and more than a few girls.

They drove up on to the main road and followed the signs for Fort William, Roddy with his window down again and the wind buffeting the interior of the car. Irvine began to feel cold on the back of her neck but she said nothing. This was supposed to be about him, not her.

'You know,' Roddy said after they'd been driving for ten minutes, 'I've probably got way more money than I'll ever need and my taxes are all up to date. Maybe I could just retire. Buy a place up around here somewhere.'

'Sounds good,' Irvine said. 'Why not?'

'I'll need some company, though. I'd go crazy if I was on my own.' He looked at Irvine and she tried to ignore him. 'How about it, Becky Reid; wanna get married?'

'Sure.'

'Seriously?' He sounded weirdly enthusiastic.

'No, Roddy. Not seriously.'

'Aw, come on. Look how good we are together. And you used to dig me once, right?'

'You forget that I also dumped you once, so the answer is no. Look, Roddy, I like you just fine but if you have some hope of anything happening on this trip or any other time you'd better just forget it.'

'I can take you away from everything you hate. The stuff that got in your head and messed you up yesterday.'

'You know what, Roddy? If you weren't such a tool that might just have done it for me.'

He slumped back in his seat and pouted.

'Can't blame me for trying,' he said.

14

Five and Three had stayed at the largest hotel they could find on the road to Fort William; better to be anonymous than stand out in a small B&B. Five was still pissed off at Three for jumping out of the car last night and talking to the cop when clearly there was no realistic prospect of getting to her at that point. But they had argued enough and there was no point in going on about it any longer.

Five had the GPS tracker with him at their breakfast table and saw that the cop and the guy were on the move and heading their way. Maybe they would get the chance to do something later today.

'Is that one of them iPhone things?'

Five looked up from his bowl of fruit and yogurt. The waitress had black hair with a pink stripe through it.

'Something like that,' he said, smiling at her.

The girl rolled her top lip over the metal ball pierced through her lower lip and then flicked at it with her tongue.

'Can I see it?' she asked, reaching for the tracker.

'No,' Five said, putting his hand on top of it.

The girl looked annoyed, but said nothing except to ask if they wanted coffee or tea. After she had left, Three asked what they were going to do today.

'Get this over with and get the hell out of this country,' Five told him. He held the tracker up so that Three could see the screen. 'They're coming over here now. Let's try to be ready this time.'

Three nodded and looked out of the window at the front of the hotel to the distant clouds rolling their way.

15

Cemeteries are for winter, when the sky and the mood match the grey granite of the headstones.

Logan and Ellie walked together up the shallow incline towards the new plots at the top of the hill, an extension of the original cemetery to cope with the increasing numbers of its occupants. Ellie was quiet, as she always was here. She would talk in her own time.

The headstones stretched out on all sides in neat, parallel rows. Logan read the stones as he walked, checking off the ages of those interred in the ground as he went.

Seventy-four.

Twenty-three.

Forty-one.

Eighty-five.

Two.

It was always the kids that got him the most: too little time.

He remembered the last time he went to a funeral – one of his grandparents – walking along a similarly desolate pathway and seeing a stone for a baby of three months old. Never getting any older.

Night night, wee man.

That was the inscription below the name and the dates. Someone's loving words at the end of each day. Implicit in them, *see you in the morning*.

Logan swallowed, emotion sticking in his throat as he looked at Ellie walking past all these reminders of the dead and heading towards Penny's place with them. They neared the top of the hill and Ellie reached out to take his hand, squeezing hard.

They stood side by side facing the plain stone – Ellie's choice. Logan would have paid for whatever she wanted but the simplicity of it made him think more of his daughter. No need for ostentation; remembering Penny the way she was in life.

'I'm going to see her,' Ellie said, stepping on to the grass and walking to the stone.

She kneeled and set the flowers on the ground, resting against the stone. Then she took the card and put it down by the flowers.

Logan looked down the hill and saw a number of stones lying flat on the ground, knocked down by kids who had no respect. No understanding of the pain it caused the husbands and wives, sons and daughters, who came to see their loved ones and instead found the senseless vandalism: desecration.

Ellie was talking in a low whisper, telling her mother how she was doing and that Logan was taking care of her. Logan stepped further away, not wanting to eavesdrop on her moment of privacy.

When Ellie was done, she kissed the top of the stone and said that she'd be back soon. Then she walked to Logan and buried her face in his chest, wrapping her arms around him. He felt her tears soak through his T-shirt, warm against his skin, and held her. Told her everything would be fine and that he would always be there for her. Not really knowing if that was true – who did? But it was what you said.

When she pulled back and wiped at her eyes and nose with her hand he put his palms on her cheeks and leaned down till their noses touched.

'I love you, Ellie,' he told her.

She had never responded in all the times he had said that to her – and there had been many times. He said it anyway, unafraid of rejection or shame.

He said it because she needed to hear it.

He said it because it was true.

They walked down the hill and away from the grave and Logan saw the clouds forming to the north as the unseasonal warmth prepared to surrender to the rain.

'Me too,' Ellie said as they made their way towards the gates.

They went to a local café in Shawlands for breakfast: a proper greasy spoon and a regular Sunday morning treat. French toast for her with plenty of brown sauce and scrambled eggs on toast for him.

'Do you want me to call you Dad?' Ellie asked with her mouth still half full. She didn't look up at him, but concentrated on cutting another square of the bread and dipping it in the sauce.

'Call me whatever you like, Ellie. I don't mind.'

She looked at him now. 'Honest?'

'Sure. Logan's my name so call me that if you want.'

'But you're my dad.'

'So long as we know that, you don't need to say it.'

She smiled and he reached across the table to wipe a smear of sauce from the side of her mouth with a napkin.

'Thanks, Logan.'

Somehow it sounded right.

16

Hudson was with Two and Four at their flat in the east end of the city when he heard his mobile ringing in the living room. He went through and picked it up, not recognising the number on the screen except that it had a London dialling prefix.

'How are the preparations going for tonight?'

For a moment Hudson felt his stomach flip, wondering how anyone could know about what was planned. Then he realised that it was the boss's voice. 'Where are you calling from?' he asked.

'From home, of course. Just enjoying Sunday morning on the terrace following a very satisfying evening with some female company, if you know what I mean?'

'You shouldn't be calling me from that phone,' Hudson said. 'It's not safe.'

'What are you talking about? Safe from whom?'

'It's up to you how you conduct your business, I suppose,' Hudson told him. 'Me, I never use a traceable phone to discuss work.'

'I like that you're cautious, Carl, I really do. But stop being such a pussy or you'll begin to annoy me.'

'Whatever you say,' Hudson said, breathing slowly.

'So, like I said, how are things?'

'We're good. Final preparations will be done this morning and we'll be in position tonight. And then . . .' Hudson trailed off, reluctant to finish the sentence.

'I like your subtlety.'

Hudson said nothing, wanting the call to be over.

'So you got the stuff from my man yesterday?' the boss asked.

'Yes.'

'And it's suitable for the task at hand?'

'It's fine.'

'What's the matter, Carl? Not in the mood for idle chat?'

Always the power games with this guy; the need to show that he was in control and that everything ran to his timetable.

'Look,' Hudson said, 'I need to go. Things to do.'

'OK, Carl. I get the point.'

'I'll call you after it's done.'

'I look forward to it.'

They left the flat together and drove in a nondescript Mazda to the industrial unit they had rented out of town, paying cash on a no-names basis. It was located at the end of a row of five similar units in a small commercial park and was perfect for their needs.

Once inside, Four put on a pair of dark blue overalls and went to work on the thing, adding the final component that Hudson had collected yesterday. Hudson always felt nervous being this close and marvelled at Four's apparent ease with his materials. This had been Four's specialism in the army and so maybe he was blasé now about the risk.

Two stayed outside, smoking casually and trying not to look like he was guarding the place. He did a good line in nonchalant.

'How long?' Hudson asked Four, hating the taste of the air in the place – oil, burnt solder and the faint whiff of the cigarette smoke from outside.

'Just about a half-hour. It needs to appear as if this was the key part. I've got to wire it in carefully, so it looks right but it doesn't interfere.'

Hudson went outside to get some fresh air and walked into a billowing cloud of exhaled smoke from Two.

'Fuck's sake,' Hudson said, coughing and turning his face away.

'Sorry, boss,' Two said, dropping the cigarette and grinding it into the concrete with his shoe. 'You should've said you were coming out.'

Hudson breathed in some fresh air to clear the taste from the back of his throat.

'How's it going in there?' Two asked.

'Won't be long.'

'Gives me the heebie-jeebies, that stuff. Why in the hell does it have to be done like this? I mean, it's risky for everybody.'

Hudson looked across the road at the low, brick-built commercial units with their faded signs for low-cost businesses, a printer and a car mechanic among them. A plastic Tesco bag wafted by on the gentle breeze, hugging the ground.

'I think I'm getting out after this,' Hudson said. 'I know it's not enough to retire on, but I can't face working for this guy any longer. Plus, I've got my son to think about now.'

'Not like the movies, eh?' Two asked, glancing sideways at Hudson.

'Hardly,' Hudson snorted.

They stood quietly for a moment, listening to the river running behind the units across the road and hearing the distant hum of traffic as cars passed by on the motorway half a mile away.

'What about you?' Hudson asked eventually. 'You can have it if you want. The team, I mean. They'll follow you without any question.'

'I know. And I appreciate the offer, boss, I really do. But you know me, one job at a time. I don't like to have to think too hard.'

Hudson nodded and turned to go back inside.

'You going to tell the boys?' Two asked.

Hudson paused with his hand on the door handle. 'After,' he said, and then went inside.

Two pulled out a packet of Marlboros and slid another cigarette out, holding it in his mouth for a moment before lighting it.

'It's a bad business all right,' he said to no one.

17

Irvine found a decent hotel at the north end of Fort William and pulled in to see if they had any rooms. Funny, she thought, how you settle so quickly into holiday mode; nothing mattering except where the next meal or bed was.

This time she got lucky and was able to find two rooms for the night. After booking in and getting their bags stored she went to Roddy's room and asked if he wanted to go and explore the hotel facilities. She'd seen a sign for a leisure club and hoped that maybe there was a pool.

'Nah,' Roddy said. 'I'm pretty beat actually. I think I'll just crash out for a bit before we head for dinner, if that's OK.'

'Sure,' Irvine said. 'You take it easy and I'll come get you for dinner.'

He pulled his feet up on to the duvet and took his cap off, putting it on the little table by the bed. Irvine went to the window and pulled the curtains closed. 'You want to eat here or go into town?' she asked.

'You decide. I'm buying.'

*   *   *

Irvine looked in on the restaurant to see what it was like. It was as she had imagined. Two elderly couples were drinking late afternoon tea with plates of assorted scones and cakes. She didn't think Roddy would fit in here.

The leisure club was in the basement and had an indoor pool. Irvine had not packed a swimming costume but she saw that there were a few for sale on the wall behind the reception counter.

The girl at the counter was no more than twenty, her skin clear and glowing in the absence of any make-up. Her blonde hair was tied up in a pony-tail and she could not have been more helpful or courteous, even suggesting a smaller size for Irvine at one point. A girl always appreciates that.

There was a family splashing in the shallow end of the pool, the father throwing his toddler son high in the air while the mother looked on with mild concern. An older girl was sitting glumly in the Jacuzzi, no doubt wishing she was somewhere else. Irvine smiled at her as she walked along the side of the pool heading for the changing rooms but all she got back was a sullen stare.

Suit yourself.

There were no other guests in the changing room so she was able to change without feeling self-conscious and then examine herself in the full-length mirror to see how she looked in the costume. Having her son had changed the shape of her body irrevocably, but she managed to keep in decent enough condition. She was convinced that her breasts were different now, even though she'd only breastfed for around six weeks, and there was no doubting the traces of cellulite on the backs of her thighs in the harsh strip-lighting. Still, not bad all told.

Irvine eased herself into the pool at the deep end and then swam lengths for twenty minutes, enjoying the effort involved in the exercise. After she was done, she floated face up with her hair like a halo around her head.

The family sharing the pool with her left noisily and she was alone, enjoying the rare moment of tranquillity. Over in the corner, the Jacuzzi began to froth and bubble, obviously set to go on and off automatically. Irvine swam to the shallow end and then slipped into the Jacuzzi, relishing the warmth of the water after the cooler temperature of the pool.

She ran her mind over the events of last night – the two goons in the car park of the hotel – and chided herself for being so sensitive and, if she was honest, a little scared. She had not been a beat cop for more than two years now and had lost that street awareness, the radar sense of when things might kick off. Maybe she was still a little on edge after the concert and the panic that had ensued when Roddy took his dive off the stage.

Resting her head back on the edge of the Jacuzzi, she closed her eyes and allowed the warmth to embrace her, soothing away her concerns.

Back in the room after her swim, Irvine changed out of her clothes and lay on the bed in her underwear. She closed her eyes to conjure a more pleasant image and remembered the previous day at Logan's flat. Her thighs tingled at the images in her head and a warm glow spread inside. Rolling on to her side, she grabbed her phone and called him.

Ellie answered.

'Oh, hi, Ellie, it's Becky here. How are you doing?'

'Fine.'

'Good.' Not awkward at all, then, Irvine thought. 'Is your dad there?'

'Logan,' she heard Ellie shout. 'It's for you. It's Becky.' She knew that if she was going to make this thing with Logan work, she would have to address her relationship with Ellie.

'Hey,' Logan said. 'Where are you?'

'Fort William.'

'Nice. You drive up through Glencoe? Beautiful, isn't it? I love that drive.'

'It's good.'

'You don't have to sound so happy about it, you know.'

'Sorry. It's just that . . . I think there's a couple of guys following us and I bumped into them last night.'

'What do you mean, following you?'

'Journalists or something, I think. It's got me on edge.'

'Don't worry about them, OK. You're already famous after they got you at the hospital, so how bad can it get?'

She felt better that he could joke about it. 'If that's supposed to cheer me up, it's not working.'

'What would cheer you up? Want me to talk dirty?'

'Well, I am in my underwear so that might work for me.'

Logan was quiet.

'No need to be shy,' Irvine said. 'I've seen you naked now, remember?'

'Yeah, well, phone sex is all well and good but I don't think Ellie would appreciate it if she walked in mid-act. Can I take a rain check for the real thing next time I see you? Whenever that might be.'

'Sounds good. And maybe we should talk about Ellie as well.'

'What do you mean?'

'This is new for her. You and me being together, I mean.'

'She's already been asking me about you *and* about her mum. We were at the cemetery today. But I think she'll be OK. She's tough.'

'Maybe so, but we need to be careful. That's all I'm saying. We need to involve her in it so that she feels a part of it and not just a spectator.'

'It's all still new for us. We'll work through it. I mean, if we can get past what happened before then we can get past this, right?'

'Probably. Listen, I'm going to get some rest before we head out for dinner.'

'OK. Let me know when you think you'll be coming home and I can set something up for when you get back. Grab some food maybe.'

'What you up to tonight?' Irvine asked.

'Nothing much. But guess what.'

'What?'

'Alex is doing a job for Tara Byrne tonight. Some film premiere in Glasgow. How cool is that?'

'You're joking. Tara Byrne the actress?'

'Yeah. Want an autograph?'

'How does she look in real life?'

'Don't know – I never got the chance to meet her. But I'm guessing she's still smokin' hot, you know.'

'You'll just have to make do with me.'

After the call, Irvine washed her face, applied some make-up and got dressed in black jeans, a short-sleeved black top and a pale-blue cotton cardigan. She messed with her hair for a few minutes before deciding that the water in the pool had totally ruined it for the day and settled for tying it back off her face.

Roddy sounded groggy when she called through to his room but agreed to meet her down in the lounge in half an hour.

It was busy in the lounge but she found a table in the corner and ordered a glass of dry white wine, sipping at it slowly and enjoying the chatter around her. The conversations with Logan had helped her forget the two men from the car park, and she was determined to relax tonight and enjoy some good food and a few more glasses of wine.

She would have been less happy had she known that within twenty-four hours her image would once again be broadcast over the news channels.

18

The make-up and hair stylists had finished their two-hour session with Tara, and Cahill got the nod from Phil Hanson that they were ready to go. He told Tom Hardy and Carrie Richardson to check outside the room. They would be the rear team and would follow Hanson, Cahill and Tara after they were safely in the lift. Downstairs, in the lobby, Bailey Judd and Chris Washington were the point team, and had already done a thorough sweep of the underground car park and all the ground-floor facilities.

After Hardy and Carrie had left the room, Cahill pulled out his mobile and called ahead to the cinema where Harry Shields, one of the Scots in the CPO team, had spent the day scoping out the arrangements.

'Harry, it's Alex. How are things there?'

'It's all good. They're pretty organised and the event security staff are a decent bunch.'

'They cooperated with all your requests, then?'

'Yeah, no worries. There are crowd barriers all the way up the hill to the entrance from Sauchiehall Street, so that will keep everyone on the pavements and off the road. Plus the top of the road's been blocked off and there's a cop car up there in case anyone gets too annoyed.'

'What's it like inside?'

'Old-school cinema; bit of a rabbit warren. But I got them to lock and double-check all the exterior doors. As long as we have control over entry we should be fine.'

'OK. Listen, we're just about ready to head out so it shouldn't take us more than five or ten minutes to get there.'

'Copy that. See you soon.'

Cahill turned at the sound of Tara's bedroom door opening. He had to admit, he could see why she was in demand. If she wasn't the most beautiful woman he had seen up close, she wasn't far off. There was something of the Audrey Hepburn about her in a fitted black dress.

'All set?' she asked, looking at Cahill. He heard the nerves in her voice; the smallest hint of a tremor.

'We're good,' he said. 'Just waiting for the all-clear from outside.'

She glanced at Hanson and appeared to relax when he smiled at her.

Hanson would be at Tara's side all night. He was the very visible deterrent, looking imposing now in his black suit and black open-necked shirt. Cahill was more casual, more anonymous, in a mid-grey linen suit with a plain white shirt. He was supposed to look ordinary, as if he was her regular driver. The suit was expensive, bespoke, and cut to hide his powerful physique as best it could: deliberately just a little on the big side.

Carrie, Tom and the other CPO team members were more casual still, to blend in with the crowd attending the premiere. It wasn't a black-tie event but more of a cool indie thing, so they wore jeans and jackets.

Cahill's earpiece clicked as Hardy's voice came on line. 'All set out here.'

His microphone was clipped under the lapel of his jacket and he could speak quite normally without giving the impression that he was communicating remotely. 'Copy, Tom. We'll be out presently.'

He turned to Tara. 'OK,' he said. 'We're ready when suits you.'

'I'm fine right now,' she said.

'Mr Leonard not joining us?' Cahill asked, looking at Hanson.

'No,' Hanson said. 'I guess maybe he's a bit nervous about the whole added security thing.'

'Figures,' Cahill said. 'All mouth, that one.'

He ushered Tara forward before speaking again to Hardy. 'We're coming out now, Tom.'

The walk out of the hotel was uneventful from a security perspective, with only photographers and journalists outside the entrance to contend with. After that, the convoy of three cars proceeded slowly along the hotel's crescent driveway.

Cahill drove, with Hanson in the passenger seat beside him. Tara was alone in the rear. The car was a large, silver saloon of German origin, solid and smooth.

'Nice car,' Hanson said. 'Is it armour-plated?'

'No,' Cahill said, shaking his head. 'I mean, we've got one of those if we need it but tonight's not one of those kinds of nights.'

'Thank God for that,' Tara said, laughing nervously.

Cahill's eyes never rested on one location for long, always sweeping across his front field of vision and then checking the mirrors at the side and rear. The town was quiet: low tide on a Sunday evening.

Hardy and Carrie were in their car twenty-five yards behind

with Washington and Judd a similar distance ahead. Both teams drove similarly nondescript vehicles: small, European saloon cars in popular colours and a couple of years old; blending in.

They pulled on to the west end of Sauchiehall Street and, up ahead, Cahill could see people condensed at the bottom of the short hill that led to the cinema. He could hear the murmur of crowd noise already.

'Harry,' he said, speaking into his mike. 'We're on the approach now.'

'Copy. I'm at the door. All clear so far.'

'Good. Do me a favour and walk the barriers outside. See what you can see.'

'Will do.'

Cahill looked in the rear-view mirror at Tara and told her that everything was good up ahead. Nothing to be concerned about.

Not yet, anyway.

19

Hudson entrusted delivery of the package to Four because he was the expert with it. Or at least that's what Hudson told himself. In reality, he hated being close to it and was glad that he had someone else to get it in place. He'd seen more than one of his fellow soldiers killed by a malfunction.

Hudson sat in the passenger-seat while Two drove to the position they had chosen.

'You sure the boss was clear about what's to happen?' Two asked. 'About who was fair game?'

'Crystal,' Hudson sighed.

Two shook his head and laughed. 'You really don't like this guy,' he said.

'I'd be laughing as well if I wasn't so worried that he was going to drop us in it. I should've realised when I met him that time at the coffee shop. The way he talked about it there: way too public.'

'He's nuts.'

'Did I tell you that he called me from his house this morning?'

Two turned to face Hudson. 'What, on the land-line?'

'Yeah.'

'Jesus.' Two turned again to look out of the windscreen as he drove. 'That's not good. Does he have your home number?'

'Fuck, no. Nobody does. Not even you.' Hudson looked out the side window at the city moving past. I think maybe all of us have to cut loose from this guy once we're done on this thing tonight.'

'I don't know,' Two replied. 'I mean, he doesn't strike me as the kind of guy you just say cheerio to. So long and thanks for the memories.'

'What are the options? The guy is going to go down sooner or later and he'll have no problem in fingering us if it helps him any. And I know the type. You do too. We've both seen it in theatre. Am I right?'

Two nodded.

'Some jumped-up Sandhurst prick,' Hudson went on. 'Sitting in his tent directing forward operations with no clue and when it goes to shit he covers his own back and it's us grunts that get screwed over.'

They were quiet for a moment, and Hudson saw that they were making the last turn to get to their chosen vantage point.

'What is it you're saying?' Two asked.

'Maybe I don't know what I'm saying. It's just that . . .' Hudson trailed off.

'This guy's got connections from what I hear, you know?' Two said. 'We have to be really sure about what we're getting into if we're gonna do anything about it.'

'I know.'

Two pulled in to the side of the road and eased the car to a stop. Hudson opened the glove compartment and took out a pair of high-end binoculars. 'I'm just thinking out loud,' he said. 'That's all.'

Two raised his eyebrows at Hudson. 'Whatever you say, boss,' he said, then opened his door to get out.

Here we go, Hudson thought: point of no return.

20

It was past summer season now, so the centre of Fort William was quiet enough to give Irvine and Roddy their pick of where to eat. They eventually settled on a little Chinese place just off the main street, in a narrow alley that sloped down towards the road running along the bank of Loch Linnhe.

The clouds that had threatened rain earlier in the day had not amounted to anything, blowing over and dispersing by mid-afternoon. It was cooler now than it had been in the last few days and Irvine found herself drawing her cardigan across her chest. In the distance, gulls circled and whooped above the water.

Inside, the restaurant was surprisingly light on the usual clichés of Chinese restaurants on the west coast, with subtle décor in white and grey. Irvine kind of liked it and Roddy's only current concern was getting some food.

A tall waitress showed them to a table at the back of the place, which was fine as there wasn't much of a view from the single window except the other side of the alley. They ordered water and a bottle of Sancerre and settled down to scanning the menu. Irvine mentioned the daily fish specials to Roddy.

'Good for me,' he said. 'But a toast first.'

Irvine braced herself for something cheesy, but wrapped her hand round her glass of wine anyway.

'To friends and quiet times away from it all,' Roddy said.

Irvine waited for the punch-line, but it appeared he was serious. Roddy saw the hesitation in her body language.

'Look,' he said, 'I know I can be a bit hard to take sometimes . . .'

'A bit . . .' Irvine said, raising her eyebrows.

'OK, I deserved that. But this has been good for me and I know that you're doing it just because you're a good person. And I want to say thanks, you know.'

Irvine waited to see if there was any more.

'So, thanks,' he said. 'And I mean it.'

'You're welcome,' Irvine said, deciding that he was being sincere.

They touched glasses and sipped at the chilled wine.

'You know,' Irvine said, 'this is probably not entirely selfless on my part.'

Roddy watched her but said nothing.

'I mean, I've had a difficult couple of years. For a whole variety of reasons. What with my divorce and . . . some other stuff.'

'What stuff? Maybe I can help you with it.'

Irvine smiled. 'No, Roddy, I don't think you can. Anyway, I was just going to say that this has been as much about me getting away as it has about you. I'm not some angel descended to light the way for you.'

'It doesn't matter to me what your motivations are.'

The waitress came back over and Irvine ordered sea bass with fried rice for two. When it arrived after the starter the smell of ginger, oil and spring onions set her salivary glands to overdrive.

'Wow,' Roddy said. 'That smells great.'

They shared the food and drank all of the wine and relaxed fully for the first time since they had embarked on the trip, settled into their roles now and comfortable with what they were doing.

'How *is* your love life?' Roddy asked after they had ordered coffee.

Irvine squinted at him, feeling just about tipsy enough to tell him about Logan.

'Come on, spill,' Roddy pressed her. 'You got the gory details about me.'

Irvine held up her hand, palm out, not wanting to hear any more tales from the tour bus from him. 'Fine,' she said. 'Where do I start?'

'Anywhere you like.'

'He's got a daughter.'

'OK, so he's divorced as well. Or is he still married?'

'He's never been married.'

'I'm intrigued. Doesn't sound like your kind of guy.'

'I know, right? But he is.'

Irvine lifted her glass and drained the last few drops of wine, looked at her watch and saw that it was close to ten. It was almost completely dark outside.

'It's a really long story,' she said. 'But he didn't know he had a daughter until recently and he's now looking after her full time.'

'What happened to her mother?'

'She died.'

'Maybe you shouldn't tell me this.'

'No, I want to. Anyway, the girl is thirteen now and I think they're both still struggling to come to terms with their own relationship. I knew them before we got together and she and I got on great.'

'But now that you're competing with her for her dad . . .'

'God, it sounds like *such* a cliché, doesn't it?'

'There are a lot of single parents out there and lots of messed-up kids.'

'I know.'

'Is he worth the effort?'

Irvine leaned back in her chair stretched her arms above her head. 'They both are,' she said.

'Then there's nothing to talk about. You just get on with it and try to make it work. There's no such thing as the perfect relationship.'

'Except maybe the tour bus groupies?'

'Well . . .'

21

Cahill slowed fifty yards from the bottom of the hill, looking past the lead car as it indicated and started to turn. His eyes scanned in stages: far, mid-distance, near.

Everything looked good so far.

'I see you now,' Harry Shields' voice sounded in his ear as the car in front completed its turn and disappeared behind the crowd. 'All clear.'

'Copy,' Cahill replied. 'Keep your eyes open, everyone.'

Hardy and Carrie closed the gap behind them and they turned almost together. Cahill had anticipated a big crowd and wasn't surprised to see that he was right. Hands reached out from behind the barriers, straining to touch the car as it glided slowly past. Lights flashed from camera phones, lighting the way on both sides of the road like an airport runway.

Washington and Judd had stopped their car opposite the entrance to the cinema, giving cover from that side of the road. They were both out of the car now and watching the crowd closely.

The car behind slowed and then stopped, blocking off anyone

approaching from the street. Two more cars turned up from Sauchiehall Street and stopped behind them, the occupants no doubt wondering what the hell was going on.

Cahill steered his car into the space outside the entrance, the more powerful flashes from the professional photographers' cameras bursting in front of him in waves.

As he stopped, Hanson turned in his seat to speak to Tara.

'Everything OK?' he asked.

She nodded and smiled, her nerves under control.

'Wait here,' Cahill said, opening his door and stepping out on to the street.

As Cahill opened his door, Hanson reached back and grabbed Tara's hand, squeezing it gently before opening his own door.

Another wave of flashes went off as Cahill went to open the rear door, not looking at Tara in the back seat, his eyes focused on the crowd. Always alert. He saw that some of the press had been allowed to bring their vehicles inside the security perimeter and was annoyed; he'd made it clear that that was not supposed to happen.

Hanson came round the car, shielding Tara from the crowd as Cahill opened the door.

The flashes became as one: a burst of light like the sun. Everyone shouted her name, wanting her to look down their lens. Needing that front-page shot.

Tara stood and turned to the crowd across the street, waving at them and holding her position like a true pro so that everyone could get a picture.

Cahill kept his attention on the crowd at the entrance; saw Harry Shields walk out and nod. All clear inside.

One of the cars stuck on the hill behind the rear car sounded its horn and Cahill, from the corner of his eye, saw Hanson look that way, taking his eyes off the crowd around him.

'Phil,' Cahill said sharply. Hanson's head whipped back around. 'Eyes front,' Cahill told him. 'Don't get distracted.'

Hanson nodded.

It took discipline and training, Cahill knew, to keep the distractions at the edge of your awareness. You had to trust your team.

Cahill started to walk forward and Tara followed with Hanson just behind. Shields pointed to the right-hand door where a member of the event security staff was waiting to usher them inside.

Tara stopped on the pavement for a last photo opportunity, turning and smiling so that everyone got the angle they needed.

Cahill and Hanson stood at opposite sides with their backs to her, scanning the photographers and fans grouped five deep.

Then Tara walked inside and Cahill relaxed just a little.

Part one over, he thought. Get her back home and then we're done.

He looked down the hill and spoke into his mike. 'OK, Tom,' he said. 'You can clear the road and let them on through now. We're done up here.'

'Copy, Alex,' Hardy replied. 'Keep it smooth.'

Cahill smiled and nodded at Washington and Judd across the road.

'Good job,' he said, turning to follow Hanson inside the cinema.

22

The restaurant emptied by around ten-thirty, leaving Irvine and Roddy alone with their coffee. The staff lurked behind the bar counter, waiting for them to leave so that they could close up for the night and get home.

'How are you feeling?' Irvine asked, conscious that he was still far from fully recovered.

'Yeah, not bad,' Roddy replied. 'I mean, my head's starting to throb a bit, but that's maybe just the wine.'

Irvine nodded at one of the staff behind the bar and made the universal sign for the bill, signing her name in mid-air with an imaginary pen. For the first time in her life she was aware of how faintly ridiculous that act was and pulled her hands down into her lap.

The waitress who had served them brought the till receipt over on a white side plate and set it down in front of Irvine. She pushed it across the table to Roddy.

'What's the damage?' she asked.

'A gentleman never tells.'

'That's why I asked.'

'You're funny. Anyone ever tell you that?'

Irvine looked out of the window as Roddy pulled out his wallet and looked through his collection of gold and platinum credit cards.

There was a weak lamp above the door of the restaurant and it cast a pale circle of light into the alley, barely reaching the opposite wall. Irvine thought she saw someone standing against the far wall; the merest hint of movement in the blackness. She leaned forward and strained to see better, but there was nothing there. If there had ever been anything in the first place.

'Paranoid,' she said aloud.

'What?' Roddy looked up from the chip and PIN machine that he was using to pay the bill, the waitress looking bored beside him.

'Nothing,' Irvine said. 'I think I'm just tired.'

Roddy shrugged and the machine silently printed out a receipt. 'We going to head now?' he asked.

'Sure,' she said, pulling her cardigan off the back of her chair and slipping it on. 'You going to behave like a gentleman and walk me back to my room?'

He stood and bowed with a flourish, his hat falling on to the floor.

'OK, slick,' she said, laughing. 'Don't overdo it, OK.'

He looked a little disappointed, bent to lift his cap from the floor and fitted it back over his head. 'Give a guy a break,' he said.

'Aw, don't go in the huff.' Irvine nudged him in the ribs and pushed him in the back towards the door. 'Let's get to bed,' she said.

He looked back at her over his shoulder and pushed the brim of the cap up on his head. She tutted at him. 'You just don't ever stop, do you?' she said.

Roddy turned the handle of the front door, pulled it open and stepped out into the alley.

23

Cahill never relaxed once during the build-up to the film showing. He and Hanson stayed close to Tara as she mingled with the other guests before being ushered to her seat in the main auditorium. Cahill noticed that once or twice Hanson put his arm round her waist to guide her through the crowd.

They had decided in advance that only one of them would sit with her during the film, the others being stationed at various entry and exit points. Cahill had reluctantly agreed that Hanson would sit with her, but after seeing him being distracted outside on the street and being too tactile with her inside he changed his mind and called Carrie over before they went to their seats. While Tara was finishing an interview with a journalist in the bar of the cinema, he took Hanson aside, leaving Carrie to watch her.

'I'm pulling you from your seat,' he said.

Hanson frowned. 'Why? Because of what happened outside? I only looked away for a second. Anyone would have.'

'I didn't,' Cahill told him.

'But—'

'None of my team did.'

Hanson looked back at Tara and Cahill saw in his face that he was unhappy about the decision.

'Look, Phil,' he said. 'You're not a bad guy, but this is my op and I decide how it runs.' Hanson continued to avoid eye contact. 'I've been doing this for a while. It takes years to learn how to do it properly and it's more than just being a veteran.'

Hanson turned back to him. 'What makes you so good?' he asked, starting to get angry. 'You're just an ex-grunt like me.'

Cahill kept his voice level. 'No, Phil. I didn't go straight from the service to this. I've had proper training, that's all you need to know.' Hanson looked like he wanted to argue some more, but Cahill held his hand up. 'It's done, Phil. You're too close to this and I need to make sure that the focus is on her.'

Hanson looked at the floor and breathed heavily through his nose.

'Fine,' he said after a moment. 'Where do you want me?'

Cahill stood at the back wall of the auditorium for the duration of the film. That way he was able to see everything and monitor each member of his team. Hanson did exactly what he was told to do and Cahill was pleased that he had put their argument behind him. With a little more time and some training, he thought, Hanson might be a good guy to have around.

He was only vaguely aware of the film and realised it had ended when the crowd stood and applauded, the lights going up and everyone looking at Tara. She looked relaxed for the first time, smiling and waving.

'Keep her in her seat till the place clears,' Cahill said into his mike. 'We don't want to try to control her in the crowd. It'll be too tight.'

'Copy,' Carrie said.

Cahill stayed where he was, watching Tara as she spoke to a number of guests and making sure that the team continued to cover the crowd, looking for abnormal movement patterns. Again, there was nothing out of the ordinary and the place cleared in ten minutes. Cahill started down the stairs towards Tara's seat.

'Phil,' he said, 'you swap places with Carrie now. Tom, you and Carrie get outside to check things out for the departure. Chris and Bails go to the lobby and clear the interior. We'll hold here.'

Everyone acknowledged and then moved to carry out Cahill's directions.

'How was it?' Tara asked when he got to her seat.

'How was what?' Cahill asked.

'The film. What did you think of it?'

'I didn't really notice.'

'If you thought it was bad,' she said, 'just say so. I won't be offended.'

'No, for real. I didn't see it. I was busy looking out for you.'

'You're *so* serious,' she said, smiling.

'I sure am.'

24

Roddy started walking up towards the main street but Irvine wanted to go down the hill towards the loch, where the moon was sparkling silver on the black surface of the water.

'Let's go down and walk along that way,' she said.

He stopped and turned.

Behind him, shadows moved out from the wall, forming into the shape of two men.

Irvine's heart convulsed.

The emergency exit of the restaurant opened beside the men and someone threw a bag of rubbish out into the alley. A shaft of light from the doorway illuminated one of the men's faces — except there were no discernible features, just a black, formless mass.

The door slammed shut.

Irvine was still a little drunk from the wine, unsure if what she was seeing was real.

'Roddy . . .' she said.

One of the men swung his arm round sharply.

From ten feet away, Irvine heard the slapping sound of the blow and saw Roddy's head snap to the side. The man swung his arm again and this time Roddy fell from the force of it.

The other man started towards Irvine.

She saw now that they were both wearing masks to obscure their faces. Beyond them, the light from the main street glowed weakly.

Roddy was on his knees and making a noise Irvine had not heard before, his hands clawing at his throat.

Still the second man advanced towards Irvine.

She was stuck, unable to move.

Roddy leaned over and placed his hands on the ground, dark liquid pouring from his face and neck. Then the man above Roddy raised his hand and Irvine saw it.

The knife.

The man brought his hand down on to Roddy's neck. Raised the knife up and struck again. And again.

Irvine stepped back, caught her foot on something and went down, landing painfully on her backside.

She scrabbled backwards using her hands, her shoes scraping on the concrete as the other man bore down on her, his own knife flashing by his thigh.

Roddy was flat on the ground now, the other man kneeling on him and . . .

Irvine blinked, hoping that it would all just go away.

But it would not.

Her hand slipped on something moist – a container half full of takeaway rice from the restaurant – and she fell on to her side.

The man quickened his pace and was on her, his arm ready to strike.

Irvine shouted, 'No,' and kicked out at him. Her foot connected with his knee; she felt it pop. Heard an audible crack as it bent unnaturally backwards.

He grunted, choked back a scream and went down, the knife clattering on the surface of the alley.

She pushed herself up on to her feet, while the man in front of her grabbed at his injured knee. The one with Roddy stood up and looked to see what was happening.

Roddy was still now, blood pooling on the ground around him. Too much blood.

Irvine stepped forward and stamped down hard on the fallen man's knee. Stamped again. Kicked at his groin, screaming.

The other man moved fast towards her.

She reached down, grabbed the knife and threw it at him as he advanced on her. He put his arm up to shield his face and the knife bounced off his forearm and over his shoulder.

Hissing, he stopped and grabbed at his arm with his free hand; a strip of flesh was visible through the dark material of his sleeve where the blade had sliced into it.

'No,' Irvine screamed at them, holding her hands up.

The man beneath her swatted ineffectually at her leg. She pulled her foot out of his weak grasp, raised it up and stamped down on his mask, hearing the back of his skull crack against the ground.

She shouted something, not even sure what it was, and backed away. She blinked tears from her eyes, smearing make-up as she wiped her arm across her face.

The man on the ground was still, his leg twisted all wrong. The other one looked down at him, his head tilted to one side. He looked back up at Irvine and she saw his eyes through the holes in the mask.

They stood that way for an age; a second.

He started towards her again, the knife held out in front of him.

Irvine was glad she had her trainers on and not heels. She was pretty quick.

Turn and go.

But Roddy . . .

Roddy's gone.

But . . .

Move. Now.

The door to the restaurant opened and the man looked at the staff who stepped out into the alley, ready to go home after a long shift.

Irvine swivelled and ran.

Cars passed by on the road ahead.

Could she stop herself; did she want to?

Just go and keep going. Over the road, over the fence and on to the water, moving fast enough to skip across to the other side like a flat stone thrown hard.

Noise behind her. Don't look back.

She hit the corner going too fast, tried to turn and lost her footing. She slid and cracked into a parked car; it stopped her from going out into the road as a car flashed past. A face at the window blurred by, seeing her but not seeing her.

Irvine turned and looked up the alley. Someone screamed.

She felt pain jab in her hip where she had hit the car.

Then she was running again.

25

The convoy turned on to Waterloo Street, heading for the Hilton. Tara was in the back of the car, talking on her mobile to her mother, still new enough to all of this to get a little giddy about it and want to share it with her family. Cahill hoped that she would hold on to that for as long as possible, because he knew it wouldn't last. He'd been on close protection details for enough actors and musicians to know that the pressure and the lack of privacy eventually took its toll.

'Yeah,' Tara was saying. 'It was great, Mum. Everyone was so nice about the film after.'

Hanson had been quiet since his confrontation earlier with Cahill; still a little sore about being told off. But he was keeping his focus much better now, not distracted by Tara any more.

Up ahead, the car carrying Washington and Judd veered right and went down the hill towards the rear of the Hilton and Cahill followed. There was no other traffic in sight.

Still on the job, Cahill told himself. Keep it tight for a few more minutes.

'How we doing back there?' he said into his mike.

'It's all good,' Hardy's voice answered.

'Almost home.'

'Copy that. You're buying the beers.'

'So what's new?'

They turned right at the bottom of the hill and Cahill saw the sign at the entrance to the Hilton. He drew up behind the lead car and had to slow sharply as the red brake lights burned bright in front of him. The three cars stopped together, the lead one having just made the turn on to the Hilton's driveway.

'What's the hold-up?' Cahill asked.

Quiet for a beat.

'Some kind of bust up with the taxi drivers,' Judd said. 'They're blocking the road.'

'Anything obvious?' Cahill asked.

'Nope. Don't see anything.'

Cahill put his hands on the steering wheel and waited, certain that the taxi drivers would clear out of the way when they saw the cars waiting. He wasn't concerned. Not yet, anyway.

'We're moving again,' Judd said finally.

Cahill lifted his foot off the brake and eased forward, turning into the driveway. He had just straightened his car up when Judd braked hard again.

'What's wrong with these guys?' Judd's voice sounded in his ear.

Cahill looked at Hanson. 'Go see what's going on,' he told him.

Hanson nodded, then opened his door and got out, walking up the shallow incline past Judd's car. Cahill could see a group of the taxi drivers standing just in front of the lead car arguing and pointing along the line of stationary taxis.

'Why are we stopped?' Tara asked.

'Looks like the taxi drivers are having a bit of an argument about where they are in the queue.'

Tara leaned forward, resting her hands on the tops of the front seats. Cahill could smell the light perfume she was wearing and glanced at her face in the rear-view mirror.

'Typical,' she said, slumping back in her seat.

Up ahead, it looked like Hanson was getting caught up in the argument. Washington opened his door and got out of the lead car.

Cahill's instinct for trouble started to kick in.

26

Cahill stood in the open door of his car and turned to Hardy in the car behind. He motioned for him to reverse and go round to the other side of the driveway, going in the wrong way. Hardy nodded at him and started to back up.

Cahill got into his car and waited while Hardy straightened up and drove forward again.

Cahill reversed into the road. He put the car in first gear and paused, looking again at the commotion up the hill. He noticed that there were two free spaces in front of one of the taxis – a plain black one, with no advertising colours on it. One of the drivers went over to it, cupped his hands against the glass and peered in the side window.

Hanson looked back at Cahill and shrugged his shoulders.

Judd waited in his car while Washington walked up to the crowd.

Something about the plain taxi bothered Cahill, but he couldn't quite figure out what. 'What's going on up there?' he said into his mike.

'The drivers say this cab's been blocking the rank and they're getting pissed about it now,' Washington said.

'Who cares?' Cahill said. 'Tell them to get out of the road, for Christ's sake.'

He looked along the row of taxis again and saw what it was that was bothering him. The plain taxi had not been there when they left for the premiere; and it had no city council licence plate on the back.

Suddenly it felt all wrong.

'Get back in the cars and let's get out of here,' he said urgently.

'Copy,' Washington said.

Hanson turned to head back down and bumped into one of the drivers, who shoved him hard. Hanson squared up to him.

'Phil, back off,' Cahill said over the radio.

Washington moved towards Hanson. Judd shifted into reverse, waiting for Washington.

Cahill looked over at Hardy's car, which was now stopped just short of the exit from the driveway. Beyond that, he saw a car in the distance on the far side of the motorway. He looked hard at it, trying to see in the dark. It looked like a man was leaning on the bonnet.

Hanson was still squaring up to the guy he had bumped into.

Cahill got out of the car and stood looking over to the far side of the motorway; he thought he saw the man leaning on the car lift a pair of binoculars to his eyes.

Washington reached Hanson, pulling him away from the crowd of taxi drivers.

Cahill was conscious that Tara was alone in the car. He looked around but saw no one in the immediate vicinity and started to walk up to meet Hanson and Washington, glancing over at the car in the distance, unsure of how he felt, except that something wasn't right.

'Phil,' he shouted, breaking into a jog now. Hanson turned to him.

Cahill felt the hairs on the back of his hand stand on end, as if an electric charge had passed through the air.

Something flashed white from the plain taxi, air expanding faster than the speed of sound as the bomb wired to the engine detonated.

Cahill was aware of feeling like he'd just run head first into a brick wall; then he was lifted into the air.

His breath was knocked out of him, his diaphragm crushed as his ribs compacted from the force of the explosion.

He tasted blood in his mouth.

Heard the sharp crack of the bomb; the screech of metal being torn apart.

Then he was falling.

It turned black.

Still he kept on falling.

27

Irvine's hip throbbed as she ran away from the alley and towards the hotel, not really sure exactly where it was. Twice she turned up streets heading away from the loch's edge expecting to see the hotel only to discover that she hadn't picked the right one. She was starting to panic and was conscious of the few people out on the streets staring at her.

When she turned the third corner she saw the small park in front of the hotel and the lights glowing from the downstairs windows; people sitting there drinking wine and coffee, oblivious of the terrible things that one human was capable of doing to another. She walked unsteadily to the edge of the pavement, bent down with her hands resting on her knees and vomited into the storm drain. Her stomach continued to heave even when there was nothing left to come up and her eyes filled with tears at the effort.

After she was done, Irvine limped through the park, pushed open the glass reception door and went slowly up to her room. She sat on the bed and felt her stomach heave again, forcing her to run to the bathroom and sink to her knees by the toilet, spitting yellow bile into the water and flushing it away. The tears came again, this time not from the convulsions but from the dark realisation of what had just happened to her; and to Roddy. Leaning on the seat, she sobbed helplessly.

Then she heard low male voices outside in the hall; soft footsteps approaching her door. She stopped crying and sat up straight, close to panic again. But the voices came and went as they passed by her room and a door opened further down the hall.

The realisation came to her that maybe the men in the car park the previous night were not reporters after all, but assassins. The word sounded ridiculous even in her head and she laughed almost involuntarily. But all melodrama aside, perhaps they were after Roddy, somehow related to his drug habit. Had he left a large debt unpaid and this was the payback? She'd heard of pushers using violence, of course; but to just kill him like that without trying to get any money. Why? It didn't make any sense to her.

What if it was more personal: a jealous husband or boyfriend?

Whatever it was, Irvine knew that she would have to report what had happened. And she could not get changed or cleaned up for fear of destroying any evidence that might be on her.

She went back to the main part of the room and called 999 from the phone on the table beside her bed. She was put through to the local police office and explained that she had been attacked in town, gave them the location and told them that she thought her companion was badly injured and might still be there. She couldn't quite bring herself to say that she thought he was dead.

Too much blood.

Too much.

The operator offered to send someone to pick her up and she gladly accepted, giving him the hotel name and room number before hanging up.

Irvine slumped back on the bed. Looking up at the light-fitting in the centre of the ceiling, she saw a cobweb filled with the remains of insects. She suddenly felt more tired than she ever had in her life. Her eyelids fluttered and she thought, just as she lost consciousness, that maybe she was fainting.

part three: aftermath

1

Logan opened his eyes in the dark and sat up. His head was fuzzy from too little sleep. He strained to listen, expecting to hear the sounds of Ellie in the kitchen or bathroom, but there was nothing.

He reached out and straightened his digital alarm clock and saw that it was just before midnight. He'd only been asleep for about an hour but found it hard to shake the feeling that something was wrong. He was startled when the door to his room opened and Ellie came in.

'What was that noise?' she asked.

'What noise?' he said, his eyes still adjusting to the dark.

'Dunno.'

She sounded groggy, rubbing at her eyes. Logan pushed his covers off and swung his legs out.

'You have a bad dream?' he asked her.

'No,' she said. 'I thought I heard something.'

'Like what?'

He wondered if she was having one of her sleep-awake moments.

'You awake, Ellie?'

'Uh-huh.'

Logan stood and walked to the door, stepping past Ellie and switching on the hall light. He winced in the glare, blinking until it was no longer painful.

'It was like a bang or something,' Ellie said. 'Like fireworks, but far away.'

'It was definitely outside, you think?' he asked her, worried that maybe somebody was trying to break into the flat.

She nodded, looking down at the floor and shading her eyes from the light.

'OK,' Logan said. 'Go back to bed and I'll have a look around.'

She padded slowly back to her room.

Logan checked each room, making sure that the windows and front door were secure. Everything looked fine; nothing tampered with. When he was done he went to the living room and pulled the blinds aside, peering outside. The street was empty except for a young couple walking unsteadily on the opposite side of the street. On the way home from the pub, he thought.

Back in his bedroom, he picked up the BlackBerry and checked to see if someone had tried to call him, but there was nothing. His e-mail list had not expanded since he last checked it around eight that night.

Ellie was curled up under her duvet when he went to her room and he thought that she had gone back to sleep until she spoke.

'What was it?' she asked.

'Nothing,' he said. 'I mean, I couldn't see anything.'

'Did you look outside my window?'

He went to the window and pulled her curtains aside to check the latch, which was secure. The window faced the city centre and he saw nothing out of the ordinary.

Ellie got out of bed and walked over to stand beside him, her hair tangled and mussed and falling down over her face. She pushed it back behind her ears and leaned her head against his arm.

'What made the bang?' she asked.

'I don't know, honey. I don't know.'

2

Something stirred at the edge of Cahill's consciousness.

He couldn't breathe, afraid to open his mouth and take a breath. Afraid that the darkness might rush into his lungs through his mouth and nose. Clog his airways and fill his blood. And you don't come back from that.

Not ever.

Fire crackled, the heat of it on his face, the raw, red and gold tongues licking at the air and scalding it.

He couldn't see anything where he was.

Couldn't feel anything, except numb.

He realised that he was no longer falling, but floating; held up by nothing. Felt the fire again, hot against his skin.

Something tugged at him from below. He looked down and saw a shape begin to form, colours coalescing. The colours of his past: green and brown and beige.

You're in the army now, son.

The colours multiplied and became many. Arms clad in desert camo reached out for him and he felt the call in his head.

Come join us. There's no pain down here; no pain.

He watched them, unable to move as they faded away below him and their cries became weaker until he couldn't hear them any more. And he realised that it wasn't them sinking, but that he was rising.

He kicked out, firm and strong, and saw the fire crackle above him. Felt the heat again.

He heard voices above him, now those below were gone. But the ones above were not welcoming, not seeking to embrace him. The voices above knew only pain.

He kicked again for the surface, the red and orange and gold of the fire blurring into focus. He felt heavy; knew that he had to be strong to break the surface.

'Nothing worth having is easy.' His father's voice from the past.

'I know that,' he replied, but only in his head. 'Don't you think I know that?'

He kicked again, this time with all the strength he could muster. But he felt so heavy. For a moment he didn't think that he would make it; felt himself slip back and saw the light above begin to fade.

'Fuck you,' he roared, again in his head. 'Fuck all of you. I've been down here before and you couldn't keep me then.'

And then he's moving fast, climbing up. The darkness rushes by, light funnelling towards him. And the faster he moves the heavier he gets.

Then the pain comes in waves, bursting inside him.

The light is within touching distance.

One last push, he thinks. Then I'll make it.

He looks down and sees them all beneath him again, arms stretching up for him and voices keening; sees that they are trapped in a rising tide of red.

'You can't have me. Not now.'

Turning his face away from the bloody tide racing from below to engulf him, he reaches out and pulls himself up into the light.

3

Cahill opened his eyes.

Blinked hard.

Everything was fuzzy.

He wiped at his eyes; felt blood slick against his hands. Could feel the heat of the fire on him; taste the smoke.

He coughed and realised he couldn't hear, his ears buzzing. Wiped again at his eyes, this time with his sleeve.

His vision cleared.

A fire was burning across the road.

He felt metal railings at his back and pushed himself up till he was sitting. Breathing in he felt something jagged and jerked at the pain.

I'm in shock.

Breathed again, trying to get oxygen into his bloodstream. Felt the pain again, hard and sharp in his side.

It's just broken ribs. You've had worse.

All the lights in the hotel had gone out.

The buzzing stayed in his ears but he filtered it; heard screaming.

Footsteps hard and fast against the tarmac, getting closer. Then a face in front of his; someone talking, shouting.

Tom Hardy.

Always Tom.

'Get me up,' he said.

Hardy put his hands on Cahill's shoulders and told him to stay put, to wait for the ambulance.

'No,' Cahill said. 'Get me up, Tom.'

Hardy leaned in until his lips were at Cahill's ear. 'You stay put,' he shouted, pulling back and jabbing a finger in his face.

Cahill knew he was right and nodded. Hardy put a hand on his shoulder and looked back across the road. Cahill followed his gaze and saw a human arm lying on the road, charred and alone.

'What happened?' Cahill asked. Hardy turned back to him.

'A bomb,' he said. 'A goddamned car bomb.'

4

Cahill did what he was told and sat on the ground with his back against the railings, wrapped in Tom Hardy's jacket to keep his temperature up and guard against going any deeper into shock. Hardy had checked him out and found that his only external injuries were a long gash in his head and assorted scratches and cuts on his arms, hands and face.

Hardy had looked at him solemnly when Cahill explained that he thought he'd broken a few ribs in the blast and felt pain whenever he tried to breathe. They both knew that he could have blast lung; the pressure wave from the explosion rupturing a lung.

'You know the plan,' Hardy had told him. 'They won't send ambulances or paramedics in here until they're sure that there are no secondary devices.'

Cahill nodded. He knew.

'Your skin tone is good, considering,' Hardy said. 'Beyond that you'll just have to sit tight for now, OK?'

He knew what Hardy was saying: you *look* OK, but there's nothing more I can do for you now.

Some comfort.

Hardy left him sitting there, staring at the arm in the road.

His memory flitted in and out, making it difficult to remember what had happened exactly. He remembered being at the premiere, guarding that actress.

What was her name?

He turned his head and scanned the area around him. There was a big silver car in the road, only twenty feet in front of him, and he couldn't believe he hadn't noticed it before. A young woman was sitting in the rear seat, staring uncomprehendingly at the scene outside; the front doors of the car were wide open and all the window glass was shattered. He thought maybe that was the actress but he couldn't recall her name.

She turned and looked at him, holding his gaze for a few long moments. Her face was devoid of emotion and her skin so pale as to be almost translucent.

Looking beyond her, his eyes were drawn to the burning wreckage of the taxi that had been rigged with the bomb. It was little more than a metal frame now, twisted and scorched and lying in a shallow crater in the tarmac.

He had a feeling someone else had been in the car with the woman; couldn't remember who it was.

Not one of his team. But somebody.

There was another car . . . one of his? . . . on the entrance slope, again with no glass in the windows. It was empty. He tried to remember who had been with him from CPO. His mind fought him.

Where were the people from that car?

His people.

He looked around for Hardy and saw him to the right, leaning over someone lying on the ground.

A woman kneeled in front of Cahill: small, but compact and solid.

A voice cried out in pain behind her, rising to a scream and then stopping.

'Carrie?' he asked.

She nodded and stretched her neck to look at the gash on his head, investigating it with her hands. He let her do it and said nothing, feeling no pain as she probed the wound.

'It's not too bad,' she said finally. 'A few stitches and you'll be good as new.'

Everyone sounded to him as if they were talking underwater, his hearing muffled and that buzzing still echoing in his head. Carrie smiled at him, or at least that was what it looked like she was trying to do. Her face was smeared with dust and blood and he could see tear tracks on her cheeks. He reached out and touched her cheek with his fingertips. She grabbed his hand, squeezing it hard as another tear leaked out from one of her eyes.

'Who was here?' he asked. 'How many of us?'

She looked down at the ground and he felt her grip on his hand tighten, saw tears fall from her face on to the ground.

'Carrie,' he said.

Her shoulders heaved as she tried to keep her emotions in check. She straightened up and sniffed back phlegm, wiping her arm across her face, streaking tears and dirt and blood like war paint.

'Chris is in a bad way,' she said, her voice wavering. 'I don't know if he's going to make it. Bails isn't much better.'

Cahill heard the words but found it difficult to comprehend what she was saying. Or perhaps he just didn't want to.

'Hanson's gone,' Carrie said.

'Who's Hanson?' Cahill asked, vaguely aware that he knew the name but unable to form a picture of the person it belonged to.

She ignored his question and looked over to where Hardy was tending to the man on the ground. Cahill followed her gaze and saw Hardy waving at her frantically. She looked down at Cahill.

'What?' he asked.

'It's Chris. I've got to go.'

Cahill watched as she sprinted towards Hardy; the empty sound of death filled the night air.

5

Cahill could no longer sit and do nothing while his team suffered in front of him. He reached back and grabbed the railings, trying to slide up to a standing position, but when he got halfway up a wave of nausea struck him and he fell back down, landing heavily on his rear.

He heard again the voice scream in pain ahead of him, but couldn't see anyone through the thick black smoke still belching from the ruined taxi.

He closed his eyes, took a deep breath and pushed up, this time making it all the way to his feet.

The nausea hit him again. He bent over and vomited on to the road.

He looked at the contents of his stomach spattered on the street and was pleased to see that there was no blood. Concussion, he told himself. That's all.

He leaned back against the railings and tried to get some more air into his lungs, each breath rasping in his throat. He gathered saliva in his mouth, trying to rinse away the taste of the vomit, and then spat it out.

The woman sitting alone in the car was still watching him impassively. Sirens sounded, distant to him, and blue lights flashed on the overpass above and on the motorway to the west as police cars arrived to take up viewing positions from a safe distance.

Cahill had spent nine months with Strathclyde Police as a civilian counter-terrorism security adviser and knew that they would keep their distance until the bomb disposal team had cleared the area. They were on their own until then.

He walked gingerly towards the woman in the car, stopping every few feet as feelings of dizziness and nausea washed over him. When he reached her, he pulled open the rear door and sat on the edge of the seat. She gave no indication that she was even aware that he was there.

'Miss,' he said.

She glanced at him, startled by his voice.

'We have to get out of here,' he told her. 'It's not safe.'

She frowned at him and reached up to pull a piece of glass from her hair. A single line of blood made its way slowly out of her hairline and down into her left eye. She blinked and wiped at it, a look of annoyance passing across her face.

Tara. That was her name, he remembered.

'Tara, we need to get out of here. Do you understand?'

He reached out and grabbed her hand, the other one still wiping at the blood in her eye.

'Come with me,' he said.

She shuffled along the seat and swung her legs out into the road. Cahill noticed how perfect her shoes looked, as if they had just come out of the box. Funny the small things you notice.

He moved back to give her room to get up, still holding her

hand. When they were both standing, he put his arm round her waist and held tight, as much to support his own weight as hers as his head swam again.

'Where are we going?' she asked. 'Where's Phil?'

Phil Hanson. Cahill remembered now.

'We have to get out of here.'

'Where's Phil? Where is he?'

Her voice started to rise. Cahill pulled her round to face him and reached up to put a hand on her cheek, biting back the pain from his ribs.

'Let's just take care of ourselves for now. Then we worry about the others.'

She tried to pull away from him, squirming in his grasp, but he was much too strong for her.

'Tara, relax,' he told her, his voice firm. 'We'll get Phil, OK. But you need to come with me for now.'

Her shoulders slumped and her eyelids fluttered; Cahill thought that she was going to faint. But she straightened again and nodded at him.

Cahill turned his head sharply at the sound of a car coming their way fast. He instinctively stepped around to shield Tara. The car skidded to a stop beside them, Hardy driving with Judd barely conscious in the passenger seat. Carrie was in the back; Washington lay with his head resting in her lap. Washington looked the worst, blood masking his face and his clothes torn and blackened.

Cahill hoped that the blood made it look worse than it was.

Hardy reached over, pushed the front passenger door open. 'Can you drive?' he shouted at Cahill.

'I'll just have to.'

Hardy nodded, his face grim. 'You need to get Tara in the other car now and follow me.'

Hardy drove forward, then stopped and ran back to help Cahill get Tara in the passenger seat of the silver car before Cahill eased into the driver's seat, his ribs screaming at him. Hardy went back to his car and pressed on the accelerator as Cahill turned the other car to follow.

They veered right under the building next to the hotel and turned quickly left to go up the hill towards Bothwell Street. The top of the road was blocked by unmarked police cars and four armed officers trained their weapons on the car. An ambulance waited on the street behind them, pulsing cold, blue light.

Hardy stamped on the brake and the car slid to a halt; Cahill did the same behind him and just stopped before colliding with the car in front. Tara reached out with one hand on the dashboard to brace herself. The armed policemen were crouched down behind the cars, only their Kevlar helmets, tense faces and weapons showing. Cahill could see that they were shouting but his hearing was still impaired and he had no idea what they were saying. Hardy got out of the car in front of Cahill.

'They're telling us to get out of the cars and get down on the ground,' Hardy shouted back at Cahill.

'We can't move Chris,' Carrie screamed from the back seat of the lead car. 'He needs to get to a hospital.'

Hardy huffed out a breath, raised his hands and then laced his fingers behind his head. 'We're not armed,' he shouted up at the police barricade. 'We have people here in need of immediate medical attention.'

Cahill watched as one of the policemen stood and waved with his hand for Hardy to get down on the ground. The other three kept their weapons trained on the cars.

Please don't let us get killed by these guys, Cahill thought.

6

Hardy motioned for Cahill to get out of his car and on to the ground as he went down on to his knees, wrapping his hands back behind his head. Cahill pushed his door open and told Tara to get out and do just as Hardy had done, but she looked over at him with scared eyes and shook her head.

'It's OK,' he told her, his own voice muffled by the constant buzzing in his ears. 'We need to get out to show them that we're not a threat. I'll be right out after you.'

She faced forward and shook her head violently, her body tense, ready to resist any attempt to move her.

'Tara,' he said. 'My friends are dying in that car and I need to get them to a hospital right now. I need you to move. Please.'

She remained tensed, her hands on the dashboard in front of her. Cahill knew that he was really in no shape to forcibly remove her from the vehicle, and that would probably prove counter-productive anyway. If she got out and refused to cooperate with directions from the armed police she was likely to get shot. And maybe get the rest of them shot too. The cops would be treating this as a terrorist attack and everyone in the cars was potentially a threat to them.

Cahill looked out at Hardy who was lying on the road, staring back at them.

'She won't move, Tom,' Cahill shouted through the open space where the windscreen used to be.

Hardy put his nose against the tarmac and blew out a breath before looking up the hill again towards the road-block at the top. 'There are injured people in these cars,' he shouted. 'We can't move them.'

Cahill felt sweat start to bead on his forehead and upper lip, the salt water stinging his burned skin.

The policeman who had stood started to move around his vehicle. One of his colleagues followed behind. They walked slowly towards Hardy, their weapons pressed firmly to their shoulders and aimed at the cars.

Tara began to shake and then cry, her body heaving against her seat. Cahill reached over to her, but pain bolted through him, causing him to jerk and shout out. The policemen stopped and crouched, still in firing position.

'Tara,' Cahill said through gritted teeth, 'I know this is like nothing you've ever been through before, but I need you to calm down. Do you understand?'

She didn't respond except to put her hands to her face, sobbing heavily and bending forward. Cahill knew that the movement in the car would unnerve the officers out on the street.

'Alex.' Carrie's voice sounded from the car ahead of him. 'Chris's pulse is really weak. We need to get the hell out of here.'

Cahill looked out of the windscreen and saw that the two officers had stood and were again advancing slowly towards them, only fifteen feet away now.

'I can't do anything,' Cahill said, looking at Hardy. 'I can't shift her.'

'Then we just have to sit tight till they get here,' Hardy said, his lips set in a thin line.

'Armed police,' the lead officer shouted. 'Nobody move or we *will* shoot.'

Cahill watched as they came forward, the man at the rear aiming his weapon at Hardy and the lead one keeping his trained on the front car. They were both dressed in black overalls with heavy black boots and padded Kevlar vests that had POLICE printed on them in white. The helmets were tight to their heads and Cahill knew from experience that they restricted their movement and hearing, but it was a small price to pay to stop a live round taking their skulls apart.

The lead officer came up to Cahill's car and Cahill followed him with his eyes. The barrel of the gun was pointing directly at his head.

'Armed police,' the man shouted again. 'Get out of the car one at a time and get on the ground, now.'

Tara put her hands to her ears and sobbed, shaking her head from side to side.

The second officer reached Hardy and motioned for the two other men at the top of the hill to come down. They did so quickly, moving to cover their colleagues.

'Armed police. Get out the fucking car. NOW.'

He almost screamed the last word and it finally pulled Tara out of her panic. She lifted her hands and swivelled her legs out, stepping on to the road.

'Slowly,' the lead officer said, backing away a step. 'Now get on the ground.'

Tara did as she was told and Cahill did the same on his side of the car.

Two of the officers trained their weapons on Carrie and Judd while the other two checked Hardy, Cahill and Tara for any weapons. Cahill's broken ribs screamed at him as he was pushed on to the road and his hands were bound with plastic ties. He gritted his teeth as they pulled him upright and waited for it to be over.

Carrie came out of the car and told them that Washington was unconscious and in bad shape before she too was cuffed with the ties. All four were then made to stand with their backs against the wall of the building at the side of the road while one of the officers leaned in to check Judd and Washington.

The cops were sweating heavily and the strain of the night showed in their faces. The lead officer turned to them, finally recognising Tara.

'Are you Tara Byrne?' he asked.

She nodded.

'Who are the rest of you?' he asked Hardy.

'We're her CP team,' he said. The cop looked blank. 'Close protection,' Hardy said quickly. 'We're her security team.'

'You armed?'

'No.'

'They with you?' pointing at Washington and Judd in the lead car.

'Yes. Look, we got caught in the explosion and they need to get to hospital.'

'What happened back there?' the officer asked.

'Car bomb,' Hardy answered.

'*Jesus.*'

'Yeah, now can you get that ambulance down here? Please.'

The cop stared at Hardy then waved up at the ambulance, motioning for it to come down to meet them.

Cahill felt light-headed and slid down to a sitting position with his back against the wall.

'Can we get these cuffs off?' Carrie asked.

'You got any ID?' the lead officer asked.

'In the glove-box,' Cahill said, sounding to everyone like he was shouting because his hearing was still affected. 'Letter of authorisation and photo ID.'

The officer nodded, lowering his weapon and then pushing it round to his back where it hung, secured by the strap. He went into the silver car and got the papers from the glove-box, flicking through and reading them closely. He turned to Cahill.

'This is from 10 Downing Street,' he said, holding up the letter of authorisation.

Cahill nodded, then bowed his head.

So tired.

7

Logan couldn't sleep after getting Ellie settled. He got up and went back round the flat checking again that the front door and all the windows were secure. When he was done, he went to the living room and switched on the TV. It was tuned to the BBC 24-hour news channel.

'. . . reports of an explosion in the centre of Glasgow tonight,' the anchor said, tilting her head to the side and putting her finger on the device fitted in her ear, listening to the input from the production booth above her in the studio.

Logan sat on the couch and stared at the screen.

'We understand that casualties are unknown at this time,' the woman went on. 'Emergency services have been unable to get on scene at the Hilton hotel pending a sweep of the area for secondary devices.' She was struggling to use what little information she had to form complete sentences.

'. . . treating it as a suspected terrorist attack.'

Logan grabbed his phone and called Cahill's mobile. It went

straight to voicemail. He waited for the short message to end and for the beep so that he could leave a message.

'Alex, it's Logan. Give me a call when you get this, OK?'

Unsure of what to do next, he called and got Hardy's voicemail.

Same for Bailey Judd and Chris Washington.

He pressed the phone to his forehead; felt an increasingly heavy knot of emotion settling in his stomach.

Ellie came into the room and leaned against the doorway, rubbing at her eyes and watching the TV.

'What's going on?' she asked. Logan said nothing.

The woman on the screen was talking now about the planned responses that UK police forces have in place for terrorist attacks.

'Did something happen?' Ellie asked.

Logan nodded.

'What?' she said, sounding a little scared.

Logan walked over and hugged her. 'Something bad.'

8

Hudson was still pumped full of adrenalin from the explosion; his pulse was racing and his heart thudding in his chest. He tried to breathe regularly to slow his heartbeat.

'How much ordnance did he use in that thing?' Two said. 'It went up like I don't know what. Jesus.'

'It just looked bad 'cause of it happening in the city like that. Wasn't really that big.'

'Still.'

'Yeah.'

They were quiet as they drove along the motorway heading south, Hudson being careful to stay within the speed limit all the way, but not going slowly enough to attract attention. He wanted to get well clear before stopping, maybe even waiting until they crossed the border into England. He remembered that there was a service station at Gretna and thought that they would pull in there.

His phone trilled on the dashboard and he saw that it was Five calling – hopefully to report success with the woman cop. A good night's work all in. Hudson pressed the button to answer the call. 'All done?' he asked.

There was quiet for a moment and Hudson wondered if the call had connected properly. Then he heard breathing over the speaker mounted in the roof of the car.

'What's up?' he asked this time, glancing at Two.

'We screwed up,' Five said.

Hudson closed his eyes for an instant. 'Tell me,' he said.

'We got the guy.'

'Which guy?'

'The singer guy, you know? From the hospital.'

Hudson had almost forgotten about him. 'But not the cop. Is that what you're doing such an awful job of telling me? That she's still around?'

'Yes.'

Hudson braked and swung the car on to the hard shoulder. He slammed his hands on the steering wheel.

'There's something else,' Five said.

Hudson leaned his forehead against the wheel. 'What?'

'Three's in a bad way. Got his knee done. And he got kicked in the head. I mean, he's up but he can't walk too good. I think he got a concussion.'

'A woman and a junkie did this to you pair of fuckwits? Is that what you're telling me?'

Five did the smart thing and stayed quiet.

'This was supposed to be the easy part,' Hudson said, looking at Two. 'How is it that what we just did went down so smooth and yet a simple shank and run got screwed up?'

Two didn't answer.

Hudson tried to clear his head and focus on what was left to do with the cop. 'You still have the GPS on her?' he asked.

'Yeah,' Five said.

'Is it switched on?'

They heard Five fumbling around on the other end of the line.

'Where are you?' Two asked.

'We're back at the hotel. Don't worry, nobody saw anything to get worked up about.'

'"Don't worry", he says.' Two shook his head.

Hudson fought a sudden urge to laugh.

'Yeah, the GPS is still working,' Five said. 'Her car's still in the town but it's not moving. Maybe she's heading to the cop shop on foot?'

'Wouldn't you?' Hudson asked.

Five knew better than to answer.

'Well, it needs to get done,' Hudson said. 'I mean, none of us gets any more money until the whole thing is finished. So you stay put and keep an eye on her, but take it easy and keep a low profile. Use the GPS. You two idiots get locked up and it is over.'

'What are we going to do?' Five asked. 'I mean, we can't just walk into a police station and go to war, can we?'

'The only thing I do know is that somebody has to do what you couldn't.'

'You're coming up here, then?'

Two looked at Hudson, the corners of his mouth turning down.

'Yes, we're coming up there,' Hudson sighed.

9

Cahill was sitting on the pavement waiting for another ambulance to transport him to the hospital. Carrie hovered by the medical teams working on Washington and Judd, asking the odd question but otherwise letting them get on with their job. One of the team had tried to give her a quick check, but she had brushed him off, telling them to concentrate on her colleagues.

After a while, Cahill couldn't tell how long, the first ambulance left with Washington in it, siren and lights at full power.

More ambulances arrived a few minutes later and the crew that approached Cahill, an older man and a young woman, quickly got him up and on to the stretcher. They pushed the stretcher into the back of the rig to give him some oxygen through a mask and to hook him up to an ECG monitor to check his heart. Hardy came over and stood at the open rear doors to watch as the ambulance containing Judd peeled away. Cahill's hearing was still messed up but his head was clearing and he motioned with his hand for Hardy to come closer.

'Call my wife,' Cahill said, pulling the oxygen mask away from his face. 'Call Sam.'

Hardy studied his face for a moment before replying. 'And tell her what?' he asked.

One of the paramedics pulled Cahill's hand away from the mask and fitted it back on his face, fixing him with a stern look and telling him not to do that again.

'Tell her there's been a car accident, that I'm OK but they're taking me to the hospital to check me out. It's kind of true.'

'She won't believe me. This will be on the TV already.'

'Just tell her, OK. I mean, the important thing is that she knows I'm fine.' Cahill tried to sit up but winced when his broken ribs grated again and decided he was better off lying still for now.

'You don't look fine,' Hardy said.

'I'm alive. Right now that qualifies.'

Two blue-grey Land Rover Defenders roared past outside, going down the hill towards the bomb site. They looked like they had been heavily modified with plated armour and Cahill figured that it was the bomb disposal squad from the naval base at Faslane, twenty-five miles north-west of the city. That meant that the Major Incident Plan must have been put into effect by the police almost immediately following the blast and that one of the hospitals in the city centre would have been evacuated, its existing emergency patients transferred elsewhere leaving the unit free to deal with any casualties from the incident.

They were moving to deal with this fast; at least that was a positive. Maybe the emergency services had learned something after the Glasgow Airport attack.

It also meant that the Strathclyde Police Special Branch unit would have been called in to handle the criminal investigation; probably Neil Livingstone and George Kelly, both known to Cahill and seasoned members of the unit.

Down at the bottom of the hill, the Defenders slowed, their brake lights burning red, and then followed the directions of the four armed police officers round the corner.

Hardy stepped back as the ambulance doors closed.

'Which hospital?' he shouted before the doors had closed all the way.

'The Royal.'

The doors crunched shut and the ambulance started to move, Cahill suddenly realising that he had no idea where Tara Byrne was; so much for looking after your client.

The ambulance rolled and rumbled towards the Royal Infirmary in the north-east corner of the city centre, the interior intermittently bathed in blue and the siren howling outside. Cahill watched quietly as the male paramedic worked on and around him while the woman drove.

'Heart rate looks good,' the man told him, the ambulance bucking as it turned a corner sharply. 'Any pain other than from the ribs?'

Cahill shook his head.

The man leaned over him and checked with a pen-light to see that his pupils were dilating. He looked again at a printout from the ECG machine, nodding to himself and scrunching the paper into a ball.

'Still good,' he said, lightly patting Cahill's chest.

They had not put any sort of ointment or mask on his face, which Cahill took to mean that any burns he had suffered were minor and could wait till they got to the hospital. They were more concerned about getting oxygen into him.

He pulled the mask away from his face to speak. 'What did they tell you?'

'Explosion,' the paramedic shouted back, Cahill straining to hear over the sound of the siren and the noise in his ears. 'Possible terrorist attack, so only move in once the police had cleared it for us. Lucky you guys got out.'

Cahill nodded and put the mask back over his face.

It didn't feel like they had been lucky.

The ambulance jerked to a stop and the crew moved quickly to open the doors and pull his stretcher out.

Once inside the building, Cahill looked right and saw that the waiting area was deserted, a product of the evacuation no doubt. The rows of blue plastic chairs lay empty, the vending machines untouched. He was pushed left past the triage window and bumped through heavy double doors into the treatment area.

Cahill had expected chaos and noise, but it was relatively calm except for the team of medics working on Washington in a curtained area in the far right corner of the large room. Judd was on a bed to his right and Cahill was relieved to see that his eyes were open and he was communicating with the hospital staff. He strained to see what was happening with Washington, but was pressed gently back down on to the stretcher.

'They're looking after your friends,' the woman paramedic said. 'You need to take care of yourself for now.'

They stopped the stretcher and applied the holding brakes before helping Cahill shuffle painfully on to a bed. A new face appeared above him: an Asian woman dressed in blue scrubs.

He lay still and listened while the green-suited crew from the ambulance relayed all the information they could about his condition to the doctor. They spoke in a particularly incomprehensible mix of colloquial Glaswegian and technical medical terminology and Cahill gave up trying to follow the conversation. When they were done, the man patted his shoulder and told him to let the doctor look after him; then he left, no doubt to head back to pick up the next casualty from the site.

Time passed interminably, with Cahill desperate to find out how Washington was doing and what had happened to everyone else. As he lay there getting poked, prodded, bandaged, smeared and injected – thank you diamorphine – he heard the entrance doors bang open with increasing regularity and the sounds of a large number of medics going to work on the injured. The lights overhead were intended to be bright enough for the staff to see exactly what they were doing, but as far as Cahill was concerned they just hurt his eyes.

After a while they told him they were moving him to a room and giving him a sedative. He complained but knew that they were doing their best for him, and than he surrendered to the warmth of the drug as it coursed into his blood.

He slept.

Cahill heard the voices before he opened his eyes. He couldn't make out what they were saying, but he recognised Sam straight away.

It took a while for him to float up out of the drug-induced sleep, and as he came to the pain in his ribs began to throb and his face felt weird. He raised a hand to his face and felt it sticky with ointment. He had no idea how much time had passed.

Someone grabbed his hand and said his name.

He heard his kids' voices; heard them crying.

Opened his eyes fully and saw Sam and the girls; felt his own tears well up.

Sam leaned in and kissed him gently on his lips and it was like the first time all over again.

'I love you,' she whispered, her breath soft against his ear.

Then the girls were in his arms and he pulled all three of them in tight, never wanting to let go ever again.

10

Irvine jerked awake. Someone was banging on the door of her room.

'It's the police. Are you all right in there?'

She wasn't sure how long she'd been out; looked at the clock and guessed that it must have been close to two hours.

What took them so long?

It took all of her strength to push up off the bed and walk to the door. Through the peephole she saw the familiar, comforting black of the uniform.

'Can you hold your warrant card up, please,' she said. Watched him as he got his card out and held it up so she could see it. Opened the door.

He was only young, no more than twenty-five, muscles knotting in his strong forearms when he took his hat off. They all went to the gym these days, the young cops. Wait till they get a family, she thought; then the gut will start to bulge like the older guys'.

'I'm with Strathclyde CID,' she told him.

He looked confused, lines pinching between his eyes. 'Um, you called in an assault, miss?'

'Yes. Sorry. I just thought that . . .'

What was she saying? Poor guy probably thought she was drunk. Which, of course, she was after all the wine: just a little bit.

Nice first impression: make-up streaked across her face and smelling of booze and puke.

His face softened and he put his hat back on, turning his face to look down the hall at his partner, a woman PC about Irvine's age.

'I think you're in shock,' he said, looking back at her. 'Let's get you to the station and we'll get you sorted, OK?'

She nodded, shivering slightly, though it wasn't cold.

'Are you injured?' he asked as he stepped into the room, causing her to back up. For a moment she had an irrational fear that maybe they weren't real police at all.

'No, I don't think so,' she said, as the woman PC followed her partner in. 'Just, you know . . .'

The female officer nodded, putting on her best sympathetic face. 'You should bring a change of clothes, because we'll need to keep yours for evidence,' she said.

'Of course, yes.'

The officers stood and watched as Irvine rummaged in her bag for a fresh pair of blue jeans, a plain T-shirt and a black hooded sweatshirt. She handed them to the man and followed them out into the hall.

The woman PC stayed behind Irvine as they walked down the stairs and out through reception. The night porter's eyes followed her as she went; it looked like she was being arrested.

It was how she felt.

Sitting in the back of the police car watching the town go by, she realised that they had not said anything to her about Roddy. She leaned forward.

'Did you find him? Did you find Roddy?'

The man was driving; turned his head to look at his partner in the passenger seat. Then looked straight ahead.

'What does that mean?' Irvine asked, knowing already what it meant.

The woman turns in her seat, softens her features; just like they teach you. Irvine knows it's true, but suddenly she doesn't want to hear it; wishes she'd never asked the question.

'I'm sorry,' the woman says. 'I'm really sorry.'

Irvine feels it all drain out of her and falls back in the seat. Streetlights flash by.

Dark then light.

Dark then light.

There then gone.

Roddy.

11

The police station was bigger than Irvine had expected for a town this size: three storeys high and sitting back off the main street. They took her in through the front door to a small waiting area with a glass counter. At least they weren't taking her in the back to the charge bar.

The woman behind the glass was obviously a civilian employee and wore a pale-blue shirt with NORTHERN CONSTABULARY printed on it. She nodded at the male officer as he came in through the door and pressed a buzzer under the counter to open a door that took them into the working part of the station.

Irvine was led into a room with a Formica-topped table, a sink and an area for making tea and coffee. She sat in a plastic chair and accepted the offer of a cup of tea. She'd never been on this side of it before: a victim.

Closing her eyes, all she could see was an image of the knife being thrust down into Roddy's neck. She rubbed at her eyes, as if that would wipe away the memories, and hoped that she wasn't developing post-traumatic stress, cursed by some trigger of the brain to relive the awful moment again and again.

No wonder the soldiers coming back from Iraq and Afghanistan were so screwed up. What they must have seen.

The woman PC came back and sat opposite Irvine, placing her hat on the table and smoothing her dark hair down on her head.

'Drink up,' she said. 'It'll do you good.'

'Make it all better?' Irvine asked.

'Sorry. I suppose it'll take more than a cuppa.'

Irvine nodded and drank some of the tea, glad of the hot, sweet taste of it.

'When you're ready,' the woman said, 'we'll have to get some details. CID will be here to take a statement.'

Irvine nodded again.

'And we'll need you to get changed and hand over your clothes.'

'I know,' Irvine said.

'Of course. You're with Strathclyde CID, right? Where you based?'

Irvine knew that she was being deliberately drawn into conversation to get her to relax a bit, but was happy to indulge the standard psychological manipulation. It made her feel at home.

'Nowhere just now. I mean, I'm on leave.'

'Why?'

'I got divorced and my super told me to take some time. Recharge.'

'Is that what you were doing up here?'

Irvine sipped again at the tea and looked at the PC through the steam rising from her cup.

'Is this you taking my statement?' she asked.

'If you want to do it now, we can. But we're just talking.'

Does she think I'm somehow involved in this? Or am I being paranoid?

'No,' Irvine said after another sip. 'I was helping an old friend, or at least I was trying to. It didn't turn out so well.'

'How did you know him?'

Irvine wasn't sure if they knew yet who Roddy was: famous rock star. God, that sounded so weird in her head.

'You know who he is?'

The PC nodded slowly. This is definitely an interview of some kind, Irvine thought.

'We used to go out,' she said. 'When we were teenagers.'

'And now?'

'He needed help, so I helped.'

'Help with what?'

Too soon for blood tests to have been done, Irvine thought. But she's probably Googled him already and seen the drug stories.

'He got into some trouble with drugs. But I think you probably know that already.'

More nodding; even when it's one of your own, you keep a professional distance. No, make that *especially* when it's one of your own. Too much bad press over the years meant that cops got treated more carefully sometimes than the real bad guys.

'Anyway,' Irvine went on, 'he was getting better, you know. Been clean for a while.'

'Maybe he was running away from something,' the PC said. 'From someone.'

'I don't know. I don't think so. But that was my first thought tonight. I mean, after it . . .'

Breathe.

'After it happened.'

The PC leaned forward, clasping her hands.

'Do you want to tell us about it now?' she asked Irvine.
'OK.'

Irvine was left alone with a brown paper evidence sack to put her clothes into. She felt vulnerable and alone as she stripped down to her underwear, leaving the clothes in a heap on the table while she got dressed, anxious not to be standing there in her undies when CID came along.

She put the clothes in the bag, folding them neatly first, then sat at the table and drained the now tepid tea from her cup. The woman PC came back into the room without knocking and took Irvine to a more formal interview room where they had set up an old tape recorder to take her statement. After that, the woman left to log Irvine's clothes into evidence.

Looking up at the corner of the room, Irvine saw a camera trained on her and wondered if this was what it felt like to be a suspect.

12

When the door opened again, a tall, thin man dressed in a charcoal suit came in, followed by the woman PC. His hair was receding slightly to a widow's peak and combed straight back on his head.

Irvine stood and held out her hand, taking it as a positive sign when he shook it and introduced himself.

'I'm DS Campbell,' he said. 'Please, sit down. I know this must have been a terrible night for you.'

'It has been.'

'Is there anyone we can call for you?'

'I think it's probably a little late to call anyone now.'

'Of course,' he said, smiling. 'You can lose track of real time on a shift, can't you?'

Irvine nodded, but was thinking that it was unlikely that the CID were on shifts in this part of the world on a Sunday night and that he had probably been called at home to come in on this.

Campbell turned his attention to the tape recorder, checking to make sure that both decks were working and that the tapes had been rewound to the start. When he was satisfied, he pressed record on both decks, paused for a moment and then spoke, first giving the date and time.

'This is Detective Sergeant Campbell for the interview of Rebecca Catherine Irvine in connection with the death of Roddy James Hale.'

Irvine told them everything: from the concert to the hospital and beyond. She saw in their eyes, in the quickly exchanged glances, that they were sceptical about her theory that the two men she had encountered in the hotel car park had somehow tracked Roddy here: wee bit too James Bond for the Scottish Highlands.

'Had you ever seen these men before the hospital?' Campbell asked, making his own notes with a cheap-looking fountain pen in a black notebook on the table in front of him.

'No, I don't think so.'

'Well, now, which is it? No, or you don't think so?'

'It's no.'

'And you're absolutely certain that it was the same men you saw in the car park of the hotel during your stay in Ballachulish?'

'I'm certain of it, yes. Or at least it was one of them I saw at the hospital.'

'But it was dark, right?'

'It was night, yes. But there were lights on in the car park.'

'Uh-huh.'

Irvine said nothing, waiting for a question.

'But, correct me if I'm wrong, and I do know that hotel, the light is pretty poor in the car park, isn't it?'

'It wasn't great, but I have no doubt it was the same man.'

'Right. The same man.'

He paused and wrote something else in his notebook. Irvine suspected it was a tactic he used just to buy thinking time. If it was, it was a good one and she thought maybe she would adopt it once she got back on the job.

'And what makes you think that it may have been the same men who attacked you and Mr Hale tonight?'

'Well, nothing really. I suppose I'm just speculating. Trying to understand in my own mind why someone would want to do that.'

'Of course. Entirely understandable.'

Again with the writing. Irvine looked at the woman PC, who held her gaze firmly.

'But they were wearing masks tonight and you didn't see their faces?'

'Correct.'

'You didn't happen to see what kind of car they drove, did you? Or the registration number?'

Irvine said no and felt foolish; a police officer should have noted those things. But she wasn't on duty and had put the whole incident down to something else. Now it felt as if Campbell was deliberately trying to get to her.

It was working.

'Is there any reason you can think of,' Campbell went on, 'that perhaps the attack was directed at you? Not at Mr Hale.'

Irvine had not even considered that as a possibility and said so.

'You're on compassionate leave, is that right?' Campbell asked.

Irvine nodded, realising that Campbell had been briefed before the interview started.

'Why is that?'

'Isn't this going a little off the subject? What's that got to do with what happened tonight anyway?'

'Just trying to get all the facts, you know.' Campbell waited for her to answer his question, tapping his pen on the table surface.

'I just got divorced from my husband and I have a little boy to look after, so my super thought it would be good if I got some time off.'

Campbell's eyebrows went up at that and Irvine hated how defensive she was beginning to sound.

'So let me get this straight,' Campbell said. 'You're divorced, you have a young son and you're up here on your own with your former boyfriend who's in a rock band and has a history of drug problems. Is that correct?'

Irvine leaned forward, resting her hands on the table. 'Correct,' she said, her tone even.

'Where's your son?'

'At my parents' house. It's a holiday for him.'

'Mmm hmm. A holiday.'

Irvine sat back in the chair, putting her hands in her lap and pleased that she had not let him rile her with his cheap innuendo. No doubt he was a decent detective, but she felt angry all the same at being treated like this for no good reason.

'How does your husband feel about all this?'

'I don't know. We don't speak much any more.'

'Does he see his son?'

'Not really, no.'

'That seems odd, don't you think?'

'No. It's entirely in keeping with his character.' Irvine was pleased to see that Campbell seemed a little surprised by that response.

'Right,' was all he said.

She rubbed at her eyes, feeling fatigue begin to take its toll on her and wanting to get out of there.

'Is your husband the type of man,' Campbell said, 'who might not take too well to you seeing someone else so soon after the divorce?'

'If you're asking me if I think he put someone up to this, attacking me, then the answer is no. That's absurd. We've been separated for a while now and he seems quite happy to be free to screw as many women as will have him. And, anyway, I wasn't seeing Roddy in the way that you mean it.'

'OK,' Campbell said, standing and looking a little uneasy. 'I think we can conclude the interview now.'

'Can someone drive me back to the hotel?'

'Of course. How long will you be staying there?'

'Is this where you tell me not to leave town?' Irvine laughed as she said it; a Hollywood joke.

'You know I'm in no position to do that,' Campbell replied. 'But obviously it would assist in our inquiries if you were around to answer some more questions if necessary.'

'I live in Glasgow,' Irvine said. 'It's not really that far and we can do anything else on the phone, can't we?'

'Well, of course we can. But, I mean, if you've already planned to be away for a few more days it would really be helping us out if you could be here.'

Irvine was in no mood to pander to any idea he might have that she, or her ex-husband, was somehow involved in this, but didn't want to get into a fight with him.

'I'm only booked in for tonight, but I suppose I can stay another day.'

'That would be very helpful.' Campbell took a business card from his wallet and handed it to her, telling her to call him any time if she had any more thoughts. Irvine took that to mean when she had a more sensible story to tell him.

13

Logan rubbed at his eyes as he drove Ellie to school the next morning. The traffic stop-started as the rush hour drew to a close. He'd finally got to bed around three, when it was clear that there was little else the news teams could find out about the explosion because the scene was still heavily secured. What he had learned from the reports – that it was at or near the Hilton – and the lack of contact from any of the CPO team convinced him that Cahill and the others had been caught up in it. He had slept little as a result.

He kept the radio off in the car, not wanting to upset Ellie, though he was desperate to find out what was going on. Ellie, however, seemed largely impervious to what had happened and was busy texting one of her friends on her mobile, laughing and shielding the phone from Logan's view. She jumped out when he stopped the car and shouted goodbye, running off to join a group of girls in red blazers and tartan skirts standing at the entrance to the school.

Logan turned the radio on and started the drive into town, having decided that the best thing he could do was go to the office to find out what was happening. He flicked between the pre-set stations on his radio until he found a news show.

'. . . in other news today, the shocking murder of singer Roddy Hale who was stabbed to death in Fort William last night . . .'

Logan slammed on his brakes, forcing the driver of the car behind him to swerve to avoid a collision.

'Police are working on the theory that he was involved in an altercation in the street after leaving a restaurant in the town.'

Logan pulled his car over to the side of the road and listened to the rest of the story, hoping that there would be some mention of Irvine, but there was none. He muted the sound on the radio and called Irvine's mobile. It rang out and then switched to voicemail. Logan checked his watch and saw that it was close to nine. He sat for a moment watching the traffic crawl past him, unsure of what to do.

His phone was sitting on the passenger seat when it rang, the display telling him that it was Irvine calling him.

'Becky!' he said. 'God, I just heard about Roddy on the radio. Are you OK? What happened?'

'Logan,' she sighed, sounding half asleep. 'It was awful.'

'But you're OK, right?'

'I'm fine, yes. Just tired. I was at the police station here and didn't get to bed until after two.'

'They said on the radio it was some kind of street fight or something.'

Irvine was quiet for a while. 'I don't know,' she said finally. 'I mean, we just came out of the restaurant and these two guys were waiting for us. They were wearing masks and . . .'

She trailed off and Logan could hear the emotion in her voice.

'Jesus,' he said. 'You think maybe it had something to do with drugs?'

'I don't know what to think, I really don't. The CID were asking me about Tom and whether he might have been jealous of me seeing someone else. It was tough.'

'Tom? No way. Not his style.'

'I know that.'

Logan was about to ask her if she had heard about the explosion, but she spoke again before he had a chance to say anything.

'How's things with you? How's Ellie?'

'We're good. I just dropped her off at school.'

'Sounds normal.'

'Not really.'

'What do you mean?'

'You didn't hear about what happened here last night?'

'No. I was kind of occupied.'

'Of course, sorry. There was an explosion at the Hilton and they're treating it for now as a potential terrorist attack.'

'Christ, it just gets worse.'

'There's more to it than that. The actress that Alex was covering last night . . .'

'Tara Byrne?'

'Uh-huh. She was staying at the Hilton and I haven't been able to contact Alex or any of the team that was on her detail.

'You don't think . . . What are you going to do?'

'I'm heading into the office. See if anyone there knows anything about it yet.'

'You better get going then. I'm fine, so go check on the others.'

'I will. When are you coming back?'

'I'm going to stay here another night then probably head home tomorrow.'

'All right. Listen, I'll call you later when I know what's going on. Look after yourself, you hear?'

Logan noticed a hugely increased police presence as he neared the city centre: armed officers standing on the street and vehicles on the roads. Traffic here was quieter than normal; no doubt many people had decided to stay at home with their families until they understood the nature of the attack.

There was an armed police officer standing at the entrance to the underground car park at the CPO building on St Vincent Street and an unmarked car blocking the ramp down. Logan slowed as he approached and buzzed his window down. The officer motioned with his hand for Logan to keep moving, but he stopped and told him that he worked in the building and needed access to the car park.

'No one's getting into the car park today, sir,' the officer said, leaning down to look into the car. 'What's your name and who do you work for?'

'Logan Finch and I work at CPO.'

'Well, you can't park here. All CPO employees are being interviewed in the third-floor office suite and so I need you to find somewhere else to park and report in for an interview.'

Logan felt a knot in his stomach. 'This is about the attack last night?'

'I can't tell you anything else, sir. Please just report to the office suite and someone will be able to speak to you in more detail there.' He stepped back from the car and waved Logan on.

Discussion over.

14

'Where are you?' Tom Hardy asked when Logan answered his call.

'I'm on my way to the office, Tom. What the hell is going on? I couldn't get anyone on the phone last night and now there are armed cops at the office telling me that everyone has to be interviewed.'

Logan was sitting in his car having parked in a shopping centre, the nearest public car park to the office.

'You heard about the explosion?' Hardy asked.

'Of course I did. It's all over the news.'

'Right. I haven't seen any TV since yesterday.'

'Where are you? Where's Alex?'

'We're at the hospital, the Royal Infirmary.'

Logan didn't like the way that Hardy was avoiding talking about anyone. 'Tom,' he said, 'tell me what happened. Is everyone OK?'

'No, Logan. Everyone is not OK.' Hardy cleared his throat. Logan waited for him, his heart beating faster. 'Chris is in a bad way. He's in surgery now.'

'And Alex?'

'As well as can be expected. Tough old bastard got a couple of broken ribs and some low-level burns on his hands and face, but he's going to be fine.'

'What happened?'

'Car bomb at the hotel. Detonated when we got there.'

Logan didn't know what to say; couldn't conceive of such a thing in the city centre. Didn't want to believe that anything could happen to Washington; that he might die.

'One of Tara's security team got killed,' Hardy told him.

'It wasn't aimed at her, was it?' Logan asked.

'Why not?'

'I don't know. I mean, it just sounds so . . . unlikely.'

'Yeah, well, there are certainly easier ways of going about it if she was the target, that's for sure.'

'Is she OK?'

'Other than suffering some shock, she seems fine, but they're keeping her in for now to monitor her.'

'So, what? It was just bad luck you got caught up in a terrorist attack?'

'I don't know. No one does. The cops won't answer any of our questions and CPO is locked down so we can't access our people or our systems.'

'They can't think that we were involved in this, can they?'

'I doubt it. They're just keeping everything under control until they're in a position to start analysing the evidence. Given that we were at the site and the nature of our business, it's only natural they would take the time to look at our operation.'

'What about the warehouse on Scotland Street?'

'Officially, CPO has no connection to that building. Ownership is hidden in a series of overseas shell companies.'

'Have you guys been interviewed or cautioned or anything? Do I need to organise a criminal lawyer for anyone?'

'Nothing like that, no. Special Branch will be in charge of this thing while it's still classified as a terrorist attack and we know those guys pretty well; trained some of them actually. We're good for now.'

'OK. Look, I'm going to go into the office and speak to the police there. See what I can find out about this.'

'Yeah, just treat it like business as usual. That's what we've been telling everyone. Go into the office and answer all their questions.'

'There's nothing at the office about, you know, what happened up at the loch?'

Hardy said nothing.

'Tom?'

'Logan, everything's fine. Alex and I will be out of here today and we'll talk then.'

Logan realised he'd broken a cardinal CPO rule – don't speak about anything of any importance or sensitivity over the phone, especially using a mobile. Cahill was paranoid about surveillance of telephone and computer communications. Any time they had a meeting he always took the battery and SIM card out of his phone, claiming that they could be tapped into remotely and used as listening devices unless that was done. Logan never really knew if that was true, but Hardy had clearly been annoyed at his mention of the warehouse and the loch.

'I understand, Tom,' Logan said. 'We'll catch up later.'

'Be careful,' Hardy said.

It sounded like a warning.

15

Irvine called the hotel reception and made arrangements to keep her room for another night, then went for a shower. She stood with her face in the strong jet of water, running her hands through her hair to smooth it back on her scalp. The hotel had provided some cheap, generic shampoo and shower gel combination that smelled of chemicals more than the orange blossom advertised on the label.

As she massaged the liquid into her hair emotion hit her unexpectedly hard and she bent over with her hands on her knees, images from the previous night flashing vividly in her mind. The thing that hit her hardest was the sound and feel of the man's head under her foot as she stamped down on him.

She dried herself quickly and dressed in the clothes she had taken with her to the police station before blow-drying her hair and applying the minimum amount of make-up required to make her feel ready to face the world.

There was no one at home when she called her parents' house, so she left a message on the answerphone trying to sound upbeat and saying that she would call later to talk.

Irvine sat at a table by the bay window in the restaurant and ordered breakfast to kick-start her day. She just caught the kitchen in time and was the last resident left in the place by the time her order arrived. It was surprisingly good and she started to feel better as the food hit her stomach, thinking about the night before and trying to analyse it; taking control of it rather than being afraid of it.

There was no doubt in her mind that the two men had followed them to the restaurant and waited for them to leave. The masks meant that they had planned it in advance. But the attack had been a little chaotic and she figured that if they were professional criminals, which they had to be, they were probably at the junior end of the scale.

She couldn't convince herself that it was about an unpaid drugs bill. If Roddy had been telling the truth about getting clean – and she was convinced of that – then he had been free of drugs for a while. So why an attack now? And he clearly still had plenty of money to pay any debt. Those in the drug trade were interested really in only two things – getting rich and staying out of jail. Forcing Roddy to pay up would have fulfilled both aims better than having him killed.

The sun was up today, but with more cloud cover than there had been in previous days, and Irvine was sure that the warm spell was about to end. After breakfast, she walked down to the lochside and watched the activity on the water, enjoying the bracing breeze and the sound of the birds that chased the boats hoping for scraps of food.

She bought a late edition newspaper to see what was being written about the explosion back in Glasgow. As ever with the papers, there was a lot of speculation but little by way of fact; probably because the police did not know much yet and would not want to comment until they had a firmer grasp on the evidence.

There was plenty of ink devoted to Tara Byrne's involvement in the events, giving the editor an excuse to print photos of her and fulfil his daily quotient of titillation, and making Irvine regret buying a tabloid rather than a broadsheet.

The official word from the police was that there were four fatalities and ten injured, the fatalities being described as three taxi drivers and one member of Tara's 'entourage'. That was one of the tabloids' favourite words for the team of people that looked after major celebrities, insinuating that it was excessive and unwarranted – driven by ego and too much money.

Back at the hotel, Irvine settled down on a sofa in the lounge with a pot of tea and read the main stories again, trying not to worry too much about what was going on with Logan and the CPO team back in Glasgow.

16

Hudson leaned on the car enjoying the cool breeze and the sun on his face while Two spoke to Five on his phone inside the car. They were in a car park at the south end of Fort William's town centre. Hudson was tired of having to deal with the failure to address the situation with the woman cop and had told Two to speak to Five and work out where they were going to meet. He sure as hell was not going to their hotel, because if Three and Five had been seen or if anyone had any suspicions about them he wanted to remain distant. They would be cut loose in an instant if necessary.

Two got out of the car after finishing his call and stood quietly, waiting for Hudson to speak before saying anything. He'd seen Hudson in this kind of mood before and knew better than to push him.

'What's up?' Hudson said finally.

'He says Three looks better this morning, though his knee needs proper treatment.'

'He'll just have to wait.'

'And he still thinks that they're OK in terms of anyone being suspicious. Says he went down to breakfast and they were all talking about the thing in Glasgow more than what happened in town.'

'And what's his plan for making this right, so that I can get my money?'

'I thought *you* were going to . . .'

'Never mind,' Hudson said, cutting him off. 'I wouldn't trust either of those clowns to come up with anything sensible considering what they've managed so far.' He turned to face Two. 'What's her location?'

'Stationary at the hotel,' Two told him. 'Has been since last night.'

'We need her to get out of here. I don't want anything else to go down here, not after last night.'

'I told him you'd say that.' Two waited for Hudson to speak, but he remained quiet. 'What do we do now?'

'Call those idiots back and tell them to get close to the hotel and watch her. I don't want to have to rely on some GPS device they fitted. As soon as she moves, I want to know about it.'

'Then what?'

'Then I'll see to it myself this time. Make sure it gets done. If that guy hadn't taken a header off the stage in the first place . . .'

He didn't finish the thought, aware that it was entirely redundant.

I was *that* close to her. It would all have been done now, he thought.

That close.

17

An armed police officer was stationed at the front entrance of the CPO building, along with two uniformed officers. One of the uniforms, an earnest-looking young woman, took Logan's details, checked his name off against a list she held on a clipboard and told him to go up to the third-floor reception and wait there until someone came to speak to him.

Logan did as he was told, standing alone in the lift and noticing the dark circles under his eyes in the mirrored walls. The lift pinged to indicate that it had reached the third floor and the doors slid open to reveal yet another uniformed officer sitting at the reception desk. Plenty of overtime on this one, Logan thought.

'Name?' the officer asked.

'Logan Finch.'

'Position?'

'I suppose you'd call me in-house counsel.'

'You're a lawyer, then,' the officer said, barely able to conceal his contempt as he looked up at Logan.

'Yes.'

'Take a seat please, sir. Someone will be out to speak to you shortly.'

Logan sat on one of the sofas in the reception area while the officer spoke into the radio mike fixed to his uniform, explaining to someone that Logan was there and ready to be interviewed. There were no other CPO staff members around, but plenty of cops moving back and forward between the lift and the interior of the office suite with boxes full of papers, collecting evidence.

After about ten minutes, a slim man in a plain navy suit with a white shirt and a red patterned tie came into the reception area and went straight to Logan.

'Mr Finch?'

'Yes,' Logan said, standing and extending his hand, which the man took firmly and then released.

'I'm George Kelly, with Strathclyde Police Special Branch.'

Logan nodded, noting that the man's hair was almost white.

'If you'll follow me, please, and we can have a chat, OK?' He smiled as he spoke, though his eyes were entirely devoid of humour.

Logan followed him to the main boardroom and walked in as Kelly held the door open for him. There was another man sitting at the big table in the room, shuffling through some papers and writing notes in a pad. He was younger than Kelly by maybe ten years and wore an almost identical navy suit and white shirt combo, though he had a pink and blue striped tie. He was stocky, not quite fat, with blond hair.

'Neil, this is Logan Finch,' Kelly said as he closed the door of the room. Logan walked round the table and shook the younger man's hand.

'Neil Livingstone, Special Branch.'

Logan nodded and went to the sideboard to get a bottle of water, trying to steady his nerves. He took his time pouring the water into a tall glass with his back to the table. He took a drink and turned to sit opposite the two men.

'How can I help?' he asked.

Livingstone leaned forward and flipped through his notepad as Kelly sat back in his chair with his hands clasped in his lap.

'How's DC Irvine?' he asked.

Logan wondered why they would ask about Irvine but decided to play it straight and just answer whatever they asked.

'She's good.'

'Uh-huh,' Kelly said. 'And your daughter, Ellie?'

'Also good. Why?'

'Must have been a tough year for you,' Kelly said, ignoring Logan's question. 'I mean with what happened to Ellie and her mother.'

Logan knew that the police had initially been suspicious of the story about Ellie just turning up at his flat, but thought that they had got past that when the Russian had been identified as Penny's killer.

'We're both still coming to terms with it, but I take comfort from the fact that Ellie's with me.'

'Difficult for a girl that age. I mean, first she loses her mother and then she's living with you. And you'd never met till after her mother's death.'

'Like I said, we're coping together. It takes time, you know.'

Kelly nodded, like he knew all about it.

'At least they caught the guy,' Livingstone said. 'Right?' He flipped through his pad some more and spoke again without waiting for a response from Logan. 'Vasiliy Renko. Got himself shot in a bar in town not far from here.'

'That's right,' Logan said, still unsure of where they were going with this.

'Funny, that,' Livingstone went on. 'It happening so close to this place.'

Logan shrugged, though he was beginning to feel uncomfortable at the line of questioning.

'You won't have heard this yet,' Kelly said, coming back into the conversation. 'But apparently this guy, this Renko, was linked to some people that got killed up north. At Loch Awe.'

Logan held his gaze.

'Yeah,' Livingstone said, smiling. 'Place they found the bodies was torched so it's taken a while to get any useful DNA results. But we got them eventually. Just this week, in fact.'

'Turns out,' Kelly said, 'that Renko was part of a Russian outfit that was operating over here. A right bad lot by all accounts, you know. Drugs and guns and all the rest. One of them had a conviction back home for indecency with a minor too.'

'You deal in that kind of stuff,' Logan said, pleased by how even his voice sounded, 'and you can't complain if you wind up dead, can you?'

18

Kelly and Livingstone watched Logan in silence for a moment. Logan knew that they were waiting for him to say something more but he was determined to wait them out.

'What was your involvement in providing security last night for Tara Byrne?' Kelly asked eventually.

Logan was pleased to have moved off the subject of Loch Awe.

'I got a call from Alex on Friday night to come in here on Saturday and help draw up the contract. That's my job here: the legal stuff.'

'Alex is Alexander Cahill?'

'Yes. Anyway, I came in and Tara's manager provided a draft contract which I revised, and it was completed and signed at the meeting. Pretty straightforward.'

'And what was your knowledge of the actual operation last night? The details, I mean.'

'Nothing. That's not my field of expertise.'

'Are these kinds of operations planned on paper, and are the plans kept here?'

'It varies,' Logan said. 'Maybe for the bigger or longer jobs there will be paperwork, but probably not for something like this.'

'What do you mean, "like this"?'

'A one-nighter.'

'Did you have any contact with Alex or anyone else on the security detail for Miss Byrne last night?'

'No.'

'Not even a phone call or an e-mail or anything?'

'Nothing. I mean, there's no need for me to be involved once the contract is signed, because the actual security is Alex's thing.'

Kelly looked at Livingstone and Logan sensed frustration building in them. They had clearly thought that they would get more from him. He decided that the best option was to stay quiet.

Livingstone pointed at something in his notepad which Kelly leaned over to see. He looked up at Livingstone and nodded before leaning back in his chair.

'Are you still in contact with Robert Crawford at Kennedy Boyd?' Livingstone asked.

'No,' Logan said, shifting in his seat.

'Do you see anyone from your old firm, professionally or socially?'

'Not socially, no. But sometimes if the stuff we need to do here is complicated or outside my field than I'll use Kennedy Boyd.'

'But not Bob.'

'Correct.'

'Any particular reason for that?'

'You mean for not using Bob?'

Livingstone nodded slowly.

'I've known Bob for a while – since university . . .'

'We know,' Kelly interjected.

'. . . but we've kind of grown apart over the years. Plus he doesn't really do the kind of stuff that I use the firm for.'

'Nothing to do with his reputation, then?'

Logan had heard from a couple of lawyers he knew at Kennedy Boyd that there were rumours that Crawford was involved in some questionable deals. And Logan knew that there might be some truth in it given what had happened with the people who had taken Ellie.

'Look, I've had a long night,' Logan said. 'And I'm not really very sure what Bob Crawford has to do with all this.'

'We're not sure either, Mr Finch,' Livingstone said. 'We're just looking at everything until we know where the evidence is going to lead us. You understand the need for us to do that, right? To look at everything.'

'Of course, but . . .'

'So do you know the stories about Crawford?'

'I've heard.'

'And is that the reason you don't use him for outside legal work?'

'I've answered that already. But if Bob was able to do the work I wouldn't use him, if that's what you're asking.'

'We keep an eye on that kind of thing, you know; lawyers up to their necks in it.'

'I'd expect you to.'

'Are you aware of any specific deals that Crawford has been involved in that have any ties to any kind of organised crime? Or foreign nationals?'

Logan maintained eye contact with Livingstone and wondered just how much they knew about Crawford and the Russians. He was keenly aware that any investigation into the matter could lead the police to the deal he had completed with the men who had taken Ellie. And the only outcome for that would be that Logan and Crawford would both end up in jail.

'By foreign nationals do you mean terrorists?' Logan asked, trying to deflect their questions.

'Not necessarily, no.'

'I don't know of any, no. I mean, obviously he'll have done deals with people outside the UK, but nothing illegal so far as I'm aware.'

Livingstone looked at Kelly and then back at Logan.

'OK, Mr Finch,' Kelly said. 'I think that's all we need from you for now. If you leave us your contact details we'll be in touch.'

19

'Special Branch will be taking the lead if they're treating it as a terrorist attack,' Irvine told Logan over the phone.

She was back in her room watching some awful daytime TV chat show where the host wandered amongst a crowd of people who could only have been rounded up from the local jail and discussed the hot 'issue' of the day. Today's topic – 'I slept with my mother-in-law and now she's pregnant'.

Irvine had started off watching the news but when she saw her own picture from the hospital again she looked for something innocuous. This just about passed the test. She tried to feel guilty about watching it, but couldn't muster enough enthusiasm to hate it.

'But why were they asking me about . . . all that other stuff?' Logan asked her.

'I don't know. Maybe they were just trying to get you out of your comfort zone – get you unsettled.'

'Tom Hardy says they know the Special Branch guys so why would they be having a look at CPO when they know what Alex is all about? Doesn't make sense to me.'

'They've got superiors to answer to and they need to demonstrate that they looked at everything, turned over every rock. I wouldn't worry about it for now.'

'Yeah?'

'Sure. I mean, if they'd seriously been looking at you or at CPO you would still be in there with them now. Sounds like you got off kind of light really.'

'That can't be said about everyone.'

Irvine heard emotion in his voice, a rawness that had been lurking there since the start of the call but she had missed until now.

'What do you mean?' she asked, sitting up straighter in her chair by the window. 'What happened, Logan?'

'Chris Washington was badly injured in the explosion. They don't know if he's going to make it.'

Irvine opened her mouth to speak, but everything that flashed through her mind was a cliché and so she said nothing.

'He's in surgery was the last I heard,' Logan said.

'God, Logan. I didn't know. What about Alex and the others?'

'OK so far as I can tell, but I don't have much to go on except a short call from Tom before the Special Branch grilling. I'm going to call Tom again now and see what my chances are of getting into the hospital to see them.'

'There's no way you'll get in there just now, Logan. You know that, right?'

'What else am I supposed to do?'

She knew that the worst of it for Logan would be his sense of being powerless; unable to help his friends. Particularly those who had saved his daughter. She was acutely aware of his need to repay the debt that he felt he owed them, because he had talked about it to her more than once.

'I feel so helpless,' he said eventually.

'I know.'

'I mean, you're stuck up there after what happened and Alex is in hospital. I just want to see him and know that he's all right . . .' He was quiet again.

'And what, Logan? Tell me.'

'And be with you.'

'Me too.'

Irvine pressed the off button on the TV and stood to look out the window.

'Look,' she said. 'Call Tom Hardy and then go see Alex if you can. I'm fine and you'll see me soon, OK. Then we can catch up where we left off.'

She smiled, watching a small car ferry ploughing through the water of the loch as the clouds overhead darkened the sky.

20

'I need a doctor to look at my knee, man,' Three told Five as they sat in the car outside Irvine's hotel.

'Christ, would you shut your whining. We're lucky not to be in jail or in the ground, so let's get on with this and get it done.'

Five looked at Three in the passenger seat. He was gingerly touching the cut on his swollen lip where the woman cop had stamped on him last night. The blood had dried and clotted almost black and his lip was twice its normal size, making him look as if he was permanently pouting. He pulled a tissue from his pocket and dabbed at it.

'We need to get out of this place,' Five said. 'Especially with that face of yours.'

'There she is,' Three said suddenly, pointing up at the woman's room.

Five saw her standing at the window looking out over the loch with her phone to her ear. She put a finger on the inside of the window and appeared to be tracing a pattern on it that only she could see. He thought back to last night and how she had reacted in the alley. In some ways he kind of admired her. Most people, never mind most women, would have crumbled. Not her.

'She's not bad-looking for a cop,' Three said. 'It'll be a real shame when she's dead.'

Five looked at Three, the grin on his face twisted into a grotesque leer by his injuries.

I couldn't say the same for you, Five thought.

21

Cahill was sitting up in bed in a private room in the hospital talking to Sam when two men came in. It was just after eleven in the morning.

Sam stood uncertainly. She had been with her husband long enough to recognise police officers when she saw them.

'Morning, guys,' Cahill said, nodding at the men as they stood beside his bed.

'Alex, good to see you again,' the older of the two men said.

'Sam,' Cahill said, 'this is George Kelly and Neil Livingstone of the Special Branch.'

Sam Cahill nodded at both men and said hello, then turned to her husband. 'I'll leave you alone to talk.'

Cahill opened his mouth to protest but Sam shushed him and left. He felt unnaturally vulnerable sitting in the bed and conscious of the pain in his side every time he tried to move as the broken ribs grated. He'd much rather that Sam had stayed with him.

'You don't look too bad, considering,' Kelly said, looking closely at his face.

'Yeah, they had some stuff on my face to treat it overnight. Turns out it's just superficial.'

Cahill's palms were wrapped in bandages and his hair was matted from the explosion and the ointment that had been put on his face. He looked like he'd spent a little too long in the sun, but no more than that.

'You guys going to sit down?' he asked.

'No, Alex,' Kelly said. 'Actually we didn't really know what kind of shape you were in so we only came to get your fingerprints for now.'

'Well, as you can see, I'm doing OK, so we can talk now if you like.'

Kelly looked at Livingstone before speaking again. 'We heard about what happened with your team, Alex.'

Cahill looked down at his hands and flexed his fingers open and shut.

'Sorry,' Livingstone said. 'I hope it turns out all right.'

'Listen,' Kelly said. 'We need to get prints off all of you guys so we have samples to eliminate against whatever we can pick up from the scene. You understand, right?'

'You found anything yet?' Cahill asked. 'I mean, anything useful like a receiver or anything?'

'You think the device was remote detonated?' Livingstone asked.

Cahill thought that he detected surprise in the tone of the question, as if they knew something about the device already and it didn't involve a receiver component.

'I thought I saw someone over on the other side of the motorway before the explosion,' Cahill told them. 'I figured maybe they were watching and detonated it remotely.'

'So you think your client was the target? Tara Byrne?'

'I don't know. But I was hired to look after her, guys. Doesn't that tell you something about the threat level her management thought she was facing?'

'We had thought about that, but . . .' Livingstone trailed off.

'What?' Cahill asked.

'Look, Alex,' Kelly said. 'This is a highly sensitive ongoing investigation so, notwithstanding our history, there's a limit to what we can reveal to you. You understand that, right?'

'Sure, but I thought maybe you'd be interested in any information that could help catch whoever did this. You are, right?'

'Of course.'

Cahill recounted to them what he had been told, and shown, at the CPO offices by Tara's security detail on Saturday and tried to describe as best he could from memory what he had seen just before the explosion.

'I hear what you're saying,' Kelly said when he had finished. 'But the stuff that Miss Byrne received doesn't make it sound like the kind of person who would do this. Sounds more like a personal attack might be in his mind.'

'In the past I would have tended to agree, but look at what happened.' Cahill spread his arms out and immediately regretted it as pain jagged in his side. 'So you're going to look at that angle, aren't you?' he asked, hissing a breath in through his teeth.

'You know we will.'

'We've already got the Met involved,' Livingstone said. 'They're going through her flat in London to see if they can find anything there that might help.'

'Neil . . .' Kelly said, indicating that he was unhappy about his younger colleague saying too much.

Cahill couldn't understand why they were being so furtive. 'I just told you that I saw someone close to the scene,' he said, anger creeping into his voice now. 'You don't seem very interested.'

'We spoke to your doctor,' Kelly said, putting on his best concerned-for-the-patient look. 'She says you have some short-term memory problems which is entirely understandable after what happened.'

'So you're saying you don't believe me?'

Kelly sighed at him. 'No, that's not what I'm saying. It's just that we can't trust your memory for now. It's entirely possible that what you think you saw is not a memory at all.'

'So I made it up?'

Kelly could sense Cahill's anger rising and held both his hands up. 'You know that's not what we're saying, Alex. We need to get the all-clear from your doctor before we can get accurate information from you. All we want is your prints.'

'There's something you're not telling me, right? Something about the device. I heard it in your voice when you talked about it earlier: when I mentioned a receiver component. That's why you don't think I really saw anyone there, isn't it?'

Neither of the men spoke for a moment.

'Just the prints, Alex. That's all for now.'

Cahill wanted to challenge them further; to know what it was they had and how it would help to find the person who had attacked his team. He wanted to be first to find whoever it was; to give them true justice. But looking at the two detectives he knew that he was not going to get anything else from them now and he sank back against his pillow, resigned to being helpless. It was not a state of being that suited him and he couldn't help but wonder what it was that Kelly and Livingstone were holding back.

And what the repercussions of that information might be.

part four: escalation

1

After speaking to Irvine, Logan spent the rest of the morning locked out of the CPO office while the police carted away box after box of papers, and unable to get much information from the hospital either. Ellie had called him on her mobile at lunchtime to say that she was going to a friend's house after school and that he could pick her up from there for dinner. Logan heard more than one girl laughing in the background and said it was fine by him.

He went back home after grabbing a sandwich for lunch and called Hardy close to four in the afternoon.

'Chris is out of surgery,' Hardy told him. 'But it's still too early to know if he'll be OK. He hasn't regained consciousness yet.'

'How bad was it?'

'I don't know all the details, but the surgeon who worked on him told me it was pretty dicey – internal bleeding was the biggest danger. And he has a fractured skull.'

'What about burns? I mean, if he was that close to the explosion . . .'

'He seems to have missed the worst of that.'

'Did you see him?'

Hardy paused. 'Only for a moment. When they were wheeling him out of theatre and taking him to the intensive care unit.'

'How was he?'

'Didn't look like the same guy, you know.'

Logan waited for Hardy to say more.

'They shaved all his hair off and his face was swollen and cut.'

'How's his wife?'

'I don't know. The cops won't let us talk to her. They're being real pricks about the whole thing.'

'Tell me about it. I met two charmers from Special Branch when I was at the office this morning.'

'Yeah, they were here earlier – took fingerprints from all of us. Even Chris after he was out of surgery.'

'Why would they do that?'

'To eliminate our prints from whatever they recover from the scene. Or at least that's the official line.'

'They can't think any of us were involved in this, can they?'

'Who knows with cops? I mean, you know what they're like; treat everyone like a suspect until they can't. Guess they've got to get their kicks somehow.'

Logan closed his eyes and remembered the last time he saw Irvine and how her voice sounded on the phone.

'Alex is getting out tonight,' Hardy said. 'Maybe even in the next hour or so.'

'That's good. How is he?'

'Like you'd expect after what's happened: feeling equal parts mad as hell and guilty. Says he blames himself for not seeing it sooner than he did.'

'He saw something?'

'Says there was a guy, or guys, over on the other side of the motorway just before it happened.'

'Does he think they were waiting for Tara?'

'Waiting for something.'

'What are the police doing about it?'

'Nothing, far as we can tell. No one's seen the Special Branch twins since before lunch and they were being super-cryptic back then.'

'I got the same routine from them too. They even grilled me about . . . other things.'

'What do you mean?'

'They say they've made a connection with the Russian killed in the bar to the bodies at Loch Awe.'

'How?'

'Said they recently got some degraded DNA samples from the remains and that they were all part of the same outfit.'

'That's not so good.'

'They were just trying to bait me.'

'Did it work?'

'No, Tom. It didn't. Logan was a little annoyed that Hardy even felt that he had to ask the question.

'They haven't got a thing.'

'I know,' Logan said.

'This mess will just have to play itself out and we'll get back to business as usual.'

'It won't be the same, though.'

'I've buried more than my fair share of friends. I just hope it won't be one more this time.'

2

Sam Cahill was helping her husband get dressed in his room at the Royal Infirmary. Being a former nurse herself, she was used to the moans and groans of the recently injured. It was close to five in the afternoon and Cahill was relieved not to have to spend any longer in the hospital than was absolutely necessary.

'I hate these places,' he told Sam.

'I know you do.'

Cahill closed his eyes and grimaced as Sam put a fresh T-shirt on him, dropping his hands to his side and sitting on the bed as the pain ebbed and flowed in his body. Sam crouched in front of him, putting a hand under his chin and lifting his head up.

'If you're not up to going home just say so. I can speak to the staff here about keeping you in another night.'

'No. I want to get home.'

'We all know you're a tough guy, Alex. You don't have anything to prove on that score. Certainly not to me.'

Cahill leaned forward until his forehead touched hers. 'I know that. And I love you. But I really want to get the hell out of here and spend the night in my own bed.'

Sam stood and pulled his head around, looking at each of his ears in turn. 'How's your hearing? You said it was bad last night.'

'Better,' he said. 'Still ringing but I can hear pretty good now.' He tried to lean down to tie his shoe laces but sat back up quickly, grabbing at his injured ribs.

'Let me do that,' Sam told him. 'Just sit back.'

Cahill leaned back on the bed and watched through the open door as a variety of medical staff walked past the room. The place smelled like every hospital he'd ever been in.

Even army field hospitals were the same: stinking of disinfectant, blood and human waste.

'I ever tell you *why* I hate these places so much, Sam?'

'I just assumed you'd seen your fair share when you were in the army.'

'I did, that's for sure. But that's not it.'

'Nobody likes being in hospital.'

'My family was pretty healthy when I was growing up out in Colorado, you know. It's all that open air and high altitude. Makes you healthy 'cause your lungs have to work harder to process oxygen out of the thin air.'

'Denver's a mile above sea level, I know. You've told me often enough.'

'Anyway, first time anyone was in hospital was when I was fifteen and still at school. My dad's mom got cancer, real aggressive it was too. Took just four weeks from when they found it till she died.'

Sam finished tying the laces and stood in front of Cahill, running her hands over his head and down on to his neck. 'It's never easy,' she told him.

'My dad wouldn't let me go with them to visit her. I reckon he thought we would have enough death to see in our own time and he wanted to protect us from it as long as he could. He was like that with us, my brother and me.'

'He did OK bringing you up, didn't he?'

'I suppose so. In his own way.'

'When was the last time you spoke to your brother?'

'Couple of months, maybe.'

'You should call him when you get home.'

'I will. That's a good idea.'

'What were you saying – about your dad's mum?'

'Yeah, well, I bunked off school one day and got on a bus to go to the hospital. I'd heard my parents talking the night before about how she didn't have long to live and I wanted to go see her. She'd been good to us when we were younger, always bringing us comic books and chocolate. I felt I owed it to her.'

Cahill bowed his head and let Sam massage his neck. She waited for him to finish his story.

'So I got there and even though it wasn't visiting time officially I snuck past the nurse's station and found her room. Security wasn't so tight back then.' He looked up at Sam and grabbed her hands. 'It was like she wasn't the same person, Sam. I hardly recognised her any more. This woman that used to be full of life and love and there she was wasted away to nothin'. Dying a little bit more every second I stood there watching her. I went over to her and kissed her forehead. It was like brushing against paper, her skin was so thin and dried out. And the worst of it was . . .' Cahill looked away and blinked hard several times. 'She didn't even know it was me. Her eyes just looked through me like I wasn't there. And I don't think I ever forgave my parents for that. For keeping me away from her and not letting me say a proper goodbye to the woman I knew.'

'They were doing what they thought was best, Alex. You can see that now, can't you?'

'That's the worst part of these places, Sam. Not that you come here to die. But that they steal your essence; turn you into something unrecognisable before they kill you.'

'It's just a building.'

'Not to me it's not. I signed up to join the army soon as I turned sixteen and I think that was why. I blamed them and wanted to get away from there. Be my own man. Broke my mother's heart, I know.'

'She got over it, Alex. You know that. She was as proud as any mother can be of her son. Of you and Michael. I saw that in her at our wedding and when they came over here for Jodie's birth. And for Anna. I only ever saw her love for you.'

'You're right. But I was young back then and it took me a while to grow up. I wasted those years for all of us and now they're both gone.'

'They got to see what's most important to any parents: their sons successful in their own right and with their own families. Don't torture yourself over it.'

Cahill finished dressing on his own while Sam went to get the car to drive it round to the front entrance. He was carefully pulling on a light-weight jacket over his T-shirt when Tara Byrne walked into his room and leaned against the wall. She was still dressed in her clothes from the previous night, though she had no jewellery or make-up on. Her face was pale and she looked tired.

'How are you?' Cahill asked, unsure why she had come to see him.

She shrugged and her chin trembled.

'I heard about Phil,' Cahill told her. 'I'm sorry. I know you two were close.'

She sniffed and wrapped her arms around herself. 'You guys didn't get off lightly either.'

'Nobody ever comes out of these things the same. We just have to carry on.'

She walked towards him and sat on the bed, her fingers twisting in her lap. Cahill was standing above her and saw the sutures in her hair where she had been cut by flying glass.

'Are you OK?' he asked. 'I mean, is someone coming to pick you up or what?'

'Yes. My dad's here. I told him to wait down the hall because I wanted to come and see you before I left.'

'You're going to stay with your parents?'

'Yes.' She looked up at him. 'You don't seem too concerned about my security arrangements right now. Why is that, after what happened last night?'

He shrugged and sat beside her. 'I don't think I'm in any shape to help right now. Plus, I don't know if last night was anything to do with you.'

'Then what was it?'

'I don't know. No one does.'

'You've spoken to the police then?'

'I have, and they're none the wiser so far as I can tell.'

She got up and walked to the door, stood facing out into the corridor with her hand on the doorframe. It looked to Cahill like she wanted to say something else so he waited.

'I just wanted to say that I don't blame you,' she said, turning her head, but not quite looking at Cahill. 'For Phil.'

Cahill didn't know how to respond.

'I remember him last night,' she said, wiping a tear from her cheek. 'How he got out of the car and then into an argument with the taxi drivers. That was just like him: a little bit too hot-headed for his own good sometimes.'

'He was only looking out for you.'

She turned and looked at him. 'I know,' she said. 'I mean, that's what makes it so hard.'

Cahill nodded. 'I'm sorry this happened,' he told her. 'If I can do anything . . .'

She tried to smile, but didn't quite manage it. 'It's nice of you to say,' she said. 'Maybe we'll meet some other time.'

'Take care of yourself,' Cahill said, knowing that the chances of their ever meeting again were slim.

She left, and Cahill didn't know if he had made it better or worse for her.

A porter came into the room and helped him into a wheelchair, telling him it was hospital policy and he would have to do what he was told. The porter then chatted cheerfully all the way down to the entrance while Cahill listened. Guy could talk for Britain.

Sam pulled away from the hospital and Cahill watched it recede in the wing mirror on the passenger side of the car, glad that he had come out of it still breathing instead of in a box.

3

Sam turned the stereo on in the car and fiddled with the controls on the steering wheel until she found a song that she liked – some piano-playing singer-songwriter that Cahill found acceptable in a bland kind of way. In the same way that beige is an acceptable colour.

Resting his head on the seat, he closed his eyes and tried to think back to the previous night; to the moments just before the explosion. His mind refused to cooperate, giving him just brief shards of images and noise.

His BlackBerry chirped faintly somewhere in the car, telling him that he had a text message.

'Where's the phone?' he asked Sam.

'Um, I think it's in the bag on the floor behind your seat.'

Cahill tried to turn round but a bolt of pain stopped him.

'Want me to stop so I can get it?' Sam asked.

Cahill nodded and Sam brought the car to a halt at the side of the road as the traffic rumbled by. She undid her seatbelt and stretched behind his seat, rummaging in a blue sports bag and handing the phone to Cahill.

He checked his list of missed calls as Sam pulled back into the traffic and saw that Logan had tried to call several times, late last night and this morning.

'Did you speak to Logan?' he asked Sam.

'No, but Tom did, I think. He said Logan had been into the office today and got a bit of a grilling from your pals in the Special Branch.'

Cahill checked his text messages and frowned.

'There's a text from the alarm company,' he said. 'It says the alarm was triggered earlier this afternoon. Did you know about this?'

'Oh, that. Yes, I spoke to the alarm company when they called. I was on the way back home from the hospital to pick up your clothes but they said that they had contacted the police and were told they checked the place and found nothing.'

Cahill frowned some more. 'Not like the cops to move so fast for a domestic alarm.'

'You can be so paranoid sometimes,' Sam said, smiling. 'Would you relax? There was no one there with a big knife waiting to cut my throat.'

'Was anything out of place at home? Or, I don't know, anything just a bit off?'

'Not that I could see, no.'

Cahill began to relax.

'Oh, wait,' Sam said. 'The side gate was open and I thought I closed it this morning when I left for the hospital.'

'You mean you didn't lock it. Sam, I've told you . . .'

'I know, sorry. I don't think I locked it. Maybe that's what set the alarm off.'

'They told you it was an external sensor?'

'No. I mean, I never thought to ask.'

Cahill was careful about his home security. More so since Ellie's rescue at the loch, although he had eased off a little in the last six months. Still, he didn't like the idea of someone being at the house and opening the gate, prowling around.

He pulled down the sun visor above his head and looked in the vanity mirror, angling it so that he could look out of the back window at the cars behind. There was a plain blue Vauxhall saloon three cars back with what looked like two men in it. Nothing particularly unusual in that, but it struck him as the kind of ordinary vehicle that the police might use if they were trying to be inconspicuous. 'Trying' being the operative word, because the cops were notoriously bad at covert surveillance.

It was also the kind of car that someone might use if they were up to no good.

Cahill put the sun visor back up and watched the blue car in his wing mirror. After a minute or so he scanned the road ahead but saw nothing else that caught his interest.

'Sam, honey, pull over at the next store so I can grab a drink.'

'Sure. Want me to get it?'

'No, I'm fine.'

A corner newsagent came up on their side of the road after half a mile and Sam pulled over. Cahill got out gingerly, pulling himself up by the doorframe and grimacing all the way. Sam watched him, thinking, boys will be boys. Always trying to show that it didn't hurt.

Cahill stood and watched as the Vauxhall passed by. The man in the passenger seat stole a quick glance at him and Cahill saw that they were both wearing suits and ties. He followed the car's progress as it carried on down the road, making a mental note of the licence plate.

After buying a Coke in the shop he went back outside and

stretched a little, looking back in the direction of the hospital. A silver saloon of indeterminate make with two more men in the front seats was parked on this side of the road about fifty metres behind them.

Now he was convinced they were being followed: two teams working in stages. At least they got that part right.

He eased himself back into the car and watched intently in the mirror as the silver car pulled out behind them and kept a steady distance. Cahill did not want to alarm Sam, at least not yet, by calling Hardy or anyone else at CPO.

The new guys were no better than the last pair, though at least they varied their speed and the gap between the two cars. Cahill watched them for a couple of minutes in the wing mirror and then scanned the road ahead again.

As they passed by a turning on the left, he saw the blue Vauxhall waiting to pull out. He watched it without turning his head and then pulled his sun visor down again. The blue car waited for the silver one to pass and then joined the traffic behind it. Cahill couldn't be sure, but he thought he saw the passenger in the silver car lift a radio mike to his mouth.

Cops, Cahill thought. Probably the same ones who were at the house earlier and set the alarm off. They were always clumsy about that kind of stuff.

But why are they looking at me?

4

Irvine spoke to her mum and to Connor, trying not to cry as she lay on her bed and listened to her son as he burbled and chirped in the way that only a two and a half year old can about what a great time he was having at 'Gamma's'. Hard consonants were mostly still a challenge for him.

She had to endure another semi-lecture from her mum about her choice in men. She had to concede that there was probably some justification, the way things had turned out. She listened in silence and then said goodbye.

Irvine couldn't help but regret the decision to stay on for another night. Having spent the day reading the newspaper cover to cover and watching daytime TV, she felt entirely useless and increasingly angry at the way she had been treated at the station last night. The thought occurred to her that she could just check out now and drive home. She'd have to pay for the extra night but that would be a small price to get back to normality.

She called DS Campbell: the one who had grilled her the night before. He answered after the first ring.

'It's Rebecca Irvine,' she said, unsure if he would recognise her name. 'I gave a statement last night about Roddy. Mr Hale.'

'DC Irvine, yes. I spoke to your super this morning. Told me you were a straight shooter and that if you said it, then it must be true.'

Irvine smiled, getting the impression that her super, Liam Moore, had taken to Campbell about as much as she had last night. That was to say, not much at all.

'That was good of him,' she said.

'What can I do for you?' he asked.

'I was just wondering if you've made any progress. I know it's still early, but . . .'

'We're doing all we can.'

'I didn't mean to imply that you weren't.'

'The results of the post-mortem aren't back yet and the other physical evidence is being transferred to Strathclyde CID for analysis. We don't have the forensics capabilities up here.'

'Right,' she said, realising she really had nothing to say to this man.

'How are you bearing up?' he asked after a pause.

Irvine felt that he was asking out of some sort of sense that he had to maintain civility with a fellow officer, rather than any genuine concern for her well-being.

'I'm OK,' she said.

'I suppose that's the best you could hope for. Considering.'

'I was thinking,' Irvine went on, 'that if you didn't need me for anything immediately maybe I would just head back to Glasgow. Get home, you know?'

Campbell said nothing for a moment. 'Your super said you would cooperate as best you could to assist us,' he said finally.

Irvine was sure that Moore would have said that, but he would not have meant that she should be at Campbell's beck and call for no good reason.

'And I will,' Irvine said. 'It's just that I don't see the need for me to be here any longer.'

'I'd appreciate it if you would humour me.'

Irvine put her hand over the phone and breathed out slowly. 'Fine. My room's booked for the night anyway.'

'Thank you,' he said, before hanging up.

Irvine lay back on her bed and tried to block out the memories from last night that lurked in the dark at the edge of her mind.

5

Give these cops some credit, Cahill thought, they were better than some of the others he'd seen try to undertake covert surveillance. The cars following them switched position and varied their speed as they made their way north towards home. This level of attention meant that their interest in him was more than casual; more than just as a witness. He was going to have to tell Sam soon.

After another ten minutes, they passed by the big supermarket close to their road and then turned right, nearing their house. Cahill had no idea why he would be treated as a suspect, except that he was there when the device went off and would have been seen at the hotel the night before.

But that wouldn't be enough on its own; there had to be something else.

'Sam,' Cahill said as they turned on to their street.

He saw another two cars he didn't recognise, but which were obviously unmarked police cars. One was parked at the bottom of the road and the other past their house. Both were empty.

'What is it?' Sam asked.

GJ Moffat

'Don't be alarmed, OK, but the police have been following us since we left the hospital.'

Sam looked at him quickly and frowned. 'Well, considering what happened . . .'

'No, it's more than that.'

'What do you mean?'

They were only about a hundred and fifty metres from their house now.

'I think that they may be here to arrest me.'

'What!' Sam braked hard and was about to stop.

'No,' Cahill said. 'Keep going. Go to the house and park in the driveway.'

She looked at him and continued to slow the car.

'Sam,' Cahill said sharply. 'Get to the house or it's going to become messy. He put his hand on top of hers on the gearstick. 'Please, Sam. Just do what I say.'

She looked at him and nodded, accelerating gently and indicating to turn in to the driveway. Cahill glanced in his wing mirror and saw the two cars that had been following them pull across the bottom of the street, blocking it off from any further traffic.

This is it, he thought.

Sam brought the car to a stop, the wheels crunching on the gravel of the driveway.

'What now?' she asked.

'Where are the girls?'

'They're at a friend's house.'

'Good.'

'Alex, what is this all about?'

'I don't know. I really don't.'

He leaned over towards her, ignoring the pain in his side, and kissed her.

'Go in the house and let me do this quietly. It'll be better if I volunteer.'

'But why?'

He saw tears forming in her eyes and felt anger at the police: for doing it this way, at his home. It was showy and unnecessary.

Overhead, he heard the *whup-whup* of a helicopter as it settled into position above the house.

'It'll sort itself out, Sam. Please, just go in the house.'

She wiped at her eyes, smudging her make-up, and grabbed his hand. 'I'll call Logan,' she said. 'He'll know what to do.'

Cahill nodded as she squeezed his hand and got out of the car. He watched as she went quickly to the door and went inside, not looking back.

'OK, guys,' Cahill said to no one. 'Here I come, ready or not.'

He stepped out of the car, again levering himself out using the doorframe, and walked to the opening of the short driveway. A light wind had picked up and he saw dark clouds drifting in from the north, carrying with them the promise of more rain.

He looked up and down the street and then went slowly on to his knees and put his hands behind his head, interlacing his fingers.

He heard them before he saw them: heavy boots thudding on the tarmac. Metallic *click-clacks* as their weapons shook while they ran.

'Armed police, don't move.' The voice cracking with tension; more scared than him.

'Get down on the ground,' a different voice said.

Déjà vu.

Cahill took his hands from behind his head and used them to lower himself face first on to the ground, putting his hands back on his head when he was done.

The sweet summer smell of rain drying on the pavement filled his nostrils.

Then they were on him.

Sitting on his legs; a knee in his back.

Broken ribs screaming, causing him to buck against them.

'Don't you fucking move.'

A gun barrel pressed into the back of his head.

Cuffs pinching the skin of his wrists.

Strong arms under him, lifting and pulling. His vision flashing white stars at the pain in his side.

Don't show them the pain. Don't give them the satisfaction.

Now he's standing, one stormtrooper on each arm and one in front. Their weapons pointed at his head.

George Kelly of the Special Branch walked into view, Livingstone following a short distance behind.

'Alexander Cahill,' Kelly said. 'I'm detaining you under section fourteen of the Criminal Procedure Scotland Act because I suspect you of committing an offence punishable by imprisonment, namely murder . . .'

Kelly's voice filtered out; something about being taken to a police station.

Murder. How can this be happening?

Behind him, Sam Cahill stood at the window with tears streaking her cheeks and her hands covering her mouth.

6

Cahill sat quietly, trying hard to regulate his breathing and keep his emotions in check. He'd been to prison before, or a military stockade at least, and it held no particular fear for him. Even with his injuries, he was confident of being able to handle himself physically if things turned violent. But what did scare him was the thought of not getting out again; of seeing Sam and the kids only in brief, stolen moments in the visiting area. The loss of his family was something he truly feared.

He had no concept of the British legal system; of whether he would be taken to a prison tonight or simply held at a police station. He had noted the language Kelly had used: *detaining* and not arresting. It was unclear to him what the difference was, but given the legal requirements for precise language he had no doubt that detention was distinct from being under arrest.

He was alone in the back of a police van, inside a cage specially built into the van's interior. The place was clean enough, but the lingering stink of incarceration was there. That smell was hard to get rid of. But compared to the military transports he'd been in, the back of the van was almost comfortable.

After a while – the concept of time was fleeting – the van turned and stopped, the vehicle shaking as the cops in the front opened their doors and got out.

He sat patiently waiting for the rear doors to open. When they did, cool, fresh evening air flooded in. He breathed deeply, aware that it would probably be his last chance to experience it tonight.

Looking outside as the inner cage door was being unlocked, he saw Kelly and Livingstone chatting to a couple of the armed police. Both of the Special Branch men turned to walk towards the back of the van when they heard the cage being opened and the armed officers stayed back, entirely at ease and carrying only their sidearms in belt holsters now that Cahill was in cuffs.

The detectives stayed behind Cahill as the uniformed officers from the front of the van helped him down from the cage. He looked around quickly and saw that he was in a large courtyard, sealed off from the world outside by a pair of tall steel doors. Around him was a fairly modern, low-rise office building only a few storeys high with a taller tower at the front of it.

The uniformed officers walked him round the side of the van and through a secure door into the interior of the building. They waited with him in the small space by a wooden counter.

Kelly and Livingstone disappeared up a corridor to the left of the counter without saying anything. A uniformed sergeant stood behind the counter and Cahill wondered if the level of the floor behind it was raised because the man towered above everyone else. If it was not raised, he was somewhere in the six-five range. He had the look of an ageing rugby player: big shoulders and arms, broken nose and the beginnings of a belly creeping over his belt.

'This is the guy for the Hilton,' one of the cops at Cahill's side said. 'Section fourteen.'

'Right,' the sergeant said, glancing at paperwork on the counter in front of him. 'You have the right to have a lawyer advised of your detention. Do you have one?'

'Yes.'

The sergeant picked up a biro from the counter, his hand hovering over a sheet of paper. 'What's the name and number?'

Cahill gave him Logan's mobile number and said that his wife would already have called him anyway.

'Do you want me to call him or not?'

'Yes, sir. I want you to call him.'

'"Sir", he says.' The sergeant spoke to the officer to Cahill's left and raised his eyebrows. 'Not often we get that, eh, boys?'

The cops either side of him laughed.

'OK, let's get the pockets emptied and the belt off and a quick once-over before we get him to his room so's he can order room service.'

Cop humour; same the world over.

Cahill remained calm and quiet throughout the rest of the process. The big sergeant opened the locked gate that led to the cells and the other two walked with him, taking him into a small, airless room where he was photographed and swabbed for DNA sampling. He recognised the digital fingerprinting equipment that he'd been printed on at the hospital – no longer the sticky black ink of the old school. Everything was digitised now.

Cahill heard the cops talking about putting him in a 'legalised' cell. He had no idea what that meant and said nothing, preferring to maintain his silence until Logan got here. He was taken to his cell – a soulless, concrete slab with the thinnest mattress he had ever encountered, a scratchy-looking blanket and a pillow. There was also a stainless steel toilet with no seat and a sink. He was glad, at least, to be alone and not having to share.

The door clanged heavily and he sat on the mattress, staring at the graffiti on the walls and trying not to think of Sam and the girls; trying desperately hard not to think of them.

7

Logan had been stacking dinner plates in the dishwasher when Sam Cahill called him. He had to close Ellie's door on the way to the living room to shut out the sound of her piano practice.

Sam's voice was thick with emotion and he knew that she had been crying. His first thought was that Cahill had relapsed at hospital and he felt the full weight of that thought sink down into the pit of his stomach before she told him that he had been arrested.

Sam was not able to tell Logan what Cahill might have been charged with. He stayed on the phone with her for a while, calming her as best he could and promising that he would find out what was going on.

He sat on the sofa when the call was finished, trying to make sense of what had happened, and figure out what to do about it. He had not practised criminal law for ten years and the only criminal lawyer he knew was the one that Kennedy Boyd referred all their corporate clients to when they got in trouble. Logan had had some dealings with the man and remembered being impressed, though he couldn't immediately remember the name.

He was scrolling through the address book of his BlackBerry looking for the criminal lawyer when it rang. He didn't recognise the number, except that it had the Glasgow dialling code.

'Is this . . .' pause while looking for name on piece of paper, '. . . Logan Finch?'

'Yes. Who's this?'

'Sergeant Collier at Helen Street police station. We have an Alexander Cahill in detention and he requested that as his lawyer you be informed of his detention.'

'Right. I'll be down there to see him.'

'I expect that's what he wants.'

Logan was about to thank him when the phone on the other end clattered down and the dial tone sounded.

Logan called Sam back and told her that the police had been in touch and that he was going to see Cahill right now. He thought that was best; show him a friendly face, find out what was happening and then get him a *real* lawyer. He knew that Cahill would not be taken to court to be charged with anything officially until the next day, when the duty court sat for all prisoners arrested the previous night. So he had a little time to play with.

Next call was to his parents' house to see if they could take Ellie. He was vague about why he had to go out but persuaded his dad to make the short trip north from Ayrshire. Not that he needed much convincing where his newest grandchild was concerned.

Logan explained to Ellie that he had to go out on urgent business and that Pops would be over to stay with her, maybe even overnight. This caused more excitement than dismay.

He got ready for the trip to the station by printing off directions and a map from the internet even though his car was equipped with a satnav system. He wanted to make sure he had covered everything. He filled a bag with his laptop, a blank pad and some pens. He anticipated that he would not be allowed to take the laptop into the station, but better to have it with him than not.

While waiting for his dad to arrive, he scanned the news channels for anything new, but they were all running the same old footage, trying to put a different spin on the information. It was the curse of the twenty-four-hour news era: stuff recycled endlessly to no useful effect. Irvine's face flashed on screen briefly as the presenter spoke about the hunt for Roddy's killers.

The intercom buzzed and Ellie ran to answer it before Logan had even managed to get to the hallway.

'Hi, Pops,' she shouted into the intercom, pressing the button to release the external door downstairs before getting a reply.

'Ellie, Jeez,' Logan said as she opened the door of their flat and stepped on to the landing. 'You should at least make sure it's him first before you open the door.'

He continued to be surprised by how quickly she had been able to overcome what had happened to her. It was true enough: kids *were* resilient.

'Hey, Ellie-bee,' his dad called up the stairs.

Ellie shouted in reply and Logan went inside to get his jacket and bag. When he came back into the hall his dad was handing over his usual bag of treats for Ellie and struggling to break free of her hug. Logan went over, kissed Ellie's cheek and told his dad thanks, before going out the door.

'What's this about?' his dad shouted.

'Tell you later.'

Once in the car, Logan typed the address for the station into his satnav and waited for the system to acquire the satellites, which

GJ Moffat

always took longer than he expected. While he waited, he turned on the car radio just as the Clash's 'I Fought the Law' was ending.

Isn't that just the way the world works, he thought.

8

Logan followed the directions of the voice on his satnav and passed by the police station on the other side of a narrow dual carriageway. He turned right at a roundabout at the end of the road and parked at a KFC restaurant a short distance away.

He jogged to the station and went into the front reception area. The space behind the public counter was empty and he could not find any service bell to attract attention, so he paced back and forward looking at bland community policing statements and no-smoking signs pinned to the bare brick walls until a woman PC appeared and asked how she could help. He explained who he was here to see and was asked to take a seat.

The woman left again through a door at the back of the public area. A middle-aged man in a shell-suit with a bad comb-over came in reeking of booze. He shouted for a bit and then left when no one came to see him.

After another few minutes, Neil Livingstone came in through the door that the PC had used and indicated with his hand that

Logan should follow him. They walked through a series of corridors and then came out into another area with a counter. Logan was startled by the appearance of a giant of a man in a police uniform.

'Bag,' the giant said, holding out his hand. It looked to Logan as though he was moving in slow motion, so disproportionate in size was he to any other person in the station.

Logan gave him the bag and wondered if he turned green when he got angry.

'You can't use that in here,' the Hulk said. 'Or your phone.'

He held out his hand again and Logan fumbled in his pocket for his BlackBerry and handed it over. He saw the three stripes on the black pullover the man wore as he rummaged in Logan's bag, eventually producing the pad and one pen, which he handed back to Logan.

The Hulk inclined his head and told Logan to follow him. Logan went after him and waited while he opened a secure door and then walked down a short corridor and through another door, this one of heavy metal. Logan stepped cautiously into the room and saw two plastic chairs on opposite sides of a table.

'He'll be here in a minute,' the Hulk said, then left, pulling the door shut with a jarring clang.

Logan put his pad and pen on the table before taking his jacket off and draping it over the back of one of the chairs. The walls, where not covered in graffiti, were painted white and the floor was bare polished concrete. Every noise seemed to echo. Logan sat in the chair and waited until the door opened again and Cahill came in.

Cahill walked to the table and sat opposite him in the empty chair. Logan thought that he looked much like his usual self, except that his face still bore a red blush from the explosion.

'Some fucking thing, this,' Cahill said, trying to smile but not really making it.

'They treating you OK?'

'Apart from the fact that I've been locked up like a criminal; yeah, not too bad.'

Logan smiled at the joke. 'I guess I asked for that,' he said.

Cahill looked around the room and then back at Logan. 'So what happens now?' he asked.

'I'll get a proper criminal lawyer for you tonight. Those guys always have twenty-four-hour telephone lines. Night time is probably their busiest period, you know.'

'They said I was being detained. Is that different from being under arrest?'

'Yes. It means they can hold you without charge for a maximum period and then they either have to release you or charge you.'

'And *charging* me means that then I'll be under arrest?'

'Yes.'

'How long can they hold me before they make their minds up?'

'Six hours. So you'll get charged or released before the night is over.'

'And if I get charged . . . ?'

'You'll be held here until tomorrow morning and then they'll take you to the duty court for overnight prisoners at Glasgow Sheriff Court.'

Cahill nodded, his eyes alert and direct. 'I appreciate you not trying to make it out to be better than it is,' he told Logan.

'You wouldn't want it any other way.'

Cahill leaned forward, resting his elbows on the table and sighing. 'Listen,' he said. 'This is about the explosion. I heard them say that to the big sergeant when they brought me in here. That and the armed police at the house to pick me up means that they think

I was involved in setting the bomb. They said I was being detained on suspicion of murder.'

He paused to let that sink in. Logan shook his head and opened his mouth to speak, but Cahill held up a hand, cutting him off.

'It doesn't matter whether it's true or not for now,' he said. 'What does matter is that if I'm going to be charged it will be with murder and I'm assuming I won't get bail for that.'

Logan nodded.

'So I'll be locked up in a proper prison until the trial. I mean, assuming we get that far.'

'Barlinnie,' Logan said. 'It's the remand prison for the west of Scotland.'

'What's remand?'

'It just means that you're in prison awaiting trial. You'll be an untried prisoner, but Barlinnie also holds convicted ones.'

'Great.'

'You can handle yourself, Alex. It won't be a problem.'

'It's not the prisoners I'm worried about.' He didn't elaborate, and sat back in his chair.

'I don't understand this,' Logan said. 'What evidence can they have that justifies picking you up like they did? And so soon after the explosion.'

'They'll have my prints all over our cars and witnesses seeing me the night before checking the place out.'

'That's not enough. Not by a long way.'

Cahill agreed.

'There has to be something else,' Logan said.

'But what?'

Before Logan could answer, the locking mechanism in the door crunched open and Kelly came in with Livingstone. The Hulk stood behind them.

'Mr Finch,' Kelly said, 'We're going to interview your client now. Would you like to be present?'

Logan stood and said that he would accompany Cahill.

'Let's go,' the sergeant said, walking towards the table.

9

The interview room at Helen Street was much smaller than the one Logan had just been in with Cahill and had cheap grey carpet tiles on the floor rather than bare concrete. There was also a window, though it was barred on the inside. The room smelled faintly of cigarette smoke.

Kelly and Livingstone went round to sit on the far side of the table, the surface of which was scarred by many years of use. There was a digital recorder set up and Livingstone was getting it ready for the interview.

The Hulk waited in the room until Cahill and Logan were sitting then left, closing the door lightly. Logan expected to hear it being locked, but all he heard were the man's footsteps as he went down the corridor and back to his post at the counter.

Kelly smiled benignly at Logan and flicked through the pages of a small notebook on the table in front of him. After another minute or so, Livingstone indicated that he was ready and pressed the necessary buttons to start the recording. He spoke to identify the people in the room, the date and the time and then waited for

Kelly, who continued to leaf through the notebook for a moment before closing it and looking at Cahill.

'Tell me about the contract for Tara Byrne,' he said.

'So there's no misunderstanding,' Logan said, 'do you mean the contract for her security at the film premiere?'

'Yes, that contract.'

Logan nodded to Cahill.

'I got a call from her manager, Devon Leonard, last Friday,' Cahill said. 'He told me it was urgent and that because of some unspecified threat to her he needed a security presence at the premiere on Sunday.'

'He called you direct?'

'Yes.'

'Did he say how he came to choose you?'

'Said it was a recommendation, but he didn't say from whom. Which, before you ask, is not that unusual.'

'And you'd never met him, or Miss Byrne, before?'

'No.'

'Never been to Miss Byrne's flat in London?' Livingstone asked, interrupting Kelly's flow.

Logan was surprised by the question.

'No, I've never been to her flat,' Cahill said.

'Can you explain how we found your fingerprints there?'

Logan felt Cahill tense beside him.

'What?' Cahill said, not really meaning it as a question. 'That's not possible.'

'It's been confirmed,' Kelly said, taking over again. 'What is your relationship with her?'

'I didn't have one until this weekend.'

'Your fingerprints were also on some of the things that were sent to her. One of the dolls, for example. Can you explain that?'

'Yes. Her security guy brought them to our meeting on Saturday and showed them to me. I handled one of them.'

'Phil Hanson?'

'Yes.'

'He died in the explosion.'

Cahill said nothing and it looked to Logan as if Kelly and Livingstone were waiting for a reaction. They got none.

'Did you know that Miss Byrne and Mr Hanson had feelings for one another?'

'Yes. I spoke to Phil about that on Saturday night. Told him he couldn't be effective if he was emotionally involved.'

'So it turned out,' Livingstone said.

Cahill remained impassive. 'Look,' he said. 'What's the story with this? You guys know I wouldn't be involved in something like this.'

Kelly looked as if he wanted to agree.

'We all have superiors,' Livingstone said. 'And we have to follow wherever the evidence takes us.'

'And did the same superiors tell you to go to my house this afternoon and bring an army to arrest me outside my home? In front of my wife like that? You could have come to the hospital and I'd have gone quietly.'

'We were told to do this the right way; not to allow our relationship with you to cloud our judgement. You can understand that.'

Cahill could, but it didn't make him any less angry at being treated like that.

'We're entitled to know what evidence it is that you think you have,' Logan said.

'We found his fingerprints on a bottle in her flat,' Livingstone said. 'And we're checking it for DNA samples also.'

'We can have any of your evidence independently examined,' Logan said.

'You'll get your chance to do that.'

'A bottle in a flat isn't much to go on, guys,' Logan said, 'I mean, if that's what you're hoping to hang a murder charge on.'

'That's not all. We've got more,' Kelly said, maintaining eye contact with Cahill.

'You've got witnesses who saw me at the bomb site on Saturday,' Cahill said. 'And in the hotel and specifically in Tara's room. And you've also got my prints on the cars. Am I right?'

'That's correct,' Kelly said.

'All entirely necessary for me to do my job as her head of security for the premiere, as anyone in my business would tell you. And as you both well know.'

Logan was impressed by how calm Cahill was; no doubt his heart rate was not far above normal. Logan could feel his racing inside, every beat like a bass drum.

'That's accepted, Alex,' Kelly said. 'But how do you explain your fingerprints being on the timer for the explosive device?'

10

Cahill remained remarkably calm, lifting his hands up and placing them flat on the table top. Logan watched Kelly and Livingstone and their reaction to Cahill. Kelly was impassive but Livingstone frowned and leaned forward in his chair.

'Do you have an answer for that?' he asked.

Cahill released a shallow breath before he spoke. 'Have you boys ever investigated a bombing before?'

Logan couldn't help but think that Cahill had used the word 'boys' deliberately; letting them know that he was the only one there experienced in these things.

Neither man replied.

'I'll take that as a no,' Cahill said.

'What's that got to do with anything?' Livingstone asked.

Cahill went on. 'If you had any experience you would realise how ridiculous it would have been for me to set a timer before I left for the premiere and arrange for it to detonate at the precise time we returned to the hotel. Those premieres never run to schedule and this one was no exception. If the device was on a timer, I didn't set it.'

'I understand what you're saying,' Kelly said. 'And I can see the sense in it. But that doesn't detract from the fact that we have your prints on the device. That can't be argued away. Either your prints are there, or they are not.'

'If I wanted to take someone out, there are much easier ways to do it. I certainly wouldn't have risked the lives of my people.'

For the first time Logan heard emotion in his friend's voice.

'I can kill a man easily and with minimal fuss. That's not an idle boast; it's a fact. I've been trained to do it by some of the most able men in the world and, believe me, the last thing I would do if I wanted anyone dead would be to rig a bomb on a timer and get as close to it as I was.'

'Alex,' Kelly said. 'I'm not saying that any of that doesn't make sense. It does. But the prints . . .' He opened his hands on the table top.

'Do you have any explanation for that?' Livingstone asked.

An incessant clicking started in Logan's mind; something in his memory trying to catch his attention. He couldn't quite reach it, but the clicking persisted.

'Your bosses are just looking for an easy result on this thing, aren't they?' Cahill asked, leaning back in his chair. 'Keep everyone calm; convince them it's not terrorists. Why don't you go do your job properly instead?'

'That's what we're doing.'

'What possible reason do I have for doing this?' Cahill asked, his voice rising in volume. 'Has anyone here even thought about that?'

click-click-click-click

Cahill stood now, causing Livingstone to sit back.

'Sit down, Alex,' Kelly said softly.

Cahill looked from one man to the other.

'Alex . . .'

'I told you,' Cahill said, 'that I saw someone across the way from the hotel. Have you looked into that yet? Because I'm telling you now that what you have is not the truth.'

click-click-click-click

'You're not helping yourself behaving like this, Alex. Please sit down.'

Cahill looked away, and lowered himself slowly into the chair again. Livingstone relaxed, relieved that nothing was going to come of it. There were few people who could match Cahill when it came to the exercise of physical violence.

'You can see the logic in what Alex is telling you,' Logan said. 'I mean, it just doesn't add up.'

'This is the story,' Livingstone said, glancing at Kelly. 'You knew Tara Byrne. Intimately. You've been in her flat in London. You also just admitted that you knew she was in a relationship with her security chief, Phil Hanson. He was killed in the explosion. Your prints are all over the place, including on the device.'

'Are you saying I did this out of some sort of jealous rage?' Cahill asked. 'Is that it? That I was involved with Tara and this was to get Phil out of the way?'

Livingstone looked almost embarrassed.

'You do realise how ridiculous that sounds?' Cahill said.

Kelly nodded, agreeing with Cahill but not wanting that to be recorded on the tape.

'Motivation is secondary,' Livingstone said. 'We'll get to that eventually. For now, all the evidence points straight at you. And we still haven't heard an explanation from you about your prints on the watch.'

Logan realised now that it wasn't a clicking sound at all; it was the ticking of a watch.

'You never said it was a watch before,' he said. 'What kind of watch was it?'

Kelly leaned forward, interested again at the urgency in Logan's voice. 'A Rolex,' he said.

A movie projector started up in Logan's mind; one of those old ones that whirred and hummed as the reel spooled round. The image was jerky and incomplete.

The CPO boardroom.

Tara's manager, Devon Leonard, sliding his watch across the table at Cahill.

His Rolex watch.

Cahill taking a bottle of water from the fridge and giving it to Leonard.

Leonard taking the bottle with him after the meeting.

It had been a set-up all along.

11

'I need to speak to my client right now,' Logan said.

'Logan—' Cahill started.

'I said now.' Logan cut across his friend.

'We're not finished with our questions,' Livingstone said.

'Well,' Logan said, 'you can stop the recording now and allow me to speak to my client and we'll see where that takes us, or you can keep going and ask him as many questions as you like. But I'm telling you right now that I will advise him to exercise his right to silence.'

'That's not going to look so good for him later,' Livingstone said.

'That's just the way it is. So what's it to be?'

Livingstone looked to Kelly for the answer. Kelly stared across the table at Cahill before he looked at Logan and nodded.

'OK, Mr Finch,' he said. 'You can have your time with your client. But before you go, there's something I need to say.'

'What's that?' Logan asked.

Kelly looked wearily at Cahill and flipped open the notebook on the table in front of him. He ran his finger along a few lines on one of the pages.

'Alexander Cahill,' he began, his voice a dull monotone, 'I'm arresting you for the murders of Philip Hanson and three others. You are not obliged to say anything but anything you do say will be noted down and may be used in evidence.'

He paused and the weight of his words resonated in the room.

'Do you understand?' he asked.

'I understand,' Cahill said, all of the fight having left him for now.

'Do you have anything to say?'

Cahill looked at Logan, who shook his head. 'No.'

Kelly flipped his notebook shut. 'Let's get you some privacy so you can have a chat. Then we'll get you off to the court tomorrow.'

'It's a set-up,' Logan said when he and Cahill were back in the other room.

'I know that,' Cahill said.

'No, I mean I think I know who did it.'

'What?'

Logan was surprised that Cahill had not made the connection himself.

'It had to be Devon Leonard. He threw his watch at you when we met him on Saturday so that you would handle it. Remember? It was a Rolex.'

Cahill nodded slowly.

'And the bottle. You gave him a bottle of water and he took it away with him after the meeting. That's how he did it. It must be.'

Cahill went to one of the chairs and sat down, rubbing his hands up over his head.

'Why?' he asked. 'What's it all about? I never met the guy. Never met any of them until this week.'

'I don't know that part,' Logan said, pacing the floor. 'But at least we have somewhere to start looking.'

'If he did do this, and I hear what you're saying, he'll be long gone by now and I'll bet he has enough money to stay hidden.'

'But at least we can keep you out of jail. We have to tell these guys right now.'

Cahill held up a hand and shook his head. 'It's not about those two; it's about the ones at the top of the chain of command. It won't be enough for them, Logan. Not to keep me from getting charged today. They've got their story and it fits with enough of what they know to go with it for now. We need to run this down ourselves and make sure of it before we do anything with it.'

'But . . .'

'Don't worry about me. I can handle time in jail; so long as it's not a lifetime. I don't want this getting screwed up because we jumped the gun on it.'

Logan sat in the other chair and rested his elbows on his knees. 'You're right,' he said.

'You remember anything else about the meeting right now that could help?'

'No.'

'No matter, we can get it looked into. You need to speak to Tom Hardy about this. He'll know who to call.' Cahill laughed and squeezed the bridge of his nose between his thumb and index finger.

'What's so funny?' Logan asked.

'Nothing. It's just that in all my life, in all the things I've been through, I've never gotten into so much trouble as since I met you. You are bad news, my friend.'

Logan managed no more than a smile. He realised again that however much he knew now about Cahill, there was still a lot that his friend kept hidden. Maybe that was a good thing.

'I looked up Tara and Leonard on the internet,' Logan said. 'Something should have clicked for me then, you know.'

'Why?'

'Leonard went to every event with her. I mean, he was always right by her side, basking in the reflection of her celebrity. But he didn't go to the premiere on Sunday, did he?'

'I guess he knew what was coming.' Cahill looked at Logan. 'That's going to change.'

Logan told the sergeant that they were done with their break and Kelly and Livingstone came back to the holding cell. If anything, they looked even more solemn than before.

'Do you want to continue the interview?' Kelly asked.

'No,' Logan replied. 'We're done for now.'

'You're sure about that? You realise what it means?'

'We do,' Cahill said.

'OK. But there's one more thing we need to do tonight.'

'What's that?' Logan asked.

'An amendment to the charge.' Kelly stepped forward and opened his notebook, clearing his throat before he spoke.

'In addition to Philip Hanson and others yet to be identified, I'm charging you with the murder of Christopher Washington. You are not obliged to say anything but anything you do say will be noted down and may be used in evidence.' He closed the notebook and looked at the floor.

'What?' Logan said.

'I'm sorry you had to hear it like this,' Kelly said.

'Chris died?'

Cahill was silent. His lips parted, but no sound came out.

'I'm sorry,' Kelly repeated before turning to leave with Livingstone.

The door thudded shut.

12

Irvine spent the evening after the call with Campbell restless and uneasy about her decision to stay in the town. Her dinner consisted of a few mouthfuls of something in the hotel restaurant – she found it hard to even remember what she had ordered – and then she went back to her room to lie down. But sleep didn't come and so she paced the floor getting increasingly frustrated. When she started arguing with herself out loud, she knew that she'd reached the end of her tether.

It was eleven-thirty when she tried calling Logan. After a few failed attempts she called again and this time waited for his voicemail to click in. She was glad to hear his voice and left him a message saying that she had decided to come home after all and that she'd see him in the morning. When she finished the call, she gathered up all her things, stuffed them in her bag and went down to check out, resolved to get home tonight and to hell with Campbell.

She got a strange look from the woman at reception and still had to pay full rate for the room. She did so gladly, to get out of the place as fast as she could, and went to the car.

There wasn't much petrol left in the tank when she turned the engine over so she drove to a petrol station just past the hotel. It was part of a small commercial centre with a supermarket and a burger place. She pulled up to a pump behind an old Mazda with a man sitting in the passenger seat. At this time of night the place was quiet and the only other car drove away as she opened her door and stepped out.

She pressed the 'pay at pump' button so that she did not have to go into the station itself and stood looking back at the town while the machinery thrummed behind her, petrol sloshing into the car and the fuel counter ticking over. The air was thick with the smell of petrol and she saw rainbow colours where it had spilled on to the concrete of the garage forecourt.

Irvine turned at the sound of footsteps and saw a man with his head down wearing a baseball cap walk to the driver's door of the Mazda and open it. He took the cap off, revealing his closely shaved head, and Irvine thought for an instant that she recognised him from somewhere. She couldn't place him and smiled when he glanced at her. He smiled back, got into the car and drove off. She watched the car for a while as it pulled out into the traffic and took the road down along the loch, heading out of town to the south.

Irvine finished filling her car and replaced the pump, shivering as a light rain started to spot on the ground around her.

Back in the car, she was pulling her seatbelt back on when it hit her who the guy was. She *had* seen him before.

At the concert.

When Roddy fell.

And now he was here.

13

Hudson drove away slowly from the petrol station, watching Irvine in his rear-view mirror. It was clear from the look on her face that something had sparked in her memory. She got in the car and he watched as the car sat there much longer than it should have. He started counting and gave up when he got to twenty and the road they were on curved away until the station was out of sight. He pulled over at the first turn-off and stopped, slamming a hand against the steering wheel.

'What?' Two asked.

'It's like anything that could go wrong will go wrong,' Hudson said through gritted teeth.

'What the fuck?' Two said. 'Tell me.'

Hudson shifted in his seat to face Two. 'The woman cop?' he said.

'Uh-huh.'

'Well, she just pulled into the petrol station behind us and saw me when I came back to the car.'

Two looked perplexed. 'So?'

'So? Is that it?' Hudson's voice started to rise in pitch.

'She doesn't know you. What's all the fuss about?'

Hudson bowed his head and rubbed the stubbly hair on his scalp. 'She saw me at the concert,' he said. 'And now she's seen me here.'

Two's face fell.

'After what happened last night,' Hudson said, 'her nerves will be on a razor's edge, and seeing me is going to send her off on one.'

Two turned in his seat and looked back. 'She hasn't followed us,' he said.

Hudson laughed: a harsh, barking sound that made Two recoil slightly. 'Would you?' he said. 'If it was me, I'd turn the car round and drive in the other direction as fast as I could.'

'What if she goes to the cops?'

'I don't know.'

'So what do you want to do?'

'You say that like I've got a choice.'

Two nodded but said nothing.

'You and I both know that in addition to not getting paid we'll likely get a bullet between the eyes if this doesn't get fixed,' Hudson said. 'The boss is not a man to be screwed with. He hires us, for Christ's sake. That says it all.'

'I'll call the others.'

'You do that. And while you're at it maybe you could find out why they didn't call to tell us she was on the move and headed right towards us.'

'Yeah.'

'I'll kill those idiots for free when this is done.'

Hudson opened his door and got out of the car while Two called Five. He walked away, breathing steadily and trying to ease the anger he felt. The last thing he needed was to be chasing a target all over the Highlands. Especially a cop who knew he was after her.

He stood in the rain, feeling it cool on his head and face, and watched Two speaking on the phone. When he was done, he got out of the car and shouted to Hudson. 'She's heading north. Says she's moving pretty fast.'

'No shit,' Hudson said. 'Let's go.'

14

Irvine panicked. She swung her car out of the petrol station and gunned the engine as she turned sharply away from the town and the two men in the Mazda. The wheels spun for an instant, complaining at the burst of power as they tried to grip on the damp road, and then the car shot forward.

It was just too much of a coincidence: seeing him at the concert and again up here. She had no doubt that the man had recognised her; had felt it in the brief moment when their eyes had met at the pumps. He had been cool and detached, showing no sign of panic, just getting in the car and driving away. Which scared Irvine more than if he had panicked.

From this end of town the road swept up into the hills, with the mountain reaching into the cloud on her right. Trees whipped by on both sides, still lush and green. The rain was that maddening kind that couldn't seem to decide if it wanted to be there or not, alternating the odd spit with a quick burst of heavier drops. Irvine spent more time varying the speed of her wipers than anything else.

As the minutes passed and she saw no sign that she was being followed, Irvine's breathing started to ease and she slowed the car as the road snaked through the trees. She tried to regulate her breathing, glancing in the rear-view mirror every few seconds. When she had been driving for about fifteen minutes she saw a makeshift lay-by: really no more than a grass verge that had been used as a place to stop so frequently that the ground was now hard and brown. She thought for a moment about stopping there and trying to call someone, but decided that it would be smarter to wait until she found somewhere more public, just in case the men were following her.

She pressed the button on her door to lower the window and then inclined her head so that the wind whipped some of the rain into her face. Her legs felt like jelly, not quite responding to the signals being sent from her brain to operate the pedals.

She tried to remember the men who had attacked her and Roddy, their height and build. But it was mostly just a blur; memories of shock and panic only. Clearing her mind of extraneous thoughts, she rewound to the moment when the men stepped out of the dark and she saw them for the first time. Before . . .

She couldn't be sure, but she didn't think that the guy from the concert and the petrol station was one of them. He was broader through the chest and shoulders, and taller.

Maybe.

But what did that mean: that there were four men after Roddy? Why would it take so many?

Nothing seemed clear to her. She wiped a hand over her face, enjoying the cool, slick sensation of the water on her skin.

She looked in her rear-view mirror and then ahead: there were no other cars in sight. She could not remember ever feeling quite so alone.

15

It was after midnight when Logan finally left the station at Helen Street. It was dark outside and the rain was falling heavily, bouncing off the ground in fat splashes. He ran from the station entrance across to his car, past two kids who worked in the KFC. They were huddled under the building's canopy, no doubt waiting for their ride home.

He sat in the car with the engine running and the heat turned up, still not able to comprehend Washington's death.

A gust of wind caused a flurry of rain on the windscreen, the noise pulling Logan from his thoughts. He had work still to do tonight and would have to leave his grief until later.

He checked his BlackBerry, seeing that he had four missed calls: three from Becky and one from his dad at around ten. Becky's last call was only a half hour earlier and he thought about calling her back but decided not to. She'd probably called him just before going to bed and anyway she'd be back home tomorrow and he would see her then – if he could find the time, given the situation Cahill was in.

Logan went to his contacts list to look for the criminal lawyer when he noticed that his voicemail light was flashing. He dialled into it and listened to Irvine's message, smiling at the sound of her voice, though she did sound more than a little pissed off.

He went back to his contacts and stopped when he saw a name he thought might be the lawyer he was looking for. He clicked on the name and it took him to the full contact details, including the name of a law firm and an emergency number. He had the right man.

'Is this Joe Shaw?' Logan asked when the phone was answered on the third ring.

'Yes.'

'Listen, I'm sorry to call this late. You don't know me but I used to be with Kennedy Boyd and I need a criminal lawyer.'

'Um, OK.'

'Not for me personally.'

'Go on.'

'I work in-house now for a security firm, and the owner, who is a good friend of mine, just got arrested.'

Logan could hear the shuffle of papers on the other end of the line.

'OK, what's the charge and where is he right now?'

'Murder. He's being held at Helen Street station.'

There was a long enough pause to make Logan think that he had lost the connection before the lawyer spoke again.

'Helen Street is for, ah, sensitive cases,' Shaw said. 'What's your friend involved in?'

'It's to do with the Hilton bombing.'

Another long pause.

'Are they saying that he was responsible for the explosion?'

'Yes.'

'OK. So he's going to court tomorrow in Glasgow?'

'That's what I understand, yes.'

'Has he been interviewed?'

'He has. I stayed with him for that.'

'Good. He didn't confess, did he?'

'No,' Logan said seriously.

'That was my best joke,' Shaw said.

'Sorry. It's been a long day.' Logan would have laughed if he had any energy left.

'No problem. Does your friend know that you're arranging for me to see him tonight?'

'Yes. I mean, I told him that I'd get someone but I couldn't remember your name at the time.'

'Leave it with me and I'll get organised and go see him in the next hour or so. Now the really hard question: can he afford to pay for me and the best QC I can hire?'

'He can. That's not an issue.'

'Good, because for a case like this he's going to need the best.'

Logan felt better now that he had spoken to someone who could help Cahill more than he could. He didn't know much about the lawyer, but he liked his low-key confidence on the phone. At least he *sounded* as if he knew what he was doing.

The rain remained constant all the way from the station to Logan's flat in Shawlands and he switched the wipers to their highest setting. Traffic was light at this time on a Monday night, with most people inside or in bed before the next working day. But not Chris Washington. He thought about Chris's wife and family and what they would be going through now. He decided to check in with Tom Hardy when he got home, no matter what the time.

He pulled into an empty space on the opposite side of the road from his building. There was a Bentley saloon with heavily tinted windows parked across from him, directly outside the door to his building. As Logan switched the car engine off, a large man in a dark suit got out of the front of the Bentley and looked over at him.

Logan stared at the man, who was indistinct through the heavy rain, no more than a silhouette. The man held up a hand and beckoned Logan forward.

Logan got out of his car and looked warily up and down the empty street, wondering who this man was. And who else might be in the car.

He stood where he was and the man walked across the road, stopping ten feet short of Logan's position. Logan tensed, unsure what to expect.

'My boss needs to speak to you,' the man said in an English accent, pure London East End.

'Who's your boss?'

'He'll tell you everything. Just get in the car.'

Right now, that was the last thing on Logan's mind.

The man stared at Logan and then turned and went back to the car. He opened the rear door and leaned inside. Logan heard him speak to someone but couldn't make out what was said. The rain hammered down, plastering his clothes to his skin.

The man came back and spoke again.

'He wants to speak to you about Mr Cahill. About his predicament.'

The words scraped their way down Logan's spine. The man turned to go back to the Bentley and this time Logan followed him. The man opened the rear door and held it, ready to usher Logan inside. Logan saw that there was another man in the car. He did not recognise him.

Logan paused in the street, looking at the man holding the door and feeling the rain soak his hair and run down over his face. He looked up at his flat and saw his dad standing in the bay window staring at him. Then he stooped into the door of the car and sat next to the man inside.

The man wore what looked like a very expensive grey suit, cut to fit him perfectly. His pale-blue shirt was open at the neck and he had a matching handkerchief in the breast pocket of his jacket. His thick grey hair was swept back from his tanned face and he smiled at Logan as he sat down, handing him a small towel.

The door clunked solidly shut and the driver moved back from the car. Logan turned to watch him open a small umbrella and walk away down the street.

'Terry understands that sometimes I need a little privacy,' the man next to Logan said in an English accent.

'What's this about?' Logan asked, rubbing his hair with the towel and drawing it down over his face. 'Is it about Alex?'

'In part,' the man said. 'Perhaps if I formally introduce myself it'll make things a bit clearer.'

The smile remained on his face, streaked by distorted light refracted through the rivulets of rain running down the windows of the car. It looked to Logan as if he wore the smile as a mask; as though his real face was hidden behind it. The man held out his right hand and Logan shook it, the man holding on firmly for a little longer than was comfortable.

'I'm Gabriel Weiss,' he said.

The White Angel grinned.

part five: revelations

1

'Have you seen the film *Sophie's Choice?*' Weiss asked.

Logan shook his head, no; unable to speak.

'Great film,' Weiss went on. 'Very dark.'

Logan saw a light glimmer in Weiss's eyes, and guessed that many people would mistake it for a keen intelligence. Logan saw it for what it really was: the spark of insanity.

'Meryl Streep plays this Jewish mother who gets taken to a concentration camp by the Nazis. She's got her little boy and girl with her. The film's set in the present day and you only get the full story of what happened in the concentration camp slowly as the film progresses. In flashback, you know.'

He paused, looking for a response. Logan nodded, thinking, *What the hell are you talking about?*

'Anyway, the crux of it is that in the camp one of the guards, a real nasty piece of work, tells her that she has to choose between her son and her daughter. One of them can stay with her and one of them they will take away from her.' Weiss shook his head and looked out into the night for a moment. Logan waited for him to continue.

'So, Meryl, she's screaming and crying and acting up a storm. I mean, that woman can act. And eventually she has to give the guard one of her children. Can't remember if it's the boy or the girl; doesn't matter, really.' Weiss turned back to face Logan, sweeping a hand through his hair. 'And she never sees that child again. Totally destroys her. Ends up committing suicide. Like I said, very dark.'

Pause.

'So, it got me thinking about the choices we make in life and the consequences. For example, I chose to bring those Russians into my organisation and put them in charge of the deal up here. You remember it, right?'

'Is that rhetorical?' Logan asked, finding his voice and surprised at the edge in it when he spoke.

Weiss watched him for a moment and then continued as though Logan had said nothing. 'And they chose to kill your old girlfriend and take her daughter. Little Ellie. You do remember that?'

'I do. I also remember putting a bullet in one of them.'

'Of course you do.'

Weiss reached into his jacket and took out a cigarette and a small, expensive-looking lighter. 'You mind?' he said, lighting the cigarette without pause. The smoke penetrated Logan's airways, cloying and hot.

'So, where was I?' Weiss said. 'Oh, yes. Choices.' He nodded, agreeing with himself. 'You *chose* to shoot one of my men. And every action has an equal and opposite reaction.'

'I did it because they had my daughter. I was reacting to that.' As if reasoning with him would work.

'Fine. Have it your way. But that wasn't the end of the chain reaction.'

'What do you mean?'

'Well, it took some time. Initially just minor annoyances from some of my competitors. Nothing I couldn't cope with. So I let it go; allowed you to have your life. I had my money after all, but eventually people started taking grander liberties with me. I haven't made an exact calculation, but in the last six months your affront to my reputation has cost my business six figures. Word got around that Gabriel Weiss was soft. That he let some cunt lawyer . . .' He stopped and shook his head. 'I must apologise for my language.'

Logan noticed that Weiss seemed to relish the use of profanity; as though he had only just discovered the joy of swearing. Like a child.

'Bottom line is that there are certain people out there who have encroached on my business interests as a result of my allowing you and your friends some latitude in what happened up here. And so I need to demonstrate to these people that I am not to be messed with, you know?'

'You got your money,' Logan said. 'I saw to that. And at great risk to my career and freedom.'

'Not enough, my friend. Not nearly enough. You see, the people in my world do not understand the finer points of negotiation. They see only weakness, and they pounce.'

'Why not fight back? They're the real bad guys.' Logan hated the way he sounded: like he was pleading with him.

'Good and bad,' Weiss said. 'Outmoded concepts.'

'Not to me.'

Weiss took a long draw on the cigarette and blew a smoke ring. 'Which brings me back to choices,' he said, shifting in his seat until he was square on to Logan. 'Let's call it "Logan's Choice". Your chance to save someone.'

Pause.

'And damn another.'

Logan felt fear rise in him, the taste of bile bitter in his throat; remembered his father standing at the window above the car, motionless. Was someone up there with him?

With Ellie?

Was he too late already?

Not now, a voice screamed in his head. Not after all that we went through to get here.

Please. Not now.

2

Weiss appeared to relish the emotions flitting across Logan's face. He reached out to flick some ash into the ashtray in front of him.

'Let me lay it out for you,' he said. 'First up, I'm afraid that when it comes to the police officer there is no choice.'

Logan frowned, not immediately understanding what he was talking about.

'Detective Irvine,' Weiss said.

And suddenly Logan understood.

'She dies. There's no stopping it.'

Not Roddy; he just got in the way. They were after Becky.

'Sorry. I know you and she were looking to start something.' Weiss looked at his watch. 'Maybe she's dead already. Whatever; she won't survive the night.'

Logan's whole body felt like it was shaking, but when he looked down at himself there was no movement. He tried to remember when he last spoke to Becky; remembered seeing that she had left a message on his voicemail not long ago. Maybe forty-five minutes. That probably meant she was OK at least for now.

'How?' he asked Weiss.

'How did I find out about her?' Your old pal Bob Crawford, of course. Bob has made a lot of money out of me since our first little adventure. I'm sure you've heard the rumours about him. Well, they're all true. He is my money-laundering lawyer of choice now. You see, when you get into business with me there's no going back; no rewinding to the beginning. Once I have you, it's either do as I ask or . . .' He leaned forward and stubbed out his cigarette, the last of the smoke lingering in the air in the back of the car.

'Bob understands how it works,' he continued. 'And when I asked him for information concerning you and what happened at the loch, he told me about Mr Cahill and how you now appeared very friendly with a certain lady detective. It doesn't take a genius to work out that you needed someone inside the police force to cover your tracks with Ellie.'

'Bob,' Logan said.

'Turns out he enjoys the money more than he does a clear conscience. But, listen, it's not his fault, so don't hold it against him. It's all me.'

Weiss spread his hands as wide as the confines of the car would allow. Logan saw the soft tissue of his throat exposed and recalled the training in personal attack and defence that Chris Washington had been giving him. His muscles twitched as he fought the urge to strike out.

'Back to your choice, though,' Weiss said. 'Do you want to hear this?'

Logan looked at him.

'I have no desire to harm that little girl of yours. Or you, for that matter. I'm content that the two of you live out the rest of your lives as best you can.'

Logan didn't know if he could believe what he was being told, or if he was just being set up again for a body blow.

'I mean it,' Weiss told him. 'But Mr Cahill is a different story altogether, you know. He's a professional and so he has to accept the risks that come with the job.'

'The bomb,' Logan said. 'That was you?'

Weiss nodded.

This was the man who had killed Chris.

Had killed Penny.

'And Leonard: he's in your pocket too? He set it all up with the watch and . . .'

'Of course.'

'Why?'

'Mr Leonard started his fledgling business with a loan from me when no one else would give him the time of day. So he owes me. And, like I said, when you get into my bed . . .' Weiss smiled.

'No,' Logan said. 'I mean why the elaborate frame on Alex? Why not just kill him?'

'Because uncertainty breeds fear,' Weiss said, leaning forward. 'And something like that, the bomb, was so terrible, inducing so much fear, that the man responsible would be for ever reviled. And his family too.'

Logan shook his head. Clearly Weiss *was* insane.

'You see,' Weiss went on, 'I don't want those people I mentioned to think that it's only death that I deal in. I want it so that they don't know what I'll do to them. Maybe I'll let them live, but ruin their whole lives. Or maybe I'll just kill them.'

Pause.

'Look, your choice is this, Logan. Option number one: you say nothing and you do nothing. Events take their course. Detective Irvine dies. Mr Cahill probably gets convicted and spends the rest of his useful life in jail. You and Ellie live happily ever after.'

'And option two?' Logan asked flatly.

'You go to the police and tell them everything: about me, about events at the loch. About what you really did to get your little girl. And maybe they believe you. Maybe Mr Cahill gets the charges against him dropped.'

'Except that we all go to jail for our part in the murder of those men at the loch, is that it? And concealing evidence; perverting the course of justice.'

'Just for starters, yes. Smart boy.'

'And even if that doesn't happen, they take Ellie away from me?'

'Can't have a man with your capacity for violence and deceit caring for a vulnerable young girl.'

Logan wasn't convinced that Weiss was correct about the consequences of choosing option two; and maybe the police would turn a blind eye to all that had happened. But he knew that however it played out, the road to be travelled if he went with that choice was not an easy one.

Yet how could he chose the first option and damn his best friend and the woman he . . . *loved?* . . . wanted to be with to death or worse?

He could not.

'Sophie's choice, Logan,' Weiss said. 'One or the other. Nothing else. Of course, if you go with option two, I'll have you *all* killed.'

Logan stared at him. 'So you're saying I have no choice at all?' he asked finally.

'There's always a choice. And there are always consequences.'

He laughed, and Logan thought that, for the first time, the joy was genuine.

3

Irvine pulled into a petrol station that had a small coffee shop inside. She thought that it would be a good place to collect her thoughts and get something to eat, and there were enough late-night travellers there to give her some hope that even if the men following her found her there they may not do anything more than just watch.

There was a selection of hot foods at a counter in the back corner of the place. She bought a bacon and cheese croissant, a cereal bar and a bottle of water and sat on her own at a table by the window to eat them. That way she could see any cars that pulled into the station.

The sound system was playing Classic FM. She was not really a fan, but it was easy to listen to and it filled the silence more pleasantly than the sound of her eating and drinking. She glanced along the road beside the garage at regular intervals, still feeling her nerve ends on alert and unable to relax.

After finishing the food, she went for a walk around the garage forecourt and started to feel a little better. The world felt less like some weird, nether place that was filled with killers and bombs.

She went back inside and ordered a coffee to pick herself up, expecting that she would be in for a long night whatever happened. Sitting at the same table, she called Logan to tell him what had happened. She hoped that he would tell her either to stop being paranoid or that he would speak to Cahill because he knew what to do in these situations.

Her relationship with Cahill was getting better, but remained strained. She knew that he was Logan's best friend and that he would always be close to Logan, not least because he had been instrumental in getting Ellie back from the men who had taken her. But his capacity for violence scared her. Being around him, she couldn't help but sense that he was always alert; always looking at the world in a different way from any normal person.

Logan's mobile diverted straight to voicemail and she left a brief message asking him to call her urgently. She was going to put the phone away in her bag when she thought that maybe he would answer his home phone.

'Hello,' a male voice answered.

Irvine thought that he sounded a little different tonight. 'Logan, it's Becky. You sound weird. What's up?'

'This is Logan's dad, Becky.'

'Oh, sorry. Is Logan there? Only I couldn't get him on his mobile.'

'No, he's not here. He had to go somewhere urgently. I'm looking after Ellie for him.'

'Do you know where he went?'

'I don't, no. He didn't wait long enough to tell me before he ran out the door. Can I tell him you phoned?'

'Please, yes.'

Irvine said thanks and ended the call.

She tried Logan's mobile again before giving up. The idea of calling Cahill direct occurred to her; talking to someone with the capacity to do harm to another human being might be no bad thing. She knew that Logan had been bulking up a little in the gym, getting leaner and stronger. And she knew that Washington had been teaching him, or at least trying to teach him, some martial arts. But she also understood that Logan was not the kind of man Cahill was. And maybe he never would be, or could be. However much he changed his body and learned the techniques, she sensed in him an innate gentle quality. Saw it in the way he was with Ellie.

In the end she didn't make the call. She didn't mind sounding crazy to Logan, but this might be a conversation that would permanently lower her in Cahill's eyes. And she got the impression he didn't hold her in the highest regard in the first place.

'She's not moving,' Two said to Hudson, looking at the GPS tracker he'd taken from Three.

'She doesn't know what to do with herself,' Hudson said.

'Good news for us.'

Hudson nodded, checking his rear-view mirror and seeing the car with Three and Five in it parked behind them.

The four of them had met up in the town and then driven after Irvine. When she stopped at the garage they had pulled up a mile away and waited to see what she would do next.

'Smart thing for her,' Two said, 'would be to check in to the nearest cop shop and not move.'

'Yeah, well, it's too late for that now,' Hudson said. 'No more playing it cautious. I need this thing done now and her time just ran out. When she gets back on the road, we take her.'

4

Weiss turned in his seat and motioned to the driver, who was standing outside some distance away, smoking a cigarette under his umbrella. He dropped the butt and ground his heel into it before walking back to the car and opening Logan's door.

'I know you'll make the right choice, Logan', Weiss said.

'Right for who?' Logan asked.

Weiss put a hand on Logan's arm as he moved to get out of the car. 'There are no perspectives in this,' he said. 'There is only the right choice and then all the other choices.'

'And *they* all end the same way?' Logan asked.

'This is how it has to be. If you make your peace with that, it'll all work out.'

Logan held his gaze, again wondering what would happen if he struck at Weiss. Maybe he'd be able to do some permanent damage before the driver could intervene.

'And this time there's no white knight to ride over the hill at dawn,' Weiss said, sensing Logan's resistance. 'Or if there is, I'll cut him in half.'

Logan turned and stepped out into the rain without responding. The driver closed the door and walked round to get in, nodding at Logan as he opened his door in a grim parody of courtesy.

Logan stood on the pavement watching as the car pulled out and moved away, gliding powerfully and quietly through the rain, water spraying from its rear wheels as it went. He tilted his face into the rain and closed his eyes.

I thought all this was behind us.

When he opened his eyes, the car was gone and the street was empty.

Looking up at the window of his flat he saw that the blinds were closed now, light glowing warmly behind them. He wondered what his father had thought when he saw him get into the car – especially after being called to look after Ellie at such short notice.

In the deepest recesses of his mind he had always worried that something about what had happened when he found Ellie would come back to haunt them. He didn't have any experience of dealing with men like Weiss before Penny's death, but he had hoped that giving Weiss his money would be enough. He had never been entirely sure that it would be.

And what to do now? If he did as Weiss suggested – threatened – then he would lose Becky, and Cahill would most likely be destroyed.

And if he didn't do as Weiss wanted?

Maybe they would all end up dead: victims of Weiss's own personal war. And Logan had no doubt that he would follow through with his promise to kill them all.

Or, maybe, they would pull together and see this thing out to its final ending. Because this was not a new situation; just a continuation of all that had gone before. Logan had committed to it one hundred per cent so far and saw no reason to depart from that course. No reason to desert his friends and family now.

And CPO was not completely disabled; Tom Hardy was still out there. They had already been up against the best that Weiss could produce and come out on top. Of course, that time they had had surprise on their side. Maybe they would have now as well – so long as they moved quickly.

5

Irvine was swirling the dregs of her coffee around the bottom of her cup when her phone lit up and an instant later the ringtone sounded. She saw that it was Logan calling from his mobile and grabbed the phone off the table.

'Logan,' she said. 'Thank God it's you. I've been trying to call.' She heard the tremor of emotion in her voice and didn't care.

'Becky. Are you OK?'

'Not really, I mean . . .'

'Wait. Just listen to me for a minute.'

'But I need to tell you—'

'No.'

It came out more sharply than he had intended, but had the effect of silencing her.

'The thing with Roddy,' Logan said. 'Those men were not after him. They were after you.'

Irvine opened her mouth to speak but no sound came out.

'It's about Ellie,' Logan told her. 'It's Gabriel Weiss.'

'What? But how?'

'I don't really have a lot of time to explain, Becky. Everything that's happened with you and with the bomb here – it's Weiss. He's coming after us. All of us.'

'But I was never involved in it. At least, not that he would have known. What's it got to do with me?'

'Bob Crawford's been working for Weiss; doing his dirty deals up here. Bob told Weiss about you and me. It wasn't hard for him to put it together from there.'

'My God.'

'Where are you now?'

'I don't really know.'

'What do you mean? What's happened?'

'I decided to leave and come home tonight. I was at a petrol station and I saw someone I recognised from the concert; from when Roddy fell. It just freaked me and I bolted. I mean, why would he be up here unless he was one of the ones after . . .' She was about to say 'Roddy' and stopped herself. 'After me. And I don't really know where I am except that I'm somewhere north of Fort William. I'm in a sort of mini service station. Thought it would be better if I got off the road and stayed somewhere public.'

She heard Logan blow out a breath.

'Can you call Alex?' she asked.

'I can't,' he said. 'Weiss framed Alex for the explosion. He's been arrested for murder.'

'What?' Irvine said, feeling panic start to rise in her.

'I'm going to call Tom,' Logan said.

For a mad instant she thought that he meant her ex-husband.

'He's got just as much experience as Alex and I know he can handle himself. I've seen it up close, remember.'

'Tom Hardy?'

'Of course Tom Hardy. Who did you think I meant?'

Irvine shook her head.

'Becky, are you OK?'

'No. I'm about a million miles from OK. I don't know where I am and there are men out there, professionals, who want to kill me. And they're between me and you and anyone else who can help me.' She felt claustrophobic; the rain was hammering on the window beside her. 'I'm scared, Logan. Really scared.'

He hated the way she sounded. Hated being so far from her; wanted to just pull her in and wrap his arms around her and tell her it would be OK.

'Becky,' he said, 'whatever it takes you will make it through this, you hear me? We'll make it through this together.' His throat felt full of fluid; drowning in his feelings for her.

'I'm going to come and get you,' he said. 'We'll work out where later, after I've spoken to Tom.'

'Logan . . .'

'I won't let anyone get in my way.'

'I love you,' she said.

He didn't reply. Couldn't reply.

'I don't care if you don't feel the same way,' she said. 'And maybe it's not real. Maybe it's everything that's happening, everything we've been through. I don't know. But it's how I feel right now.' She felt tears spill out on to her cheeks and wiped at them with the back of her free hand.

'I love you too,' Logan told her. 'And I know it's real.'

'Come for me, Logan.'

'I have to go now,' he said. 'I need to call Tom.'

'Go. Do it. I'm going to head back to the town. I don't think it's too far.'

'OK. Stay alive, Becky. You hear me? Stay alive.'

6

'What the hell is going on?' Logan's dad asked as he opened the door.

Logan came into the hall past him, trailing wet footprints on the wood, water dripping from his hair. He went to the bathroom and grabbed a towel, rubbing at his hair and face for the second time that night.

'Did you forget that you've got a daughter to take care of?' his dad asked, standing in the doorway looking at Logan over glasses perched halfway down his nose.

Logan dropped the towel into the bath and came back into the hall as his father was closing the front door. He looked into Ellie's room; saw that she was asleep. He pulled the door of her room all the way closed and motioned for his dad to follow him to the living room. His dad went to the fire and stood in front of it.

That was what Logan always remembered about his dad: the smell of fire. He'd been a fireman for thirty years while Logan was growing up, retiring on his pension at age fifty-one and then spending a year driving Logan's mum crazy by moping around the house. Eventually he happened on a second career as a driver for a chauffeur company. He didn't make much money out of it, but at least he was happy.

'So,' his dad said. 'What's the story?'

Logan moved to the couch and sat down, peeling off his wet jacket and letting it fall to the floor. 'I need you to look after Ellie for a day or two, Dad. Can you do that?'

His dad pushed the glasses back up on to the bridge of his nose and folded his arms. 'Why?'

'Can't you just do it without knowing?'

His dad moved away from the fire and sat beside him. 'No, I can't,' he said. 'Listen, son, I've stood at the side of your life for the past year or so and not once have I asked you about what happened with Penny and Ellie. I mean, what *really* happened.'

Logan looked at his dad but said nothing.

'I know when you're telling the truth and when you're not. Maybe you can hide it from the police because to you that's just part of the act of being a lawyer: never quite telling the whole story to everyone. But you can't do that with me.'

Logan rubbed his hands together, hearing one of his knuckles pop as he did it.

'And I've seen you change in the time since Ellie's been with you. You go to the gym with Chris and I can see you getting stronger. And I know that he teaches you some things because Alex told me when we were all here at New Year. I think maybe he was a little bit drunk.'

'I've always gone to the gym, Dad. That's not new.'

'But this is,' he said, grabbing Logan's arm and feeling the extra bulk of muscle under his skin. 'What are you doing that for? Who is it that Ellie needs protecting from?'

Logan stood and went to the fire, looking into the flames as they jumped and danced over the coals.

'It's not over, Dad,' he said after a moment. 'What happened with Penny and Ellie. It's come back and everything is at risk. Everyone is at risk.'

'Then go to the police and let them handle it.'

'It's not that easy. We had to do some things to get Ellie safe; things that have to stay hidden.'

'You mean stay buried?'

Logan sighed and turned to face his dad. 'Dad, I need you to be with Ellie. Please just do this for me.'

'And where will you be, Logan? She's the one you should be looking after.' He stood and pointed at the door and at Ellie's room beyond. 'What about your daughter?' His voice was rising in anger.

Logan clamped his mouth shut, grinding his teeth together. He felt all the emotion of the day hit him at once and his legs went weak, his head sparking with light.

'You don't understand, Dad.'

'So tell me. Make me understand.'

'I need more than this,' Logan said, throwing his arms out. 'I know that sounds selfish and petulant but it's how I feel. I can't help it.'

'What do you need? A woman? You think that's what you need? Maybe it's just what's behind your zip that's doing the thinking.'

Logan knew that his dad's anger was not directed at him, but at the fear he felt for Ellie. But it still stung.

'Don't do that,' he shouted. 'You had your life; your wife and your kids and everything else. I'm just as entitled to it. I've done my bit for that girl. Risked my life for her, Dad.' He stopped, fearful of saying too much.

'What did you do?' his dad asked quietly.

'More than anyone should have to. And ever since then I've given everything I have to make a life for her. For us. No one can criticise me for that.'

'You're right and I'm sorry. But—'

'No, Dad. There's no qualification.'

His dad fell silent.

'Becky and I have resisted what we've felt for a long time, and now that we're finally together I'm not going to let that slip away. I already lost Penny and I can't lose her.'

'So this *is* about Becky? You're choosing her over Ellie?'

'Christ, Dad, you know I'm not. I'm choosing both of them. Becky's life is at risk right now and I'm wasting time arguing over it with you. I have to go to her and that's all there is to it.'

'And who looks after Ellie?' His voice was rising again. 'Because I can't do it if there are bad people out there who want to do her harm.'

'I'll make sure someone comes here: one of Alex's team.'

'It's that easy?'

'No, Dad. It's *so* far from easy. That's what I'm trying to tell you. But there is no other choice.'

Gabriel Weiss saw to that.

'I have to go *now*. There's no more time. Will you stay and help me or not?'

His dad walked over and stood in front of Logan. He was a few inches shorter and had to tilt his head back to look into his son's eyes.

'Of course I'll help you,' he said. 'You know I will.' He turned and went to the sofa, picking up the phone on the table beside it. The embrace they had shared earlier was as much emotion as his dad could show, and there was no room now between them for anything else.

'I have to call your mother.'
'What will you tell her?'
'I don't know.'

7

Logan went to see Ellie. Leaving the door to her room ajar to allow some light in from the hall so that he could see her properly, he knelt beside her bed and lifted strands of hair out of her face.

She looked so different now from when he first saw her. It wasn't just that the injuries to her face had healed; she was older now, though the memories of what she had been through were still visible in her eyes. And she was changing all the time, growing up fast.

'We'll have our time together, Ellie,' he said. 'I'll make the life for you that Penny would have wanted. I promise.'

Sitting there beside her, the rest of the world melted away until it was just the two of them. And he felt a yearning so strong that he was shocked by it: to spend the rest of his life there with her and to keep her safe from harm. It would be easy to convince himself that she was his only responsibility and everyone else would have to look after themselves.

But he did not believe it.

He and Ellie would not have had their chance at this life without

Alex and Tom and Irvine and all the others. They risked their lives for Ellie, a stranger to them. And they did it because he asked them to. The debt had to be repaid.

But more than that, he could not lose Irvine as he had lost Penny, to these men of violence.

He leaned forward and kissed Ellie on her cheek and as he did so she opened her eyes. He smiled at her, unsure if she was really awake; knew that she was when she returned his smile.

'Hey, honey,' he said. 'Go to sleep, OK. It's late.'

She nodded, her eyelids heavy.

'I love you,' he said.

Her eyes closed, but a smile remained on her face.

He went to his bedroom and changed into a pair of combat trousers, a plain T-shirt and a black zip-up fleece. He grabbed his gym bag and stuffed an extra set of clothes in it. When he was done, he dialled Tom Hardy's number on his BlackBerry. Hardy sounded wide awake when he answered.

'Tom, it's Logan. I need to see you tonight.'

'OK.'

'Can you meet me at the building on Scotland Street?'

Pause.

'Is this about Alex?'

'You know what happened to him?'

'Yes, Sam called me.'

'It's about everything,' Logan said. 'Becky too. And Chris. Did you hear about him?'

'Yeah. I spoke to his wife. It wasn't easy.'

'So, can you meet me there?'

'Scotland Street,' Hardy said slowly, trying to make sense of what Logan was telling him. 'I take it that we need some . . . supplies?'

Always careful on the phone.

'We do. And I need someone at my flat as well. Just in case.'

'We're thin on the ground right now, but I can get Harry Shields there.'

'Thanks, Tom. I'll wait till he arrives and then I'll see you at the warehouse.'

'I'll be there.'

8

Hudson looked at his watch, feeling tired and angry. The cop hadn't moved for a while now and he was beginning to wonder if she would stay there all night.

'We got movement,' Two said, looking at the GPS tracker in his hand. 'Coming this way.'

'I was beginning to think she was settling in for the night,' Hudson said. 'If we're going to have any luck on this damn job maybe it'll finally be now and we can take her nice and easy.'

Two looked at Hudson and raised his eyebrows.

'Feels like I've been saying that a lot on this one?' Hudson asked.

He looked in his mirror again and saw Five get out of his car and walk quickly through the rain to get into the back.

'Where is she now?' he asked, wiping rain from his face.

'On her way towards us on this road,' Two said. 'Just over a mile north and closing.'

'Are we waiting for her to pass and then going after her?' Five asked. 'Should be a piece of cake.'

Hudson twisted in his seat until he was looking at Five. He

stared at him until Five looked away, then turned back to face the front without saying anything. Two stole a quick glance at Five, who shrugged at him.

Hudson pulled at the handle of his door and got out. He stood for a moment in the rain and then went round to the boot. He looked at Three sitting in the other car and saw him lift a hand in greeting. Hudson ignored him, found the latch under the tailgate and pulled it open.

Hudson's usual stash was intact so he reached in and pulled out one of his handguns, letting the magazine drop out of the hand-grip to check it and racking the slide to make sure there were no rounds already in the chamber. Satisfied, he pushed the magazine back in until it clicked into place, and got back into the car.

'We do it like this,' Hudson said, holding up the gun. 'That way there are no mistakes.'

'When?' Five asked.

Hudson lowered the gun, fighting an impulse to turn and shoot Five through his mouth and see the back of his head explode on to the rear windscreen. He decided against it, mainly because he'd only have to clean up the mess.

He was about to say 'Now' when his phone rang. He picked it up from the centre console and answered it with a curt 'Hello'.

'I think you boys had better get a move on and finish this,' Weiss said.

'Why is that?' Hudson asked, impatient.

'I just told them what's been happening.'

'What do you mean?'

Weiss sighed. 'What's left of the team in Glasgow after your little adventure there. I told them you were going after the cop.'

Hudson felt anger flush quickly in him; felt his head go light for an instant. Then he had it under control.

'Why would you do something like that?' he asked Weiss.

'Keeps life interesting,' Weiss said. 'Plus, I needed to let a certain person know that it was me that did this to him. That was always part of the plan.'

'It wasn't part of *my* plan.'

'Did I not tell you that part? Sorry, I thought I had.'

Hudson knew that he had been played all along. 'I think you know that you didn't. And I think that was deliberate.'

'You may be right, Carl.'

'Because I would never have taken it on if I knew it was *this* personal and that our identities could be compromised. It's not a smart way to work.'

'Oh, come on now, Carl. Don't be so self-righteous. I mean, you're a hired killer who is getting paid handsomely to do what you always do. Far more handsomely than anyone has ever paid you before. You're in no position to complain.'

Hudson closed his eyes and tried to breathe evenly. Weiss was at least half right: he had known that this job would be more risky and he had taken the big pay-day with that knowledge. But what he had not known was that Weiss was willing to put all of them at risk to satisfy a personal vendetta.

That was unacceptable.

'How are things with the cop now?' Weiss asked.

'We're just about to move on her.'

Weiss laughed. 'Where have I heard that one before?'

'Do you want it finished or not?'

'I do. Finish it now.'

Hudson ended the call, thinking, *You and I are going to have a serious talk when this is all said and done.*

9

'Less than a half mile now,' Two said, watching Irvine's car moving towards them on the screen of the GPS device.

Hudson turned to Five.

'OK,' he said. 'We're going to pull out and head south. I want you to get back in the car and wait. As soon as she passes, follow her. Then we'll box her in between us and you can pull out level with her and force her off the road. After that, I'll make sure it gets finished right.'

Five nodded and got out, running back through the rain to join Three in the other car.

Hudson turned the key in the ignition and pulled a U-turn, then drove south at a steady thirty miles an hour.

Irvine had seen a sign for Fort William indicating that it wasn't too far now: about twenty-five miles. There were few other cars on the road and she was glad of that, moving along quickly when the road allowed for it. She felt she was making good time.

She glanced at the side of the road as she whipped past a

lay-by, seeing a car sitting there with no lights on. She turned in her seat to see it, but was gone too quickly.

She watched the road behind in her rear-view mirror and saw the car's lights go on before it pulled out to follow her.

Not good.

'She should be past their position by now,' Two told Hudson. 'How long till she reaches us?'

'Any time now.'

Hudson's eyes flicked between the road ahead and his mirror, waiting for the cop's headlights to appear.

'Come on, you bitch,' he said aloud. 'Let's get this thing over with.'

Irvine pressed down on the brake pedal as she approached a bend in the road, looking in her mirror and seeing the car behind approaching fast.

As she came round the bend, she accelerated, wishing that her car was more powerful than it was.

She looked again in her rear-view mirror, watching the car behind for just too long. When she looked back at the road ahead, there was another car in front of her, its brake lights burning red in the dark. She had to make a decision – brake immediately or swerve round it and hope that nothing was coming the other way.

She went with the second option and pulled out to overtake. The car in front mirrored her manoeuvre and blocked her path. She slammed her foot on to the brake pedal and leaned back in her seat, her hands gripping tight on the steering wheel.

The rear wheels of her car lost traction and swayed out behind her, threatening to take her off the road and into the trees. Her police driver training took over and she steered into the swerve, pulling the car back level and slowing as the car in front did.

The car behind roared up and the driver switched its lights on to high beam.

Irvine looked in the mirror and then quickly away again as the lights flashed bright in her eyes. She realised that they had pulled a classic two-car manoeuvre, something that the police drivers do all the time.

She eased her car back over to the left-hand lane and the other cars followed her movements.

She knew that the one thing they were missing that would really have meant she had nowhere to go was the crucial third car, to complete the box with the trees rushing by on the other side of her. That meant one of the cars would have to make a move on her: force the situation. She anticipated that it would be the rear car, because they wouldn't want the front to open up for her, and if the lead car braked hard to cause a collision it was possible that she could clip it on one corner and send it spinning off the road and out of her way.

Hudson applied pressure to the brakes, seeing the cop's car draw closer in his mirror, wanting to slow her down because a high-speed collision was risky and unpredictable. He slowed further and saw the front of the cop's car dip as she too braked.

OK, he thought, time for those idiots to make up for their earlier screw-ups.

Irvine watched the car behind close up on her as she braked. This wasn't good, allowing them to dictate the speed. It would be better if they were going faster when they made their move.

She swallowed back the fear she felt rising in her and tried to draw on her driver training.

Time to take control.

She accelerated as sharply as her car would allow and moved up on the car ahead, hitting the bumper with a crunch that caused her head to jerk back against the seat.

Did it again.

Pulled out as if to overtake.

The front car accelerated and moved right to block her, the speed picking back up again. Behind her, the following car moved over as well.

'She's good,' Hudson said.

Two had his hands braced against the dashboard and looked back at Irvine's car as they all moved into the right-hand lane.

'Crazy more like,' he said. 'Jesus.'

Hudson saw a car approaching in front of him, flashing its lights to warn him to get out of its lane. He made a sudden decision to change the plan of attack, taking advantage of the circumstances that presented themselves to him.

'Let's see how she likes this,' he said.

He held the line as the car in front advanced on them, Two getting ever tenser beside him. At the last moment, he swerved back over to the left-hand lane.

Irvine saw the car ahead move sharply and the road open up. Then she saw the lights of the car bearing down on her; heard the driver press his hand on the horn and hold it there.

Instinct took over and she pulled the steering wheel hard to the left, her body tilting as though she was physically moving the car with her will.

Tensing, she waited to hear the screech of metal ripping through metal as the oncoming car ploughed into hers.

10

Five had not anticipated Hudson's move; was too busy concentrating on Irvine's car in front of him.

He heard the roar of the car engine a fraction too late; past the point where it would have made a difference before he started to turn his steering wheel.

Irvine's car veered into the left-hand lane as the approaching car's brakes locked, smoke from its tyres pluming into the air. She heard a faint metallic *shink* as her wing mirror was sheared off and spun away high into the night, then a loud crunch as the car passing her in the opposite direction slammed into the offside rear quarter panel of the one behind, caught mid-manoeuvre in its desperate attempt to regain the left-hand lane.

She looked in her mirror and saw the car that had gone past her skid off the road and into the trees.

The car following her rocked from the collision and was shunted into the side of the road.

Five looked up and saw the cop's car receding in the distance.

He pushed his foot down on the accelerator, intending to pull back out on to the road and catch her.

The engine roared and screeched but the car would not move.

He shifted to second gear and again tried to gun the engine. All he got was the same screeching sound.

'What the fuck was he doing?' Three shouted. 'Could've killed us.'

'I don't think he'd have lost any sleep if he had,' Five said, shutting the engine down and opening the door to get out.

Hudson had seen the collision in his rear-view mirror; he heard the crack of the cars coming together and then the entirely wrong sound of Five's car wailing to no practical effect.

'What the fuck, man?' Two shouted at him. 'What are you doing?'

Hudson took the gun from his belt and pushed it into Two's face. 'This is what I'm doing,' he shouted.

Two recoiled, pushing at Hudson's arm. 'You've lost it,' he said.

Hudson smiled, put the gun away and looked in his mirror, seeing the cop's car slow down behind him and come to a stop in the road. Then her lights went dark.

Hudson braked and stopped. 'Now we're talking,' he said, stepping out into the road.

He stood beside the car and looked up the road at Irvine's car. She was maybe fifty metres away and he could hear the engine ticking over as the rain started up again, misting the air in front of him.

Hudson raised his arm and motioned with his hand for Irvine to come forward.

Irvine watched as the man she had seen at the petrol station stepped out of the car ahead and appeared to wave her forward. She frowned.

What's he doing now?

Her attention was drawn to another set of lights appearing behind her. She did not think there was any way that it could be the other car that had been trying to catch her, judging from the noise it had been making after the crash. As it approached she saw that it was a large Mercedes saloon.

The car slowed behind her then pulled past, the driver looking at her. He was a middle-aged man with a tie loosened at his throat; looked like a businessman coming back from a late-night engagement.

He continued down the road until he was almost level with the car ahead and then his brake lights came on.

'No,' Irvine said aloud. 'Don't do that.'

The Mercedes stopped beside the man standing in the road.

The man in the road turned to the Mercedes and bent over, like he was going to talk to the driver.

There were three flashes of light and simultaneous sharp *cracks*.

He had just shot the driver of the Mercedes.

Now the road was blocked; no way to get past the two stationary cars. Irvine almost admired his tactical brain.

Almost.

Hudson looked for a moment at the bloody mess that had been the man's face and straightened up. It felt good to get his gun off after all the crap he'd had to put up with on this job.

He heard Irvine's car accelerate and looked back up the road. Her car was bearing down on his position fast. He barely had time to react; looked like she was going to ram the back of the Mazda.

He started to move sideways and brought his gun up; fired at the car.

Fired again.

11

Irvine saw the muzzle flash as the man shot at her; instinctively moved her head while keeping her foot pressed on the accelerator and aimed at the back of the car ahead of her.

If there was no way round the cars, she was going to go through them. The Mazda that the men were driving was not large: a mid-sized hatchback. She was prepared to gamble on the weight of her Mondeo being enough. If both cars that had pursued her were incapacitated it would give her some breathing space.

She heard two more gunshots but nothing hit her car; handguns were not very accurate, she knew. Especially at night when both the gunman and his target were moving.

She braced for impact and angled her car slightly at the last minute, trying to hit the rear edge of the Mazda to move it out of the way.

It worked.

The Mazda spun and bumped against the trees at the side of the road.

Irvine's car continued on, the airbag in the steering wheel exploding in her face.

She held the wheel straight with one hand and pulled at the airbag until she could see the road ahead. Glancing in her mirror she saw the man walk into the middle of the road and the muzzle flash of his gun as he fired at her again.

The remaining wing mirror on her car shattered as a bullet tore through it.

Then she was round a corner and out of sight, still fighting with the partially deflated airbag and feeling like she wanted to throw up.

Hudson stared down the road after Irvine's car as Two climbed into the driver's seat of the Mazda and tried to start the engine. It coughed for a moment before it started. Just as Two was easing back in his seat, smiling, the engine faltered and died. He tried again, with the same result.

Two got out of the car and looked around at the glass and metal lying on the road and then at the dead man in the Mercedes. He pulled a phone from his back pocket and called Five.

Hudson went round the Mercedes, opened the driver's door and pulled the body of the man out and over to the side of the road where he rolled it down a short, steep hill. He went back to the Mercedes and looked inside. The interior was splattered with blood.

'It'll clean up just fine,' he said to himself.

Two walked round the car to Hudson.

'Their car is done,' Two said, nodding his head back up the road in the direction of Three and Five. 'It won't budge. Same with ours.'

'We'll take the Merc,' Hudson said. 'You get down there and cover up that body. Tell those idiots to push their car off the road out of sight and deal with anyone that's still alive inside the one that hit them. Then we'll go pick them up when we're finished here.'

Two looked from Hudson's face into the Mercedes and back again. 'We can't take that,' he said.

'Why not?'

'Well, for one thing, it's covered in blood.'

'We can wipe it down.'

'More to the point, when the driver doesn't show up wherever he's going someone is going to call the police and then the car will be marked well and truly. I mean, we can't risk getting pulled over.'

Hudson stooped and peered inside the Mercedes again. He straightened up and felt the weight of the gun in his belt; thought for a moment about how it would feel to grab it, put it to his own head and pull the trigger.

'Fine,' he told Two. 'Let's get this off the road before anyone else comes by and then you get our car fixed.'

They released the brake on the Mercedes and pushed it over to the side of the road where it seemed to pause for a moment before rolling down the hill and crunching into the inert body of its owner.

12

It had taken much longer for Harry Shields to make it to the flat than Logan wanted – more than two hours. Logan wanted to get word about Weiss to Cahill, so he called and left a coded message on Joe Shaw's voicemail for him to pass on. He spent the rest of the time pacing between rooms, unable to relax. When Shields finally arrived, Logan quickly introduced him to his dad and left with Shields sitting in a chair in the hall with his coat on his lap and his hand resting on the gun underneath. His dad saw this but said nothing, resentment still lingering from their earlier argument.

'I'll be back, Dad, don't worry,' Logan told him from the open doorway.

'Will you?'

'I have to be.'

It was close to four in the morning and the dark streets were virtually empty so Logan made it to the warehouse on Scotland Street quickly. He waited in the road while the electronically operated gates swung slowly open and then drove in to park beside Hardy's battered old jeep.

The rain was still coming down hard and Logan felt it cold on his head and neck as he stood outside the security door and punched in the entrance code. Hardy was waiting inside and nodded a greeting before turning and leading Logan to the armoury. Logan had been there many times for target practice, but still found it otherworldly; the smell of metal, gun oil and cordite unmistakable.

Hardy had laid out the gear on a table. Two Heckler & Koch MP5 sub-machine guns, SIG Sauer handguns, additional ammunition magazines and ballistic vests.

'Feels like we've been here before, Tom,' Logan said, recalling a similar night not too long ago when he had followed Cahill into the armoury for the first time.

Hardy nodded. 'You've been trained on the MP5, right?' he asked, resting his hand on one of the small rifles favoured by SWAT teams the world over.

'Yes.'

'OK, then. I've set them both to continuous fire mode but you remember what you've been taught?'

'Short, controlled bursts.'

'Correct. It's easy to press the trigger and hold when you're in a firefight, but you've got to stay focused or you're liable to hit something you don't want to, OK?'

Logan nodded. He remembered all of this from when Cahill had taken him through his training for the weapon. It was a very different beast from a handgun.

'Just the two of us?' Logan asked.

'There's no one else,' Hardy said, looking down at him.

'Will it be enough?'

'Logan,' Hardy said, sounding like a schoolteacher. 'One step

370

at a time, OK. You haven't even told me where it is that we're supposed to be going, what we're up against or what it is we're supposed to achieve. Let's sit down and have a coffee, and you can tell me everything first.'

They moved to the small meeting room that Logan remembered was where he first heard anything significant about the White Angel – Gabriel Weiss. He sat at the table and looked at the laptop that was sitting open on it while Hardy got two black coffees from a vending machine. He saw that Hardy had been searching the Net for news on the bomb and had settled on an article from the BBC website. The report said that Tara Byrne had been treated for shock and then released otherwise unharmed, and there was a video clip of Devon Leonard sitting comfortably in his London office and trying to look concerned.

'So that's where he went,' Logan said.

'What?' Hardy asked, coming back to the table. He set down two cardboard cups, steam rising from them, thick with the hot, bitter aroma of the coffee.

'Tara's manager,' Logan said, pointing at the screen where Leonard's face was freeze-framed. 'He must have gone back to London to plant the bottle.'

'You've lost me, Logan.'

'Sorry, Tom. Maybe I should rewind a bit.'

Logan tried to explain it all as logically as he could, starting with his meeting in the police station with Cahill and ending with his conversation in the Bentley with Weiss. When he finished Hardy leaned back in his chair and stretched his long arms above his head, looking even taller than his lean, six-foot-four frame.

When he was done stretching, he sat quietly in the chair and closed his eyes. Logan said nothing for a few minutes but as time moved on he began to wonder if Hardy had actually fallen asleep.

'Tom,' he said, when he couldn't wait any longer, 'are you OK?'

'Just thinking,' Hardy said, but did not open his eyes.

Logan waited and eventually Hardy leaned forward, placing his hands flat on the table.

'How much has Alex told you about our past?'

Logan thought for a moment. 'Not much, really. I know that you were in the army together but that's about it. I kind of assumed that after you came out you went straight into the close-protection business.'

Hardy shook his head. 'Very different skill sets,' he said. 'The army doesn't teach you the core skills needed for CP work. It teaches you how to kill efficiently and how to survive.'

Logan had never really thought about it before, but he could see that it made sense. Still, he was wondering what this had to do with recent events and glanced at his watch, conscious that Irvine was still out there alone and scared.

'Alex was twenty-eight when we left the army together,' Hardy said. 'I was a little bit older. We were kind of struggling with what to do next, you know, and I suggested that maybe we should apply to join the police force. But being a cop didn't really appeal to Alex that much.'

'So what did you do?'

'Well, we were good soldiers and that gave us some connections. I mean, army officers make good politicians. Or at least some of them do. Our last chief went on to become an adviser to the NSA – you know what that is?'

'I know what it stands for: National Security Agency.'

'Correct. So, anyway, he was looking for some veterans for a task force he was putting together and got in touch with us. Seemed like a decent gig so we took him up on his offer. And it worked out pretty well for a while, you know. We were soldiers so we knew what it meant to have a chain of command and how to follow orders. Plus, we got results.'

From the way he said it, Logan felt that 'results' probably meant that some bad guys were no longer around to make trouble in the world.

'Then what?' he asked.

'We got the call to join the Secret Service.'

Logan had only a vague understanding of what that particular organisation did, and said so.

'Basically,' Hardy said, 'we were the President's CP team. I mean, don't get me wrong, not everyone gets to guard the man. But we looked after some pretty important people: the VP, SecDef. People like that.'

He spoke in an even tone, not boasting. Like it was just a job. It made Logan believe what he was being told.

'Which is where you learned the CP skills, right?'

'Correct. And we met some interesting people along the way. People all over the world.'

Logan finally started to see where this was going. 'People here?' he asked. 'In the UK?'

'Yes,' Hardy said. 'Me and Alex were part of a small advance team that came over to London to make preparations with the British security services for a visit by one of our charges. We got to know some of the British guys pretty well. In fact, we even trained with them a little bit at Hereford.'

'Hereford,' Logan said. 'That's the SAS, right?'

'Yes. And others too. Have you heard of the DET?'

Logan shook his head.

'No reason you would,' Hardy said. 'They don't get the same publicity but they are real serious people. Or at least they were when Northern Ireland was still a major trouble spot. Soldiers trained to be plain-clothes operatives skilled in firearms, covert operations, extractions: the works.'

A light went on for Logan. 'And your experience here gave you the idea to set up your business in the UK, rather than in the States?'

'Yes. We knew that we would have a shot at being market leaders over here whereas there are plenty of guys like us in the States already. And it was actually the senior DET guy that suggested it to us when we were talking over a few whiskies one night. He was about to pension out and said he knew the right people to get us in under the radar.'

'So you could get this place kitted out without any questions?'

'That's part of it, yes. But also so we could get some jobs to start us off. Cover for HMG when they were a bit too stretched.'

'What's HMG?'

'Her Majesty's Government. Sorry, Logan. We tend to slip into the jargon too easily.'

Logan was struggling to understand how all of this was going to help them with the task in hand, and he said so.

'The DET guy I told you about?' Hardy said. 'He lives on Mull, not far outside of Tobermory. You know it?'

'Yes. You get the ferry to the island from Oban?'

'That's it. Which can't be too far from where Becky is. I mean, if she started out at Fort William, right?'

'I suppose so.'

'Look,' Hardy said, his Texas drawl coming on strong. 'We can at least direct her to a safe place until we can get there. I can make a call to my guy and he can meet up with her at the ferry. I mean, we need to get Becky out of her car because that's probably how they've been able to keep tabs on her. With a GPS tracker device most likely. It's how we would do it.'

'And your guy has what's needed to combat these guys?' Logan asked. 'He has guns, right?'

'No,' Hardy said, making a face like he was wincing at a sudden pain. 'He doesn't. Claims he no longer believes in those things.'

Logan frowned.

'He's, ah, a little bit eccentric,' Hardy said. 'But it's the best I can do at short notice.'

'What age is he?' Logan asked, suddenly picturing a stooped old man waving a walking stick at a gunman.

'Oh, he's still got all his faculties,' Hardy said. 'He must be fifty-five or so now and still strong as an ox. Just a little bit divorced from modern society. He has a phone, but that's about it; one of those old-school ones with the dial on it.' He made a circular motion with his index figure as if using the dial. 'Don't worry. If it comes to it he'll put himself between Becky and those guys.'

'And what if that's not enough?'

'Then we just have to get there on time.'

'So we're going after her?' Logan asked, the sick buzz of adrenalin starting inside him.

Hardy nodded.

'I'll check the ferry timetable,' Logan said.

'Good.'

'But what about Alex?'

'He's not going anywhere just yet, is he? And, anyway, he can take care of himself.'

'But getting Becky doesn't take us any closer to Weiss and he's the one pulling the strings. Even if we take out the team following Becky he'll just hire more of them and Alex will still be in jail. This time we know that we have to get to him; cut off the head of the organisation and kill it once and for all.'

'I know that,' Hardy said. 'I'm still working on it.'

13

Irvine stared at the entrance to the police station, still unsure if she'd made the right decision to come back to the town. The police were already sceptical about her story of hitmen running around the Highlands after Roddy and telling them what had happened now might just lose her all credibility.

She was parked in the station car park, thinking that it was safer to be here than trying to drive home through the night when she didn't know how close behind her those men might be.

She decided to hell with it and that she would just have to put up with the condescending DS Campbell until they found the mess up the road. She had grabbed the handle of her door to get out when her phone rang, seeming both incredibly bright and very loud. She was startled by it and knocked it on to the floor of the car, and had to scramble around to find it. She didn't recognise the number on the screen and when she pressed answer and said 'Hello' the voice that replied sounded distant and tinny.

'Who is this?' she asked, pressing the phone harder against her ear.

'It's me, Becky. It's Logan. I'm with Tom Hardy.'

'Jesus, Logan. You scared me.'

'Sorry.'

'Becky, hi.' Hardy's voice came on the line. 'We've got you on a speaker which is why it might sound a bit faint.'

'It's OK, I can hear you.'

'Do you want to talk her through this, Logan?' she heard Hardy ask.

'No,' Logan replied. 'You go ahead.'

'OK, listen, Becky. Time is probably getting a little bit tight on this so I'll be brief. These guys that have been after you probably have a tracker fixed to your car somewhere. That's how they've been able to follow you without always being right behind you.'

'That explains a lot,' Irvine said.

'What do you mean?' Logan asked.

'They found me, out on the road. I was heading back to the town when these two cars tried to box me in and force me off the road.'

'Jesus. Are you all right?'

'I'm fine, Logan. Just a little shook up. My car got banged up but I think they're worse off. My driver training came in handy and I managed to get out of there. Your tax money at work.' She tried to sound light-hearted and failed.

'So they might be very close now?' Hardy asked.

'I don't know,' Irvine said. 'Maybe. But I left their cars in pretty bad shape.'

'OK, we're going to come and get you, but there's someone who can help you not too far away and so I'm going to ask you to get to the ferry at Oban and head over to Mull. Do you think you can do that?'

'I think so,' Irvine said, thinking that it seemed a little over-elaborate.

'Good. I'll have my guy meet you on the other side, so you're on your own until then. Stay in public places where there are people around and you'll be fine.'

'Look, why can't your guy come over to meet me on this side? Or why can't you guys just come up here right now? I mean, I'm in the police station car park and I'm sure they would let me wait inside. I was just going to go in anyway.'

Hardy was quiet and Irvine wondered if they'd been cut off. 'Tom,' she said. 'Are you still there?'

'Yes.'

Irvine thought that maybe he was angry at her for questioning his plan. She didn't really know him very well, only through meeting him a few times with Logan, and couldn't read his mood.

'What if I just keep moving instead, you know?' Irvine said, thinking that an alternative suggestion might go down better. 'Drive down to meet you guys.'

'I agree with Becky,' Logan said. 'I mean, it's probably just as quick for us to meet halfway. Maybe even quicker.'

'You're both right,' Hardy sighed. 'I thought that I could get this past you, but obviously not. I should have been more open with you and I apologise.'

'What are you talking about, Tom?' Logan asked.

'Becky,' Hardy said, 'do you know what happened with Alex? That he's been arrested for the bombing in Glasgow?'

'Yes. But what has that got to do with . . .'

'What that means is that we need a plan that not only gets you safe, but one that allows us to get Alex out of the mess he's in as well.'

'I understand that, Tom. But I still don't see how that has any bearing on my situation. Or why I have to put myself at further risk to get on a ferry quite possibly with the men who are trying to kill me right there with me.'

'Those men are probably the same ones who were responsible for the bomb. Or, at least, they're part of the same team. And so they're our only link to the real bad guy. To Gabriel Weiss.'

Irvine was still confused, lack of sleep making her thinking fuzzy. She couldn't see where all this was going.

'Spit it out, Tom,' Logan said.

'We need at least one of these men alive.'

'So?' Irvine said.

'We need to know where they are going to be,' Logan said, finally realising what Hardy was proposing. 'Somewhere remote, so that we can plan to intercept them. Isn't that right, Tom?'

'Yes.'

'You're saying you want me to let them follow me; to lead them into a trap?' Irvine asked, her voice rising. 'To be your bait?'

'That's exactly what I'm saying,' Hardy replied.

14

Logan and Hardy sat quietly, waiting for Irvine to say something more.

'I know that you don't owe Alex anything,' Hardy said, when there was no response on the speaker phone. 'But it's—'

'Tom,' Irvine said, cutting him off. 'There's no way you can make this sound any better than it is so don't even bother to try.'

'Fair enough.'

The line was quiet again.

'Do you want me to do this, Logan?' Irvine asked finally.

'I can't ask you to do it, Becky.'

'So it all comes down to me?'

'Yes.'

Hardy looked at Logan and raised his eyebrows in a question. Logan couldn't answer him; didn't know what her response was going to be. He shook his head and stared at the phone, waiting for Irvine to reply.

'You're right, Tom,' she said, '*I* don't owe Alex anything. But Logan does. And so does Ellie. I guess that means I don't really have a choice. I mean, I haven't really had a choice since I helped you guys get Ellie back.'

What went unsaid: since she broke the law and played a part in the cover-up of the deaths of the men who had taken Ellie.

'There's no pressure,' Logan said. 'It's your choice, Becky, and no one would hold it against you if you said no.'

'This man,' Irvine said. 'The one who's going to meet me on the island. Do you trust him, Tom? Enough to put my life in his hands?'

'No. I trust him enough to put *my* life in his hands.'

'That's a difficult statement to argue with. I think you know that.'

'I'm not saying it to persuade you to do this. That's not my style. I'm saying it because it's the truth.'

Logan believed him and hoped that Irvine would too. They waited.

'In for a penny . . .' she said at last.

Logan couldn't tell how she felt about the choice she had made. He felt sick to his stomach.

'Tell me about your man,' Irvine said.

'He's a little eccentric,' Hardy told her. 'But he'll make sure you're safe. He's a retired soldier. Best of British, believe me.'

'I guess I'm not really in a position to be picky. What's his name?'

'Roger Purcell.'

'He has equipment to deal with this?'

Logan looked at Hardy, wondering whether he was going to tell her that Purcell had no guns.

'Yes,' was all that Hardy said.

'What's the plan, then?'

Hardy looked at Logan and pointed at the laptop in front of him.

'The first boat to Mull is at seven,' Logan said. 'It's just gone five now so you'll need to get moving and get over to the ferry terminal.'

'Get back on the road, in this car? With the tracker?'

'We need them to follow you. That's part of it.'

'I know it is. I was just talking to avoid the sound of silence. It makes me think too hard about what I might have to go through. Best if I don't think about it at all and just do it, you know. Do you want me to take the car on the boat or leave it over here?'

'On the boat. If they miss the first ferry they'll need to know where you went.'

'And how will she recognise Roger when she gets over there?' Logan asked Hardy.

'We'll tell him your car make and registration number,' Hardy said. 'And that he should signal you with three flashes of his lights.'

'Right.'

'Be safe, Becky,' Logan said. 'We'll be there for you as soon as we can. We'll aim for the next ferry after yours at nine.'

'OK. I'm heading off now.'

15

Logan stood up after the call to Irvine, anxious to get on the road.

'Where are you going?' Hardy asked.

'We need to move,' Logan told him. 'You said so yourself. That time is tight.'

'Sit down, Logan.'

Logan couldn't understand Hardy's attitude and told him so.

'Logan,' Hardy said, 'you're not thinking straight. First up, we need to speak to Roger and get him on board.'

Logan sat again and felt fatigue pull his shoulders down, as if there was someone sitting on them. 'Of course,' he said, rubbing at his eyes. 'What was I thinking?'

'After that we'll use the cots here to have a quick, micro nap; no more than half an hour but it's better than nothing. *Then* we head out.'

'Isn't Roger going to be in bed and none too happy to hear from us?'

'He doesn't sleep much. Touch of insomnia. If I know Roger, he'll be glad just to have someone to talk to.'

Hardy used his BlackBerry to find Purcell's number and paused before punching it into the speakerphone on the table.

'Why did Weiss do it?' he asked. 'I mean, why did he go all Blofeld and lay it all out for you; why not just let it happen?'

'I thought about that,' Logan said. 'And truth is I don't really know. I think that maybe it isn't enough for him to let us know about it after the fact. What he really wants is to torture us; make us feel helpless and then guilty that we couldn't save our friends. Couldn't save the ones closest to us. It's all about the pleasure he gets from the misery of others.'

Hardy nodded, his eyes fixed on a point in the distance: a point well beyond the walls of the warehouse and the shores of the country that he now called home.

'I know the type,' was all he said.

Hardy turned out to be right about Purcell; he answered the call wide awake and could not hide the delight in his voice when he heard Hardy's distinctive accent.

'Tommy,' he said in the typically clipped English of the officer class. 'How long has it been?'

'Too long, Roger. Far too long.'

'Well, we've all got lives to lead, haven't we? You youngsters have, anyway. Not an old fart like me.'

'Roger, you're only ten years older than me.'

'Old before my time, Tommy.'

'Roger, listen. I hate to impose on you, especially after all this time . . .'

'Spit it out, Tommy. Whatever it is you know that I'll do what I can.'

'OK, here goes . . .'

Hardy spoke quickly and outlined the situation as briefly as he could. There was no preamble or attempt at rationalisation for a story that would have seemed unbelievable to any normal person. Logan guessed that both of these men were used to such things.

'You can never kill enough of 'em, eh?' Purcell said when Hardy was done. 'There's always more waiting under the next rock.'

'True.'

'You know I won't go to the mainland?'

'I know, Roger. I'll get our woman over to the island on the ferry and you can take it from there.'

'What does she look like?'

'She's about five-six. Trim, with dark hair,' Hardy said.

'Blue eyes,' Logan added.

'Is she a looker?'

'Yes, sir,' Logan said. 'She is.'

'And you have a special interest in her, son? Don't deny it 'cause I can hear it in your voice.'

'I wouldn't want to deny it. And you're right.'

'It clouds your judgement. I've seen it.'

'I know that, but—'

Purcell cut across him. 'Tommy,' he said. 'You trust this lad to do right?'

Hardy looked at Logan for a beat before speaking.

'I do. And even if I didn't, I don't have a choice because we're all that's left.'

Logan smiled at Hardy's honesty.

'Good enough for me,' Purcell said.

'Roger,' Hardy said, 'the men who are following her probably have a tracker on her car but we don't know if they'll be close enough to be there when she boards the ferry. So unless you see them when the boat docks you'll need to take her car rather than your own to your place so that they can still follow.'

'A tracker sounds about right. If they are professionals.'

'We can't get there in time for the first boat,' Logan said. 'And the next one is at nine. We'll be a couple of hours behind you.'

'So,' Purcell said. 'I'm going to be putting myself in harm's way.'

'Yes,' Hardy replied. 'You'll be on your own for a while.'

'It won't be the first time.'

'You understand that these guys are just the hired guns, right?'

'I do.'

'Alex is in jail because they set him up to take the fall for the bombing. Killing all of them won't get him out of that jam. We need to be smarter than that. We need to go after the guy at the top.'

'That's why you need to set the trap, with your woman right in the middle of it? To take someone alive?'

'Yes.'

'You don't trust the plods to do this?'

Hardy laughed without humour. 'No,' he said. 'They're generally useless at this kind of thing and they're not trained for it.'

'I don't disagree. But, tell me, what's on your mind if we do succeed in taking one of the foot soldiers into captivity?'

Hardy rubbed at the stubble on his chin, not wanting to appear foolish in front of Purcell.

'Come on,' Purcell said. 'We're all friends here. Spit it out.'

'How much do you know about Echelon?'

'I know enough to tell you that it's not as sophisticated or as far-reaching as the media would have you believe.'

'So tell me what you do know.'

'It's a signals intelligence network which the UK and the US, amongst others, operate to intercept communications all over the world. Primarily with the aim of combating terrorism.'

Logan listened in silence, feeling the way he did when they were planning the rescue of Ellie: like a little boy playing at soldiers who suddenly realises that it's not a game any longer.

'Is it sophisticated enough to be able to monitor mobile phone transmissions in this country?' Hardy continued.

'You boys still taking the batteries and memory cards or whatever they're called out of your mobiles?'

Hardy heard Purcell laugh. 'Yes,' he said.

'And so you should.'

'Does that mean that Echelon can monitor the transmissions?'

'Yes. But how does that help you?'

'To run the operation in Glasgow they would have had to communicate somehow and I'm guessing it would be via cloned mobile phones that they would use only for this job and then destroy. That way they don't leave a lasting trace.'

'I agree.'

'So I was thinking that if we . . . if *you* knew someone in or close to the Echelon operation in the UK who would be able to check the records and capture some of the chatter over their mobiles it would maybe give us enough evidence to clear Alex. Or at least give us a place to start.'

'His name still carries a little weight in the corridors of power, you know.'

'So does yours. And if we can get anything from Echelon maybe it will be enough for someone in HMG to have a word in the right ear and pull the charges against him. They won't believe that he did it anyway, but they will need something concrete.'

Purcell was quiet for a little while. Although he did not use, in fact despised, mobile phones, his previous job meant that he had to know how the technology worked. Hardy wondered if Purcell was coming to the same conclusion that he had.

'To do what you're suggesting and achieve the desired goal,' Purcell said, 'we would need at least one and preferably more of those phones so that we have the numbers they were using.'

'Correct.'

'And the reason you want one or more of the men who has been operating them to be still breathing and able to function as a human being is in case the phones are security protected or there's some code that needs deciphering.'

'Again, correct.'

'Which leads us right back to where we started – setting the trap.'

'I can't ask you to do this if you don't want to, Roger. You know that.'

'I would not expect you to have to, Tommy. It would be vulgar and beneath both of us for you to have to remind me of my obligations to you and Alex.'

Hardy said nothing.

'I'll be your trap.'

'Thanks, Roger.'

'I can waste time on the drive to my place,' Purcell said. 'Give you boys a chance to catch up a bit. Maybe even stop off for some breakfast with the lady. If she *is* a looker then it would be my pleasure.'

Logan smiled.

'That's still going to mean I'll have time to kill, so to speak, before you boys can get here.'

'It's not without risk,' Hardy said. 'For both of you.'

'Tommy,' Purcell said. 'You know me. I haven't had this much fun in years. It'll be good to get one last fright.'

part six: hunted

1

Irvine sat in her car in the line for the Mull ferry, waiting for the crew to finish preparations for the first voyage of the day so that she could roll on, get her car secured and then find something to eat.

She had followed the signs for Oban and got there not long after six; first in line. The boarding operation was a very civilised affair with cars lined up in a grid so that everyone knew their place in the queue. She had taken some time after she arrived to get out of the car and wander up and down looking to see if she recognised any of the cars from last night. She was pleased not to see them.

The rain had eased to no more than a light drizzle, but it was persistent, nagging at her whenever she got out of the car. She had the heater turned up but found it difficult to get warm.

Her phone chirped to life, displaying Logan's mobile number.

'We're getting ready to head out after you,' Logan said, no time being wasted on formal greetings. 'Have you made it to the ferry yet?'

'Yes. I'm there now.'

'Any sign of them?'

'Not so far, no.'

'We should be there in plenty of time for the next ferry at nine.'

'Hope you booked online to get your discount.'

Logan was amazed that she was so calm. 'This will all work out,' he said.

'I believe you.'

Over a hundred miles south-east, Hardy and Logan packed their gear into the rear of Hardy's jeep, Hardy finishing by throwing a canvas sheet over the small pile of equipment.

'How good is this guy?' Logan asked. 'Purcell, I mean. Is he up to this? I mean, if he has to hold them off before we get there?'

Hardy squinted at Logan in the glare from the powerful halogen security light fixed to the outside wall of the warehouse. 'He's up to it. Believe me. She's in good hands, Logan.'

Logan nodded, satisfied with the response. They got in the car and Hardy slid the key into the ignition. 'Do you love her?' he asked.

Logan paused and the security light went off, leaving them in darkness.

'I think I do,' he said finally. 'Yes.'

He couldn't see Hardy's face in the dark, but saw his head nod once before he turned the key and the engine rumbled to life.

Logan remembered how Hardy had looked when he first met him: worn down by the business of war and the tragedy that he had seen. But in the time since their rescue of Ellie he had seen him change; had seen the fatigue slowly ebb away to be replaced by something else. And in the moment before the light had gone out he realised what it was that gave Hardy his reason to go on; it was the job he loved more than anything else.

'You're a good man, Tom,' Logan said. 'Don't let anyone ever tell you any different.'

Hardy turned his face to Logan, his features lit now by the reflection of the car's headlights against the warehouse walls. 'I underestimated you when we first met, Logan. I thought you were just some soft lawyer and that Alex was crazy for putting his life on the line for you. And for asking me and the rest of the team to do the same.'

'You never said anything at the time.'

Hardy shrugged. 'I did it for Alex. Like I've always done.'

'It doesn't change what I just said.'

'This time,' Hardy said, 'I'm doing it for you.'

2

'She's been in the same place for about half an hour now,' Two said to Hudson.

Hudson was driving the Mazda with Two beside him and Five and Three in the back. He looked at them in the rear-view mirror, Three's eyes darting off to the side when they locked with his.

Repairing the car on the fly by the side of the road had proved challenging and time-consuming. And Hudson knew that when dawn finally came it wouldn't be too long before the three wrecks (and the bodies that went with them) would be discovered. He needed to get this finished quickly.

'How far?' Hudson asked.

'Couple of miles or so.'

'What is she doing? Why isn't she running? I thought she would have been back in Glasgow by now.'

Two shrugged, then pointed to a left-hand turn in the road for Hudson to take. As they came round the corner, they saw a signpost for Oban and beside it a picture representing the ferry.

'You think she's heading for the boat?' Two asked. 'Trying to put the water between us?'

'Smart move if she is. It would probably give her a few hours' breathing space.'

'Where does it go from here, the boat?'

'How should I know? Why don't you go online on your phone and check.'

'Can't,' Two said. 'We just got these basic phones. No internet access.'

'I'm beginning to think she's more resourceful than we anticipated. Either that or just plain lucky.'

Hudson pressed down on the accelerator, urging the car to move on. If she was able to get on the boat ahead of them and cross the water to wherever it was she was going, then . . .

He knew that the boss would not find any outcome other than her death acceptable.

There was no option but to keep going.

3

Irvine drove on to the ferry and waited for a steward in a luminous work vest to signal to her that it was all right to get out of her car. When she stood up, she looked back and saw from the volume of traffic boarding that the boat was likely to be full. Which meant that if the men who were following her were going to get on they would be stuck at the back.

The guy in the luminous vest was pointing at the door to the side and telling her to get off the car deck. She smiled tightly at him and did as she was told.

The stairs up were narrow and the interior of the boat painted in plain colours. Even when she got to the main covered seating area there were few or no home comforts, though there was at least a small serving hatch selling drinks and basic snacks.

Irvine went up to the top deck and sat in the chill morning air, thankful that at least it had stopped raining for now. The other passengers were a mixture of all sorts: businessmen in suits, families and what looked like foreign backpackers. After five minutes she decided to go back inside and get something hot to drink.

She stood at the back of the queue that had formed at the refreshment hatch and checked her watch. It was almost time for the ferry to move. She looked around again and was relieved still to see no one that she recognised.

The milk she got to accompany her tea was horrible long-life stuff in tiny plastic containers and the tea itself looked as if it had been left to stew for at least half an hour. She sat at one of the tables by the window and poured the milk into her tea. As she lifted the plastic cup to her mouth she felt the boat shift and saw the landscape outside begin to move by slowly as the ferry left the dock and started to turn.

The tea was strong and hot, though not particularly tasty. But it was just what she needed after the last night. She snapped a Kit-Kat in two and ate it slowly, savouring the chocolate and washing it down with the last of her tea.

The boat was starting to gather speed when she finished and put her rubbish in a bin by the refreshments hatch. Feeling a little better, she decided to go back out on to the deck and try to enjoy the rest of the hour-long journey.

The slow progress of the ferry meant that the view did not change very much, and after a while, with the cold wind biting at her exposed face, Irvine stood and turned to go back inside. As she opened the door she saw a shaven-headed man standing with his back to her waiting in the refreshment line. He was talking intensely to another man.

Irvine could not be certain, but it looked as if it might be the man from the concert and the petrol station. She stood in the open doorway and stared at him, unable to make a decision on what to do next.

'Hey, lady,' a male voice shouted to her from a bench seat to her left. 'Close the door, would you? It's cold out there.'

The two men in front of her turned and she saw that it *was* him. He looked at her for a moment, maintaining eye contact the whole time, and then turned back to his companion as they shuffled forward in the queue.

'The door,' the voice to her left said again.

She turned and saw a man sitting with his leg up on the bench as if resting an injury. He had a swollen top lip and a cut that extended from just below his nose to halfway down his chin. The man beside him was the one who had asked Irvine to close the door. He was looking at her in a way that made her feel very uncomfortable, and she recognised them as the men from that night in the hotel car park.

It seemed so long ago now.

'In or out?' he asked her.

Irvine stepped back on to the deck and allowed the door to swing shut. Through the glass she saw the man with the shaved head turn his face to her. He watched with a blank expression as she backed away from the door. Irvine moved slowly until she felt the hard wooden back of one of the deck seats against her legs telling her she could go no further.

The man continued to stare at her through the glass door and then, just before turning away from her, he nodded.

Irvine pulled her jacket tight to her body and looked out over the wide expanse of water.

I hope Purcell lives up to his billing.

4

Cahill had slept in far worse conditions than his cell in the Helen Street station. Many times, in fact. But that had always been by choice and he had been able to exercise some sort of control over his environment and the events going on around him. This time he had no control and that made for a restless night for him.

The lawyer Logan had talked about had come to see him and he seemed like an able kind of guy. Cahill had nothing against him; it was just that he knew it would take more than a lawyer to get him out of this. He had to hope that Logan and Hardy had worked out what they were going to do.

He was wide awake when the man-mountain sergeant came to get him at seven-thirty the next morning.

'Your transport awaits, dickhead,' the sergeant said, smiling at him.

Cahill stood as two private Reliance security guards came into the cell, cuffed him and then walked him out of the station to a waiting van in the courtyard. Everything's privatised these days, he thought, even the prison transports.

There were two other prisoners in the van already when Cahill got in, neither of them older than nineteen and both trying their best to look tough. One of them was making not too bad a job of it and Cahill decided that he'd have to keep an eye on him.

It wasn't far to the Sheriff Court, but rush-hour traffic made for slow going. Cahill no longer had a watch on, but he thought that it must have taken about half an hour to make the trip before the van slowed and came to stop.

Outside, he saw that the van had descended a steep ramp from the guarded entrance to the court at street level and walls stretched high above him. He shuffled along last in the line into a dark corridor in the basement of the building. It was lined with barred cells where the prisoners waited until their case was called.

The three of them from the van were put together in a cell on the right, along with four other inhabitants. Most of them didn't look much older than Cahill's travel companions and sported an assortment of tattoos. Two of them had prominent facial scars from knife attacks. Cahill had seen better sutures applied by an overworked army field-surgeon verging on a breakdown than these guys had received, so uneven and jagged were the scars.

Everyone did their best to avoid eye contact and Cahill was no exception. The last thing he wanted was to get into it with one of these thugs. Not that he couldn't handle himself; he just didn't want a serious assault charge hanging over him in addition to everything else.

The cell door clanked shut.

Cahill waited.

5

Logan managed to get some broken sleep in the jeep on the way to the ferry terminal at Oban. Hardy drove fast and assuredly, always right on or just above the speed limit. They made good time, arriving shortly after eight.

They were third in line and got out of the car to stretch in the grey morning, breathing deep lungfuls of the sea air.

'Lucky they don't do metal-detectors or hand searches of the cars,' Hardy said as he leaned over to stretch out his hamstring muscles.

'I don't think Mull is seen as a prime terrorist target,' Logan said.

Hardy smiled and then stood to his full height and stretched his arms above his head before rolling his head to loosen his neck.

Logan looked out to sea. 'Do you think they'll have reached the landing on the other side yet?'

'Yes. If it's running on time.'

'I thought maybe Becky would have called.'

'Be surprised if there's any phone signal, at least on the trip over. And probably the coverage is not that great on the island.'

Logan nodded, lines crinkling his forehead.

'Don't worry,' Hardy told him. 'Roger is a man of his word. He'll look after her.'

They got bottles of water from the jeep and stood on the dock drinking as other cars slowly started to form up in a line behind them. Hardy had an old khaki army cap on and pulled it low over his head as the drizzling rain turned to a fine mist.

Logan wondered if there would ever be a time when they were free from the repercussions of what happened eighteen months ago. Maybe all of this was an echo of his break-up from Penny. It seemed to Logan that it was Penny leaving him that day almost fourteen years ago that ultimately led everyone down the road to Loch Awe, to Ellie and now to here. Were they damned to be always running just to catch up?

'What's up?' Hardy asked, reading his face and screwing the cap back on his bottle of water.

'I was just thinking,' Logan said. 'About how we got here and whether it will ever be over.'

'And?'

Logan turned his face to Hardy. 'I don't know, Tom. I really don't.'

Hardy nodded and clapped a hand on Logan's back. 'We're gonna finish it this time. Otherwise there's no point in us being here.'

'Or Becky putting herself in harm's way.'

6

Irvine was still out on the deck when the boat started to slow and the announcement came over the PA system that they would be docking soon and everyone should get to their cars. She moved quickly to join the massed ranks of passengers shuffling down the stairway to the car deck below, happy that for now at least there was safety to be had in the crowd.

She sat in her car with the doors locked and watched the rest of the passengers work their way to their vehicles. The four men were last in line and stared over at her before moving to their own car at the back of the boat.

Irvine assumed that there would be a large area on this side where cars congregated for the outward-bound ferry, so she would drive round that until she saw the signal from Purcell. There would be too many people about for the four men to try to take her there: too public. She felt reasonably secure for now at least.

When the boat finally came to a rest, the doors in front of her opened, flooding weak light into the interior. She drove out slowly, following the directions of the stewards, tension knotting in her stomach as she bumped down on to the tarmac. She tried to take deep breaths but it didn't help.

She quickly scanned the waiting area for a car flashing its lights but saw none. Some of the cars coming off the ferry were turning in for a brief stop before travelling on. She did the same and saw a lone car parked at the far north of the area. She drove through the traffic towards it and as she passed the last vehicle in front of her the lights of the lone car flashed quickly three times. She felt herself relax and drove forward to park beside it.

The driver of the car nodded at her before getting out and walking round to meet her. Irvine opened her door and stood behind it: a shield just in case.

The man stopped not far from her. He was just under six feet tall with a lean frame and long hair that looked as if it hadn't seen a brush or a comb in a few days. He had the wind-blown complexion of someone who enjoyed being outdoors whenever possible.

'I'm Roger,' he said. 'I take it that you're Rebecca?'

Irvine nodded. 'So what do we do now?' she asked.

Purcell paused and turned to scan the stationary cars in the waiting area. Irvine waited.

'OK,' he said, turning back to her. 'I see our boys are here, then.'

'How do you know?'

He smiled. 'Practice.'

He stepped forward and held out his hand. Irvine reached into the car and grabbed her bag before closing the door and taking it, feeling comforted by the hard, calloused palm.

'We'll take my car,' Purcell said.

Irvine didn't know what to say so just nodded and smiled, feeling like a child again, going for a quiet morning drive with her father to get ice cream and sweets. He took her bag and put it in the boot of his Saab and then got into the driver's seat beside her.

'I'm going to level with you,' he said, twisting in his seat to face her and looking serious.

'OK. I've been through a lot so I can take it.'

He took her hands in his. 'Your man Logan was right. You *are* a looker.'

Irvine didn't know quite how to take that, and blushed. Purcell went on without pause.

'Tommy tells me that we need to put an end to this thing and the only way to do it is to draw these fellows in and take at least one of them alive.'

Irvine nodded. Purcell was watching her reaction closely.

'You have guns and stuff for this, right? I mean we'll need those kinds of things.' He pursed his lips. 'We'll do fine,' was all he said. 'Shall we get going?'

Irvine wasn't quite sure what he meant by that, but she let it go and said yes.

Purcell winked at her. 'Forward march,' he said, twisting the key in the ignition and revving the powerful engine of the car.

7

'What's this guy up to?' Hudson asked Two, following Purcell's car at a moderate forty miles an hour, a small queue of cars forming up behind them. 'I mean, he picked us out at the ferry car park and now it's like he doesn't even want to try to lose us. I don't get it.'

'Beats me,' was all Two said.

'Maybe he's a nobody,' Three said from the rear seat. 'Never been in the game, you know?'

'He's been in the game all right,' Hudson said. 'He definitely spotted us and he knows we're here.'

Three said nothing more.

Hudson knew that this job had unravelled way beyond a mere screw-up and that it was now a full-blown disaster. Here they were on a little island and now the cop had back-up. Professional back-up.

'I should've known,' he said to Two, 'that if someone is willing to offer top dollar for a job like this it's because the chances of its going badly wrong are pretty high.'

'She's been lucky,' Two said. 'Nothing more.'

Hudson smiled. 'How does that saying go? The more you practise, the luckier you get?'

'Something like that.'

'She's been lucky, it's true. But she's also been good.'

'Luck always runs out, though.'

'But ability doesn't. That's what I'm worried about.'

8

Purcell drove steadily along the winding road towards Tobermory, putting a Led Zeppelin CD in the stereo and playing it loudly. Irvine hated Led Zep.

Purcell tapped out the drumbeat to 'Kashmir' on the steering wheel, apparently oblivious of both Irvine's presence and that of the car following them. Irvine suspected that it was only an act and that he was well aware of everything that was going on around them.

He slowed the car as they approached a small roadside café and sighed when he saw that it was closed. 'Guess we'll just have to go into town instead,' he said, more to himself than to her.

'What's that?' Irvine asked.

He turned his head and looked at her as if he had only just realised that someone else was in the car with him.

'We need to give Tom and your boy time to catch up with us so we'll stop off for a cuppa. I was going to do it here but looks like it's shut.'

He accelerated again and then eased back when the speedometer touched forty. They continued at that speed until the town came into view. The buildings fronting the harbour were painted in bright pastel shades. Purcell slowed the car as they descended on to the waterfront and pulled in to stop in front of a café in a pale-blue building.

'Here we go,' he said, pulling on the handbrake and opening his door to get out.

Irvine felt that he was much too blasé about the whole situation; her own stomach was flipping around inside her. A cuppa was just about all she might be able to manage to hold down. She got out of the car and immediately felt the wind cutting in from the sea. Her T-shirt and sweatshirt provided nothing like enough protection against the cold.

She followed Purcell into the café, pausing in the doorway and looking back along the street as the car that had been following them approached. She stepped inside, out of view, and walked to the counter where Purcell was ordering two fried breakfasts and a pot of tea. 'Need to keep our strength up, eh?' he said, winking at her.

She was beginning to question Tom Hardy's faith in this man.

Logan tried to call Irvine from the ferry but though his phone was showing at least one signal bar none of the calls connected. He was frustrated and impatient and asked Hardy to try, with the same result.

'Must be no signal where they are,' Hardy said. 'Roger will call from his landline when he gets to the house.'

'What do we do until then?'

'Nothing except what we planned to do.'

Logan left Hardy inside and went out on to the deck. His fleece didn't keep the cold out but he was glad of that; he needed to be alert and the bracing wind whipping in off the sea certainly helped ward off any fatigue that he might have felt from lack of sleep.

He stayed out on the deck until he felt the boat slow for the approach to the dock and then went inside to find Hardy again. They both got coffee from the refreshment bar and drank it quickly before going down to the car deck.

In the car, Logan checked his watch and saw that it was almost ten.

'Alex will be in court soon,' he said. 'Then it'll be off to Barlinnie.'

'He'll be fine,' Hardy replied. 'Don't worry about him. I mean, he's been through a lot worse than that.'

'That's what he said.'

The boat's engines rumbled and the sound of the churning water was audible inside the car.

'Did you get word to Alex?' Hardy asked. 'About Weiss?'

Logan nodded. 'I told the lawyer to tell him.'

'How?'

'Just the two words. White Angel.'

9

Joe Shaw had come down to the holding cells in the basement of the court to see Cahill and go over again what was likely to happen at the hearing that morning. Cahill noticed as they were led to a private interview room that a lot of the court security officers and some of the prisoners knew the lawyer and he took some comfort from that; Shaw was clearly a veteran of this kind of thing.

Cahill had understood everything when they had spoken for the first time at the police station in the early hours of the morning, but he said nothing and listened again dutifully.

The lawyer was about to leave when he turned back to Cahill. 'Your friend Logan told me to pass on a message,' he said.

Cahill asked him what it was.

'"White Angel".'

It took a moment for the name to register with Cahill.

'Does it mean anything to you?' the lawyer asked.

'It means everything,' Cahill said.

*　　*　　*

He waited quietly in his cell until they called his name just after nine-thirty and then followed two Reliance guards up the stairs out of the basement and into the dock of the courtroom. His mind was buzzing following the message from Logan.

He was surprised at how small the courtroom was. He had been expecting some grand, vaulted ceiling. Instead, it was more like a meeting room in a nondescript council building constructed out of concrete in the sixties. The only things that marked it out as a courtroom were the jury box and the judge's elevated bench beneath the court crest on the wall.

Shaw had explained to Cahill that this appearance was in private and so there were no representatives of the press or members of the public in the room. This was not because of the nature of the offence that he was charged with; it was routine for all these types of hearing. Cahill recalled the lawyer saying something about his being 'on petition', but it was all just jargon to him.

He sat on the hard wooden bench in the dock between the two Reliance men. There was an older man sitting next to Shaw dressed in the full regalia of wig and gown: his QC. The man sported a magnificent grey beard that was stained around the mouth from tobacco use. Cahill imagined that it was from smoking a pipe, though the truth was his QC was a chain smoker of cheap cigarettes.

A door opened at the back right of the court and a court officer came in ahead of the judge, who was dressed just like Cahill's QC.

'Court,' the officer shouted, and everyone stood up. The judge sat and the three lawyers in the room – the two men on Cahill's side and the prosecutor – bowed before they too sat down.

The court clerk, who sat below the judge, shuffled some papers and formally called out the case name. He stood and handed the papers to the judge, who peered at them over his glasses. The judge was a small, rotund man who looked bored for the duration of the proceedings.

The prosecutor, an impossibly young-looking woman with short blonde hair and precipitous high heels, stood and read out the various charges. It was a long list and much more detailed than what had been said by the cops at the station when Cahill had been charged. When she had finished, the judge looked at Cahill's QC, who stood and held the lapels of his gown.

'I appear with the accused, m'lud,' he said. 'He emits no plea and makes no declaration.'

'Very well,' the judge said. 'Remanded. No bail.'

The Reliance guards motioned for Cahill to stand and then led him back down the stairs into the cell area.

'I was expecting something more,' Cahill said to them on the way down.

He got no reply.

They put him back in the holding cell where he knew he would have to wait until all the other prisoners had been processed.

So far, he thought, there hadn't been a lot of ceremony for something that might result in his being put in jail for the best part of the rest of his life.

10

Purcell attacked his breakfast with gusto, but Irvine had only a few forkfuls of scrambled eggs before giving up on hers and settling for some buttered toast with her tea. She spent the whole time looking out on to the street, half convinced that the men following them would burst into the café and kill them both in a hail of gunfire.

But the men did not appear at all through the hour or so that they took over breakfast. Irvine didn't know what that meant, if anything. Purcell had turned out to be not much of a talker, contrary to the initial impression he had given at the ferry dock. Irvine was beginning to wonder if he suffered from some sort of psychological disorder.

After paying the bill, he led Irvine outside and stood for a full minute looking along the street in both directions. Irvine did not immediately see the car that had been following them, but Purcell's gaze seemed to have locked on something at the far end of the street ahead of them. She recognised the Mazda and realised that all four men were sitting inside waiting for them to come out of the café.

Purcell watched the car, motionless.

'What do we do now?' Irvine asked.

Purcell said nothing. Irvine waited.

'I guess we go back to my place,' Purcell said finally, turning to face her. This time there was no smile or wink.

'And do what?'

'Wait.'

'That's it? That's the big plan?'

'The simple ones are often the best.'

'I hope you're right.'

Purcell unlocked the car and got in. Irvine stayed outside and took her phone out of her pocket, checking again for a signal and finding that there was no reception.

'No luck?' Purcell asked when she got in beside him.

'No.'

'We can use the landline at my place,' he said.

They drove along the street, the speedometer barely touching twenty miles an hour. Purcell glanced at the car as they passed by.

Irvine stared at Purcell. His eyes flicked to her. 'What?' he asked.

Irvine shook her head but said nothing. This is the man I've trusted my life to, she thought. I hope Tom Hardy knows what he's doing. I really do.

Purcell continued on to the end of the street and took a hairpin turn leading up the hill out of the town and into the countryside again. The other car followed steadily about fifty yards back. Irvine turned in her seat and watched it.

'Still there,' Purcell said.

'I don't like this,' Irvine told him.

'Nobody does. But it's not as if we have any choice.'

She faced forward again, clasping her hands together between her legs to try to stop them from shaking too hard.

'It comes for us all,' Purcell said, patting her knee. 'It's how we face it down that really matters.'

'You're talking about death?'

He nodded.

'I'd much rather not have to face it down at all.'

'What? Go quietly in your sleep when your time is up, is that it?'

'Something like that, yes.'

'Don't you think everyone wants that?'

'I suppose.'

'I mean, the boys out in Iraq and Afghanistan. The boys that were in Vietnam and Korea. The Second World War. The Great War.'

'I get the picture. But there's a difference, you know. They choose to sign up for it. Soldiers, I mean. I didn't.'

'Of course you did. You're a police officer, aren't you? It's just a different kind of uniform.'

'It *is* different.'

'Look, we're here now so there's no use crying over it.'

'I'm not crying. I'm scared.'

'I am too. I'm not stupid. I've just learned how to deal with the fear.'

'Maybe that's all that being brave is.'

'That and being prepared as best you can to face it.'

There was a terrible logic to Purcell's argument and Irvine had no more energy to debate it with him. She tried to relax back in her seat. Rain was starting to spot the windscreen. Irvine peered out and saw heavy black clouds rolling in above them.

'How much farther is it?' she asked. 'To your place, I mean.'

'Maybe ten minutes.'

Irvine looked outside as the clouds quickly darkened the sky, turning the day almost to night. 'Doesn't look like there's much around here by way of other houses,' she said.

'That's the beauty of it.'

'Normally I'd agree. But not today. Not when we really need people to be around.'

'We don't need just any people. Ordinary folks would be no use to us anyway. And Tommy will be here soon.'

'Soon enough?'

Purcell shrugged, but did not make eye contact.

Outside, the clouds rolled on over the fields and hills and the rain started to come in driving sheets, slapping hard against the windscreen. Purcell reached out and switched on the headlights before turning the wipers to their highest setting. They swished across the glass, barely able to keep up with the rain.

'Looks like a storm,' he said, peering up at the sky. 'A bad one too.'

Irvine didn't know if he was talking about the weather or what lay ahead for them.

Hardy drove off the ferry as fast as he could and turned on to the road leading to Tobermory. Logan drummed his fingers on his knees and looked anxiously up at the sky and the black clouds that filled it.

The rain started slowly, and then it was as if someone ripped open a jagged cut in the sky and all the water it was holding spilled out.

Logan suddenly didn't feel so certain about their plan: about Purcell and the trap they were setting. It didn't feel to him as though they were the ones in control. He said so to Hardy.

'Roger has certain skills that make him the best person for this,' Hardy said.

'What do you mean, Tom? Don't talk in riddles.'

'He wasn't just a soldier for your government. He was in black ops. Stuff that was done under the radar.'

'Are you saying he killed people for the government?'

Hardy shrugged. 'That's not what I said.'

Logan figured that he was being told to drop the subject.

11

Purcell slowed the car as it dipped over a rise and Irvine saw a large house sitting just below the brow of the next hill. It looked like an old farmhouse set back from the road along a driveway that was maybe fifty feet long. The front door was in the centre of the building with two windows on either side on both floors – almost exactly symmetrical except that the left hand side looked a little wider to Irvine. Lights were on in two of the downstairs rooms and smoke drifted into the storm from the chimney.

'Is that it? she asked.

'Yes. What do you think?'

Like she was going on a holiday: *Is everything to your liking, madam?* Was he for real?

'You don't like it?' he asked when she did not reply.

'You're serious? Really?'

He looked at her almost as if she had offended him.

'Listen,' she said. 'It's a beautiful house. But you'll excuse me if in the circumstances I'm not giddy with excitement.' Her voice rose more than she had intended; she realised she sounded almost angry.

'It's not like I'm here to relax and enjoy myself, is it?' she asked more softly.

'I suppose that's right. Still . . .'

Still what? Jesus.

As the car started up the hill, Irvine saw headlights catching in the wing mirror on her side of the car as their pursuers continued inexorably after them.

'How are we going to do this?' she asked, feeling the nausea of fear rising again. 'I mean, what if they speed up to us and go for it as we pull up at the house?'

'Don't worry, I've got electric gates. Big old iron ones. They'll have to come across the driveway or the fields on foot to get to the house.'

'And you're going to pick them off then?'

How unreal did that sound?

'No.'

'I meant with your gun.'

'I know what you meant. And I don't have any. Guns, I mean. Did I not tell you that?'

Irvine looked at him, unable to answer. How much worse was this going to get? 'So what the hell are we supposed to do? These guys *will* have guns.'

'You're right.'

'So?'

'So, I know that house inside and out. I've been a soldier and more for most of your life and I know how to kill a man without a gun. Know how to disable him and stop short of killing him. I know more about it than you would ever want to know.'

Irvine heard something in his voice. 'You're enjoying this, aren't you?'

Purcell lifted a small plastic handset from the door pocket on his side as they approached the gates at the mouth of the driveway and pressed the top button on it. The gates eased back and he slowed the car to allow the operation to complete.

Irvine turned and looked back. The car behind them had stopped and shut off its lights; it was barely visible now through the rain in the dim light of the storm.

When they were through the gates, Purcell pointed the device over his shoulder and pressed the other button. The gates swung back and clanked shut.

He pulled the car round in a circle in front of the house so that Irvine's door was closer to the entrance. Ever the gentleman; keeping the lady as dry as possible. She unsnapped her seatbelt and waited for him.

'To answer your question,' he said, facing her, 'yes, I am enjoying this. And I'll enjoy it even more once it starts in earnest.' Irvine started to speak but he held up a hand to shush her. 'Look, I know that my behaviour might appear a little odd to you, to most people. But we're each of us unique so you're in no position to judge me.'

Irvine watched his eyes closely in the dark interior of the car.

'The reason I thrived as a soldier, and after, was that I didn't mind the killing. I say it without shame or pride. It's just the way I was. The way I am. Which of us is without fault?' His eyes were flat and emotionless.

'I suspect the men in that car back there are the same,' she said.

He looked over his shoulder for a moment. 'No,' he said finally. 'At least not all of them. Otherwise you and I would not have met and you'd be dead right now.'

'So why do they do it?'

421

'For money.'

'And where does that leave us?'

'With an advantage. You see, I won't hesitate even for a fraction of a second and that will be enough. If the killing instinct isn't there people like me will always win.'

'Even if you don't bring a gun to a gunfight?'

'We'll see, won't we?' He pulled at the handle of his door.

'You've been in this situation before, haven't you?'

He winked at her again; the gesture of a madman. Only this time it was strangely comforting.

Logan was holding his BlackBerry up trying to improve on the single reception bar when the screen glowed brightly and an unfamiliar number appeared on the display, the handset vibrating in his hand.

He turned the face of the phone to Hardy, who glanced at the screen and nodded. Logan answered the call and heard Irvine's voice, aware of the tension that constricted his throat.

Feels too much like I've been here before.

'It's me, Logan,' she said. 'I'm at Roger's place. They're right outside.' The same fear that he felt was all too apparent in her voice.

'We're not too far away,' he told her. 'We're coming as fast as we can.'

'They'll come for me before you get here, I know they will.'

'We'll be there soon. You'll be fine.'

It sounded unconvincing even to his own ears and he hated not being able to say anything more than that.

'Put Tom on,' Irvine said. 'Roger wants to speak to him.'

Logan handed the phone to Hardy.

'Roger?' Hardy said. 'How do you want to play this?'

'Can't say, Tommy. I'll have to play it as I see it when it happens.'

'What do you want me to do when we get there?'

Purcell laughed drily. 'You do what comes naturally: kick the door in, shoot anything that moves. When the dust clears, pray that you didn't shoot either of us.'

12

Hudson drove slowly up the incline with the car lights off. He stopped ten feet short of the gates and looked at them through the rain that sheeted down from the charcoal sky.

'Car won't get through those,' Two said to him from the passenger seat.

'I know.'

'So what do you want to do?'

Hudson ignored the question and moved the car on, accelerating over the brow of the hill and down the other side until they were out of sight of the house. All that he could see was the grey slate roof above the thick grass of the fields.

'Two teams of two,' Hudson said, unclipping his seatbelt and turning to speak to all of them.

'The old boy's going to have firepower in there,' Five said. 'Got to have.'

Hudson nodded. 'We have to assume so. And he'll have been watching us drive by.'

'So we flank the house?' Two asked.

'Yes,' Hudson replied. 'You and me will go along the bottom of the slope on this side out of sight of the house and move up on the far side. You two' – he jabbed a finger at Three and Five – 'go the long way round on the opposite side so that you're never visible at any time from the rear windows of the house.'

There was no way that Hudson wanted to be partnered with either Three or Five for this kind of direct assault. He knew that splitting up into a weak team and a strong one was not ideal, but that was just the way it was going to be. Three and Five put them in this mess so they would just have to deal with it together.

'And then what?' Five asked.

'You go in the back and we go in the front. Take out a window but do it smart. Smash one window but don't go in it. The other one of you goes in through the one furthest from the first one you smash real quick and opens up if need be. Got it?'

They all nodded.

'Right,' Hudson said. 'Let's get it done.'

He opened his door and felt the full force of the rain on his face as he stood up to go round to the boot of the car, never taking his eyes off his surroundings and scanning all round just in case the old boy had decided to come down to them.

He got his other Glock handgun out of the boot of the car, slipping it into the waistband of his jeans next to the one already there. He tucked them under his T-shirt and jacket to keep them dry; the metal of the barrels was cold against his stomach. When he had done that, he pulled on his ballistic vest. Finally, he closed the boot till it latched but did not shut it all the way, keeping noise to a minimum.

'You guys head off first, because you've got the longest walk and you're a gimp,' he said, looking at Three. 'We'll signal to each other by hand where the side wall meets the back wall when we're in position. Then we move.'

13

'How far?' Logan asked.

'I'd say we're maybe ten minutes out,' Hardy said. 'No more than that.'

'Shouldn't we get ready? I mean, get the vests on and the weapons loaded?'

'No. There's a hill before Roger's house and I want to get there first. We'll be out of sight of the house and can approach from there on foot. Good thing about this weather is it'll largely mask the sound of our approach.'

'Is there time?'

'There's no time not to. We have to get it right. There's only one chance to do it. You know that by now, Logan.'

He nodded, aware that Hardy's plan was the right one. The only one. 'Then what do we do?' he asked.

'Same as ever. We adapt to the circumstances that present themselves. If these guys have gone in ahead of us, and we have to assume that they will, then we'll use their points of access. We don't have any comms gear or way of speaking to Roger and Becky covertly so we might just have to get noisy straight up.'

Logan understood the euphemism: shoot first, everything else comes later. He had never been directly involved in anything like this, in the first wave of an assault. Sure, he knew how to shoot and had been in the thick of it at Loch Awe. But this was different. This was proper soldiering and he was not a soldier.

'We're going in together?' he asked.

'Yes. That way we have cover. Going in separately with just the two of us would be suicide.'

Logan nodded. All colour had drained from his face, and Hardy glanced at him as the jeep pushed on through the rain.

'Don't worry,' he said. 'I'll be on point.'

Small comfort.

14

'Aren't you going to lock the door?' Irvine asked Purcell as he brushed past her, heading to the back of the house through the central hallway, motioning for her to follow. She walked quickly after him and watched as he unlocked the back door that led from the kitchen to the back garden. When he was done, he turned to face her.

'If we give them a means of access, then we'll know exactly where they're coming in.'

'Isn't it better to hold them off for longer?'

He smiled and pointed to a window. 'These things are single glazed. All it takes is a stone or a gun butt. A locked door gives us ten seconds at best. The tactical advantage of knowing where they are is worth more.'

'Won't they see it as a trap and use the window anyway?'

He shrugged. 'We'll just have to see.'

He went to the stove to check four small pots of cooking oil which were heating on gas burners.

'Boiling oil?' she asked, raising her eyebrows.

'I don't recommend it. Nasty stuff.'

Moving to a work counter, he slid two medium-sized steel knives from a butcher's block.

'Why not the big ones?' Irvine asked.

'They can be unwieldy. Better to have control than size.'

He took a sharpening steel from a drawer under the counter and worked expertly with both blades until satisfied with the cutting edge. He gave one to Irvine and kept the other for himself.

'If it comes down to it,' he said, 'go for anything soft. The throat is best. It'll be open and exposed and there's a lovely windpipe and some pretty important arteries. Don't be shy about it, OK. You stick it in hard and pull it sideways. That way you rip everything out.'

An image of Roddy bleeding in the alley flashed in her mind.

Purcell put a hand on her shoulder. 'No time to be squeamish,' he said. 'Now let's get upstairs.'

'We're not waiting down here for them?'

'And present them with an easy target? No. Never heard of the Spartans' stand at the Hot Gates? There's only one stairway so they'll have to come up that way. We can trap them in the narrow passage and defend that. We'll take the oil up with us and toss it down on the buggers. Aim for the face and blind them. Then we can get up close and personal.'

'If we have to,' Irvine said. 'I mean, if Tom and Logan don't get here first.'

'Of course.'

Irvine found it hard to believe that Purcell would wait; he clearly relished the prospect of the fight too much.

15

Hudson put his back against the side wall of the house and wiped the rain from his face. It didn't help much as the torrent continued unabated, soaking his clothes to the skin. Two came up beside him and Hudson peered round the rear corner to see if Three and Five were in place yet. He saw no sign of them but noticed that all of the lights in the house were now out.

So the old boy and the cop were getting ready for them.

Hudson considered the possibility of stopping the whole thing right now. Just sloping back to the car and heading to the ferry. But it wasn't an option. He did not really know the man who had paid him these past few years, other than that he was a very serious individual. Given what he had tasked Hudson to do this time, there was no doubt that he would not let him walk away from it without consequence.

He moved back from the corner, turned to Two and shook his head to let him know that the others were not in position yet. He checked his watch, waited for thirty seconds to tick by and then looked again for a signal.

Nothing.

Where the hell were they?

He repeated the same process twice more before he finally saw the signal from the far side of the house. He acknowledged it and then moved at a crouch with Two under the single side window on the ground floor of the house until they were at the front corner. He quickly looked round to the front of the house. There was no sign of any movement. He motioned for Two to follow him and stepped out, pulling his jacket up and gripping the handle of one of his guns.

16

Irvine waited in the dark of the main bedroom on the first floor of the house. Purcell was sitting out in the hall beside the stairs with his back against the wall and the four pots of still-smoking oil arranged beside him. His knife was on the floor between his legs. It was almost absurd and Irvine would have laughed if she had not felt so utterly terrified.

They had been like that for only a few minutes when the sharp sound of multiple windows breaking pierced the silence. Irvine sat bolt upright and stifled a shout with her hand. Purcell leaned over to look in on her and put a finger to his lips telling her to stay quiet.

Come on, Logan, where are you?

Irvine strained to hear and after a few moments could make out the sound of glass crunching underfoot. They were in the house now.

The sound of the footsteps on the broken glass stopped and the silence bore down on her again.

Purcell pushed himself slowly up the wall until he was

standing. He lifted one of the pots with his left hand and held his knife in the other.

Irvine stood herself and walked to the door of the bedroom, her own knife gripped in both hands.

Purcell turned to her and signalled with his right hand that she should get back into the room and away from the doorway. She set her mouth in a tight line and shook her head, no. He widened his eyes at her in exasperation, but she stayed firmly where she was.

She heard movement at the bottom of the stairs; wet shoes on the slate floor of the hall. The faintest of squeaks, but it was definitely there. She held her breath as Purcell inched towards the top of the stairs and began to bring the pot of oil round, getting ready to throw it into the stairwell.

17

Logan followed Hardy round to the back of the jeep when they stopped at the bottom of a small hill, the rain soaking his clothes almost immediately. He thought he heard a faint rumble of thunder in the distance.

Hardy pulled the rear door open and tossed the cover off the gear they had stowed there. They slipped on the vests as quickly as they could, then Logan waited in the rain while Hardy checked the guns. When he was done, Logan holstered his sidearm and hefted the small MP5 rifle over his shoulder. They started away from the jeep and up the hill, their feet skidding on the slick grass at the side of the road.

Hardy slowed as he approached the top of the hill and Logan did likewise behind him, trying to breathe at a regular rate to calm the blood pumping through his body.

Hardy crouched down and looked over the hill – then motioned for Logan to join him. He saw the house and the Saab parked outside. There were no other vehicles visible and no lights on in the house.

Hardy remained still and pointed at the ground-floor windows. Logan strained to see what he was being shown, and saw that two of them were broken.

'We need to move now,' Hardy said.

Logan nodded and they both ran forward at a low sprint, their rifles at port arms across their chests.

As they approached the house, Logan's whole body tensed, expecting the flare of gunfire to erupt from the windows and bullets to tear at him. But nothing came. They reached the perimeter wall, three feet high and constructed out of old stone, and crouched behind it.

'I don't see any movement,' Hardy said. 'You?'

'Nothing,' Logan replied, shaking his head.

Hardy frowned and stared at the house.

'What now?' Logan asked.

'We go straight in. Nothing else for it.'

Hardy stood and vaulted the wall with Logan following close behind. This time, as they ran, they pushed the rifle stocks into their shoulders and pointed the barrels straight ahead, ready to engage any target that came into view.

18

Irvine heard more faint noises; the sound of shoes on slate again. Then it went quiet. Purcell remained tensed at the top of the stairs.

There was a creak as the old wooden steps complained under a man's weight and Purcell moved quickly, swinging his arm round in an arc and tossing the oil down into the stairwell. He did not wait, but lifted another pot and immediately threw the contents after the first.

There was a loud shout.

Something flashed up the stairs; roared simultaneously.

Gunshots.

Then more.

Bullets thudded into the wall at the top of the stairs. Irvine pulled back instinctively as plaster and wood splinters showered her.

Purcell reached down for a third pot, blinking dust from his eyes.

Someone grunted on the stairs; hissed in pain. Footseps sounded on the slate, retreating.

Then the thump of someone running up at them.

'No.' A shout from below.

Purcell shifted his weight. More shots sounded. The corner of the wall at the top of the stairs disintegrated. Purcell turned his head to shield his face and dropped the pot. Oil spilled out on to the wooden floor.

A man appeared in the opening at the top of the stairs, his head flicking to the side where he saw Purcell. He turned, raising his gun.

Irvine shouted.

Purcell swept his knife up, slicing into and through the man's breastbone; he pushed the knife in hard as the bone broke with a crack.

The man's eyes opened wide; his mouth gaped. He dropped the gun and, as it clattered down the stairs, flailed uselessly at Purcell's hands. Irvine saw the angry red burns on his face and hands. The oil had hit its mark.

Purcell pulled the knife out and in one quick movement stabbed it into the man's throat and ripped it out sideways.

Arterial blood sprayed the walls.

Purcell stepped up and kicked the man away from him, toppling him back down the stairs.

Gunfire up the stairs; bullets ripping into the wall beside Purcell. He ducked back out of sight and smiled at Irvine, his face streaked in the war paint of dust and blood.

Irvine never wanted to see the look that was on his face ever again.

19

Logan heard the shots and saw the muzzle flashes illuminate the interior of the house as he ran beside Hardy.

Fifty yards now from the front door.

Shouts.

More gunfire.

Thirty yards.

Twenty.

Quiet now; no more shots.

Hardy got to the house and set himself against the wall beside the front door. Logan did likewise on the opposite side of the door. He looked to Hardy for direction.

'Wait,' Hardy said.

Rain dripped down into Logan's eyes. He swiped at them, desperate to know what the quiet signified. He saw Penny splayed out in her own blood. Her face warped and changed and it was Becky.

He closed his eyes and tried to shake the image from his head. But it would not leave him.

Not again.
Not so close.
Gunfire roared again inside.

20

The guns roared up at Irvine and Purcell: sustained.

Irvine ducked as more plaster exploded and dust plumed into the air.

Feet on the stairs; the gunfire to cover their approach.

Purcell, on his knees, grabbed the last pot of oil and heaved it round the corner just as another man reached the top of the stairs.

The hot liquid splashed into his face, his eyes and mouth. A scream gurgled in his throat.

Purcell snapped his arm out, stabbing repeatedly in short jabs to the man's chest and throat.

The guns below fired again.

Purcell fell back, shouting out.

The man on the stairs clawed at his wounds, unable to stop his life ebbing out in a red gush. He fell forward, his face thumping into the top stair and his body sliding back out of sight.

Purcell reached out to Irvine and she grabbed his hand, pulling him into the room with her and slamming the door shut. He clutched at his leg and Irvine saw blood pulsing over his fingers.

Footsteps sounded on the stairs as one of the remaining men closed in on them. More gunfire sounded, bullets taking chunks of wood out of the bedroom door. Irvine felt splinters in her cheeks, threw her hand up to protect her eyes.

Purcell lifted up a hand, showing Irvine the gun he had taken from the second man he had killed. He grinned, his teeth stained with blood.

21

Hudson went up the stairs, stepping over the bodies of Five and Two, not looking at either. Three fired a covering volley behind him; Hudson felt the bullets whip past him, the air contracting.

Three stopped firing as Hudson neared the top of the stairs. Hudson pointed his gun round the corner where he had seen the man who had killed the others and fired. But there was no one there.

Hudson was now on the final step, his eyes darting from side to side, assessing the terrain. A door opened just to his left and he saw the unmistakable form of a gun barrel. He had a split second decision to make: swing his gun round and shoot or drop it and hold his hands up.

He hesitated, aware that such a thing was usually a fatal mistake.

Nothing happened.

He peered into the gloom beyond the gun that was pointed at his face and saw a grinning monster, its face streaked in blood.

Hudson held his free hand up and slowly lowered his gun to the floor.

'Boss?' Three shouted from below.

The man in the room extended a hand dripping blood and curled his finger at Hudson, inviting him in. Hudson had no choice. He stepped slowly up into the hallway and walked into the room as the man backed away from him, the gun still levelled at his face.

The cop sat on the floor behind the man.

'Boss?' Three shouted again, stepping on to the bottom stair and pointing his gun up at the first floor.

22

Someone shouted from just inside the front door of the house. Logan couldn't wait any longer; he pushed past Hardy and in through the door, raising his rifle as he went.

Hardy followed him.

A man stood at the bottom of a flight of stairs that went straight up from the hall to the first floor. He turned as Logan and Hardy came into the house, a handgun held out in front of him. He had bruising to his face and a cut lip; strapping on one of his knees. His eyes opened in shock when he saw Logan step forward. He had no time to react before Logan swung his rifle around and cracked the stock of it into his face.

The man went down to the floor still conscious, but barely. He dropped his gun and flapped his hands ineffectually at his face, unable to coordinate his movements.

Hardy pulled a set of plastic ties from his rear pocket, turned the man on to his front and secured his hands behind his back. He picked up the gun and tossed it past Logan out of the door. Then he pointed his rifle up the stairs.

Logan stayed where he was, waiting for Hardy to move. They saw two bodies crumpled on the stairs.

'Tommy,' a voice shouted from above. 'Is that you?'

Hardy looked back at Logan – saw hope dawning in his face.

'Roger?' Hardy shouted. 'What's the situation?'

'I have just what you need up here.'

Logan dropped his rifle and ran past Hardy, brushing away Hardy's attempt to hold him back and taking the stairs two at a time.

'Becky,' he shouted as he ran.

He reached the top of the stairs and saw the open doorway with Purcell standing over a kneeling man and pointing a gun at the back of his head.

'Becky,' Logan said again, not seeing her.

Irvine stepped out from behind Purcell and walked forward to meet Logan, wrapping her arms tight around him and burying her face in his shoulder.

23

Hudson and Three were on the floor of Purcell's kitchen with their backs against the wall. Logan, Irvine, Hardy and Purcell sat round a big oak table in the middle of the room, Hardy with his chair turned out so that he could watch the two men.

Purcell had checked his own leg to find that the bullet had gone straight through the meaty outer part of his thigh, tearing some muscle but missing bones and major arteries. He'd cleaned himself to get rid of all the blood and then let Hardy strap his wound before dressing in a pair of hiking trousers and a fleece top.

'We've got a doctor,' Hardy said to Purcell. 'I'll get him to come up and give that leg some proper attention.'

'Appreciate it, Tommy. Thanks.'

Hardy nodded, never taking his eyes off Hudson and Three.

'What did you do with the bodies?' Purcell asked.

'They're out back, under your patio table cover,' Hardy replied. 'I have a feeling we might need them for something, though I've not quite worked out what.'

Purcell raised his eyebrows.

Irvine was staring at Three, seeing the scars on his face from where she stamped on him in the alley. He looked right back at her. She wanted to hold his gaze, to show him that she was stronger. But in the end she was the one who looked away.

'Are we letting these two go?' she asked.

'Yes,' Hardy said. 'It's got to be that way. No more killing.'

'But *he* killed Roddy,' she said, pointing at Three. 'And he tried to kill me.'

'They also killed Washington and badly injured Bails as well. We just have to live with that. That's the way it is in a war. There are priorities other than revenge.'

Logan turned to the table and looked at the phones they had taken from the four men who had mounted the assault on the house. He picked Hudson's up and scrolled through the call log, noticing that most of the calls received were marked as being from callers identified simply by numbers. There were only two callers who had not been allocated number tags, one with a London prefix and one a mobile.

'Well,' he said, 'we know they were using a numerical code system and we have all of the phones.'

'That'll be good enough for Echelon,' Purcell said.

Hardy nodded, stood and walked over to the two men sitting on the floor. He bent, placed his rifle on the floor at his feet and showed the phone's display to Hudson.

'Who are these numbers for?' he asked.

Hudson looked from the phone to the rifle to Hardy's face and back again. This gig was over. It was either cooperate or end up like Two and Five. It was an easy choice to make. In fact, given what these men seemed to be capable of, getting on the right side of this bunch seemed eminently sensible right now.

'One's from the boss,' Hudson said. 'The London number. He's the guy who paid me.'

448

'And the other?'

'I don't know.'

'I don't believe you.'

'I mean, I don't know who the guy is. All he did was give me a Rolex watch to put in the device. It wasn't even a functioning part of it. I just do what I'm told.'

'It must have been Devon Leonard,' Logan said, standing and walking to where Hudson sat on the floor. 'Did you meet him face to face?'

'Yes,' Hudson said, looking up at Logan.

'Describe him.'

Hudson described Leonard, right down to his cowboy boots.

'It's Leonard all right,' Logan said.

Hardy stood and walked back to his seat at the table. Logan stayed where he was, looking down at Hudson.

'You did all this for money?' he asked.

Hudson said nothing. Beside him, Three smirked.

Irvine walked over until she was standing beside Logan, and looked down at Three.

'Fuckin' what?' Three said to her.

Irvine slapped his face. Three shouted out. She slapped him again, harder this time, and he fell sideways on to the floor, squirming and trying to roll away.

'I think maybe you should show more courtesy towards these people,' Hudson said.

Logan put his hands on Irvine's arms and pulled her away from Three. The two of them went back to sit at the table while Three grunted and rolled around on the floor.

'So how do we do this?' Hardy asked. 'I mean, how do we sell the story?'

'I've been thinking about that,' Logan said. He leaned forward, spinning Hudson's phone on the table surface. 'If I follow what you and Roger were saying, these phones will allow the Echelon people to pick up phone conversations relating to Becky and the explosion. And then we have the calls Weiss and Leonard made direct to one of the phones, so that links them to hiring these guys. Plus, Weiss told me that he provided the money to set Leonard up in business. So that's the connection between them. And with Leonard being Tara Byrne's manager there's a link direct to the bombing.'

'Sounds good to me,' Hardy said.

Irvine continued to stare at Three, who was trying to pull himself upright again by levering his back against the wall. It wasn't working.

'Are you willing to go to London to meet your contacts and sell this?' Logan asked Purcell. 'Because it will take a really hard sell and we haven't even worked out all the details yet to make it fit together for them. You'll have to leave the island.'

'There's no other way,' he said. 'It'll have to be a face-to-face.'

'But will you do it?'

'Yes. The people I know will be able to get jurisdiction switched away from the local plods to some national organised crime thing. That'll help. No offence to local plods.'

Irvine smiled.

'There's one big problem we haven't addressed,' Logan said. 'Gabriel Weiss. He's not going to accept all of this and go to jail quietly. He's just as likely to want to tell the whole story very publicly to take us down with him, and that would defeat the purpose of it all.'

'You're probably right,' Irvine said.

'I know the type,' Purcell added. 'He'll have plenty of money and lawyers to do his bidding. We need a more permanent solution where he's concerned.' He stood and walked over to Hudson and Three. Hudson tensed, anticipating a blow.

'What do you think, son?' Purcell asked him.

'I've been thinking the same thing myself for a while now,' Hudson said, seeing a way for him to get out of this whole mess alive. 'Maybe I can help you with him?'

'I was hoping you'd say that,' Purcell said.

part seven: endings

1

Gabriel Weiss woke to the sound of his radio alarm clicking on. He reached over to the table beside his bed and pushed the button to switch the noise off. It was just after seven-thirty.

His city house was in a very exclusive part of London and extended to three storeys, each one refurbished to the highest specification when he moved in five years ago. There was a sound system through the whole place that could be controlled in each room, so as he stepped into the tiled bathroom, which was the size of most people's living rooms, he fiddled with a panel on the wall until the sound of Queen's 'Bohemian Rhapsody' filled the house. He wasn't averse to a little bit of bombast and turned the volume up high.

After a long shower, he dressed semi-casually in a black-linen Armani suit with a white shirt. He was alone today and enjoying the freedom to do as he pleased, although he knew that to maintain the façade of his legal practice he would have to show his face in the office.

'Tiresome,' he said to his reflection in the hall mirror.

When he was on his own he wasn't really one for cooking, but this morning he decided that he needed something to fill the void in his stomach. He quickly scrambled two eggs and ate them with a toasted wholemeal bagel and cup of English Breakfast tea in the kitchen extension on the ground floor of the house. It had a huge glass section in the roof and he looked up at the sound of rain falling on it.

He was a little more concerned today than he had been last night, having not heard from Carl Hudson now for close on two days. He appreciated that at the end of a job like this one, Hudson would have to stay low and be careful about communications. But two days was being disrespectful. And there had been nothing in the news about the woman cop. Maybe he would apply a discount to the fee.

Still, at least the American was languishing in jail with no sign of the press letting up on the vitriol being heaped upon him. When he saw the news footage of the man's wife and children besieged at their house by reporters he felt a deep sense of satisfaction at a job well done. Everyone would know that if you messed with Gabriel Weiss he didn't do anything as mundane as kill you: he shattered your whole life.

As he was leaning back in his chair, finishing his tea, the phone on the granite counter rang. He frowned. Not many people had this number and most of them knew better than to call him this early.

Weiss walked the length of the kitchen to answer it, looking out into the lush green foliage of his professionally landscaped garden.

'It's me,' the voice on the other end said.

'Carl,' Weiss said with genuine joy. 'Good to hear from you at last.'

'Yeah, well, it's been a difficult few days as you can imagine.'

'How did you get this number?'

'You called me from it, don't you remember?'

'Of course. How could I forget? You expressed your disappointment so forcefully, after all.'

'I want to get paid.'

'I like your direct approach. But I need to be careful about transferring that kind of money even between our legitimate corporations. So do you. And, anyway, how do I know that you finished the job? There's been nothing on the news about her.'

'It's done,' Hudson said. 'They won't find her for a while, if at all, and I'll bring you a souvenir to prove it. But my situation is that I need it in cash. And I need it now.'

'Why?'

'I just would rather it was kept entirely off the radar. How much can you get today? How much do you have there?'

Weiss considered refusing, but he was feeling ebullient now and decided to cut Hudson some slack.

'I can only let you have another hundred.'

'Fine. I can get the rest later. Where can we meet?'

'Let me get organised and I'll call you back on this number from my office when I get in, OK?'

'Good for me. When will you be there?'

'Well, I'm leaving about now so less than an hour – depending on the traffic, you know.'

'We'll talk then.'

Hudson didn't wait for Weiss to acknowledge before ending the call.

Weiss went to the top floor of the house and retrieved £100,000 from the safe expertly concealed in the floor under his bed. In his line of business he needed to have fast cash available for unforeseen emergencies. Currently his stash was at close to one million, but he wasn't about to give a bigger chunk to Hudson. He would have to wait for the rest.

He put the cash in a leather holdall and went to the lift he'd had installed in the house to take him down to the garage. He wanted to take the Porsche and feel the exhilaration of driving such a perfect piece of precision engineering.

You had to enjoy life.

He was so caught up in the moment that he failed to notice the lights on the security cameras through the house flick from green to red.

A tone *pinged* to signal that the lift had reached the garage. The doors slid open and Weiss was surprised by the man standing in front of him. It took a moment for him to recognise the face.

'Hello, Gabriel,' said Hudson.

Weiss opened his mouth to speak.

Hudson raised a pistol with a suppressor attached and fired twice. The bullets entered Weiss's mouth and exited the rear of his skull, taking blood and brain matter with them. He dropped straight to the ground.

Hudson looked down at him, watching him die.

'You brought this on yourself,' he said.

He picked up the holdall from beside Weiss's body before it was engulfed by the quickly expanding pool of blood and slipped the gun inside. He took a remote control device out of his jacket pocket. It had been programmed to match the frequency for the door to Weiss's garage. He pointed it at the door and pressed the button. When the door was halfway up, he stooped underneath and walked out into the street. He pressed the button to close the door and then put the remote in the bag to get rid of later.

Weiss had fallen so that he lay half in and half out of the lift. As the doors opened and closed against his lifeless body, the garage door slid down to cover his final resting place.

2

A week later Logan sat with Sam Cahill in the main reception area of the Sheriff Court. It was somehow both grand and uninspiring at the same time; resplendent in various tones of brown and beige and populated by equal numbers of criminals and lawyers. A couple of the lawyers nodded in passing to Logan: former colleagues at Kennedy Boyd. But no one stopped to talk.

Joe Shaw had explained to Logan and Sam that the proceedings today would again be in private and that, after it was over, Cahill would be taken back down to the cells in the basement of the court to be formally processed for release. There would be no stunning courtroom scene at the climax of this particular case.

Sam was a mass of tics and shakes, with dark shadows under her eyes from lack of sleep over the past week since Cahill's arrest. Logan put his arm round her shoulders and hugged her.

'It'll be fine,' he told her. 'Alex is getting out.'

'What if somebody made a mistake? I mean, maybe they won't do what they said they would.'

'It's done,' Logan said. 'Don't worry about it.'

It had not been easy for Purcell to convince the people he knew to use the full resource of Echelon when it appeared that the perpetrator of the atrocity at the Hilton was already locked up. Both he and Hardy had flown to London for a face-to-face, making for some very heated discussions.

The cloned mobile phones from Hudson's crew were used to recover enough of the communications between them leading up to the bombing and the attack on Roddy for the job to be effectively done. And the calls from Weiss's home number to Hudson's phone confirmed Weiss's connection to the attack.

What really helped to persuade them in the end was the extent of the ongoing Interpol investigation into Weiss's activities. And now that he was dead – in what appeared to be a gangland-style professional hit – it would never come to trial.

All of which meant that a decision was taken to do nothing about Devon Leonard, there being no point in dredging it all up for a low-level wannabe like him. A brief visit by Purcell to Leonard's house in the dark of night was enough to scare him into keeping quiet for the rest of his life.

'Did you have to tell them everything?' Logan had asked Hardy at the CPO offices when he returned from the trip. 'About what happened at Loch Awe with Ellie. All of it?'

'Does it matter?'

'It matters to me. And to Ellie.'

Hardy had looked long and hard into Logan's eyes before he spoke again.

'The people who are making these decisions have the authority to countermand anyone. They carry the highest authority, if you follow me. There's none of us need worry about any of this, and I mean going back to what happened before. Trust me and drop it, OK? It's done.'

'What about Special Branch? They made the connection between the Russian in the bar and the bodies up at the loch. If they keep looking at that it might come back against us somewhere down the line.'

'They have the *highest* authority,' Hardy repeated. 'Forget about it, OK.'

'Are you telling me that we have to rely on the government of this country effectively sanctioning the murder of the Russians and being involved in covering it up? I find that hard to believe, Tom.'

'Talk to Roger Purcell. He'll tell you that they've sanctioned much worse.'

'But who's going to come up with a story that they can go public with?' Logan asked. 'I mean, about the bombing.'

'That's for the big brains in British intelligence. And you can forget all the jokes about them; they're actually very good.'

'What about the two men who made it off Mull? Do we have anything to worry about from them now that they're free?'

'No. They were professionals. It wasn't personal for them so we're done with them. They were probably grateful that we didn't kill them or turn them in and the lead one was true to his word when it came to taking Weiss out, wasn't he? Who knows, those kinds of decisions sometimes come back positively. There's no end of gratitude a man will give you if you spare him his life.'

It turned out no one in authority cared too much for the lives or the reputations of drug dealers or assassins.

Not unless they operated on their side.

Joe Shaw came out of the courtroom to tell Sam and Logan that the hearing had gone to plan and that Cahill would be up from the cells shortly. Logan walked Shaw out of the building and thanked

him for his help. He said his bill would be in the post that night
and laughed, shaking Logan's hand. Logan knew that he was not
joking.

He went back inside and found Sam pacing the full width of
the building, unable to relax and on the verge of tears. He tried
to get her to sit, but she shrugged him off.

She was so immersed in her own thoughts that Logan was the
first to see Cahill. He came out of the heavy double doors to Logan's
left and looked around uncertainly, something approaching fear
passing across his face. It was the first time that Logan had seen
his friend anything other than entirely in control.

Logan stood and Cahill saw him. He broke into a wide grin.
He heard Sam before he saw her: her shout and the *click-clack* of
her heels on the marble floor. Then she was in Cahill's arms,
smothering his face in kisses.

Logan beamed and Cahill wrapped both arms tightly round his
wife. They stayed like that for an age as people milled around them
oblivious, having witnessed similar scenes there before. Logan
turned and walked towards the exit to give them what little privacy
he could, the sound of Sam's quiet tears staying with him as he
went.

Later, he drove them both to their house where the Cahill girls
bolted out of the front door and almost knocked their father over
with the force of their embrace. When the pure, raw emotion of
their welcome had subsided, Cahill guided Sam and the girls into
the house and walked back to the car, where he hunkered down
beside the open driver's window. He looked to Logan much the
same as he always did.

'Good to be home, man,' he said. 'Thanks.'

'It was a team effort.'

'I don't doubt it. You can tell me all about it over a beer.'

'But not tonight.'

'No. There's some people here that I'd rather spend time with. No offence.'

Logan laughed.

'Tell me one thing,' Cahill said. 'Is it done now? This thing with us and with Ellie?'

'I think it is.'

'You only *think* it is?'

'I don't know. Is there ever any way to be certain of this stuff?'

'Sometimes. How did it go down?'

Logan looked around and then opened the door, stepping out of the car and leading Cahill away from it.

Cahill smiled. 'Glad to see you're learning to be careful where you talk,' he said.

'Tom took care of it. Him and Roger Purcell.'

'Roger was in on it? Shit, then we've got nothing to fear. If it was Roger, it's over.'

'Why?'

'He knows way too much for anyone to want to piss him off. They like to keep Roger happy so that he stays quiet. It's a mutually beneficial relationship.'

'He's an odd guy.'

'Too right he is. Did you see him at work up close?'

'I saw the results.'

'That'd be enough.' Cahill shook his head and looked up and down the street, breathing in deeply as weak rays from the sun broke through the low cloud cover.

'It's good to be back,' he said. 'Damn good.'

3

Logan stood outside Irvine's front door, shifting his weight from one foot to the other while he waited for her to answer. He had only seen her briefly after they got back from Mull, with both of them desperate to get back to their children and try to put it all behind them for good.

She answered the door with Connor in her arms; he was smearing food over her top and laughing. She put him down and ushered Logan into the house. Connor ran unsteadily ahead of them and through into the kitchen, shouting two-year-old nonsense as he went.

Logan boiled the kettle and made them both a cup of tea while Irvine finished feeding her son.

'He looks happy,' he said.

'Yeah, he's a good boy.' Irvine made a face at Connor as he mashed a tuna sandwich between his fingers, mayonnaise squelching out on to the table.

'How are *we* doing?' Logan asked.

Irvine looked at him and shrugged. 'OK, I think. It's been a tough courtship so far, don't you think?'

Logan couldn't help but smile, though he didn't know if she had intended it as a joke. 'Some of it's been pretty good,' he said.

'Can't deny that,' she said, laughing. 'And wouldn't want to.'

Logan went to the kitchen window, looking out at the narrow garden as blue sky showed through the clouds. 'I was thinking,' he said. 'Maybe we could all go out for something to eat. I mean today, after Ellie finishes school. What do you think?'

Irvine took the remnants of the sandwich from her son and started cleaning his hands with a cotton wipe. 'I think that would be nice,' she said. Discarding the cotton wipe, she came and pressed herself against Logan's back, wrapped her arms round his chest and kissed him gently on the neck.

Logan felt a charge tingle through him and put his hand on top of hers.

They took Logan's car, with Connor strapped in his seat in the back. Logan parked round the corner from the school and told Irvine to wait in the car.

'Let me tell her you're both here first,' he said.

Irvine looked uncertain. 'If it's not going to work out between me and her . . .'

Logan held up his hands. 'It'll work,' he said.

He walked round to the school just as the bell rang and the pupils started to swarm out. Logan always liked how colourful and warm the place looked with all the girls in their red blazers.

Ellie wandered out slowly, talking earnestly with two of her friends. When she saw Logan, she said goodbye quickly and ran over to him.

'What was the big talk all about?' he asked her.

Ellie looked back at her friends. 'Just stuff.'

He realised, perhaps for the first time, that she was starting to develop her own life, separate from him. Which was all he could hope for: a normal life for both of them. He took her bags from her and they started to walk towards the corner where the car was parked.

'Have you talked to your friends about Alex?' he asked.

'Yes.'

'You know that he didn't do that thing? That it was all a mistake?'

'I suppose.'

Logan stopped and turned to Ellie. 'Just because of what he did for you, it doesn't mean that's what he does all the time. You understand? It was his job to protect that woman, not to hurt her.'

'The way he protected me?'

'Yes, just like that.'

'That's what I told them.'

Logan dropped the bags and hugged her, not caring that she would be embarrassed by him in front of her friends.

They started walking again. Logan told Ellie that Irvine and Connor were waiting in the car and that they were going out for dinner. He was holding Ellie's hand and felt her tense.

'Do they have to come?' she asked quietly, the tone of her voice uncertain.

'I thought it would be nice.'

They rounded the corner and saw Irvine and Connor standing beside the car. Irvine waved at Ellie and then had to grab at Connor as he toddled forward and tripped over a loose paving stone. She managed to catch him before he fell face first on to the ground. Ellie laughed. Logan didn't blame her: little kids falling over were funny.

Connor's lower lip started to twitch as if he was going to cry. Irvine lifted him up into her arms and went to meet Logan and Ellie.

'Hey, Ellie,' she said. 'How's things with you?'

'OK.'

'We going to get some dinner?'

'So I'm told.'

'*Ellie*,' Logan said.

'It's OK, Logan,' Irvine said. She put her hand on his arm and looked at Ellie.

'Ellie, honey, I'm not trying to take Logan away and I know I'm not your mum. I'm not trying to be. You understand?'

Ellie nodded impassively.

Connor squirmed in Irvine's arms and she put him down. He wobbled over to Ellie and grabbed her leg.

Ellie looked uncertainly at Irvine, who nodded at her. Ellie reached down and took hold of one of Connor's hands as he stepped back from her.

'You want to get some dinner, Connor?' she asked him, leaning forward.

'Yuh.'

'I suppose it might be OK,' Ellie said to Logan, straightening up again.

Logan and Irvine stepped to the side to let Ellie guide Connor towards the car and then followed behind them. Irvine grabbed Logan's hand for a moment and squeezed before hurrying to catch up with the children. She looked back at Logan and smiled, brushing hair from her face as the wind picked up briefly. He was struck by how beautiful she looked in that instant; wanted to freeze-frame it.

Irvine turned back to Ellie and Connor. Watching the scene, Logan thought about how much less complicated his life used to be when he was on his own.

And how much better he liked it now.

GJ MOFFAT

Daisychain

'Don't even think about stopping half-way through: this is a strictly one-sitting, white-knuckle adrenalin ride' Daily Record

Over the course of three violent, fearful days, the paths of three people's lives will intersect and change forever.

Logan Finch has just about everything he ever wanted, including a penthouse apartment and a shot at making partner in one of Glasgow's largest law firms. But there's something missing from his life: he still pines for the woman he thought was 'the one' and who left him without a word of explanation over twelve years ago.

Alex Cahill is one of Logan's clients, and probably his best friend. The profane, gregarious American owns a successful security business but has a shadowy past and a capacity for violence.

Detective Constable Rebecca Irvine, newly promoted to Strathclyde Police's CID, is stuck in a failing marriage. On her first day in the new job she is called to a murder scene in the affluent Southside of Glasgow. The victim is Penny Grant, Logan's former girlfriend.

And her eleven-year-old daughter, Ellie, is missing . . .

978 0 7553 1852 0

 hachette
SCOTLAND